Margaret Oliphant, Annie Louisa Walker

The Autobiography and Letters of Mrs. M. O. W. Oliphant

Third Edition, second Impression

Margaret Oliphant, Annie Louisa Walker

The Autobiography and Letters of Mrs. M. O. W. Oliphant
Third Edition, second Impression

ISBN/EAN: 9783744688000

Printed in Europe, USA, Canada, Australia, Japan

Cover: Foto ©Raphael Reischuk / pixelio.de

More available books at **www.hansebooks.com**

From a drawing made in 1895 by Janet Mary Oliphant

THE AUTOBIOGRAPHY AND LETTERS OF

MRS M. O. W. OLIPHANT

ARRANGED AND EDITED BY

MRS HARRY COGHILL

THIRD EDITION, REVISED

SECOND IMPRESSION

WILLIAM BLACKWOOD AND SONS
EDINBURGH AND LONDON
MDCCCXCIX

PREFACE.

IN some of the last words she ever wrote, Mrs Oliphant described herself as "a writer very little given to explanations or to any personal appearance"; and probably of no writer that ever lived was this so absolutely true a description. Her work, enormous in volume and multifarious in kind, was given to the public; her life was for her children first, and after them for the small circle of loving and intimate friends who closely surrounded her. Of these, many, in the last darkening years of her life, had passed away, and with one small exception it is in these years only that we find in her writings any personal revelations, intentional or unintentional. They were very rarely intentional, and when they were, it was of deliberate purpose and for a fixed reason, as in two recent papers in 'Blackwood'— "The Thoughts of a Believer" and "The Verdict of Old Age." The last and most touching instance is in the only preface which she ever attached to a novel —the few pages called "On the Ebb Tide," prefacing 'The Ways of Life.'

When she wrote those pages, worn out with bodily and mental suffering, she thought she felt in herself the beginnings of failure. As a matter of fact, she had never written more brilliantly than at times during the concluding year of her life; but she had never since the death of her last child been conscious of that happy mastery of her work which had supplied many of the pleasantest hours of the past. "I am behind the fashion," she said herself; "I have no longer the place or the value I had." She felt certain that the difficulty of producing good work must increase for her (as, indeed, at sixty-nine it well might), and she greatly longed to be released from her service and allowed to join those who had gone before her. But until within the last few months she had very little hope of escape. When first those who loved her were anxious, alarmed by her pallor, her inability to take food, and what they knew of her nights of sleepless sorrow, she used to smile and say, "Don't be afraid; there never is anything the matter with me." Her health had almost always been perfect, withstanding every kind of fatigue and sorrow, and she could not think that it would fail her. But when, only about ten days before the end, it became certain that she was mortally ill, she said, as she had imagined Mr Sandford saying, "God is very good; He gives me everything."

In this quiet confidence that everything had been so perfectly arranged for her, with her mind clear, even a little flicker of fun in her eyes at times, always a tender smile and word for those she loved, a great writer passed away from us, leaving a blank that there is certainly no one capable of filling. There have been, perhaps there are (and she herself would have been the first to say it with full belief), greater novelists, but who has ever achieved the same variety of literary work with anything like the same level of excellence? A great deal of her very best remains at present anonymous — biographical and critical papers, and others dealing with an extraordinary variety of subjects. But merely to divide her books into classes gives some little idea of the range of her powers. Her novels, long and short, can hardly number much less than a hundred, but these for a long time back were by no means her works of predilection; and in the three last sad years all fiction had been heavy labour to her. Next in importance come her biographies — Edward Irving, Count de Montalembert, Principal Tulloch, Laurence Oliphant, and a number of smaller ones, some involving great labour and research; while her last work of this class, two volumes of the 'History of the House of Blackwood,' occupied two years of her life. Then there are the brilliant papers on the reign of George II., collected some years ago, and those on the reign of Queen Anne; the laborious, but not entirely successful, 'Literary History of England,' and 'A Child's History of Scotland.' 'The Makers of Florence' began a fresh series in 1876; it was followed at intervals by 'The Makers of Venice,' 'Rome,' and 'Jerusalem,' each of these books involving immense labour, and all, except 'Rome,' having its materials carefully collected on the spot. The topography of Rome she knew well; every aspect of it had been engraved on her memory with the pencil of sorrow. Finally, there remains one of the most wonderful sets of writings in our language—that which began very simply and sweetly with 'A Little Pilgrim,' and went on through various 'Stories of the Seen and the Unseen,' reaching a strange poetic power and beauty in 'A Beleaguered City,' and finding, to those who were near enough to her life to guess the thoughts with which it was written, a most fitting end in 'The Land of Suspense.' Thus she had laboured in almost every field of literature, winning every kind of success, and never, in all the fifty years (except, perhaps, for one moment in the early days of her widowhood), making a real failure. One day in the last week of her life she said, "Many times I have come to a corner which I could see no way round, but each time a way has been found for me." The way was often found by the strengthening of her own indomitable courage, which, as long as her children were left to her, never seemed to flag, —it was the courage of perfect love. But it is certain that if she had had no moral qualities except courage, she could not have toiled on as she did: a saving sense of humour, a great capacity to enjoy what was really comic and everything that was beautiful, made life easier to her, and "the great joy of doing kindnesses" was one never absent from her. So that whatever suffering might be lying in wait to seize upon her solitary hours, there was almost always a pleasant welcome and talk of the very best to be found in her modest drawing-room. If the visitors were congenial, her charm of manner awoke, her simple fitness of speech clothed every subject with life and grace, her beautiful eyes shone (they never sparkled), and the spell of her exquisite womanliness made a charmed circle round her. She was never a beautiful woman at any time of her life, though for many years she was a very pretty one, but she had, as a family inheritance, lovely hands, which were constantly busy, in what she called her idle time, with some dainty sewing or knitting; she had those wonderful eyes which kept their beauty to the last minute of her life; and she had a most exquisite daintiness in all her ways and in the very atmosphere about her which was "pure womanly."

It was just at the moment when all England kept festival for the Queen's second Jubilee—in the last half of June 1897—that Mrs Oliphant lay dying in a sunny little house at Wimbledon. Happily free from acute pain, she had passed into a serene region of perfect peace, out of which she spoke to us who were about her with all her old brightness, giving such information and directions as she thought might be useful *after*. And one distinct injunction she laid upon us—no biography of her was to be written.

Many years ago she had begun in a time of great trial and loneliness to write down scraps more or less autobiographical, and later had added more cheerful pictures of her early life. Later still, to please her last surviving child, she continued this memoir, bringing it up to the time when her two sons went to Oxford. She must, it would seem, have intended to add to it some record of the remaining twenty years of her life, and possibly in her last hours she forgot how great a gap was left. At any rate she bade us deal with this autobiography as we thought best, believing that it would serve for all that was necessary.

But when those to whom she had intrusted it came to examine the manuscript, a great disappointment befell them. It had no beginning; scraps had been written at long intervals and by no means consecutively. The first entry in her book was written in 1860, and mentions, rather than records, the struggles of her early widowhood. The second, in 1864, is the outpouring of her grief for the loss of her one daughter, her little Maggie, suddenly snatched from her in Rome. After this is the long gap of twenty‑one years, till the time when in her bright house at Windsor with both her sons still left to her, and her two adopted daughters about her, she was moved to write down a more connected and less sad record.

So far, then, there is a narrative in her own writing. After 1892 there is nothing, and it seemed impossible to allow the late years of her life—full of work, full of varying scenes and interests—to remain altogether unrecorded. The best thing that could be done, therefore, was to supplement her manuscript with letters, and to connect these with the slightest possible thread of story, thus endeavouring to obey her wishes and yet gratify the many readers who have for so long a stretch of years regarded her as a friend.

A large portion of the correspondence now printed belongs to the Blackwood family. Her faithful and highly‑valued friend, the late Mr John Blackwood, his sister the late Miss Blackwood, and Mr William Blackwood, the present Editor of 'Maga,' were all recipients of letters which are very characteristic and very interesting, and give almost a connected history of Mrs Oliphant's literary work. Some others come from Mr Craik (Macmillan & Co.), and some from other business correspondents and private friends. A few letters to her sons have been added, and it has seemed advisable to furnish now and then a letter written *to* her to explain those written *by* her.[1]

Very little more than this has been attempted. Only when the end must be chronicled another hand takes up the pen she has laid down and sorrowfully records the close of a life—not faultless, indeed, but noble, loving, and womanly in the highest sense, and of a literary career full of sound, skilful, and serviceable labours.

A. L. C.

October 1899.

---

[1] In the present edition a few letters from Mrs Oliphant's younger son have been omitted. The Editor has thought herself justified in withdrawing them because she hopes later to collect into a small volume these and other memorials of the gifted and much beloved writer.

CONTENTS.

AUTOBIOGRAPHY.

I.

WINDSOR, *1st February* 1885.[1]

TWENTY-ONE years have passed since I wrote what is on the opposite page.[2] I have just been reading it all with tears; sorry, very sorry for that poor soul who has lived through so much since. Twenty-one years is a little lifetime. It is curious to think that I was not very young, nearly thirty-six, at that time, and that I am not very old, nearly fifty-seven, now. Life, though it is short, is very long, and contains so much. And one does not, to one's consciousness, change as one's outward appearance and capabilities do. Doesn't Mrs Somerville say that, so far from feeling old, she was not always quite certain (up in the seventies) whether she was quite grown up! I entirely understand the feeling, though I have had enough, one would think, to make one feel old. Since the time when that most unexpected, most terrible blow[3] overtook me in Rome—where her father had died four years before—I have had trials which, I say

---

[1] It has been thought better to print the earlier portion, or such of it as might interest general readers, after this part of Mrs Oliphant's journal, so as to preserve the sequence of the narrative. —ED.

[2] See p. 87 and footnote. —ED.

[3] The death of her daughter. —ED.

A

it with full knowledge of all the ways of mental suffering, have been harder than sorrow. I have lived a
laborious life, incessant work, incessant anxiety—and
yet so strange, so capricious is this human being, that
I would not say I have had an unhappy life. I have
said this to one or two friends who know faintly without details what I have had to go through, and astonished them. Sometimes I am miserable—always
there is in me the sense that I may have active cause
to be so at any moment—always the gnawing pangs
of anxiety, and deep, deep dissatisfaction beyond
words, and the sense of helplessness, which of itself
is despair. And yet there are times when my heart
jumps up in the old unreasonable way, and I am,—
yes, happy—though the word seems so inappropriate
—without any cause for it, with so many causes the
other way. I wonder whether this is want of feeling, or mere temperament and elasticity, or if it is
a special compensation,—" Werena my heart licht I
wad dee "—Grizel Hume must have had the same.

I have been tempted to begin writing by George
Eliot's life—with that curious kind of self-compas-
sion which one cannot get clear of. I wonder if I
am a little envious of her? I always avoid considering formally what my own mind is worth. I
have never had any theory on the subject. I have
written because it gave me pleasure, because it came
natural to me, because it was like talking or breathing, besides the big fact that it was necessary for me
to work for my children. That, however, was not
the first motive, so that when I laugh inquiries off
and say that it is my trade, I do it only by way of
eluding the question which I have neither time nor
wish to enter into. Anthony Trollope's talk about
the characters in his books astonished me beyond
measure, and I am totally incapable of talking about
anything I have ever done in that way. As he was
a thoroughly sensible genuine man, I suppose he was
quite sincere in what he says of them,—or was it that

he was driven into a fashion of self-explanation which belongs to the time, and which I am following now though in another way? I feel that my carelessness of asserting my claim is very much against me with everybody. It is so natural to think that if the workman himself is indifferent about his work, there can't be much in it that is worth thinking about. I am not indifferent, yet I should rather like to forget it all, to wipe out all the books, to silence those compliments about my industry, &c., which I always turn off with a laugh. I suppose this is really pride, with a mixture of Scotch shyness, and a good deal of that uncomprehended, unexplainable feeling which made Mrs Carlyle reply with a jibe, which meant only a whimsical impulse to take the side of opposition, and the strong Scotch sense of the absurdity of a chorus of praise, but which looks so often like detraction and bitterness, and has now definitely been accepted as such by the public in general. I don't find words to express it adequately, but I feel it strenuously in my own case. When people comment upon the number of books I have written, and I say that I am so far from being proud of that fact that I should like at least half of them forgotten, they stare — and yet it is quite true; and even here I could no more go solemnly into them, and tell why I had done this or that, than I could fly. They are my work, which I like in the doing, which is my natural way of occupying myself, though they are never so good as I meant them to be. And when I have said that, I have said all that is in me to say.

I don't quite know why I should put this all down. I suppose because George Eliot's life has, as I said above, stirred me up to an involuntary confession. How I have been handicapped in life! Should I have done better if I had been kept, like her, in a mental greenhouse and taken care of? This is one of the things it is perfectly impossible to tell. In all likelihood our minds and our circumstances are so arranged that, after all, the possible way is the way that is best; yet it is a little hard sometimes not to feel with Browning's Andrea that the men who have no wives, who have given themselves up to their art, have had an almost unfair advantage over us who have been given perhaps more than one Lucrezia to take care of. And to feel with him that perhaps in the after-life four square walls in the New Jerusalem may be given for another trial! I used to be intensely impressed in the Laurence Oliphants with that curious freedom from human ties which I have never known; and that they felt it possible to make up their minds to do what was best, without any sort of *arrière pensée*, without having to consider whether they could or not. Curious freedom! I have never known what it was. I have always had to think of other people, and to plan everything—for my own pleasure, it is true, very often, but always in subjection to the necessity which bound me to them. On the whole, I have had a great deal of my own way, and have insisted upon getting what I wished, but only at the cost of infinite labour, and of carrying a whole little world with me whenever I moved. I have not been able to rest, to please myself, to take the pleasures that have come in my way, but have always been forced to go on without a pause. When my poor brother's family fell upon my hands, and especially when there was question of Frank's education, I remember that I said to myself, having then perhaps a little stirring of ambition, that I must make up my mind to think no more of that, and that to bring up the boys for the service of God was better than to write a fine novel, supposing even that it was in me to do so. Alas! the work has been done; the education is over, my good Frank, my steady, good boy, is dead. It seemed rather a fine thing to make that resolution (though in reality I had no choice); but now I think that if I had taken the other way, which seemed the less noble, it might have been better for all of us. I might have done better work. I should in all probability have earned nearly as much for half the production had I done less; and I might have had the satisfaction of knowing that there was something laid up for them and for my old age; while they might have learned habits of work which now seem beyond recall. Who can tell? I did with much labour what I thought the best, and there is only a *might have been* on the other side.

In this my resolution which I did make, I was, after all, only following my instincts, it being in reality easier to me to keep on with a flowing sail, to keep my household and make a number of people comfortable, at the cost of incessant work, and an occasional great crisis of anxiety, than to live the self-restrained life which the greater artist imposes upon himself.

What casuists we are on our own behalf!—this is altogether self-defence. And I know I am giving myself the air of being *au fond* a finer sort of character than the others. I may as well take the little satisfaction to myself, for nobody will give it to me. No one even will mention me in the same breath with George Eliot. And that is just. It is a little justification to myself to think how much better off she was,—no trouble in all her life as far as appears, but the natural one of her father's death—and perhaps coolnesses with her brothers and sisters, though that is not said. And though her marriage is not one that most of us would have ventured on, still it seems to have secured her a worshipper unrivalled. I think she must have been a dull woman with a great genius distinct from herself, something like the gift of the old prophets, which they sometimes exercised with only a dim sort of perception what it meant. But this is a thing to be said only with bated breath, and perhaps further thought on the subject may change even my mind. She took herself with tremendous seriousness,

that is evident, and was always on duty, never relax-
ing, her letters ponderous beyond description — and
those to the Bray party giving one the idea of a mutual
improvement society for the exchange of essays.

Let me be done with this—I wonder if I will ever
have time to put a few autobiographical bits down
before I die.   I am in very little danger of having my
life written, and that is all the better in this point
of view—for what could be said of me?   George
Eliot and George Sand make me half inclined to
cry over my poor little unappreciated self—" Many
love me (*i.e.*, in a sort of way), but by none am I
enough beloved."   These two bigger women did
things which I have never felt the least temptation
to do — but how very much more enjoyment they
seem to have got out of their life, how much more
praise and homage and honour!   I would not buy
their fame with these disadvantages, but I do feel
very small, very obscure, beside them, rather a failure
all round, never securing any strong affection, and
throughout my life, though I have had all the usual
experiences of woman, never impressing anybody,—
what a droll little complaint!—why should I?   I
acknowledge frankly that there is nothing in me—a
fat, little, commonplace woman, rather tongue-tied
—to impress any one; and yet there is a sort of
whimsical injury in it which makes me sorry for
myself.

Feb. 8th.

Here, then, for a little try at the autobiography.   I
ought to be doing some work, getting on a little in
advance for to-morrow, which gives a special zest
to doing nothing:[1] to doing what has no need to
be done — and Sunday evenings have always been
a time to *fantasticare*, to do what one pleased; and
I have dropped out of the letter I used to do on
these occasions, having — which, by the way, is a

---

[1] This is exactly what Sir Walter says in his Diary, only published
in 1890, so I was like him in this without knowing it.

little sad when one comes to think of it — no one to write to, of anything that is beneath the surface.[1] Curious! I had scarcely realised it before. Now for a beginning.

I remember nothing of Wallyford, where I was born, but opened my eyes to life, so far as I remember, in the village of Lasswade, where we lived in a little house, I think, on the road to Dalkeith. I recollect the wintry road ending to my consciousness in a slight ascent with big ash-trees forming a sort of arch; underneath which I fancy was a toll-bar, the way into the world appropriately barred by that turnpike. But no, that was not the way into the world; for the world was Edinburgh, the coach for which, I am almost sure, went the other way through the village and over the bridge to the left hand, starting from somewhere close to Mr Todd the baker's shop, of which I have a faint and kind recollection. It was by that way that Frank came home on Saturday nights to spend Sunday at home, walking out from Edinburgh (about six miles) to walk in again on Monday in the dark winter mornings. I recollect nothing about the summer mornings when he set out on that walk, but remember vividly like a picture the Monday mornings in winter; the fire burning cheerfully and candles on the breakfast-table, all dark but with a subtle sense of morning, though it seemed a kind of dissipation to be up so long before the day. I can see myself, a small creature seated on a stool by the fire, toasting a cake of dough which was brought for me by the baker with the prematurely early rolls, which were for Frank. (This dough was the special feature of the morning to me, and I suppose I had it only on these occasions.) And my mother, who never seemed to sit down in the strange, little, warm, bright picture, but to hover about the table pouring

---

[1] This was but a momentary cause of sadness. All her more intimate correspondents were alive, and rejoiced in letters from her.—ED.

out tea, supplying everything he wanted to her boy
(how proud, how fond of him!—her eyes liquid and
bright with love as she hovered about); and Frank,
the dearest of companions so long—then long separated, almost alienated, brought back again at the end
to my care.   How bright he was then, how good
always to me, how fond of his little sister!—impatient by moments, good always.   And he was a
kind of god to me—*my* Frank, as I always called
him.   I remember once weeping bitterly over a
man singing in the street, a buttoned-up, shabby-
genteel man, whom, on being questioned why I cried,
I acknowledged I thought like my Frank.   That was
when he was absent, and my mother's anxiety reflected in a child's mind went, I suppose, the length
of fancying that Frank too might have to sing in the
street.   Frank, however, never gave very much
anxiety; it was Willie, poor Willie, who was our
sore and constant trouble—Willie, who lives still in
Rome, as he has done for the last two- or three-
and-twenty years—nearly a quarter of a century—
among strangers who are kind to him, wanting nothing, I hope, yet also having outlived everything.   I
shrank from going to see him when I was in Italy,
which was wrong; but how can I return to Rome,
and how could he have come to me?—poor Willie!
the handsomest, brightest of us all, with eyes that
ran over with fun and laughter—and the hair which
we used to say he had to poll, like Absalom, so
many times a-year.   Alas!

What I recollect in Lasswade besides the Monday
morning aforesaid is not much.   I remember standing at the smithy with brother Willie, on some occasion when the big boy was very unwillingly charged
to take his little sister somewhere or other,—standing in the dark, wondering at the sparks as they
flew up and the dark figures of the smith and his
men; and I remember playing on the road opposite
the house, where there was a low wall over which

the Esk and the country beyond could be seen (I think), playing with two little kittens, who were called Lord Brougham and Lord Grey. It must have been immediately after the passing of the Reform Bill, and I suppose this was why the kittens bore such names. We were all tremendously political and Radical, my mother especially and Frank. Likewise I recollect with the most vivid clearness on what must have been a warm still summer day, lying on my back in the grass, the little blue speedwells in which are very distinct before me, and looking up into the sky. The depths of it, the blueness of it, the way in which it seemed to move and fly and avoid the gaze which could not penetrate beyond that profound unfathomable blue,—the bliss of lying there doing nothing, trying to look into it, growing giddy with the effort, with a sort of vague realisation of the soft swaying of the world in space! I feel the giddiness in my brain still, and the happiness, as if I had been the first discoverer of that wonderful sky. All my little recollections are like pictures to which the meaning, naturally, is put long afterwards. I did not know the world moved or anything about it, being under six at most; but I can feel the sensation of the small head trying to fix that great universe, and in the effort growing dizzy and going round.

We left Lasswade when I was six, my father's business taking him to Glasgow, to the misery of my mother, who was leaving her boys behind her. My father is a very dim figure in all that phantasmagoria. I had to be very quiet in the evenings when he was at home, not to disturb him; and he took no particular notice of me or of any of us. My mother was all in all. How she kept everything going, and comfortably going, on the small income she had to administer, I can't tell; it seems like a miracle, though of course we lived in the utmost obscurity and simplicity. I was the child of her age

—not her old age, but the sentiment was the same. She had lost three children one after another—one a girl about whom I used to make all sorts of dream-romances, to the purport that Isabella had never died at all, and was brought back in this or that miraculous way to make my mother and myself supremely happy. I was born after that period of misery, and brought back life to my mother's heart. She was of the old type of Scotch mothers, not demonstrative, not caressing, but I know now that I was a kind of idol to her from my birth. My clothes were all made by her tender hands, finer and more beautifully worked than ever child's clothes were; my under garments fine linen and trimmed with little delicate laces, to the end that there might be nothing coarse, nothing less than exquisite, about me; that I might grow up with all the delicacies of a woman's ideal child.

But she was very quick in temper notwithstanding this, and was very far from spoiling me. I was not petted nor called by sweet names. But I know now that my mere name meant everything to her. I was her Maggie—what more could mortal speech find to say? How little one realises the character or individuality of those who are most near and dear. It is with difficulty even now that I can analyse or make a character of her. She herself is there, not any type or variety of humankind. She was taller than I am, not so stout as I have grown. She had a sweet fresh complexion, and a cheek so soft that I can feel the sensation of putting mine against it still, and beautiful liquid brown eyes, full of light and fun and sorrow and anger, flashing and melting, terrible to look at sometimes when one was in disgrace. Her teeth projected, when she had teeth, but she lost and never replaced them, which did not, I think, harm her looks very much—at least, not in my consciousness. I am obliged to confess that when I remember her first she wore a brown front ! according to the fashion of the time—which fashion she detested, and suddenly abandoning it one day, appeared with the most lovely white hair, which gave a charm of harmonious colour to her beautiful complexion and brown eyes and eyebrows, but which was looked upon with consternation by her contemporaries, who thought the change wickedness. She had grown very early grey like myself, but was at this period, I should think, about forty-five. She wore always a cap with white net quilled closely round her face, and tied under her chin with white ribbons; and in winter always a white shawl; her dress cut not quite to her throat, and a very ample white net or cambric handkerchief showing underneath. She had read everything she could lay hands upon all her life, and was fond of quoting Pope, so that we used to call her Popish in after-days when I knew what Popish in this sense meant.

She had entered into everything that was passing all her life with the warmest energy and animation, as was her nature; was Radical and democratic and the highest of aristocrats all in one. She had a very high idea, founded on I have never quite known what, of the importance of the Oliphant family, so that I was brought up with the sense of belonging (by her side) to an old, chivalrous, impoverished race. I have never got rid of the prejudice, though I don't think our branch of the Oliphants was much to brag of. I would not, however, do anything to dispel the delusion, if it is one, for my mother's sake, who held it stoutly and without a doubt.

I understand the Carlyles, both he and she, by means of my mother as few people appear able to do. She had Mrs Carlyle's wonderful gift of narrative, and she possessed in perfection that dangerous facility of sarcasm and stinging speech which Sir Walter attributes to Queen Mary. Though her kindness was inexhaustible and her love boundless, yet she could drive her opponent of the moment half frantic with half-a-dozen words, and cut to the quick

with a flying phrase. On the other side, there was
absolutely nothing that she would not have done or
endured for her own ; and no appeal to her generosity
was ever made in vain. She was a poor woman all
her life, but her instinct was always to give. And
she would have kept open house if she could have
had her way, on heaven knows how little a-year.
My father was in one way very different. He hated
strangers ; guests at his table were a bore to him.
In his later days he would have nobody invited, or
if guests came, retired and would not see them,—
but he was not illiberal.

We lived for a long time in Liverpool, where my
father had an office in the Custom-house. I don't
know exactly what, except that he took affidavits—
which was a joke in the house — having a special
commission for that purpose. We lived for some
time in the North End (no doubt a great deal
changed now, and I have known nothing about it
for thirty years and more), where there was a
Scotch church, chiefly for the use of the engineers
and their families who worked in the great foun-
dries. One of the first things I remember here
was great distress among the people, on what account I cannot tell — I must have been a girl of
thirteen or so, I think. A fund was raised for their
relief, of which my father was treasurer, and both
my brothers were drawn in to help. This was very
momentous in our family, from the fact that it was
the means of bringing Frank, up to this time everything that was good except in respect to the Church,
to that last and crowning excellence. He got interested about the poor, and began to come with us to
church, and filled my mother's cup with happiness.
Willie, always careless, always kind, ready to do
anything for anybody, but who had already come
by some defeat in life which I did not understand,
and who was at home idle, took the charge of ad-
ministering this charity, and used to go about the

poor streets with a cart of coal behind him and his pockets stuffed with orders for bread and provisions of all kinds. All this I remember, I think, more through my mother's keen half anguish of happiness and pride than through my own recollection. That he had done so poorly for himself was bitter, but that he did so well for the poor was sweet; oh! and such a vindication of the bright-eyed, sweet-tempered unfortunate, who never was anybody's enemy but his own — words which were more true in his case than in most others.

When I was sixteen I began to have—what shall I say?—not lovers exactly, except in the singular —but one or two people about who revealed to me the fact that I too was like the girls in the poets. I recollect distinctly the first compliment, though not a compliment in the ordinary sense of the word, which gave me that bewildering happy sense of being able to touch somebody else's heart — which was half fun and infinitely amusing, yet something more. The speaker was a young Irishman, one of the young ministers that came to our little church, at that time vacant. He had joined Frank and me on a walk, and when we were passing and looking at a very pretty cottage on the slope of the hill at Everton, embowered in gardens and shrubberies, he suddenly looked at me and said, "It would be Elysium." I laughed till I cried at this speech afterwards, though at the moment demure and startled. But the little incident remains to me, as so many scenes in my early life do, like a picture suffused with a soft delightful light: the glow in the young man's eyes; the lowered tone and little speech aside; the soft thrill of meaning which was nothing and yet much. Perhaps if I were not a novelist addicted to describing such scenes, I might not remember it after — how long? Forty-one years. What a long time! I could not have been sixteen. Then came the episode of

J. Y., which was very serious indeed. We were engaged on the eve of his going away. He was to go to America for three years and then return for me. He was a good, simple, pious, domestic, kind-hearted fellow, fair-haired, not good-looking, not ideal at all. He cannot have been at all clever, and I was rather. When he went away our correspondence for some time was very full; then I began to find his letters silly, and I suppose said as much. Then there were quarrels, quarrels with the Atlantic between, then explanations, and then dreadful silence. It is amusing to look back upon, but it was not at all amusing to me then. My poor little heart was broken. I remember another scene without being able to explain it: my mother and myself walking home from somewhere—I don't know where—after it was certain that there was no letter, and that all was over. I think it was a winter night and rainy, and I was leaning on her arm, and the blank of the silence, and the dark and the separation, and the cutting off of all the dreams that had grown about his name, came over me and seemed to stop my very life. My poor little heart was broken. I was just over seventeen, I think.

These were the only breaks in my early life. We lived in the most singularly secluded way. I never was at a dance till after my marriage, never went out, never saw anybody at home. Our pleasures were books of all and every kind, newspapers and magazines, which formed the staple of our conversation, as well as all our amusement. In the time of my depression and sadness my mother had a bad illness, and I was her nurse, or at least attendant. I had to sit for hours by her bedside and keep quiet. I had no liking then for needlework, a taste which developed afterwards, so I took to writing. There was no particular purpose in my beginning except this, to secure some amusement and occupation for myself while I sat by my mother's bedside. I wrote a little book in which the chief character was an angelic elder sister, unmarried, who had the charge of a family of motherless brothers and sisters, and who had a shrine of sorrow in her life in the shape of the portrait and memory of her lover who had died young. It was all very innocent and guileless, and my audience — to wit, my mother and brother Frank—were highly pleased with it. (It was published long after by W. on his own account, and very silly I think it is, poor little thing.) I think I was then about sixteen. Afterwards I wrote another very much concerned with the Church business, in which the heroine, I recollect, was a girl, who in the beginning of the story was a sort of half-witted undeveloped creature, but who ended by being one of those lofty poetical beings whom girls love. She was called, I recollect, Ibby, but why, I cannot explain. I had the satisfaction afterwards, when I came to my full growth, of burning the manuscript, which was a three-volume business. I don't think any effort was ever made to get a publisher for it.

We were living at the time in Liverpool, either in a house in Great Homer Street or in Juvenal Street —very classical in point of name but in nothing else. Probably neither of these places exists any longer—very good houses though, at least the last. I have lately described in a letter in the 'St James' Gazette' a curious experience of mine as a child while living in one of these places. It was in the time of the Anti-Corn Law agitation, and I was about fourteen. There was a great deal of talk in the papers, which were full of that agitation, about a petition from women to Parliament upon that subject, with instructions to get sheets ruled for signatures, and an appeal to ladies to help in procuring them. It was just after or about the time of our great charity, and I was in the way of going thus from house to-house. Accordingly I got a number of these sheets, or probably Frank got them for me, and set to work. Another girl went with me, I believe, but I forget who she was. The town was all portioned out into districts under the charge of ladies appointed by the committee, but we flung ourselves upon a street, no matter where, and got our papers filled and put all the authorised agents comically out. Nobody could discover who we were. I took my sheets to the meeting of the ladies, and was much wondered at, being to the external eye a child, though to my own consciousness quite a grown-up person. The secretary of the association or committee, or whatever it was, was, I think, a Miss Hayward; at all events her Christian name was Lawrencina, which she wrote L'cina. I admired her greatly, and admired her pretty handwriting and everything about her. I myself wrote abominably, resisting up to this time all efforts to teach me better; but the circulars and notes with Miss L'cina's pretty name developed in me a warm ambition. I began to copy her writing, and mended in my own from that day. It did not come to very much, the printers would say.

I was a tremendous politician in those days.

I forget when it was that we moved to Birkenhead —not, I think, till after the extraordinary epoch of the publication of my first book. From the time above spoken of I went on writing, and somehow, I don't remember how, got into the history of Mrs Margaret Maitland. There had been some sketches from life in the story which, as I have said, I burned; but that was pure imagination. A slight reflection of my own childhood perhaps was in the child Grace, a broken bit of reflection here and there from my mother in the picture of Mrs Margaret. Willie, after many failures and after a long illness, which we were in hopes had purified him from all his defects, had gone to London to go through some studies at the London University and in the College called the

English Presbyterian, to which in our warm Free Churchism we had attached ourselves. He took my MS. to Colburn, then one of the chief publishers of novels, and for some weeks nothing was heard of it, when one morning came a big blue envelope containing an agreement by which Mr Colburn pledged himself to publish my book on the half-profit system, accompanied by a letter from a Mr S. W. Fullom, full of compliments as to its originality, &c. I have forgotten the terms now, but then I knew them by heart. The delight, the astonishment, the amusement of this was not to be described. First and foremost, it was the most extraordinary joke that ever was. Maggie's story! My mother laughed and cried with pride and happiness and amazement unbounded. She thought Mr S. W Fullom a great authority and a man of genius, and augured the greatest advantage to me from his acquaintance and that of all the great literary persons about him. This wonderful event must have come most fortunately to comfort the family under new trouble; for things had again gone wrong with poor Willie—he had fallen once more into his old vice and debt and misery. He had still another term in London before he finished the course of study he was engaged in; and when the time came for his return I was sent with him to take care of him. It was almost the first time I had ever been separated from my mother. One visit of two or three weeks to the Hasties of Fairy Knowe, which had its part too in my little development, had been my only absence from home; and how my mother made up her mind to this three months' parting I do not know, but for poor Willie's sake everything was possible. We had lodgings near Burton Crescent in a street where our cousins, Frank and Tom Oliphant, were in the same house. We had the parlour, I remember, where I sat in the mornings when Willie was at his lectures. Afterwards he came in and I went out with him to walk. We used to walk through all the curious little passages leading, I believe, to Holborn, and full of old bookshops, which were our delight. And he took me to see the parks and various places—though not those to which I should suppose a girl from the country would be taken. The bookshops are the things I remember best. He was as good as he could be, docile and sweet-tempered and never rebellious; and I was a little dragon watching over him with remorseless anxiety. I discovered, I remember, a trifling bill which had not been included when his debts were paid, and I took my small fierce measures that it should never reach my mother's ears, nor trouble her. I ordained that for two days in the week we should give up our mid-day meal and make up at the evening one, which we called supper, for the want of it. On these days, accordingly, he did not come home, or came only to fetch me, and we went out for a long walk, sustaining ourselves with a bun until it should be time to come home to tea. He agreed to this ordinance without a murmur—my poor, good, tender-hearted, simple-minded Willie; and the little bill was paid and never known of at home.

Curiously enough, I remember little of the London sights or of any impression they made upon me. We knew scarcely anybody. Mrs Hamilton, the sister of Edward Irving's wife and a relation, took some notice of us, but she was almost the only individual I knew. And my heart was too full of my charge to think much of the cousin up-stairs with whom my fate was soon to be connected. We had known scarcely anything of each other before. We were new acquaintances, though relations. He took me, I remember, to the National Gallery, full of expectation as to the effect the pictures would have upon me. And I—was struck dumb with disappointment. I had never seen any pictures. I can't tell what I expected to see—something that never was on sea or shore. My ideal of absolute ignorance was far

too high-flown, I suppose, for anything human. I
was horribly disappointed, and dropped down from
untold heights of imagination to a reality I could
not understand. I remember, in the humiliation of
my downfall, and in the sense of my cousin's astonished disappointment at my want of appreciation,
fixing upon a painting—a figure of the Virgin in a
Crucifixion, I think by Correggio, but I am quite
vague about it—as the thing I liked best. I chose
that as Wordsworth's little boy put forth the weather-
cock at Kilve—in despair at my own incapacity to
admire. I remember also the heads of the old Jews
in Leonardo's Christ in the Temple. The face of
the young Redeemer with its elaborate crisped hair
shocked me with a sense of profanity, but the old
heads I could believe in. And that was all I got
out of my first glimpse into the world of art.   I
cannot recollect whether it was then or after, that
an equally great disillusionment in the theatre befell
me. The play was " Twelfth Night," and the lovely
beginning of that play—

> "That strain again | it had a dying fall"

—was given by a nobody in white tights lying on a
sofa and balancing a long leg as he spoke. The
disgust, the disenchantment, the fury remain in my
mind now. Once more I came tumbling down from
my ideal and all my anticipations. Mrs Charles
Kean was Viola, and she was middle-aged and
stout![1] I was more than disappointed, I was angry
and disgusted and cast down. What was the good
of anything if that was all that Shakespeare and the
great Masters could come to ?

I remember after this a day at Greenwich and
Woolwich, and the sight of the Arsenal, though why
that should have made an impression on my memory,
heaven knows! I remember the pyramids of balls,
and some convicts whose appearance gave me a thrill

---

[1] Probably under thirty.—ED.

of horror. I think they were convicts, though why
convicts should be at Woolwich I can't tell—perhaps
it was a mistake. And then Mr Colburn kindly—I
thought most kindly, and thanked him *avec effusion*—
gave me £150 for 'Margaret Maitland.' I remember
walking along the street with delightful elation, thinking that, after all, I was worth something—and not to
be hustled about. I remember, too, getting the first
review of my book in the twilight of a wintry dark
afternoon, and reading it by the firelight—always
half-amused at the thought that it was *me* who was
being thus discussed in the newspapers. It was the
'Athenæum,' and it was on the whole favourable.
Of course this event preceded by a couple of months
the transaction with Mr Colburn. I think the book
was in its third edition before he offered me that
£150. I remember no reviews except that one of the
'Athenæum,' nor any particular effect which my success produced in me, except that sense of elation.
I cannot think why the book succeeded so well.
When I read it over some years after, I felt nothing
but shame at its foolish little polemics and opinions.
I suppose there must have been some breath of youth
and sincerity in it which touched people, and there
had been no Scotch stories for a long time. Lord
Jeffrey, then an old man and very near his end, sent
me a letter of sweet praise, which filled my mother
with rapture and myself with an abashed gratitude.
I was very young. Oddly enough, it has always remained a matter of doubt with me whether the book
was published in 1849 or 1850. I thought the
former; but Geraldine Macpherson, whom I met in
London for the first time a day or two before it was
published, declared it to be 1850, from the fact that
that was the year of her marriage. If a woman re-
members any date, it must be the date of her marriage![1] so I don't doubt Geddie was right. Anyhow, if it was 1850, I was then only twenty-two, and

---

[1] It *was* 1849.—ED.

in some things very young for my age, as in others perhaps older than my years. I was wonderfully little moved by the business altogether. I had a great pleasure in writing, but the success and the three editions had no particular effect upon my mind. For one thing, I saw very few people. We had no society. My father had a horror of strangers, and would never see any one who came to the house, which was a continual wet blanket to my mother's cordial, hospitable nature; but she had given up struggling long before my time, and I grew up without any idea of the pleasures and companions of youth. I did not know them, and therefore did not miss them; but I daresay this helped to make me— not indifferent, rather unconscious, of what might in other circumstances have "turned my head." My head was as steady as a rock. I had nobody to praise me except my mother and Frank, and their applause—well, it was delightful, it was everything in the world—it was life,—but it did not count. They were part of me, and I of them, and we were all in it. After a while it came to be the custom that I should every night "read what I had written" to them before I went to bed. They were very critical sometimes, and I felt while I was reading whether my little audience was with me or not, which put a good deal of excitement into the performance. But that was all the excitement I had.

I began another book called 'Caleb Field,' about the Plague in London, the very night I had finished 'Margaret Maitland.' I had been reading Defoe, and got the subject into my head. It came to one volume only, and I took a great deal of trouble about a Nonconformist minister who spoke in antitheses very carefully constructed. I don't think it attracted much notice, but I don't remember. Other matters, events even of our uneventful life, took so much more importance in life than these books—nay, it must be a kind of affectation to say that, for the writing ran through everything. But then it was also subordinate to everything, to be pushed aside for any little necessity. I had no table even to myself, much less a room to work in, but sat at the corner of the family table with my writing-book, with everything going on as if I had been making a shirt instead of writing a book. Our rooms in those days were sadly wanting in artistic arrangement. The table was in the middle of the room, the centre round which everybody sat with the candles or lamp upon it. My mother sat always at needlework of some kind, and talked to whoever might be present, and I took my share in the conversation, going on all the same with my story, the little groups of imaginary persons, these other talks evolving themselves quite undisturbed. It would put me out now to have some one sitting at the same table talking while I worked —at least I would think it put me out, with that sort of conventionalism which grows upon one. But up to this date, 1888, I have never been shut up in a separate room, or hedged off with any observances. My study, all the study I have ever attained to, is the little second drawing-room, the first being where all the (feminine) life of the house goes on; and I don't think I have ever had two hours undisturbed (except at night, when everybody is in bed) during my whole literary life. Miss Austen, I believe, wrote in the same way, and very much for the same reason; but at her period the natural flow of life took another form. The family were half ashamed to have it known that she was not just a young lady like the others, doing her embroidery. Mine were quite pleased to magnify me, and to be proud of my work, but always with a hidden sense that it was an admirable joke, and no idea that any special facilities or retirement was necessary. My mother, I believe, would have felt her pride and rapture much checked, almost humiliated, if she had conceived that I stood in need of any artificial aids of that or any other description.

After this period our poor Willie became a minister of the English Presbyterian Church, then invested with glory by the Free Church, its real parent, which in our fervid imagination we had by this time dressed up with all sorts of traditional splendour. It, we flattered ourselves, was the direct successor of the two thousand seceders of 1661 (was that the date?). There had been a downfall, we allowed, into Unitarianism and indifference; but this was the real, and a very respectable, tradition. Willie went to a very curious little place in the wilds of Northumberland, where my mother and I decided—with hopes strangely wild, it seems to me now, after all that had gone before— that he was at length to do well, and be as strenuous to his duty as he was gentle in temper and tender in heart. Poor Willie! It was a sort of show village with pretty flowery cottages and gardens, in a superior one of which he lived, or rather lodged, the income being very small and the position humble. It was, however, so far as my recollection goes, sufficiently like a Scotch parish to convince us that the church and parsonage were quite exotic, and the humble chapel the real religious centre of the place. A great number of the people were, I believe, Presbyterians, and the continuance of their worship and little strait ceremony undoubted from the time of the Puritans, though curiously enough the minister was known to his flock by the title of the priest. I don't in the least recollect what the place was like, yet a whiff of the rural air tinged with peat or wood, and of the roses with which the cottages were garlanded, and an impression of the subdued light through the greenish small window half veiled in flowers, remains with me,—very sweet, homely, idyllic, like something in a pathetic country story of peace overshadowed with coming trouble. There was a shadow of a ruined castle in the background, I think Norham; but all is vague,—I have not the clear memory of what I saw in my youth that many people retain. I see a little collection of pictures, but the background is all vague. The only vehicle we could get to take us to Berwick was, I recollect, a cart, carefully arranged with straw-covered sacking to make us comfortable. The man who drove it was very anxious to be engaged and taken with us as "Miss Wilson's coachman." Why mine, or why we should have taken a rustic "Jockey-to-the-fair" for a coachman, if we had wanted such an article, I don't know. I suppose there must have been some sort of compliment implied to my *beaux yeux*, or I should not have remembered this. We left Willie with thankful hearts, yet an ache of fear. Surely in that peaceful humble quiet, with those lowly sacred duties and all his goodness and kindness, he would do well! I don't remember how long it continued. So long as he kept up the closest correspondence, writing every second day and giving a full account of himself, there was an uneasy satisfaction at home. But there is always a prophetic ache in the heart when such calamity is on the way.

One day, without warning, except that his letters had begun to fail a little, my mother received an anonymous letter about him. She went off that evening, travelling all night to Edinburgh, which was the quickest way, and then to Berwick. She remained a few miserable days, and brought him back with her, finally defeated in the battle which he was quite unfit to wage. He must have been then, I think, about thirty-three, in the prime of strength and youth; but except for a wavering and uncertain interval now and then, he never got out of the mire nor was able to support himself again. I remember the horrible moment of his coming home. Frank and I went down, I suppose, to the ferry at Birkenhead to meet the travellers. We were all very grave —not a word of reproach did any one say, but to be cheerful, to talk about nothing, was impossible. We drove up in silence to the house where we lived, asking a faint question now and then about the journey. I remember that Willie had a little dog called Brownie with him, and the relief this creature was, which did not understand being shut up in the carriage and made little jumps at the window, and had to be petted and restrained. Brownie brought a little movement, an involuntary laugh at his antics, to break the horrible silence—an angel could scarcely have done more for us. When we got home there was the settling down in idleness, the hopeless decision of any wretched possibility there might be for him. The days and weeks and months in which he smoked and read old novels and the papers, and, most horrible of all, got to content himself with that life !

I had been in the habit of copying out carefully, quite proud of my neat MS., all my books, now becoming a recognised feature of the family life. It struck us all as a fine idea that Willie might copy them for me, and retrieve a sort of fictitious independence by getting 10 per cent upon the price of them ; and I really think he felt quite comfortable on this. Of course, the sole use of the copying was the little corrections and improvements I made in going over my work again.

It was after this that my cousin Frank came upon a visit. We had seen, and yet had not seen, a great deal of each other in London during the three months I had spent there with Willie; but my mind had been preoccupied with Willie chiefly, and a little with my book. When Frank made me the extraordinary proposal for which I was totally unprepared, that we should, as he said, build up the old Drumthwacket together, my only answer was an alarmed negative, the idea never having entered my mind. But in six months or so things changed. It is not a matter into which I can enter here.

In the spring of 1851 my mother and I were in Edinburgh, and there made the acquaintance of the

Wilsons, our second cousins,—George Wilson being at that time Professor of something which meant chemistry, but was not called so. His mother was an exceedingly bright, vivacious old lady, a universal devourer of books, and with that kind of scientific tendency which made her encourage her boys to form museums, and collect fossils, butterflies, &c. I forget how my mother and she got on, but I always liked her.

George Wilson was an excellent talker, full of banter and a kind of humour, full of ability, too, I believe, writing very amusing letters and talking very amusing talk, which was all the more credit to him as he was in very bad health, kept alive by the fact that he could eat, and so maintain a modicum of strength — enough to get on by. There were two daughters—Jessie and Jeanie—the younger of whom became my brother Frank's wife; and the eldest son, who was married, lived close by, and was then, I think, doing literary work for Messrs Nelson, reading for them and advising them about books. He very soon after this migrated to Canada, and became eventually President of University College, Toronto, and Sir Daniel in the end of his life.

My mother at this time renewed acquaintance with Dr Moir of Musselburgh, an old friend of hers, who had, I believe, attended me when, as a very small child, I fell into the fire, or rather against the bars of the grate, marking my arm in a way which it never recovered. This excellent man, whom everybody loved, was the Delta of 'Blackwood's Magazine,' and called everywhere by that name. He had written much gentle poetry, and one story *à la* Galt called 'Mansie Wauch,' neither of which were good enough for him, yet got him a certain reputation, especially some pathetic verses about children he had lost, which went to the heart of every mother who had lost children, my own mother first and foremost. He had married a very handsome stately lady, a little conventional, but with an unfailing and ready kindness which often made her mannerisms quite gracious and beautiful. There was already a handsome daughter married, though under twenty, and many other fine, tall, well-bred, handsome creatures, still in long hair and short skirts, growing up. I think I was left behind to pay a visit when my mother returned home, and then had a kind of introduction to Edinburgh literary society, in one case very important for myself. For in one expedition we made, Major Blackwood, one of the publishing firm, and brother of the editor of the 'Magazine,' was of the party; and my long connection with his family thus began. He was accompanied by a young man, a Mr Cupples, of whom, except his name, I have no recollection, but who was the author of a sea-story then, I think, going on in 'Blackwood,' called the 'Green Hand,' and who, it was hoped, would be as successful as the author of 'Tom Cringle' and the 'Cruise of the Midge,' a very effective contributor twenty years before. All I remember of him was that my cousin Daniel Wilson, who was also of the party, indignantly pointed out to me the airs which this young author gave himself, "as if it was such a great thing to be a contributor to 'Blackwood'!" I am afraid I thought it *was* a great thing, and had not remarked the young author's airs; but Daniel was of the opposite camp. Major Blackwood, who interested me most, was a mild soldierly man, with the gentlest manners and drooping eyelids, which softened his look, or so at least it appears to me at the end of so many years.

I remember that one of the places we visited was Wallyford, where was the house in which I was born, but of which I had no recollection. It must have been a pleasant homely house, with a projecting half turret enclosing the staircase, as in many houses in the Lothians, the passages and kitchen down-stairs floored with red brick, and a delightful large low

drawing-room above, with five greenish windows looking out upŏn Arthur's Seat in the distance, and a
ghost of Edinburgh.[1]   That room charmed me greatly,
and in after days I used to think of becoming its
tenant and living there, for the sake of the landscape
and the associations and that pretty old room; but
before I could have carried out such an idea, even had
it been more real than a fancy, the pretty house was
pulled down, and a square, aggressive, and very commonplace new farmhouse built in its place.

The consequence of my introduction to Major
Blackwood was, that some time in the course of the
following months I sent him the manuscript of my
story 'Katie Stewart': a little romance of my
mother's family, gleaned from her recollections and
descriptions.   The scene of this story was chiefly laid
in old Kellie Castle, which I was not then aware was
the home of our own ancestors, from whom it had
passed long before into the hands of the Erskines,
Earls of Kellie—with the daughter of which house
Katie Stewart had been brought up.   She was my
mother's great-aunt, and had lived to a great age.
She had seen Prince Charlie enter Edinburgh, and
had told all her experiences to my mother, who told
them to me, so that I never was quite sure whether
I had not been Katie Stewart's contemporary in my
own person.   And this was her love-tale.   I received
proofs of this story on the morning of my wedding-
day, and thus my connection with the firm of Blackwood began.   They were fond of nicknames, and I
was known among them by the name of "Katie" for
a long time, as I discovered lately (1896) in some old
letters.   I suppose they thought me so young and
simple (as they say in these letters) that the girl's
name was appropriate to me.   I was not tall ("middle
height" we called it in those days), and very inexperienced,—"so simple and yet self-possessed," I am

---

[1] This house is the scene of the story of 'Isabel Dysart,' reprinted since
Mrs Oliphant's death.—Ed.

glad to say Major Blackwood reports of me. I was only conscious of being dreadfully *shy*.

We were married in Birkenhead on the 4th May 1852,—and the old home, which had come to consist of such incongruous elements, was more or less broken up. My brother Frank, discontented and wounded partly by my marriage, partly by the determination to abandon him and follow me to London, which my father and mother had formed, married too, hastily, but very successfully in a way as it turned out, and so two new houses were formed out of the partial ruins of the old. Had the circumstances been different—had they stayed in Birkenhead and I gone alone with my husband to London—some unhappiness might have been spared. Who can tell? There would have been other unhappiness to take its place. They settled in a quaint little house in a place called Park Village, old-fashioned, semi-rustic, and pretty enough, with a long strip of garden stretching down to the edge of a deep cutting of the railway, where we used to watch the trains passing far below. The garden was gay with flowers, quantities of brilliant poppies of all colours I remember, which I liked for the colour and hated for the heavy ill odour of them, and the sensation as of evil flowers. Our house in Harrington Square was very near: it looked all happy enough but was not, for my husband and my mother did not get on.

My child's birth made a momentary gleam of joy soon lost in clouds.

My mother became ailing and concealed it, and kept alive—or at least kept her last illness off by sheer stress of will until my second child was born a year and a day after the first. She was with me, but sank next day into an illness from which she never rose. She died in September 1854, suffering no attendance but mine, though she concealed from me how ill she was for a long time. I remember the first moment in which I had any real fear, speaking to the doctor with a sudden impulse, in the front of her door, all in a green shade with the waving trees, demanding his real opinion. I do not think I had any understanding of the gravity of the circumstances. He shook his head, and I knew—the idea having never entered my mind before that she was to die. I recollect going away, walking home as in a dream, not able to go to her, to look at her, from whom I had never had a secret, with this secret in my soul that must be told least of all to her; and the sensation that here was something which would not lighten after a while as all my troubles had always done, and pass away. I had never come face to face with the inevitable before. But there was no daylight here—no hope—no getting over it. Then there followed a struggle of a month or two, much suffering on her part, and a long troubled watch and nursing on mine. At the very end I remember the struggle against overwhelming sleep, after nights and days in incessant anxiety, which made me so bitterly ashamed of the limits of wretched nature. To want to sleep while she was dying seemed so unnatural and horrible. I never had come within sight of death before. And, oh me! when all was over, mingled with my grief there was—how can I say it?—something like a dreadful relief.

Within a few months after, my little Marjorie, my second child, died on the 8th February; and then with deep shame and anguish I felt what I suppose was another wretched limit of nature. My dearest mother, who had been everything to me all my life, and to whom I was everything; the companion, friend, counsellor, minstrel, story-teller, with whom I had never wanted for constant interest, entertainment, and fellowship,—did not give me, when she died, a pang so deep as the loss of the little helpless baby, eight months old. I miss my mother till this moment when I am nearly as old as she was (sixty, 10th June 1888); I think instinctively still of asking her something, referring to her for information, and I dream constantly of being a girl with her at home. But at that moment her loss was nothing to me in comparison with the loss of my little child.

I lost another infant after that, a day old. My spirit sank completely under it. I used to go about saying to myself, " A little while and ye shall not see me," with a longing to get to the end and have all safe—for my one remaining, my eldest, my Maggie seemed as if she too must be taken out of my arms. People will say it was an animal instinct perhaps. Neither of these little ones could speak to me or exchange an idea or show love, and yet their withdrawal was like the sun going out from the sky— life remained, the daylight continued, but all was different. It seems strange to me now at this long distance—but so it was.

The glimpse of society I had during my married life in London was not of a very elevating kind; or perhaps I — with my shyness and complete unacquaintance with the ways of people who gave parties and paid incessant visits—was only unable to take any pleasure in it, or get beyond the outside petty view, and the same strange disappointment and disillusion with which the pictures and the stage had filled me, bringing down my ridiculous impossible ideal to the ground. I have tried to illustrate my youthful feelings about this several times in words. I had expected everything that was superlative,— beautiful conversation, all about books and the finest subjects, great people whose notice would be an honour, poets and painters, and all the sympathy of congenial minds, and the feast of reason and the flow of soul. But it is needless to say I found none of these things. We went "out," not very often, to parties where there was always a good deal of the literary element, but of a small kind, and where I found everything very commonplace and poor, not at all what I expected. I never did myself any justice,

as a certain little lion-hunter, a Jewish patroness of
the arts, who lived somewhere in the region about
Harley Street, said.   That is to say, I got as quickly
as I could into a corner and stood there, rather wist-
fully wishing to know people, but not venturing to
make any approach, waiting till some one should
speak to me; which much exasperated my aspiring
hostess, who had picked me up as a new novelist,
and meant me to help to amuse her guests, which
I had not the least idea how to do.   I fear I must
have been rather exasperating to my husband, who
was more given to society than I, and tried in vain
(as I can now see) to form me and make me attend
to my social duties, which even in such a small
matter as returning calls I was terribly neglectful of
—out of sheer shyness and gaucherie, I think; for I
was always glad and grateful when anybody would
insist on making friends with me, as a few people did.
There was an old clergyman, Mr Laing, who did, I
remember, and more or less his wife—he especially.
He liked me, I think, and complimented me by saying he did not like literary ladies—a sort of thing
people are rather disposed to say to me.   And Lance
(the painter of fruits and flowers and still life), who
was a wit in his way, was also a great friend of mine.
He dared me to put him in a book, and I took him at
his word and did so, making a very artless represen-
tation, and using some of his own stories; so that
everybody recognised the sketch, which was done in
mere fun and liking, and pleased him very much—the
only actual bit of real life I ever took for a book.   It
was in ' Zaidee,' I think.

Among my literary acquaintances was the Mr
Fullom who had read for old Colburn my first book,
and whose acquaintance as an eminent literary man
and great notability we had all thought at home it
would be such a fine thing to make.   He turned out
a very small personage indeed, a solemn man, with
a commonplace wife, people whom it was marvellous

to think of as intellectual. He wrote a book called
'The Marvels of Science,' a dull piece of manufacture,
for which by some wonderful chance he received a
gold medal, *Für Kunst*, from the King of Hanover.
I think I see him moving solemnly about the little
drawing-room with his medal on his breast, and the
wife following him. He soon stalked away into the
unknown, and I saw him no more. I forget how I
became acquainted with the S. C. Halls, who used
to ask me to their parties, and who were literary
people of the most prominent and conventional type,
rather satisfying to the sense on the whole, as the
sort of thing one expected. Mrs Hall had retired
upon the laurels got by one or two Irish novels, and
was surrounded by her husband with the atmosphere
of admiration, which was the right thing for a "fair"
writer. He took her very seriously, and she accepted
the *rôle*, though without, I think, any particular setting up of her own standard. I used to think and
say that she looked at me inquisitively, a little puzzled
to know what kind of humbug I was, all being hum-
bugs. But she was a kind woman all the same; and
I never forget the sheaf of white lilies she sent us for
my child's christening, for which I feel grateful still.
He was certainly a humbug of the old mellifluous
Irish kind—the sort of man whose specious friendli-
nesses, compliments, and "blarney" were of the most
innocent kind, not calculated to deceive anybody, but
always amusing. He told Irish stories capitally.

They had the most wonderful collection of people
at their house, and she would stand and smile and
shake hands, till one felt she must stiffen so, and had
lost all consciousness who anybody was. He on his
side was never tired, always insinuating, jovial, affectionate. It was at their house, I think, that we met
the Howitts—Mary Howitt, a mild, kind, delightful
woman, who frightened me very much, I remember,
by telling me of many babies whom she had lost
through some defective valve in the heart, which

she said was somehow connected with too much mental work on the part of the mother,—a foolish thing, I should think, yet the same thing occurred twice to myself. It alarmed and saddened me terribly—but I liked her greatly. There was a great deal about spiritualism (so called) in the air at this time—its first development in England,—and the Howitts' eldest daughter was an art medium producing wonderful scribble-scrabbles, which it was the wonder of wonders to find her mother, so full of sense and truth, so genuine herself, full of enthusiasm about.

I remember a day at the Halls, which must have been in the summer of 1853. They had then a pretty house at Addleston, near Chertsey. My husband and I travelled down by train in company with a dark, dashing person, an American lady, whom, on arriving at the station, we found to be going to the Halls too. She and I were put into their brougham to drive there, while the gentlemen walked ; and she did what she could in a patronising way to find out who I was. She thought me, I suppose, the poor little shy wife of some artist, whom the Halls were being kind to, or something of that humble kind. She turned out to be a literary person of great pretensions, calling herself Grace Greenwood, though that was not her real name,—and I was amused to find a paragraph about myself, as "a little homely Scotchwoman," in the book which she wrote when she got back. Two incidents of this entertainment remain very clear in my memory. One was, that being placed at table beside Mr Frost, the academician, who was very deaf and very gentle and kind, I was endeavouring with many mental struggles to repeat to him something that had produced a laugh, and which his wistful look had asked to understand, when suddenly one of those hushes which sometimes come over a large company occurred, and my voice came out distinct—to my own horrified consciousness, at least—a sound of terror and shame to me. The other was, that Gavan Duffy, one of the recent Irish rebels, and my husband began to discuss, I suppose, national characteristics, or what they believed to be such, when the Irishman mentioned gravely and with some heat that the frolic and the wit usually attributed to his countrymen were a mere popular delusion, while the Scotchman with equal earnestness repudiated the caution and prudence ascribed to his race,—which was whimsical enough to be remembered.

Another recollection of one of the Halls' evening-parties in town at a considerably later period rises like a picture before me. They were fond of every kind of lion and wonder, great and small. Rosa Bonheur, then at the height of her reputation, was there one evening, a round-faced, good-humoured woman, with hair cut short and divided at one side like a man's, and indeed not very distinct in the matter of sex so far as dress and appearance went. There was there also a Chinese mandarin in full costume, smiling blandly upon the company, and accompanied by a missionary, who had the charge of him. By some means or other the Chinaman was made to sing what we were informed was a sentimental ballad, exceedingly touching and romantic. It was like nothing so much as the howl of a dog, one of those grave pieces of canine music which my poor old Newfoundland used to give forth when his favourite organ-grinder came into the street. (Merry's performance was the most comical thing imaginable. There was one organ among many which touched his tenderest feelings. When it appeared once a-week, he rushed to it, seated himself beside the man, listened till rapture and sentiment were wound up to the highest pitch, and then, lifting up his nose and his voice to heaven,—sang. There could be no doubt that the dear dog was giving forth all the poetry of his being in that appalling noise,—his emotion, his sentiment, his profound seriousness were indisputable, while any human being within reach was overwhelmed and helpless with laughter.) The Chinaman sang exactly like Merry, with the same effect. Rosa Bonheur, I suppose, was more civil than *nous autres*, and her efforts to restrain the uncontrollable laugh were superhuman. She almost swallowed her handkerchief in the effort to conceal it. I can see her as in a picture, the central figure, with her bushy short hair, and her handkerchief in her mouth. All my recollections are like pictures, not continuous, only a scene detached and conspicuous here and there.

Miss Mulock was another of the principal figures perceptible in the somewhat dimmed panorama of that far-off life. Her friends the Lovells lived in Mornington Crescent, which was close to our little house in Harrington Square,—all in a remote region near Regent's Park, upon the Hampstead Road, where it seems very strange to me we should have lived, and which, I suppose, is dreadfully shabby and out-of-the-way. Perhaps it was shabby then, one's ideas change so greatly. Miss Mulock lived in a small house in a street a little farther off even in the wilds than ours. She was a tall young woman with a slim pliant figure, and eyes that had a way of fixing the eyes of her interlocutor in a manner which did not please my shy fastidiousness. It was embarrassing, as if she meant to read the other upon whom she gazed,—a pretension which one resented. It was merely, no doubt, a fashion of what was the intense school of the time. Mrs Browning did the same thing the only time I met her, and this to one quite indisposed to be read. But Dinah was always kind, enthusiastic, somewhat didactic and apt to teach, and much looked up to by her little band of young women. She too had little parties, at one of which I remember Miss Cushman, the actress, in a deep recitative, without any apparent tune in it, like the voice of a skipper at sea I thought it, giving forth Kingsley's song of "The Sands of Dee." I was rather afraid of the performer, though long afterwards she came to see me in Paris when I was in much sorrow, and her tenderness and feeling gave me the sensation of suddenly meeting a friend in the darkness, of whose existence there I had no conception. There used to be also at Miss Mulock's parties an extraordinary being in a wheeled chair, with an imperfect face (as if it had been somehow left unfinished in the making), a Mr Smedley, a terrible cripple, supposed to be kept together by some framework of springs and supports, of whom the story was told that he had determined, though the son of a rich man, to maintain himself, and make himself a reputation, and had succeeded in doing both, as the writer—of all things in the world—of sporting novels. He was the author of 'Lewis Arundel' and 'Frank Fairleigh,' both I believe athletic books, and full of feats of horsemanship and strength; which was sufficiently pathetic—though the appearance of this poor man somewhat frightened me too.

Mr Lovell, the father of one of Miss Mulock's chief friends, was the author of " The Wife's Secret," a play lately revived, and which struck me when I saw it as one of the most conventional and unreal possible, very curious to come out of that sober city man. All the guests at these little assemblies were something of the same kind. One looked at them rather as one looked at the figures in Madame Tussaud's, wondering if they were waxwork or life —wondering in the other case whether the commonplace outside might not cover a painter or a poet or something equally fine—whose ethereal qualities were all invisible to the ordinary eye.

What I liked best in the way of society was when we went out occasionally quite late in the evening, Frank and I, after he had left off work in his studio, and went to the house of another painter uninvited, unexpected, always welcome,— I with my work. Alexander Johnstone's house was the one to which we went most. I joined the wife in her little drawing-room, while he went up-stairs to the studio. (They all had the drawing-room proper of the house, the first-floor room, for their studios.) We women talked below of our subjects, as young wives and young mothers do—with a little needlework and a little gossip. The men above smoked and talked their subjects, investigating the picture of the moment, going over it with advice and criticism; no doubt giving each other their opinions of other artists and other pictures too. And then we supped, frugally, cheerfully, and if there was anything of importance in the studio the wives went up to look at it, or see what progress it had made since the last time, after supper. And then we walked home again. They paid us a return visit some days after of just the same kind. If I knew them now, which I no longer do, I would ask them to dinner, and they me, and most likely we would not enjoy it at all. But those simple evenings were very pleasant. Our whole life was upon very simple lines at this period: we dined in the middle of the day, and our little suppers were not of a kind to require elaborate preparation if another pair came in unexpectedly. It was true society in its way. Nothing of the kind seems possible now.

II.

January 18, 1891.

I FORGET where I left off in this pitiful little record of my life. It was with an attempt to remember somebody worth telling about in the old life in London. We began our housekeeping in Harrington Square, on the way to Camden Town, I think, whereabouts a number of artists had established themselves; though I remember at this moment only the Pickersgills, and not even them very well. Then my Maggie was born, and my dear mother, then still living, had the joy and delight of her grandchild, the third Margaret, — one pleasure at least in that dreary ending of her life. I remember saying that there had been always something wanting to my mother, which I had felt without knowing what it was, till I saw her with my baby in her dear arms. Maggie was always a beautiful child. My dear little Marjorie was always pale and delicate, but with glorious eyes—to think of an eight months' old baby having these! But I remember that as she died she opened them widely and seemed to fix them on me as she lay on my knee, giving up her little soul in that look of consciousness, as it appeared to me. That was in 1855, thirty-six years ago, but I have never forgot the look with which that baby died.

After this we removed to Ulster Place, a larger house, which is the house in London upon which my mind dwells. I pass it sometimes going to King's Cross, when we have gone to Scotland, and

a strange fantastic thought crossed my mind the
first time I did so in these latter years, as if I
might go up to the door and go in and find the
old life going on, and see my husband coming down
the road, and my little children returning from their
walk. There was a kind of feeling of increasing prosperity when we went to that house,—more feeling
than reality; and I tried to make it pretty, though
I fear it would have looked rather dreadful to the
ideas of this changed time. It is at the corner of
Ulster Place, looking down Harley Street, and next
to a large square house with gardens, in which the
Oudh princesses or begums lived when they came to
England to plead their cause. Some of our windows
looked over this garden, and we had glimpses of the
strange Eastern figures flitting about — the white
robes and shawls, and gleaming ornaments and
dusky faces. Later Frank took a small house farther
up the road near Baker Street, I think, to make a
studio, and began to have his painted windows executed there under his own superintendence, partly
because he was not satisfied with the way in which
his designs were carried out, partly with the hope
that he might then get into a substantial business,
instead of precarious artist - work. There was a
brightness and hopefulness about the beginning.
We were both sanguine, and he dreamed of work
that might go on under his eye and keep our household going, while he might return to his painting,
which was the work he loved best. So things went
on very brightly for a time. He painted his King
Richard picture, which was sold for a tolerable
price; and then that of the Prodigal, which I have
still, and which I think a very touching picture.
And orders came in for windows. And, best of all,
our delightful boy was born. Ah, me! If I had
continued this narrative at the time when I broke
it off in 1888, I should have told of this event and
all its pleasantness, if not with a light heart, yet

without the sudden tears that blind me now, so that I cannot see the page. My beautiful delightful child, with all the little jests, that he had come too late for church, and so was unpunctual all his life after; my Sunday child, "blythe and bonny and happy and gay," as the old rhyme says. I was very anxious at his birth because of the two babies I had lost, and had implored the doctor, my old, kind, cranky Dr Allison, to examine him and tell me honestly if all was well with him. "That fellow!" he said; "he has lungs like a sponge." How well I remember the room, the doctor's look, the baby that had brought joy with him, the flood of ease and happiness that came into my heart. (The child was health itself, and vigour and sweetness and life. He was born on Sunday, November 16, 1856. And that winter was a happy and cheerful one. Sebastian Evans, then a fine young fellow fresh from Cambridge, turned aside from the current of his life because of the "doubts," then becoming a fashionable malady, which would not let him go into the Church, and drifting a little, not knowing what to do, came about a window, a memorial to his father; and he and Frank taking to each other, remained as an assistant to help with the cartoons, and by-and-by with the idea of being a partner and sharing the business. He is mixed in all this cheerful time for me. He cheered up my husband so; his great honest laugh recurs to me; his cheerful company, which drew Frank out of the worries and troubles with his workmen, and restored him to the buoyancy of youth and good-fellowship. When the idea of a partnership took shape, his brother, Mr (now Sir) John Evans, the well-known antiquary, who was also a business man — paper-maker, one of the 'Times' people—came to go through Frank's books (if he had any books), and see whether it was worth his brother's while. He came afterwards to dine, and it was not till he had gone, after all the long evening, that I heard what the decision was. After Mr Evans had seen and heard all there was to see and hear, he congratulated my husband that his circumstances permitted him to be so indifferent to profit. And there was an end of the partnership, to which I had looked forward for the sake of the companionship to Frank, I fear not with much thought of profit. We neither of us, I suppose, knew anything about business—so long as we could get on and live, that seemed all one cared for; but it was a little dash as of cold water when the business-man paid this satirical compliment, and showed us our true position. I was, of course, writing steadily all the time, getting about £400 for a novel, and already, of course, being told that I was working too fast, and producing too much. I linger upon this brief, and, as it feels to me now, halcyon time. I used the little back drawing-room, which was at first dining-room, for my work, the real dining-room of the house being Frank's painting-room, where I used to write all the morning, getting up now and then in the middle of a sentence to run down-stairs and have a few words with him, or to play with the children when they came in from their walk—my dear little Maggie, my baby-boy, two beautiful children, fresh and sweet, well and strong, reviving my heart, that had been so heavy and sore with the loss of my two infants, by the sight of their beautiful shining faces.

When I look back on my life, among the happy moments which I can recollect is one which is so curiously common and homely, with nothing in it, that it is strange even to record such a recollection, and yet it embodied more happiness to me than almost any real occasion as might be supposed for happiness. It was the moment after dinner when I used to run up-stairs to see that all was well in the nursery, and then to turn into my room on my way down again to wash my hands, as I had a way of doing before I took up my evening work, which was generally needlework, something to make for the children. My bedroom had three windows in it, one looking out upon the gardens I have mentioned, the other two into the road. It was light enough with the lamplight outside for all I wanted. I can see it now, the glimmer of the outside lights, the room dark, the faint reflection in the glasses, and my heart full of joy and peace—for what?—for nothing—that there was no harm anywhere, the children well above stairs and their father below. I had few of the pleasures of society, no gaiety at all. I was eight-and-twenty, going down-stairs as light as a feather, to the little frock I was making. My husband also gone back for an hour or two after dinner to his work, and well—and the bairnies well. I can feel now the sensation of that sweet calm and ease and peace.

I have always said it is in these unconsidered moments that happiness is—not in things or events that may be supposed to cause it. How clear it is over these more than thirty years!

In the early summer one evening after dinner (we dined, I think, at half-past six in those days) I went out to buy some dessert-knives on which I had set my heart—they were only plated, but I had long wanted them, and by some chance was able to give myself that gratification. I had marked them in a shop not far off, and was pleased to get them, and specially happy. Some one had dined with us, either Sebastian Evans or my brother-in-law Tom,—some one familiar and intimate who was with Frank. When I came back again there was a little agitation, a slight commotion which I could not understand; and then I was told that it was nothing—the merest slight matter, nothing to be frightened at. Frank had, in coughing, brought up a little blood.

And so the happy time came to an end. I don't think I was much alarmed at first, I knew so little. I was quite ready to believe, after the first shock, that it might turn out to be nothing, and to have no consequences. I was much intent upon going to Scotland that year, I remember, to Mrs Moir at Musselburgh—and I did go, Frank promising to join me in a short time. After I was gone I took a great panic in my impulsive way and came in to Edinburgh on Sunday morning and telegraphed to him to know how he was, waiting about the railway station the whole of the Sunday to have an answer, but got none,—only a letter in due time scolding me for my foolishness. We had no habit of telegraphing in those days, it being still a new thing.

But he never was well after. I thought, and perhaps he too thought, that it was the worry of the work, which began to get too much for him, and the difficulty of managing the men, who were of the art-workmen class, and highly paid, and untrustworthy to the last degree. However important it might be to get the work done they were never to be relied upon, not even when they saw him—always most kind and friendly to them, incapable of treating them otherwise than if they had been gentlemen— ill, worn-out, dying by inches; not even when it became a matter of life and death for him to get free. They were well paid, educated in their way, thinking themselves a kind of artists—and I had always been brought up with a high idea of the honour and virtue of working men. I was very indignant at this behaviour, of course, and cruelly undeceived,—and I do not think I have ever got over the impression made upon me by their callousness and want of honour and feeling. I remember most wrathfully contrasting their behaviour with that of my maids, who stood by me to the last moment; knowing we were breaking up our home and going away, and that they would be in no respect advantaged by us, yet who were as loyal and true as the others were selfish and cruel. My husband did not like it to be said—but it was so. Before we decided definitely to give up everything and go abroad, Frank went to consult Dr Walsh, who was the great authority on the lungs at that time. He lived in Harley Street, I think. I went with my husband to the door, and leaving him there walked up and down the street till he came out again. I think he was to meet Mr Quain there, who was attending him at the time. And here again there is a moment that stands out clear over all these years. I was very anxious, walking up and down, praying and keeping myself from crying, sick with anxiety, starting at every sound of a door opening. He met me with a smile, telling me the report was excellent. There was very little the matter, chiefly over - work, and that all would be well when he got away. The relief was unspeakable : relief from pain is the highest good on earth, the most exquisite feeling,—I have always said so. It was in the upper part of Harley Street that he came up to me and told me this, and my heart leapt up with this delightful sense of anxiety stilled.

Afterwards, in Rome, Robert Macpherson told me what he said was the true story of the consultation—that the doctors had told Frank his doom; that his case was hopeless, but that he had not the courage to tell me the truth. I was angry and wounded beyond measure, and would not believe that my Frank had deceived me, or told another what he did not tell to me. Neither do I think he would have gone away, to expose me with my little children to so awful a trial in a foreign place, had this been the case. And yet the blessed deliverance of that moment was not real either. The truth most likely lay between the two.

We left England in January 1859 to go to Italy. We neither of us knew anything about Italy, but that it was the sunny South—and of all places in the world it was Florence we chose to go to in the middle of winter,—Florence not as it is now, but cold and austere, without the comforts into which it has been trained since then. The journey was a dreadful one. Tom Oliphant went with us to Paris. I have no doubt that he felt he was taking leave of his brother for the last time. We were none of us experienced in Continental travelling, and in those days travellers were shut up in the waiting-rooms, not allowed to get into the train till the last moment. It was my first experience of having to take the management of things myself, and all was new to me, and my French of the most limited description. Thus it happened that what with my ignorance, and Tom's leave-taking, and the two children, and all the excitement and trouble together, our luggage was not registered, nobody thinking anything about it. We were to sleep at Lyons, and when we arrived there late at night the luggage was not forthcoming: we had no ticket,—I knew nothing about it. Nothing was to be done, accordingly, but to telegraph to Paris, and remain in Lyons till it came. We had travelled second-class, one of the few times we ever did so,—I have always had a stupid objection to this kind of economy, perhaps to all kinds of economy, though I have never been extravagant,—so I suppose our train was a slow one. I remember that there was a cheerful young fellow in our carriage who belonged to Beauçain, and who kept Frank amused, and, as it became cold in the afternoon, took off his own coat to add to the shawls and rugs that were piled upon him, and got out at one of the stations to bring a *chauffepied* or *chauffrette*—a thing filled with wood embers — for his feet: the hot - water stools which are such a nuisance now did not exist then, in second-class at least. How grateful I was to this young man, and how warmly I remember his kindness over all these years! The luggage episode made us very late. We were detained at the cold dark station at Lyons till all the other passengers

were gone, and not a cab was to be found. At last
we were allowed to share one that passed with a
single passenger in it, and so got to our hotel—a
helpless party as ever was. My poor Frank, ill and
worn out, cold and miserable, myself so unaccustomed to manage, good Jane who had never been
in a foreign country before, and the two little ones,
Maggie five, Cyril two—and nothing with us to make
them comfortable, not even a hand-bag, not a night-
gown for the children. Next day Frank insisted that
I should go out to see the place, though he would
not leave the house himself; and I drove, taking Jane
and the children with me, to Notre Dame de Four-
vières, where there was a wonderful view over the
town, and the strange little church full of ex-votos,
which I looked at with a bewildering ignorance, and
with such an aching and miserable heart! I think
that in some things I was younger than my years.
I was thirty, but with very little experience of the
world, and always shy and apt to keep behind backs.
I forget if the luggage came that night, but I think
it did, and there arose another difficulty. We were
but very sparingly supplied with money, and had
brought just enough for the journey to Marseilles
and one night's rest at Lyons. And next morning I
found that we had not enough to pay our bill and
journey, and that it was a *fête*, and the banks all
closed. This sort of thing has never been a bugbear
to me as to many people, and I went to the landlord
of the hotel and told him exactly how things were,
though with no small trembling. No one, however,
could be more kind than he was. He would not even
take from me what I could have paid him, but gave
me the address of a hotel at Marseilles where he
directed me to go, and pay his bill there. We went
away, therefore, in much better spirits, having our
boxes, and with that elated consciousness of having
been kindly treated, which, I suppose, gives one a
feeling somehow of having deserved it, of having been

appreciated, for it certainly warms the heart and im-
proves the aspect of everything. Frank must have
been better, for I remember walking down to the
harbour with him when we got to Marseilles, and
discovering—with what thankfulness!—that the boat
for Leghorn had sailed, and that we must either wait
two days for another or go on by land. I hate the
sea, and had always longed to do this, but had not,
I suppose, liked to propose it, or else had been over-
ruled by my husband. We went on accordingly to
Nice by diligence, which was not very comfortable,
for we were in the interior, the five of us, with two
other people,—a man and his son going to Antibes,
where the lad was to draw for the conscription. I
forget whether it was on this journey or when we
were approaching Marseilles that the sunrise upon
the new unaccustomed landscape struck me so—
the awful rose of dawn coming over the wide sweep
of the country, the mulberry trees all stripped of
their leaves, standing out against the growing light.
I remember, too, the delightful sweeps and folds of
the Maritime Alps, the green of the cork-trees, as I
was told, and the heavenly curves of the coast; and
Cannes, which I seem to see as little more than a
village, lying half on the hill and half on the beach,
with one great stone pine standing up against the
extraordinary blue of the sea. We must have been
about twenty-four hours in the diligence or more,
and got to Nice, I think, in the afternoon. By this
time, I suppose, my inclination to careless expenditure (such as it was, so little to anybody that had any
margin) must have got the better of Frank's wiser instincts, for we stayed a day or two at Nice, and went
the rest of the way in a vettura. So far as I recollect,
we stopped only once — at Alassio — between Nice
and Genoa. I shall never forget that night: the
hotel was an old palace, and in those days comfort
had scarcely invaded even those coasts of the Riviera.
We were taken into a huge room with a shining

marble floor, one or two rugs in front of the fireplace and by the side of the bed, and no fire. The mere sight of the place was enough to freeze the tired traveller, so ill and languid to begin with. I feel still the chill that went into my heart at the sight of this room, so unfit for him; but we soon got a blazing fire. I remember kneeling by it lighting it with the great fir cones, which blazed up so quickly, and all the reflections, as if in water, in the dark polished marble of the floor.

At Genoa we were somehow strangely fortunate. We went to what I have always supposed to be the Hôtel de la Ville, but that must have been a mistake, and I believe it was the Croce di Malta. It was one of the hotels close to the bay, looking out over the terrace and promenade that surrounds it. And here, again, the outlook being so lovely and rest so desirable, Frank wanted to stay. The landlady was English, and she offered me a beautiful suite of rooms, a great *salon*, commanding the view, with two large bedrooms attached to it. I was enchanted, but in terror for the price—when she said I might have it for eight francs a-day, the whole apartment. Why she was so good I never could tell. I think it was because of my bonnie little Maggie. Whether she had lost a child like her, or whether I only fancied so, I cannot tell. Perhaps the good woman was sorry for us all, and saw, as I did not see, how little chance there was that my husband would ever return. I recollect now the delight of the beautiful room—the walls all frescoed, not very finely perhaps, but yet the mere fact was something, the bay lying before the windows, and what was almost as beautiful at the moment — a great fire; not a few damp logs as we had been having, but a huge fire of coals and wood, which warmed my invalid through and through. I remember the glow of it and the children playing on the warm carpet, all so perfect a contrast to the

last night's chill and misery, and the feeling of
settling down in that comfort and warmth, though
it was only for two or three days.   My heart always contrived to rise whenever it had a chance,
and I think Frank was pleased.

We got into Florence in a fog, and again very
chill and tired.   I remember thinking that it might
have been Manchester for anything one saw or felt
that was like the South, and as soon as that was
possible left the hotel there for lodgings in Via
Maggio.   In all this our ignorance and want or
experience did us great harm.   The Via Maggio,
a deep street of high houses on the other side of
the Arno, was as unfavourable a spot as we could
have chosen, and to make it worse we were on the
shady side of the street.   We were on·the second
floor—a long straggling apartment with some rooms
towards the Piazza Santo Spirito, I think; and these
were sunny, and we ought· to have hired them, but
the *salon* was on the other side, and very cold.   I
had not sense to see how bad that must have been
for Frank, but used the rooms as they were arranged
in a helpless way.   I think there was a dreadful time
at first,—he suffering, unable for any exertion, sitting
silent, without even books, till my soul was crushed,
not knowing what to do or how to rouse him.   I
had to go on working all the time, and not very
successfully, our whole income, which was certain for
the time, being £20 a-month, which Mr Blackwood
had engaged to send me on the faith of articles.   To
think of the whole helpless family going to Italy,
children and maid and all, upon that alone!—but
things were very cheap in Florence then, and I don't
think I was at all afraid, nay, the reverse, always
inclined to spend.   Of course this must have added
to Frank's depression, for which I was sometimes
inclined to blame him, not knowing how ill he was.
He got rheumatism in addition to other troubles;
and I have the clearest vision of him sitting close

by the little stove in the corner of the room, wrapped up, with a rug upon his knees, and saying nothing, while I sat near the window, trying with less success than ever before to write, and longing for a word, a cheerful look, to disperse a little the heavy atmosphere of trouble. I forget how we came to know a Mr Skottowe, a lame man, who had been an artist, and who came to see us sometimes, to my great thankfulness, for he cheered Frank a little. There was also the Scotch minister, Mr Macdougall, who is still in Florence, and who sent several people to see me, a beautiful Miss M. among the rest, whose distinction was that she refused a duke! and who had dedicated herself to her old father and mother, then very old, and she no longer young, — a very attractive woman, whose sacrifice I grudged dreadfully, though she did not. I might have got into a little society, but had no desire to do so, nor any pleasure in it. I remember Frank going to see the Pitti or Uffizi for the first time, and coming back in a kind of despair: his feeling was not the *anch' io pittore*, but the other far less cheerful sense of what wonders had been done, and how far he was from being able to come within a hundred miles (as he thought) of what he saw. No doubt illness had much to do with this depression, which I, all sanguine and sure that he could do what he would, were he but well, did not sympathise in, — almost, I fear, felt to be a weakness. He recovered his spirits a little after a time, when the winter began to pass away and good weather came. I remember, however, with great and terrible vividness one scene, one day. It was the funeral day of a young Archduchess. I forget who she was : the wife of one of the Archduke's sons, who had died away from Florence and was brought home for burial. Frank, who was sometimes hard on me, as I on him, insisted that I should go out to see the procession, which I did most unwillingly all alone. It must have been very early in the year, for it was at his worst time. I walked as far as the Porta Santa Trinità, I think, and I don't think I saw any procession. It was a grey day, the sky heavy, the Arno running grey under the bridge, the hills all grey, the air tingling with the tolling of the bells, and sombre streams of people flowing towards the gate where the funeral train was to come in; as sad as any could be, a young woman forlorn, with nobody to give me even a kind look, and nothing before or about me that was not as grey and tragic as the skies. I paused a little there, having been carried so far by the instinct of pleasing him who had sent me out to see; and then I could bear it no longer and went back again, to find him sitting silent as before—by the fire.

But things brightened, as I have said, when the weather improved and it began to get warm. He thought of a picture to paint, a scene in which Macchiavelli should be the chief figure, and we began to visit the galleries, and to go out together. All sorts of strange things — not strange at all now, but wonderful then—went on in Via Maggio. Scarcely a night passed but we heard the chant of a passing funeral, and going to the window saw far below, as in a deep gorge, the torches glowing, the strange figures of the *confraternità* carrying the bier, and their tramp on the stony causeway. Sometimes it was the *misericordia*, carrying not the dead but somebody hurt by an accident; and in the day-time the deep street underneath was always a diversion, and I used to look out for the dearest sight of all—two little figures at the feet of tall Jane, or rather the one dear figure at her feet, the other always with a song or shout, in her arm against her ample shoulder. She was always very big, at this time about four-and-twenty, a finely developed, strong, large, substantial tower of a woman — the ox-eyed Juno, as we used to call her. Ah me!

would they come down from the Boboli gardens
with their hands full of anemones if I were at the
windows of the Casa Grassini now?

While we were there the revolution occurred—
which, so much as we saw of it, was more like
a popular *festa* than anything else. We had not
known, being strangers and Frank so ill, going
out little, what was going on; but a curious agitation and excitement made itself somehow felt in
the air even up in our second floor. I don't know
really except by a sort of sympathetic instinct what
it was that took us to the windows to watch the
unusual coming and going. And then suddenly
opposite us, in the Casa Ridolfi, I think, there was
unfurled a great Italian tricolour—the green, white,
and red—and in a moment like fire the whole
population seemed to blaze out in the national
colours, man, woman, child, and horse, every living
thing; and there began to be a shout of "Viva
l'Italia!" everywhere, wherever two people met in
the deep streets, a shout that my dear baby boy
took up in that little voice of his that was never
silent. I was very eager too; but Frank was rather
nervous, and unwilling to be in any way mixed up
in the crowd, with whose doings we, as strangers,
he thought, had nothing to do. I got him, however, at last to come out, and we went up to the
front of the Pitti Palace, where a great many people
were hanging about, and where at that moment
the Grand Duke was in full colloquy with the
representatives of the people. Notwithstanding the
excitement of which I was full, it was a little forlorn
to stand out there with our very faint knowledge
of Italian, and nobody to tell us what was going
on; and Frank had no desire to be in the heart
of the revolution, if it was a revolution, as I had.
Where all the cockades, the rosettes, the ribbons,
the little bouquets, all the red, white, and green
came from, at a moment's notice, or without even

a moment's notice, was an endless wonder to me; and the delight of the people, and the air of universal holiday, had none of the graver features that one expected. I am not sure that I was not a little disappointed at the entire peacefulness of the whole proceeding. We heard afterwards that the Grand Duke had given orders for the bombardment of the town, which would have had a fine effect indeed in Via Maggio had it taken place, but I don't know that the report was true. Florence was at this time the very cheapest place to live in I have ever known. We had, like most other strangers, our dinner sent in from the Trattoria every evening. It was the usual sort of meal— soup, two kinds of meat, one of them generally a chicken, a vegetable dish, and a *dolce;* plenty for us all, with fragments left over, and the price was five pauls, not quite two francs fifty centimes. I wonder if anywhere in Europe that could be had now?

We had brought an introduction to the Embassy, and the Embassy sent us huge cards in return, but took no more notice, which was just as well: what disappointed me more was, that the Brownings, to whom also we had letters, had left Florence for Rome, where we saw them subsequently. By this time I must have written, I suppose, some half-dozen books or more, and had a little bit of reputation, a very little bit in a small way, but was very anxious it should be kept to ourselves. Just before we left Florence, I remember Mr Skottowe came one day quite excited: he had heard this from Mr Macdougall, who had heard it accidentally from some one else "I thought," he said, "I had found out there was something out of the common for myself, and now it appears all the world knows." I wonder if I should have remembered that, if it had not been a compliment. I did not get many sweetmeats of the kind, so I suppose it was a little pleasure to me. I do not know that Florence itself impressed me very much: how should it, with my mind so full of other things?—my sick husband, my little children, my work, and the precariousness of our means of living (though I don't think that troubled me much). I remember nature—as I always do—more than art, and the view from Bellosguardo above all the treasures of the galleries. Frank was profoundly, depressingly, as I have said, impressed by the pictures at first—and all the glory of them. I for my part used to stray into one small room in the Pitti, I think, where at that time the great picture of the Visitation—Albertinelli's—hung alone. By that time I knew that another baby was coming, and it seemed to do me good to go and look at these two women, the tender old Elizabeth, and Mary with all the awe of her coming motherhood upon her. I had little thought of all that was to happen to me before my child came, but I had no woman to go to, to be comforted—except these two.

Florence was just becoming warm and bright and good for an invalid to live in, when Frank was seized with a desire to go to Rome. I think it very likely that, feeling himself no better, and having the doctor's verdict, which he had not told me, in his mind, he wanted me to be near the Macphersons, who would be a help and stand-by. We went on accordingly to Rome in May. I had not been very successful in my work for 'Blackwood.' I sent a story of Florence called 'Felicita,' I think (knowing nothing about Florence!), and other articles, not good, and I suppose I must have written something for Mr Blackett while in Florence, but I cannot recollect. We could not certainly have struck our tents as we did and moved on to Rome, by steamboat from Leghorn to Civita Vecchia, on our twenty pounds a-month. I remember all about the journey strangely enough, from the green water, so transluc-

ent and profound under the boat, that took us out
to the steamer at Leghorn, and the remarks of some
Irish ladies, who were the companions of the voyage,
and who made friends with the children, and suggested, perhaps guessing from some sad look in my
face, that there had been some loss between the two,
—there were but three years between them, but there
had been two babies born to die: I don't remember
their names nor anything about them except that,
and that they were kind—and Irish.   Maggie was
five and a half, with her brown curls falling on her
shoulders, and my little Cyril was two and a half,—
always the sweetest, most winning child.   He had
been called Cyril at first, then by himself when he
began to talk Tiddy, which was always his family
name all his life, though not a pretty one ; sometimes Tids, which is almost too dear, too familiar
and tender, the most caressing of all, to be thought
of now.   But I must not begin to write of my boy,
or I will not be able to think of anything else—not
five months yet since he has been taken from me !

The Macphersons had a curious position in Rome,
and it is difficult to describe them.   He always had
a curious position,—the son of a very poor man in
Edinburgh with the humblest connections, yet not
distantly related, I believe, to Cluny Macpherson,
the chief of the clan ; himself a poor painter—literally a poor painter, never good for very much, yet
always, as I have been told, in society, and with
friends quite beyond his apparent position.   There
was some romantic story about a lady in the Highlands, intercepted letters and so forth, which was
told on one side as the reason for his leaving the
country with something like a broken heart, but on
the other was made to appear like the disappointment of a fortune-hunter.   I don't know which was
true.   There was very little that was like a fortune-
hunter in his careless, hot-headed, humorous, noisy
Bohemian ways.   He had given up his painting in

Rome, and had taken to photographing; and his photographs of Rome were, I think, among the first that were executed. He had been a long time in Rome, had been there during the bombardment, and I suppose had rendered some services to the papal side, for he was always patronised more or less by the priests, and was *nero* to the heart, standing by all the old institutions with the stout prejudices of an old Tory quite inaccessible to reason. Indeed reason had nothing to do with him. He was full of generosities and kindness, full of humour and whim and fun—quarrelling hotly and making up again; a big, bearded, vehement, noisy man, a combination of Highlander and Lowlander, Scotsman and Italian, with the habits of Rome and Edinburgh all rubbed together, and a great knowledge of the world in general and a large acquaintance with individuals in particular to give force to the mixture, and to increase his own interest and largeness as a man. I could not bear him at first, poor Robert,—we used to quarrel upon almost every subject; but in the end I got to be almost fond of him, as he was, I believe, of me, though we were so absolutely unlike. Some years before I was married he had married Geraldine Bate, a niece of Mrs Jameson, very much against the aunt's will, to whom the Roman photographer seemed a very poor match for her pretty Geddie at eighteen. And so he was, and it was not a very successful marriage—chiefly, perhaps, because of the constant presence in their house of Mrs Bate, who encouraged Geddie in her little rebellions against her husband and her love of gaiety and admiration. But Robert was no meek victim, and never hesitated to tell mamma his mind. There used to be a fierce row often in the house, from which he would stride forth plucking his red beard and sending forth fire and flame; but when he came back would have his hands full of offerings, even to the mother-in-law, and his face full of sunshine, as if it had never known a cloud.

Geddie was of course full of faults, untidy, disorderly, fond of gaiety of every kind, incapable of the dull domestic life which seemed the right thing to me, ready to go off upon a merrymaking at a moment's notice, indifferent what duty she left behind, yet quite as ready to give up night after night to nurse a sick friend, and to put herself to any inconvenience to help, or take entirely upon her shoulders, those who were in need. And a pretty creature, and full of vivacity and wit, a delightful companion. A strange house it was, a continual coming and going of artists and patrons of artists; of Scottish visitors, of Italian great personages and priests, and more or less of all the English in Rome. They were, I think, in one of their best times (for they had many vicissitudes) when we went to Rome first in 1859—and saw everybody.

My husband was much revived at first by the change and by the company of Robert, to whom he had a faithful and long attachment from his boyish days, and we went with them to their *villeggiatura* at Nettuno in May. It is now, I believe, a sea-bathing place, well enough known; but then it was the rudest Italian village, one of the most curious places I have ever seen. I described it in a little sketch I made for 'Blackwood,' calling it a seaside place in the Papal States, or some such title. The rooms, the living, everything was inconceivably rough, the place like a great medieval fortress upon the rocks, with the natural agglomeration of houses hanging about its skirts. The women were handsome and wore a beautiful dress, red satin in long box-plaits, Greek jackets embroidered with gold, and beautiful embroidered white aprons and kerchiefs, with a very pretty half-Eastern head-dress. We had some very bad and some good days there. Very bad at first, and I very miserable; but later Frank took to working, and made one very pretty picture of a group of lads from the country, whom he saw and brought into the loggia, to stand to him. It hangs in my drawing-room now. He also made two sketches of the place itself, which are in my own room, his last work. This must have meant that he was feeling better. But I remember some dreadful scenes in the middle of the night, when his nose-bleeding came on, and I stood by him for hours, holding the nostril till the blood dried, he going to sleep in the meantime, while I stood with the traces all about as if I were murdering him. I remember one time when they all went off along the coast to Astura, the Macphersons and Frank with them, leaving me alone with the children, —probably my own fault, as I always had a foolish proud way of holding back,—and how I got over my little disappointment, and did my very best to get a good dinner for them to come back to, and arranged everything as nicely as possible, yet when they did come, could not keep it up, and was sulky, and injured, and disagreeable, notwithstanding that I had really taken a great deal of trouble to have everything ready and pleasant for the party. What trifles remain in one's mind! I suppose it was because I contrived to be half sorry for myself, and half ashamed of myself, that I remember this so clearly.

When we left Nettuno we went to Frascati, where we lived for more than three months, I think, and which at first was very pleasant with its great prospect over the misty Campagna, where St Peter's was visible, the only sign of the existence of Rome. We used to go out and walk on the terrace from whence there was that view,—and sometimes had a little society, the Noccioli, and Monsignor Pentini, afterwards Cardinal—an old trooper priest, who had been a soldier in Bernadotte's army, and then was supposed too liberal for promotion, having been kept back a long time from the Cardinal's hat he ought to have had. He was very kind, very benignant, the providence and at the same time the judge of all the poor people round, whom he kept from litigation, settling all their quarrels. I remember once or twice supping with him and good Ser Antonio, and his fat big Irish wife, — such good simple people, Monsignor not able to talk to me nor I to him, though he gave me many a kind look. I understood pretty well what he said, but could not express myself either in French or Italian. The Noccioli lived in the upper floor of his big old square house, with a wonderful view from the windows, and partially frescoed walls, scarcely any furniture, and a supper-table gleaming under the three clear flames of the Roman lamp, and the melons on the table, which Monsignor ate, I remember, with pepper and salt. But Frank grew very ill here. He became altogether unable to eat anything, not comparatively but absolutely; and the awful sensation of watching this, trying with every faculty to find something he could eat, and always failing, makes me shiver even now, though, God help me! I have had almost a repetition of it. We got an Italian doctor there, who was quite cheerful, as I believe is their way when nothing can be done, and spoke of our return next year, which gave me a little confidence. On the 1st of October we went back to Rome, to an apartment we had got in the Noccioli's house in the Babuino, where he got worse and worse. We had Dr Small, who brought a famous French doctor, and they told me there was no hope: it was better to tell me *franchement*, the Frenchman said, and that word *franchement* always, even now, gives me a thrill when I read it. They told me, or I imagined they told me in my confused state, that they had told him, and I went back to him not trying to command my tears; but found they had not told him, and that it was I in my misery who was taking him the news. I remember he said after a while, "Well, if it is so, that is no reason why we should be miserable." In my condition of health I was terrified that I might be disabled from attending my Frank to the last. Whether I took myself, or the doctor gave me, a dose of laudanum, I don't remember; but I recollect very well the sudden floating into ease of body and the dazed condition of mind,—a kind of exaltation, as if I were walking upon air, for I could not sleep in the circumstances nor try to sleep. I thought then that this was the saving of me. I nursed my husband night and day, neither resting nor eating, sometimes swallowing a sandwich when I came out of his room for a moment, sometimes dozing for a little when he slept—reading to him often in the middle of the night to try to get him to sleep. And when I came out of the room and sat down in the next and got the relief of crying a little, my bonnie boy came up and stood at my knee and pulled down my head to him, and smiled all over his beaming little face,—smiled though the child wanted to cry too, but would not —not quite three years old. When his father was dead I remember him sitting in his bed in the next room singing "Oh that will be joyful, when we meet to part no more," which was the favourite child's hymn of the moment. Frank died quite conscious, kissing me when his lips were already cold, and quite, quite free from anxiety, though he left me with two helpless children and one unborn, and very little money, and no friends but the Macphersons, who were as good to me as brother and sister; but had no power to help beyond that, if anything could be beyond that. Everybody was very kind. Mr Blackett wrote offering to come out to me, to bring me home; and John Blackwood wrote bidding me draw upon him for whatever money I wanted. I had sent for Effie M., my husband's niece, to come out to me, sending money for her journey; but her mother arrived some time after Frank's death, his sister, Mrs Murdoch—a kind but useless woman, who was no good to me, and yet was a great deal of good as a sort of background and backbone to our helpless little party,—for I was young still, thirty-one, and never self-confident. And there we waited six weeks till my baby was born— he as fair and sweet and healthful as if everything had been well with us. My big Jane was my stand-by, and took the child from the funny Italian-Irish nurse, Madame Margherita, who attended and cheered me with her jolly ways, and brought me back, she and the baby together, to life. By degrees, so wonderful are human things, there came to be a degree of comfort, even cheerfulness; the children being always bright,—Maggie and Cyril the sweetest pair, and my bonnie rosy baby. While I write, October 5, 1894, he, the last, is lying in his coffin in the room next to me—I have been trying to pray by the side of that last bed—and he looks more beautiful than ever he did in his life, in a sort of noble manhood, like, so very like, my infant of nearly thirty-five years ago. All gone, all gone, and no light to come to this sorrow any more! When my Cecco was two months old we came home—Mrs Murdoch and Jane and the three children and I—travelling expensively as was my way, though heaven knows our position was poor enough.

When I thus began the world anew I had for all my fortune about £1000 of debt, a small insurance of, I think, £200 on Frank's life, our furniture laid up in a warehouse, and my own faculties, such as they were, to make our living and pay off our burdens by.

Christmas Night, 1894.

I feel that I must try to change the tone of this record. It was written for my boys, for Cecco in particular. Now they will never see it—unless, indeed, they are permitted, being in a better place, to know what is going on here. I used to feel that Cecco would use his discretion,—that most likely he would not print any of this at all, for he did not like publicity, and would have thought his mother's story of her life sacred: but now everything is changed, and I am now going to try to remember more trivial things, the incidents that sometimes amuse me when I look back upon them, not merely the thread of my life.

Robert Macpherson came down with us to Civita Vecchia to see us off, and, I remember, read to me all the way there a story he had written, one of the stories flying about Rome of one of the great families, which he wanted me to polish up and get published for him. Robert introduced me to Dr Kennedy of Shrewsbury when we got on board the steamer,—a large, loose-lipped, loquacious man, full of talk, whom I liked well enough, and who talked to me pleasantly enough. He had two or three young men with him. I have always had a half-amused grudge against him, however. We were a very helpless party, the baby two months old and three other children, for I was bringing Willie Macpherson home to his aunt. In those days we had to land at Marseilles by small boats, which crowded round the steamer as soon as she came to anchor, and waited till the passengers had shown their passports and got through all the preliminaries. I saw that Dr Kennedy had engaged a large boat, and, though he said nothing to me, I was so foolish as to take it for granted that he meant me and my helpless party to go to the shore with him. It amuses me to think how astonished, how wounded and indignant I was, when, getting through before me, he and his young men stepped into their boat without a word, and left me to get ashore as I could—which, of course, I did all right, never having had any difficulty in that way of taking care of myself and my own belongings. I did not know where to go in Paris, as I could not go back to the same hotel where we had been when my husband was with me; and in our innocence we went to the Bristol!—my sister-in-law having been advised to go there, at second or third hand, through Mr Pentland. The rooms were delightful, but so were the prices, which I inquired, as we had been taught to do in Italy, before taking possession. I faltered, and said we had been sent there by Mr Pentland—but—— The name acted like magic. Mr Pentland, ah! that was another thing,—the rooms were just half the price to a friend of Mr Pentland. He was the editor of Murray's Handbooks—but of that important fact I was not aware.

After this we passed some time with my brother's family at Birkenhead, which was not very successful. I think it was rather more than I could bear to see his children rushing to the door to meet him when he came home, and my fatherless little ones ready to rush too, though it was so short a time since their father had been taken from them. I was always fantastical—and there were other things. It is a perilous business when one is very sorry for oneself, and the sight of happy people is apt, when one's wounds are fresh, to make the consciousness keener.

I was reading of Charlotte Brontë the other day, and could not help comparing myself with the picture more or less as I read. I don't suppose my powers are equal to hers—my work to myself looks perfectly pale and colourless beside hers—but yet I have had far more experience and, I think, a fuller conception of life. I have learned to take perhaps more a man's view of mortal affairs,—to feel that the love between men and women, the marrying and giving in marriage, occupy in fact so small a portion of either existence or thought. When I die I know what people will say of me: they will give me credit for courage (which I almost think is not courage but insensibility), and for honesty and honourable dealing; they will say I did my duty with a kind of steadiness, not knowing how I have rebelled and groaned under the rod. Scarcely anybody who cares to speculate further will know what to say of my working power and my own conception of it; for, except one or two, even my friends will scarcely believe how little possessed I am with any thought of it all,—how little credit I feel due to me, how accidental most things have been, and how entirely a matter of daily labour, congenial work, sometimes now and then the expression of my own heart, almost always the work most pleasant to me, this has been. I wonder if God were to try me with the loss of this gift, such as it is, whether I should feel it much? If I could live otherwise I do not think I should. If I could move about the house, and serve my children with my own hands, I know I should be happier. But this is vain talking; only I know very well that for years past neither praise nor blame has quickened my pulse ten beats that I am aware of. This insensibility saves me some pain, but it must also lose me a great deal of pleasure.

III.

December 30, 1894.

I RESUME this from the old book which contains my recollections up to 1859, when I came home from Rome with my three children, Cecco a baby of two months old. I stayed for some months, as I have said, with my brother in Birkenhead, and then went to Scotland—to Fife—for the summer, taking a small house in Elie. The Milligans (Mrs Milligan was Anne Mary Moir, a daughter of Delta, one of the girl friends whom I liked to have to stay with me in the early days of my married life in London) were at Kilconquhar, where Mr Milligan was minister, a man afterwards distinguished in his way, a well-known Biblical scholar and professor at Aberdeen. I was still only thirty-one, and in full convalescence of sorrow, and feeling myself unaccountably young notwithstanding my burdened life and my widow's cap,

E

which, by the way, I put off a year or two afterwards for the curious reason that I found it too becoming! That did not seem to me at all suitable for the spirit of my mourning: it certainly was, as my excellent London dressmaker made it for me, a very pretty head-dress, and an expensive luxury withal.

The Blackwoods were at Gibleston for the summer, a place quite near, so that I had friends within reach. I had not seen very much of John Blackwood, but he was already a friend, with that curious kind of intimacy which is created by a publisher's knowledge of all one's affairs, especially when these affairs mean struggles to keep afloat and a constant need of money. He had bidden me draw upon him when my husband died, and I was very grateful and apt to boast of it, as I have or had a way of doing; so that people who have served me in this way, even when, as sometimes happened, the balance changed a little, have always conceived themselves to be my benefactors. But he was a genial benefactor, and he and his wife used to come to see me; so that, though lonely and a stranger, I was not entirely out of a kind of society. I must, however, have been very lonely, except for the sweet company of my three little children and my good Jane, my factotum, who had gone with me to Rome as their nurse, and helped me in my trouble, and stood faithfully by me through all. I always remember, immediately after we came home, one dreadful night when my dear baby was very ill, and was laid upon her capacious shoulder as on a feather-bed, while I watched in anguish, thinking the night would never be done or that he would not live through it, when suddenly, with one of those rapid turns peculiar to infants, he got almost well in a moment! And this picture got itself hung up upon the walls of my mind, full of a roseate glow of happiness and deliverance instead of the black despair which had seemed to be closing round me.

That winter we went to Edinburgh, where I got a droll little house in Fettes Row, down at the bottom of the hill, the lower floor and the basement with a front door, in truly Edinburgh style — for "flats" were not known in England in those days. It was a very severe winter, 1860-61, and it was severe on me too. I have told the story of one incident in it in my other book, but I may repeat it here. I had not been doing very well with my writing. I had sent several articles, though of what nature I don't remember, to 'Blackwood,' and they had been rejected. Why, this being the case, I should have gone to them (John Blackwood and the Major were the firm at that moment) to offer them, or rather to suggest to them that they should take a novel from me for serial publication, I can't tell,—they so jealous of the Magazine, and inclined to think nothing was good enough for it, and I just then so little successful. But I was in their debt, and had very little to go on with. They shook their heads of course, and thought it would not be possible to take such a story,—both very kind and truly sorry for me, I have no doubt. I think I see their figures now against the light, standing up, John with his shoulders hunched up, the Major with his soldierly air, and myself all blackness and whiteness in my widow's dress, taking leave of them as if it didn't matter, and oh I so much afraid that they would see the tears in my eyes. I went home to my little ones, running to the door to meet me with "flichterin' noise and glee"; and that night, as soon as I had got them all to bed, I sat down and wrote a story which I think was something about a lawyer, John Brownlow, and which formed the first of the Carlingford series,—a series pretty well forgotten now, which made a considerable stir at the time, and *almost* made me one of the pop-ularities of literature. *Almost*, never quite, though 'Salem Chapel' really went very near it, I believe.

I sat up nearly all night in a passion of composition, stirred to the very bottom of my mind. The story was successful, and my fortune, comparatively speaking, was made. It has never been very much, never anything like what many of my contemporaries attained, and yet I have done very well for a woman, and a friendless woman with no one to make the best of me, and quite unable to do that for myself. Whether this was the reason why, though I did very well on the whole, I never did anything like so well as others, I can't tell, or whether it was really inferiority on my part. Anthony Trollope must have made at least three times as much as ever I did, and even Miss Mulock. As for such fabulous successes as that of Mrs Humphry Ward, which we poorer writers are all so whimsically and so ruefully unable to explain, nobody thought of them in these days.

I did not see many people in Edinburgh. I was still in deep mourning, and shy, and not clever about society—constantly forgetting to return calls, and avoiding invitations. I met a few people at the Blackwoods', and I remember in the dearth of incidents an amusing evening (which I think, however, came a few years later) when Professor Aytoun dined at Miss Blackwood's, he and I being the only guests. Miss Blackwood was one of the elders of the Blackwood family, and at this period a comely, black-haired, dark-complexioned person, large, and much occupied with her dress, and full of amusing peculiarities, with a genuine drollery and sense of fun, in which all the family were strong. She was full of recollections of all sorts of people, and of her own youthful successes, which, though stout and elderly, she never outgrew,—still remembering the days when she was called a sylph, and never quite sure that she was not making a triumphant impression even in these changed circumstances. She was very fond of conversation, and truly exceedingly queer in the remarks she would make, sometimes so totally out of all sequence that the absurdity had as good an effect as wit, and often truly droll and amusing, after the fashion of her family. I remember when some people were discussing the respective merits of Rome and Florence, Miss Blackwood gave her vote for Rome. "Ah," she said with an ecstatic look, "when you have read the 'Iliad' in your youth, it all comes back!" Another favourite story of her was, that when one of her brothers asked her, on mischief bent, no doubt, "Isabella, what are filbert nails?" she held out her hand towards him, where he was sitting a little behind her, without a word. She had a beautiful hand, and was proud of it.

But I have not told my story of Aytoun. Miss Black-wood had asked him to dine with us alone, and he came, and we flattered him to the top of his bent, she half sincerely, with that quaint mixture of enthusiasm and ridicule which I used to say was the Blackwood attitude towards that droll, partly absurd, yet more or less effective thing called an author; and I, I fear, backing her up in pure fun, till suddenly he burst forth without any warning with "Come hither, Evan Cameron"—and repeated the poem to us, Miss Blackwood, ecstatic, keeping a sort of time with flourishes of her hand, and I, I am afraid, overwhelmed with secret laughter. I am not sure that he did not come to himself with a horrified sense of imbecility before he reached the end.

I got rather intimate with old Mrs Wilson, a very dear old lady, the mother of my sister-in-law, Jeanie, and of Dr George Wilson and Sir Daniel Wilson—who lived at quite a great distance from me, a very long walk which I used to take every Sunday afternoon, with a complacent sense that it was a fine thing to do. She had a lonely day on Sunday, being very deaf, and unable to go to church, and her daughter much occupied by Sunday classes,

&c. Although deaf, she was an amusing and good talker, and used to give me all sorts of good advice, and tell me stories of her life. Her advice was chiefly about my children, whom she wished me to bring up on Museums and the broken bread of Science, which I loathed, pointing out to me with triumph how this system had succeeded with her own sons.

It was then I first became acquainted with the Storys, Mr, afterwards Dr, Story coming to see me in respect to my proposed Memoir of Edward Irving, which he had by some means heard about. My article in 'Blackwood' on Irving must have been published that winter: no, no, it was published much before we went to Italy, and I had been to Albury to see Mr Drummond,[1] my husband accompanying me, which was the first beginning of that

---

[1] Mr Drummond wrote to me when the article on Irving, which was in a manner the germ of the book, was published. It must have been in the end of 1848. He and all his community were much pleased with it, and had a notion, which my Roman Catholic friends always share, that since I went so far with them I must go the whole way. They gave me great encouragement accordingly, and I was supposed to be going to do just what they wanted to have done. We went to Albury on Mr Drummond's invitation, where we stayed three days, I think ; and I remember the sensation with which I sat and listened while Mr Drummond, the caustic wit and man of the world, explained to me how they were guided in setting up their church, and in building their quasi-cathedral in Gordon Square, and of the pillars called Jachin and Boaz, and a great deal more ; while Lord Lovaine, his son-in-law, now Duke of Northumberland,* a grave man, whose aspect impressed me much, listened gravely, as if to an oracle, and I looked on and wondered, amazed, as I sometimes used to be with Montalembert, at the combination of what seems to my hard head so much nonsense with so much keen sense and power—though I had much more sympathy with Montalembert, even with his medieval miracles, than with Jachin and Boaz. These good people thought, partly because of their deep sense of their own importance, and partly by a trick of sympathy which I had, and most genuine it was, that I was interested beyond measure in them and their ways, whereas it was in Irving I was interested, and listening with all my ears to hear about him, and much less concerned about the Holy Apostolic Church. They were disappointed accordingly, and not pleased with the book.

---

* Died January 1899.

project. Mr Story told me of his father's long intimacy with Irving, and promised me many letters if I would go to the manse of Roseneath to see them. I went accordingly, rather unwillingly in cold February weather, grudging the absence from my children for a few days very much. I did not know anything about the West of Scotland, and, winter as it was, the lovely little loch was a revelation to me, with the wonderful line of hills called the Duke's Bowling Green, which I afterwards came to know so well. The family at the manse was a very interesting one. The handsome young minister, quite young, though already beginning to grow grey —a very piquant combination (I was so myself, though older by several years than he)—and his mother, a handsome old lady full of strong character, and then a handsome sister with her baby, the most interesting of all, with a shade of mystery about her. They were, as people say, like a household in a novel, and attracted my curiosity very much. But when I was sent to my room with a huge packet of letters, and the family all retired for the night, and the deep darkness and silence of a winter night in the country closed down upon me, things were less delightful. The bed in my room was a gloomy creation, with dark-red moreen curtains, afterwards, as I found, called by Mr Story—witty and profane— "a field to bury strangers in." I had a pair of candles, which burned out, and a fire, which got low, while I agonised over the letters, not one of which I could make out. The despairing puzzle of that diabolical handwriting, which was not Irving's after· all (who wrote a beautiful hand), but only letters addressed to him, and the chill that grew upon me, and the gradual sense of utter stupidity that came over me, I can't attempt to describe. I sat up half the night, but in vain. Next day Mr Campbell of Row came specially to see me, a little shocked, I am afraid, to find the future biographer of Irving a young person, rather apt to be led astray and laugh with the young people in the midst of his serious talk. Mr Campbell had been a very notable character in these parts, and was at that time reverenced and admired as an apostle, though perhaps to me a little too much disposed, like everybody else, to tell me of himself instead of telling me of Irving, on whom my soul was bent. I never have had, I fear, a strong theological turn, and his exposition at family prayers, though I did my best to think it very interesting, confounded me, especially next morning when I had to catch the boat at a certain hour in order to catch the train and get home to my babies. All these details, however, gave a whimsical mixture of fun, to which, a sort of convalescent as I was from such trouble and sorrow, and long deprived of cheerful society, my mind yielded, in spite of a little resistance on the part of my graver side, which had honestly expected never to laugh again. This visit laid the foundation of a long friendship and much and generally very lively intercourse.

I saw various other people besides Mr Campbell and the Storys, in pursuit of information about Irving, and came across some amusing scenes, though they have passed out of my recollection for the most part. I remember making the discovery already noted—which, of course, I promulgated to all my friends—that every one I saw on this subject displayed the utmost willingness to tell me all about themselves, with quite a secondary interest in Irving. One gentleman in Edinburgh told me the whole story of his own wife's illness and death, and that he had reflected on the evening of her death that his children were almost more to be pitied than himself, since it was possible that he might get a new wife, while they could never have a new mother. Not an original thought, perhaps, but curious as occurring at such a moment. This was told me *apropos* of the fact that Irving, I think, had once dined in the house during the reign of that poor lady.   She had more than one successor, if I remember rightly.

One of my people whom I went to see on this subject was Dr Carlyle, whom I found surrounded with huge books,—books of a kind with which I was afterwards well acquainted—the 'Acta Sanctorum' and the like.   He was writing a life of Adamnan, the successor of Columba.   My recollection of him is of a small, rather spruce man, not at all like his great brother.   (Mrs Carlyle used to say of Dr John that he was one of the people who seemed to have been born in creaking shoes.)   It must have been he who told me to go and see Carlyle himself, who could tell me a great deal more than he could about Irving. I fancy that I must have made a run up to London from Edinburgh in the summer of 1861, and stayed with Mrs Powell in Palace Gardens—a sister of Mr Maurice, who had been very kind and friendly to me for a year or two before my husband's death.   This must have been my first visit to her after, for I remember that she questioned me as to how I was "left," and that I answered her cheerfully, "With my head and my hands to provide for my children," and was truly surprised by her strange look and dumb amazement at my cheerfulness.   I suppose now, but never thought then, that it was something to be amazed at.   I don't remember that I ever thought it anything the least out of the way, or was either discouraged or frightened, provided only that the children were all well.

It was on this occasion that, shy as I always was, yet with the courage that comes to one when one is about one's lawful work, and not seeking acquaintance or social favour, I bearded the lion in his den, and went to see Mr Carlyle in the old house in Cheyne Row, which people are now trying, I think very unwisely, to make a shrine or museum of, which I should myself hate to see.   He received me (I suppose I must have had an introduction from his brother) with that perfect courtesy and kindness which I always found in him, telling me, I remember, that he could tell me little himself, but that "the wife" could tell me a great deal, if I saw her. I forget whether he took any steps to acquaint me with "the wife," for I remember that I left Cheyne Row with a flutter of disappointment, feeling that though I had seen the great man, which was no small matter, I was not much the wiser. I remember his tall, thin, stooping figure between the two rooms of the library on the ground floor, in the pleasant shadow of the books, and subdued light and quiet in the place which seemed to supply a very appropriate atmosphere. I did not even know, and certainly never should have learned from any look or tone of his, that I had run the risk of being devoured alive by thus intruding on him. But though I was fluttered by the pride of having seen him, and that people might say "Il vous a parlé, grand'mère," I felt that my hopes were ended and that this was to be all. However, I was mistaken. A day or two after I was told (being still at Mrs Powell's) that a lady whose carriage was at the door begged me to go out and speak to her, Mrs Carlyle. I went, wondering, and found in a homely little brougham a lady with bright eyes and very hollow cheeks, who told me she had to be out in the open air for certain hours every day, and asked me to come and drive with her that we might talk about Irving, whom her husband had told her I wanted to hear about. She must have been over sixty at this time, but she was one of those women whom one never thinks of calling old: her hair was black without a grey hair in it (mine at half the age was already quite grey), her features and her aspect very keen, perhaps a little alarming. When we set off together she began by asking me if I did not come from East Lothian; she had recognised many things in my books which could only come from that district. I had to answer, as I have done on various occasions, that my mother had lived for years in East Lothian, and that I had been so constantly with her that I could never tell whether it was I myself who remembered things or she. This made us friends on the moment; for she too had had a mother, whom, however, she did not regard with all the respect I had for mine. What warmed my heart to her was that she was in many things like my mother; not outwardly, for my mother was a fair radiant woman with a beautiful complexion, and Mrs Carlyle was very dark, with a darkness which was, however, more her meagreness and the wearing of her eager spirit than from nature, or, at least, so I thought,—but in her wonderful talk, the power of narration which I never heard equalled except in my mother, the flashes of keen wit and sarcasm, occasionally even a little sharpness, and always the modifying sense of humour under all. She told me that day, while we drove round and round the Park, the story of her childhood and of her tutor, the big young Annandale student who set her up on a table and taught her Latin, she six years old and he twenty ("perhaps the prettiest little fairy that ever was born," her old husband said to me, describing this same childhood in his deep broken-hearted voice the first time I saw him after she was gone). I felt a little as I had felt with my mother's stories, that I myself remembered the little girl seated on the table to be on his level, repeating her Latin verbs to young Edward Irving, and all the wonderful life and hope that were about them, —the childhood and the youth and aspiration never to be measured. We jogged along with the old horse in the old fly and the steady old coachman going at his habitual jog, and we might have been going on so until now for anything either of us cared,—she had so much to say and I was so eager to hear.

I have one gift that I know of, and I am a little proud of it. It is that of making people talk—at

least, of making *some* people talk.   My dear Lady
Cloncurry says that it is like the art of driving a
hoop,—that I give a little touch now and then, and
my victim rolls on and on.   But my people who
pour forth to me are not my victims, for I love
to hear them talk and they take pleasure in it, for
the dear talk's sake on both sides, not for anything
else; for I have never, I am glad to say, been "a
student of human nature" or any such odious thing,
nor practised the art of observation, nor spied upon
my friends in any way.   My own opinion has always
been that I was very unobservant,—whatever I have
marked or noted has been done quite unaware; and
also, that to study human nature was the greatest
impertinence, to be resented whenever encountered.

My friendship with Mrs Carlyle was never broken
from this time—it must have been the summer either
of 1860 or 1861—till her death.   She came to see me
frequently, and I spent some (but few) memorable
evenings in her house, but at that time did not see
her husband again.

January 22.

I have been reading the life of Mr Symonds, and
it makes me almost laugh (though little laughing is
in my heart) to think of the strange difference between this prosaic little narrative, all about the facts
of a life so simple as mine, and his elaborate self-
discussions.   I suppose that to many people the other
will be the more interesting way—just as the movements of the mind are more interesting than those of
the body, or rather of the external life.   I might well
give myself up to introspection at this sad postscript
of my life, when all is over for me but the one event
to come, which will, I hope and believe, do away with
all the suffering past, and carry me back, a happy
woman, to my family, to a home,—though whether it
will be like the home on earth who can tell?   Nothing
can be more sad than the home on earth in which I
am now,—the once happy home that rang with my

boys' voices and their steps, where everything is full
of them, and everything empty, empty, cold, and
silent! I don't know whether it is more hard for me
to be here with all these associations, or to be in
some other place which might not be so overwhelming in its connection with what is past. But it is not
a question I need discuss here. Indeed I must not
discuss here any question of the kind at all, for any
attempt at discussing myself like Mr Symonds, if I
were likely to make it, only would end in outlines of
trouble, in the deep, deep sorrow that covers me like
a mantle. I feel myself like the sufferers in Dante,
those of whom we have been reading, who are bent
under the weight of stones, though I think I may say
with them that *invidiosa non fui;* but this is not to
put myself under a microscope and watch what goes
on in so paltry a thing, but only the continual appeal
I am always making to heaven and earth, consciously
or unconsciously, saying often, I know, as I have no
right to say, " Is this fair,—is it right that I should
be so bowed down to the earth and everything taken
from me ? " This makes of itself so curious a change
even in this quite innocent little narrative of my life.
It is so strange to think that when I go it will be
touched and arranged by strange hands,—no child of
mine to read with tenderness, to hide some things,
to cast perhaps an interpretation of love upon others,
and to turn over all my papers with the consciousness
of a full right to do so, and that theirs is by nature
all that was mine. Good Mr Symonds, a pleasant,
frank, hearty man, as one saw him from outside!
God bless him! for he was kindly to Cecco, who in
his tender kindliness made a little pilgrimage to Davos
the year after Mr S. died to see his family and offer
his sympathy—one of the many unrevealed impulses
of kindness he had which they never probably guessed
at all.

In the beginning of the winter of 1861 I went to

Ealing, and settled down there in a tiny house on the Uxbridge Road. It had a small drawing-room opening on a rather nice garden, a long strip of ground truly suburban, with a pretty plot of grass, a hedge of lilacs and syringas, and vegetables beyond that,—very humble, but I had no pretensions. I think by moments I must have been quite happy here. I remember the cluster of us on the grass, my little Maggie, a little mother in her way, and the two boys. We kept pigeons for the first and only time, and the pretty creatures were fluttering about, and the house standing all open doors and windows, and the sunshine and peace over all. I wrote a few verses, I remember, called "In the Eaves," and had a pang of conscious happiness, always touched with foreboding.

I had gone to Ealing to be near the Blacketts, who, much better off than I and in a much bigger house as became a publisher, lived also in the village, which was not half the size it is now. I had got very intimate with them somehow, I can scarcely tell how. Mrs Blackett was about my age, and a fine creature, very much more clever than her husband, though treated by him in any serious matter as if she had been a little girl,—a thing quite new to me, and which I could not understand. He was as good to her as a rather good-humoured but self-important man could be, very fond of her and very proud of her. She was a pretty woman, bright and full of spirit, and much his superior, knowing nothing about books, indeed, but neither did he. Through their house there fluttered a confused drift from time to time of literary persons, somewhat small beer like myself, novel-writers and suchlike. These were all very literary: our hosts were not literary at all, but with a business interest in us, along with a certain kindly contempt, such as publishers generally entertain for the queer genus writer. It was kindly at least on the part of the good Blacketts, who were the kindest folk, he always very brotherly to me, and she most affection-

ate. I was very fond of Ellen Blackett, admired her
and thought much of her. Their house was full of
big noisy boys, some of them just the same ages as
mine—a great bond between young mothers; handsome boys, wild and troublesome in later life, but
with that stout commercial thread in them which
brings men back to a life which is profitable when
they have sown their wild oats, — not the highest
motive, perhaps, but a recuperative force, such as
it was.

I had introduced Mr Blackett by his desire to
Miss Mulock in London,—he, apparently with some
business gift or instinct imperceptible to me, having
made out that there were elements of special success
in her. Probably, however, this instinct was no
more than an appreciation in himself of the senti-
mentalism in which she was so strong. He had at
once made an arrangement with her, of which 'John
Halifax' was the result, the most popular of all her
books. She made a spring thus quite over my head
with the helping hand of my particular friend, leaving
me a little rueful,—I did not at all understand the
means nor think very highly of the work, which is
a thing that has happened several times, I fear, in
my experience. Success as measured by money
never came to my share. Miss Mulock in this way
attained more with a few books, and these of very
thin quality, than I with my many. I don't know
why. I don't pretend to think that it was because
of their superior quality. I had, however, my little
success too, while I lived in Ealing. I began in
'Blackwood' the Carlingford series, beginning with a
story called 'The Doctor's Family,' which I myself
liked, and then 'Salem Chapel.' This last made a
kind of commotion, the utmost I have ever attained
to. John Blackwood wrote to me pointing out how
I had just missed doing something that would have
been made worth the while; and I believe he was
right, but the chapel atmosphere was new and pleased

people.   As a matter of fact I knew nothing about chapels, but took the sentiment and a few details from our old church in Liverpool, which was Free Church of Scotland, and where there were a few grocers and other such good folk whose ways with the minister were wonderful to behold.   The saving grace of their Scotchness being withdrawn, they became still more wonderful as Dissenting deacons, and the truth of the picture was applauded to all the echoes.   I don't know that I cared for it much myself, though Tozer and the rest amused me well enough.   Then came 'The Perpetual Curate' and 'Miss Marjoribanks.'   I never got so much praise, and a not unfair share of pudding too.   I was amused lately to hear the comments of Mr David Stott of Oxford Street, the bookseller, on this.   He told me that he had been in the Blackwoods' establishment at the time, and of the awe and horror of Mr Simpson at the prodigal extravagance of John Blackwood in giving me the price he did, £1500, for 'The Perpetual Curate.'   One could see old Simpson, pale, with the hair of his wig standing up on his head, remonstrating, and John Blackwood, magnanimous, head of the house of Blackwood, and feeling rather like a feudal suzerain, as he always did, declaring that the labourer was worthy of his hire.   Stott had the air too of thinking it was sinful extravagance on the editor's part.   As for me, I took what was given me and was very grateful, and no doubt sang praises to John. On the other side, it was Henry Blackett who turned pale at Miss Mulock's sturdy business-like stand for her money.   He used to talk of his encounters with her with affright, very grave, not able to laugh.

This was also the time when I wrote the 'Edward Irving.'   It must have been my good time, the little boat going very smoothly and all promising well, and, always my burden of happiness, the children all well. They had the measles, I remember, and were all a little ill the day of the Prince of Wales's marriage,

Cyril least ill of all, but feverish one day, when, as I stood over him, putting back his hair from his little hot forehead, he said to me with a pretty mixture of baby metaphor, which I was very proud of and never forgot, " Oh, mamma, your hand is as soft as snow." . How like him that was, the poetry and the perception and the tenderness ! Cecco too had a momentary illness, — a little convulsion fit which frightened me terribly, one of the few times when I quite lost my head. I remember holding him in his hot bath, and all the while going on calling for hot water and hearing myself do so, and unable to stop it. It was a day on which Mrs Carlyle was coming for the afternoon. When she arrived I was sitting before the fire (though it was summer), with my baby wrapped in a blanket, just out of his bath, and humming softly to him, and he had just startled me out of my misery and made my heart leap for joy, by pulling my face to him with a way he had and saying, all himself again, " Why you singing hum - hum ? Sing 'Froggy he would a-wooing go.'" He was only two and a-half. Mrs Carlyle sat by me, so kind and tender and full of encouragement, as if she had known all about babies, but did not stay very long. I think I can see her by the side of the fire, telling me all kinds of comforting things ; and by the first post possible that same evening I got a letter from her, telling me that Mr Carlyle had made her sit down at once and write to tell me that a sister of his had once had just such an attack, which never was repeated. God bless them, that much maligned, much misunderstood pair ! That was not much like the old ogre his false friends have made him out to be.

Here is a pretty thing. I should like if I could to write what people like about my books, being just then, as I have said, at my high tide, and instead of that all I have to say is a couple of baby stories. I am afraid I can't take the books *au grand sérieux*. Occasionally they pleased me, very often they did not.

I always took pleasure in a little bit of fine writing (afterwards called in the family language a "trot"), which, to do myself justice, was only done when I got moved by my subject, and began to feel my heart beat, and perhaps a little water in my eyes, and ever more really satisfied by some little conscious felicity of words than by anything else. I have always had my sing-song, guided by no sort of law, but by my ear, which was in its way fastidious to the cadence and measure that pleased me; but it is bewildering to me in my perfectly artless art, if I may use the word at all, to hear of the elaborate ways of forming and enhancing style, and all the studies for that end.

A good deal went on during that short time at Ealing. I had visitors, Miss Blackwood for two months, and much driving up and down to London to the Exhibition of 1862, which I loathed; but she enjoyed and dragged me, if not at her chariot wheels yet in the "rusty fly," which added very much to my expenses and wasted my time, with the result of being set down by her as very extravagant,—a re-proach which has come up against me at various periods of my life. Dr Story came with her, or at least at the same time, and afterwards Principal Tulloch and his wife, whose acquaintance I had made at Edinburgh, St Andrews, and Roseneath in the intervening summer of these two years, which I spent at Roseneath, for which I had taken a great fancy— the beautiful little loch and the hills. I must have gone then to Willowburn, a small house on a high bank, with a lovely view of the loch and the opposite shore, all scattered with houses among the trees, with the steamboat bustling up and down, and a good deal of boating and singing and Highland expeditions,— all very amusing, almost gay, as I had seldom been in my life before. There was always a youthful party in the manse, and the Tullochs for a time, and various visitors coming and going,—from the high respectability of Mr Edward Caird, now Master of

Balliol, and Mr Moir, to all sorts of jocular and light-minded people. I remember coming home from some wildish expedition, sunburnt and laden with flowers,—a small group full of fun and laughter sitting together on deck,—when suddenly the handsome serious form of Mrs M., always *tirée à quatre épingles*, always looking propriety itself, was seen slowly ascending up the cabin stairs, to the confusion and sudden pallor of myself in particular, to whom she was coming on a visit. I doubt if I had ever been so gay. I was still young, and all was well with the children. My heart had come up with a great bound from all the strain of previous trouble and hard labour and the valley of the shadow of death. There was some wit, or at least a good deal of humour, in the party, and plenty of excellent talk. The Principal talked very well in those days—indeed he always did, but never so well as at that time; and Mr Story, too, was an excellent talker, and his sister very clever and bright; and my dear *padrona*,[1] if she never said very much, always quick to see everything, and never able to resist a laugh. We got to have a crowd of allusions and mutual recollections after all our boatings and drivings and ludicrous little adventures on the loch and the hills, which produced a great deal of laughter even when they were not witty — Jack Tulloch's appetite, for instance, when he was taken with us on one occasion, and looked on with exquisite contempt at our admiring raptures over the scenery, but came to life whenever lunch was going, and was devotedly attended by the Highland waiters, who entered into the joke and plied him with dish after dish. He was only about eleven, poor boy. We were like Farmer Flamborough and his daughters, just as much amused by all these small matters as if they had been the most amusing things in the world. Miss Blackwood continued to make part occasionally of our expeditions, and always an amusing part. She was

―――――――――

[1] Mrs Tulloch,

full of the humour and drollery of her family, gifts in
which they were all strong, with many little eccen-
tricities of her own.

I worked very hard all the time, I scarcely know
how, for I was always subject to an irruption of
merry neighbours bent on some ramble, whom, when
they came in the evening, my big Jane, now more
cook than nurse, and general factotum, fed with great
dishes of maccaroni, which she had learned to make
in Italy, and which was our social distinction : everything was extremely primitive at Willowburn. We
had one cab in the place, which took me solemnly
now and then to dinner at the manse and other places,
and which was driven by a certain Andie Chalmers
who was our delight, who spoke in a soft, half-artic-
ulate murmur, all vowels, very tolerant of the pouring rain through which he drove us occasionally
through many a wet mile of road, allowing with a
smile that it was a "wee saft" when there was a
deluge, and who used to come to the cab door at the
foot of a hill with mild insistence, inaccessible to
remonstrance, till we one by one unwillingly, yet
with merry jests, got out to ease the horse.

I suppose after all that I only went for two sum-
mers to Roseneath, but it seems to have bulked very
largely in my life : there was a third later, but that
was in another age, as will be seen, and I was not
quite three years in Ealing. Here I had often with
me, as I had a fancy for having, a young lady on
a long visit. It would be cruel to name by name
the dear good girl, who was brought by her mother
to join us one time where we were living, the whole
party of us,—myself, big Jane, and the three children.
The girl was very tearful and pale, and her mother
whispered to me to take no notice, that she had been
praying for strength to pay me this visit, in which,
however, she enjoyed herself very much, I believe.
This was, I fear, too good a joke to be kept from
my friends.

It was in the summer of 1863 that Geraldine Macpherson came to spend some time with me at Ealing. She was much shattered with Roman fever, and she had a very bad illness of another kind, almost fatal, in my house. The high-spirited creature never gave in, kept her courage and composure through everything, but was as near as possible gone. How one wonders vainly whether, if some one thing like this had not happened, the tenor of one's entire life might have been changed. It was she who persuaded me to go back to Rome when she returned. She persuaded the Tullochs also, to my great surprise, and I daresay their own. The Principal had been ill. It was the first of those mysterious illnesses of his when he fell under the terrible influence of a depression for which there was no apparent cause. He was in the depths of this when he and his wife were with me in 1862, and he told me the whole story of it. It originated (or he thought it did) in (of all things in the world) a false quantity he had made in some Latin passage he had quoted in a speech at some Presbytery or Assembly meeting. He told it with such impassioned seriousness, with his countenance so full of sorrow and trouble, his big blue eyes full of moisture, that I was much impressed, and, I remember, gave him out of my sympathy and emotion the equally inconceivable advice to call the men together to whom that speech had been made, and make a clean breast of it to them. I remember he was staggered in the extravagance of his talk by this queer insane suggestion, and perhaps a touch more would have awakened the man's wholesome humour and driven the strange delusion away in a shout of laughter; but I was deadly serious, as was he. He was beginning to mend, and had been ordered a sea-voyage, and somebody offered him a passage in a Levant steamboat to Greece. And now, what with Geddie's persuasions and a spring of eager planning on my part how and when to go, Mrs Tulloch made up her mind to come to Rome to meet her husband, then on his way back, bringing her two eldest girls while he took his eldest boy. We set out the merriest party, ready to enjoy everything, the *padrona*, as I soon began to call her, with her daughters Sara and Fanny, Geddie, myself, my Jane, and the children, all so small, so happy, so bright, my three little things—Maggie approaching eleven. We took out a French governess with us for the sake of the children, a Mdlle. Coquelin, I think, who soon dropped out of my life after the great calamity came. But in the meantime we were all gay, fearing nothing. I remember very distinctly our journey from Paris to Marseilles, because it was a cheap journey, second class, and monstrous in length, twenty - seven hours, I think; but we were all very economical to start with. The endless journey it was! We were all dead-tired when we arrived, but when we reached our hotel and got round a table, and were well warmed and refreshed with an inno- cent champagne, St Peray, which I made them all drink, our spirits recovered. I was always great in the way of feeding my party,—would not hear of teas or coffee meals, but insisted upon meat and wine, to the horror but comfort of my companions. That, I believe, was one reason why there were never any breakdowns among us while travelling. I think with pleasure of the pleasant tumult of that arrival,—the delight of rest, the happy sleepy children all got to bed, the little party of women, all of us about the same age, all with the sense of holiday, a little out- burst of freedom, no man interfering, keeping us to rule or formality. I don't know why it should pre- sent itself to me under so pleasant a light, for I never liked second-class journeys, nor discomforts of that kind. How often have I travelled that road since, but never so free or light of heart! Heavy and sad are its recollections now, but it is a blessing of God that a happy moment (which is so much rarer) is more conspicuous in life, lighting up the long dreary lane like a lamp, than the sad ones. Oh, the bonnie little dear faces! the rapture of their wellbeing and their happiness, all clinging round mamma with innumerable appeals,—the " bundle of boys," as my Maggie said with sweet scorn, who left no room for her arms to get round me, but only mine round her. I am old and desolate and alone, but I seem to see myself a young mother, the two little fellows in the big fauteuil behind me, clinging round my neck, and their sister at my knee. God bless them, and God bless them,—are they all together now?

We went next day, I think, in the great Messageries steamboat, by Genoa and Leghorn, to Civita Vecchia, and got to Rome in three days, with time enough in Genoa to get a glimpse of the town, and in Pisa next day, making a run from Leghorn. All was well when we got to Rome, where my poor brother William was with Robert Macpherson, helping him to sell his photographs, and pouring out his stores of knowledge upon all the visitors, to good Robert's great admiration. The Tullochs and I got a joint-house in Capo le Case. We had two servants—a delightful *donna da facienda*, called Leonilda, and the only detestable Italian servant I ever saw, Antonio; but the two did everything for us somehow. We had our dinner, I think, from the Trattoria. And we had a month, or a little more, of pleasant life together. The Principal arrived from Greece—or was it Constantinople?—and all was well.

Ah me, alas! pain ever, for ever. This has been the ower-word of my life. And now it burst into the murmur of pain again.

ROME, 1864.[1]

I did not know when I wrote the last words that I was coming to lay my sweetest hope, my brightest anticipations for the future, with my darling, in her father's grave. Oh this terrible, fatal, miserable

---

[1] These pages, written in Rome at the moment of her bitter grief for the loss of her daughter, seem most suitably inserted here, though Mrs Oliphant left them detached.—ED.

Rome! I came here rich and happy, with my blooming daughter, my dear bright child, whose smiles and brightness everybody noticed, and who was sweet as a little mother to her brothers. There was not an omen of evil in any way. Our leaving of home, our journey, our life here, have all been among the brightest passages of my life; and my Maggie looked the healthiest and happiest of all the children, and ailed nothing and feared nothing,—nor I for her.

Four short days made all the difference, and now here I am with my boys thrown back again out of the light into the darkness, into the valley of the shadow of death. My dearest love never knew nor imagined that she was dying; no shadow of dread ever came upon her sweet spirit. She got into heaven without knowing it, and God have pity upon me, who have thus parted with the sweetest companion, on whom unconsciously, more than on any other hope of life, I have been calculating. I feared from the first moment her illness began, and yet I had a kind of underlying conviction that God would not take my ewe-lamb, my woman-child, from me.

The hardest moment in my present sad life is the morning, when I must wake up and begin the dreary world again. I can sleep during the night, and I sleep as long as I can; but when it is no longer possible, when the light can no longer be gainsaid, and life is going on everywhere, then I, too, rise up to bear my burden. How different it used to be! When I was a girl I remember the feeling I had when the fresh morning light came round. Whatever grief there had been the night before, the new day triumphed over it. Things must be better than one thought, must be well, in a world which woke up to that new light, to the sweet dews and sweet air which renewed one's soul. Now I am thankful for the night and the darkness, and shudder to see the light and the day returning.

The Principal calls "In Memoriam" an embodiment

of the spirit of this age, which he says does not know what to think, yet thinks and wonders and stops itself, and thinks again ; which believes and does not believe, and *perhaps*, I think, carries the human yearning and longing farther than it was ever carried before. Perhaps my own thoughts are much of the same kind. I try to realise heaven to myself, and I cannot do it. The more I think of it, the less I am able to feel that those who have left us can start up at once into a heartless beatitude without caring for our sorrow. Do they sleep until the great day? Or does time so cease for them that it seems but a matter of hours and minutes till we meet again? God who is Love cannot give immortality and annihilate affection; that surely, at least, we must take for granted—as sure as they live they live to love us. Human nature in the flesh cannot be more faithful, more tender, than the purified human soul in heaven. Where, then, are they, those who have gone before us? Some people say around us, still knowing all that occupies us; but that is an idea I cannot entertain either. It would not be happiness but pain to be beside those we love yet unable to communicate with them, unable to make ourselves known.

. . . .

The world is changed, and my life is darkened; and all that I can do is to take desperate hold of this one certainty, that God cannot have done it without reason. I can get no farther. Sometimes such a longing comes upon me to go and seek somebody, as I used to go to Frank to the studio in the old times. But I have nobody now: my friends are very sorry for me; but there is nobody in the world who has a right to share my grief, to whom my grief belongs, as it does to myself—and that is what one longs for. Sympathy is sweet, but sympathy is for lighter troubles. When it is a grief that rends one asunder, one's longing is for the other—the only other whose heart is rent asunder by the same stroke. For me, I have all the burden to bear myself.

IV.

1894.

ON the 27th of January 1864 my dear little Maggie died of gastric fever. I have written about it all elsewhere. I had escaped, I thought, from the valley of the shadow of death, and had been happy, in sheer force of youth and health and the children: now I was plunged again under the salt and bitter waves. I laid her by her father, and it seemed to me that all light and hope were gone from me for ever. Up to five years ago I could not say her dear name without the old pang coming back; since then, when there came to be another to bury in my heart, my little girl seemed all at once to become a tranquil sweet recollection; and now that all are gone she is but a dear shadow, far in the background, while my boys take up in death as in life the whole of the darkened scene. All three gone, and only I left behind! I must try not to dwell on that here. There is enough of distracted thoughts and fancies elsewhere. I have never ventured to go back to Rome. I dared not while I had still the boys to think of. Twice fatal to us, I did not venture to face it a third time. I used to say that if I knew I had a fatal disease, or was sure that they needed me no longer, I would go by myself, and would be happy to die there, but never that they should go. I feel as if I should like to go now, but not to die there, for I must, if it is possible, lie beside my Cyril and Cecco at Eton. But this belongs to a later time.

We left Rome in May, the party still together, the

Tullochs and I. I felt that if I left them then I could never bear to see them again; and thus it was that Sara and Fanny Tulloch were left with me for a year, their parents returning home. I remember very little in Rome. The people I met there, the things I saw, seemed all wiped out of my mind, except some strange broken scenes. The first week after that calamity Geddie took me out to Frascati, to their house there, for a little change; and I never can forget the aspect of that summer place, where we had once lived through the hot July and August, in the desolation of the winter and of my misery. We were on the upper storey of a great cold Italian house, the cold penetrating to the heart, cold such as never was seen or felt surely in the North,—no servants, no comforts, sitting crying over the fire through a dismal day or two in a great, gaunt, half-empty room, my heart breaking for the children. It did not last long, but I have never forgotten these dismal days. There is another day in my memory like a dream. It was then March, and we had gone to Albano and were living there. The Macphersons came out to visit us, and, as they could never be without company, asked some of their friends out from Rome on the Sunday to go to Nemi. Then, finding how I shrank from the strangers, Robert took me through the woods,—a wonderful, wild, beautiful way,—leading my donkey to the place where we were to dine. I recollect a kind of soothing in the sensation of the spring, the wild freshness of the wood; a party of charcoal-burners, whose encampment we passed, appear to me like a picture,—wild men, not safe to meet, but my kind old Robert knew them all and their dialect and their ways. Nemi, the wonderful blue lake, bound within the circle of its deep banks, and an old Palazzo with frescoed rooms looking sheer down into the wonderful metallic water, which looked something like molten sapphires, but of a warmer colour. I had half a mind, I remember, to take an *appartamento* in that house, and throw myself into the rut of artist life, though my instincts were not of that kind,—a life not exactly disorderly, but a little wild and wandering and gregarious. I wonder, if I had stayed at Nemi, and brought the boys up so—how bewildering the thought is of things one might have done.

After that we went to Naples and Capri, where we stayed a long time and got to know all the guides and people, riding about every day over all the lower island and up to Anacapri—all like a dream. And Sentella, the good hunchback maid whose face the Principal said was so full of moral beauty, and Feliciello, who was not by any means so good, but whom we liked and petted. I wrote, I think, a little sketch of it afterwards, called " Life on an Island," or some such name, in 'Blackwood.'[1]

In May we left Rome finally and moved northward to the Lake of Como, where we stayed at Bellaggio; then into Switzerland, where we spent the summer, chiefly on the Lake of Geneva; then to Paris, where we passed the winter. The Principal and the *padrona* had gone home long before, and my party in Paris consisted of my two little boys, the two girls, Sara and Fanny, Jane, and a Swiss-French governess, Mademoiselle Pricam, whom we had picked up at Montreux. In Paris we got a cheerful apartment on the Champs Elysées, the sunny side. It was at the height of the gaiety and prosperity of the Empire, and I used to say that the sight of all the gay stream of life from the windows, all the fine people coming and going, the brightness and the movement, were a kind of salvation to me in that dark and clouded time. I remember going off to St Germain to spend the first anniversary of my Maggie's death, taking my delightful boy with me; and the dark gloomy evening after I had put him to bed in the inn, once more sitting desolate and crying over the fire; but next morning the terrace in the

1 "Life on an Island," 'Maga,' January 1865.

wintry sunshine, and all the thoughts that came to
one then, and still more the going back to the cheerful rooms in Paris, which were a kind of home, and
my other dear little fellow rushing with his shout of
welcome to mamma, brought a little sunshine back;
though it was not till the 4th of April after that,
when I found the rooms crowded with flowers which
they had all gone out to get for me on my birthday
before I was up, that I began to feel as if I had
passed again from death into life. I took them all
out to St Cloud in reward for their flowers, and they
were all so gay, and the morning and the drive so
bright.

In Paris I saw a good deal of the Montalemberts.
I have described how I translated the Count's book
when I first went to Scotland after my widowhood.
He had been pleased with it, I don't know why, for
it was badly done; and by John Blackwood's desire
and introduction came to see me in Paris, and I dined
there once or twice, though under protest, for I had
never gone anywhere or cared to see anybody. There
was one party I remember which was interesting,
where were Prévost-Paradol and some other literary
people. I was too shy and out of my element to
make much of them, and have never been proud of
my French; so I did not get the good I ought out
of this glimpse of society. On one occasion Miss
Blackwood, who came to Paris and paid me a long
visit, was with me,—a little alarming in her large
bare shoulders in the small party with the other
ladies all decorously covered. There was, I remember, a pretty graceful Madame L'Abbadie, whose husband came up to me, a man with a dreadful brogue,
and said, "I speak English better than Montalembert; the reason is I am born in Dublin, and he is
born in London." Montalembert's English was delightful, perfect in accent and idiom; I don't remember any mistake of his except the amusing and
flattering one with which he expressed his surprise

when we first met to find me "not so respectable" as he had supposed. I daresay it was a mistake made on purpose; for to be sure I was still young, and perhaps, in the still lingering exaltation of my sorrow and the tears that were never far off from my eyes, looked younger than I was. It was then 1865, and I must have been thirty-seven, and had grey hair. Montalembert himself was, I think, one of the most interesting men I ever met. He had that curious mixture of the — shall I say?—supernaturalist and man of the world (not mystic, he was no mystic, but yet miraculous, if there is any meaning in that) which has always had so great an attraction for me,—keen and sharp as a sword, and yet open to every belief and to every superstition, far more than I ever could have been, who looked at him and up to him with a sort of admiring wonder and yet sympathy, not without a smile in it. He was a little like Laurence Oliphant in this, but Laurence was not a highly educated man like Montalembert. M. de Montalembert struck me as the most delightful, benign, and genial of men when I saw him first; but afterwards I used to say that he was one of the few men I was afraid of, and that he had a fine way of picking one up as on some polished pair of tongs, and holding one up to the admiration of the world around, in all the bloom of one's foolishness. I remember on one occasion, when there was great talk of vacant fauteuils in the Académie, and of the candidates, two of whom in particular were being discussed, I asked him, rather sillily, whether there were two vacancies or two candidates for one vacancy—something of that sort,—when he turned to the company and called their attention to the orderly, temperate, English mind, in which there was no rush at a prize, but a well-balanced competition of two, as I had suggested. There was a great deal of laughter, in which, of course, any shy explanation of mine was completely drowned. I doubt whether an Englishman of equally fine manners would have held up a French stranger to the gentle ridicule of the company in this way. And yet I always liked him in the midst of my alarm, and he was very kind. I gave him the ' Life of Irving,' with a little protest, which was quite true, that it was not because I had written it, but because of the man Irving that I wished him to read it, which protest he received with a little banter and look of seeing through me; but afterwards avowed that he was touched by the character of Irving and its truth, mightily apart as it was from all his own prepossessions, which were so strong, however, that he could not bear Scotland,—could not even persuade himself to permit the glamour of Sir Walter to excuse the black anti-Catholic desolation of that dreadful country, all but Iona. Happening to speak of Carlyle, he expressed great dislike for him. I had mentioned that unfortunately Carlyle had no children. "Why unfortunately?" said Montalembert; "happily, rather, for he was not a man to have the bringing up of children." I made some sort of indignant reply, but added, "I don't believe in education." He paused a moment, laughed, and said, "Neither do I." Carlyle had an equal dislike of him, and shot forth a thunderbolt at him on one occasion when I mentioned him; but spoke of Lamennais in a half tender tone,—"There is no hairm in him, no hairm in him," he said. Lamennais was tragic from the Montalembert point of view,—a name to be spoken of with bated breath.

It was Count de Montalembert who gave me tickets for one of the side chapels in Notre Dame, where Père Félix was preaching to men during Lent,—a scene I have described somewhere, and which I read a description of lately in the life of Mrs Craven. The nave was packed closely with men, a dark mass, their immovable faces whitening the whole surface of that great area under the not abundant lights, and the spare figure of the monk in the pulpit, his face whiter still, like ivory. It was very dark in the side chapels, and we did not hear very well; but the sight was very impressive, and specially so on, I think, the Thursday of Holy Week, when this immense crowd of men sang the Stabat Mater in unison,—the most wonderful volume of sound, which was quite overwhelming in the depth and strength of it, rolling like a kind of regulated and tempered thunder, or like the sound of many waters,—a perfectly new and extraordinary effect.

On the Easter morning we went very early to Notre Dame to see the communion of these men, which was also a very touching sight. There was an old lady in the gallery where we were who looked down all the time, crying and talking to herself, " Dix soldats—et un petit bon homme en blouse." I, more profane, smiled a little, and was a little ashamed of myself for doing so, at the air of conscious solemnity with which most of the men came up to the altar, very devout, but yet with a certain sense of forming part of a very great and ennobling spectacle.

I made little of the ladies of the Montalembert household on this occasion, my attention being chiefly attracted to him. The girls were quite young, and I did not see enough of them to make friends as afterwards with Madame de Montalembert,—a person to whom it is difficult to do justice in words, the fine, ample, noble Flamande, *grande dame au bout des ongles*, ready and capable to do anything in the world of which there might be need, to defend a castle, or light a fire, or nurse the sick, but helplessly unable to " do " her own hair,—a characteristic failure which amused me much when I found it out, which was not, however, till much later. I am not sure that I ever saw Montalembert again.

We had another regular evening visitor once a-week —a man whom, though I never saw more of him than those regular weekly visits, I got to think of as a dear friend, and I think he had the same sort of feeling for me—Giovanni (or, as he wrote himself, John) Ruffini, the author of ' Dr Antonio,' an Italian refugee of the

1848 times, and for years a resident in London, where he had written that delightful book in English. His written English was beautiful, but he spoke it badly and with difficulty. He was a large mild man, with blue eyes, heavy-lidded and large—large externally, and specially remarkable when they were cast down, which sounds odd but was true. He lived with an English family, with whom he had been for years—partly brother, partly lover, partly guest. I did not know them, and I don't know the rights of the story. The father had died some time before, but he still kept his place among them, and went about with the mother of the house, both of them growing old with what seemed to me a delightful innocence and naturalness. They made their *villeggiatura*, these two together, sometimes in a couple of chalets on a Swiss mountain, as if there had not been such a thing as an evil tongue in the world, which interested me exceedingly; and indeed his weekly visit, his pensive Italian mildness, the look of the traditional exile, though in so perfectly natural a man, was very interesting: that exile look with the faint air of fiction in it, and its absolute sincerity all the same, has gone out of mortal ken nowadays.

Another queer pair that I used to see were old Father Prout (Mahony, or O'Mahony, as he called himself) and the old lady about whom he circled, and who was a very quaint old lady indeed, with the air of having been somebody,—a very dauntless, plain-spoken old person in old shiny black satin and lace, and looking as if everything was put on as well as the satin—hair, teeth, and everything else. She bade her old gentleman sing me his great song, " The Bells of Shandon," which he did, standing up against the mantelpiece, with his pale head, like carved ivory, relieved against the regular *garniture de cheminée*, the big clock and candelabra. He had a fine face with delicate features, almost an ascetic face. He was one of the Fraser group, which was, more or less, an imitation of the Blackwood group, with much real or pretended rivalry, and had knocked about a great deal in his life, and was poor. There were thus two elderly romances, in old fidelity and friendship, under my eyes, made innocent, almost infantile, especially in the latter case, as of old babies, independent of sex and superior to it, amid all the obliterations of old age. I had several visitors, chiefly sent to me, I think, by Robert Macpherson,—one of them Miss Cushman, the actress, whom I had met in London and had not liked, but who touched my heart with her evident deep knowledge of trouble and sorrow. I think I have described her and others in some other places, though I can't tell where. I had visitors too from home,—Mrs Fitzgerald, Miss Blackwood, and Principal Tulloch, who came to take the girls home, and in his turn brought some odd Scotch-cosmopolitan people. Not cosmopolitan, however, was the Scotch minister, who held his little conventicle in the Oratoire, and who said sturdily, and with the courage of his opinion, that he had not learned French, and did not mean to do so, as he disapproved of it altogether.

We were about six months in Paris, in the little bright apartment which I remember cost over a thousand francs for wood and coal during that time, and was as warm as a nest. The party consisted of the two girls, my two dear little boys,—Cyril so full of wit and fun, Cecco always so original even in his babyhood, learning to read in Mademoiselle's wonderful way in a fortnight without a tear,—Mademoiselle herself, Jane, and a servant and a half—the *bonne à tout faire* and her child. The Champs Elysées, full of sun and brightness and fine carriages, and all the fine people passing in a stream every afternoon, did me much good, and it all bears a radiant aspect now as I look back, heavy though my heart often was. I heard then for the first time of our afterwards familiar and beloved cousin Annie, in reality a second cousin, whom I had never seen, but who wrote introducing herself to me, with some literary aspirations, taking at that time the shape of poetry, against which I remember I advised her, suggesting a novel instead. I cannot remember what I was then doing, nor how I was in the matter of money, but I presume I must have ¡been going on with a flowing sail, working a great deal and not requiring to take much thought of my expenses, which, alas! was my way. I ought to have been saving, of course, but I didn't, with a miraculous ease of mind which some people have thought criminal. I sometimes think, too, that it was so, and also have sometimes lately (1895) pondered upon a sadder [1] theory still, as if that had something to do with the great sorrows that have clouded the end of my life. I never had any expensive tastes, but loved the easy swing of life, without taking much thought for the morrow, with a faith in my own power to go on working, which up to this time has been wonderfully justified, but which has been a great temptation and danger to me all through in the way of economies. I had always a conviction that I could make up by a little exertion for any extra expense. Sickness, incapacity, want of health or ability to work, never occurred to me, I suppose. At the same time, I never was very highly paid for my work, and perhaps this had its effect too on my carelessness in

---

[1] This is what I thought—that I had so accustomed them to the easy going on of all things, never letting them see my anxieties or know that there was a difficulty about anything, that their minds were formed to that habit, that it took all thought of necessity out of my Cyril's mind, who had always, I am sure, the feeling that a little exertion (always so easy *to-morrow*) would at any time set everything right, and that nothing was likely ever to go far wrong so long as I was there. And my Cecco, who had not these follies, but who was stricken by the hand of God, until that too rendered further going on impossible—by the drying up of my sources and means of getting anything for him—so that I seem sometimes to feel as if it were all my doing, and that I had brought by my heedlessness both to an *impasse* from which there was no issue but one. It was a kind of forlorn pleasure to me that they had never wanted anything, but this turns it into a remorse. Who can tell? God alone over all knows, and works by our follies as well as our better ways. Must it not be at last to the good of all?

pecuniary matters. I made enough to carry me on easily, almost luxuriously, but not enough to save, never a large sum which could be partly put away at once and give one a taste of the sweetness of possessing something. I could not do this, and I fear it was not in me to practise that honourable pinching and sparing by which some women do so much. I had not the time for it, nor, indeed, I am ashamed to say, the wish. I am ashamed too to make the confession that I do not in the least remember what I was working at at this time. It is not that I have ever been indifferent to my work. I have always been most grateful to God that it was work I liked and that interested me in the doing of it, and it has often carried me away from myself and quenched, or at least calmed, the troubles of life. But perhaps my life has been too full of personal interests to leave me at leisure to talk of the creatures of my imagination, as some people do, or to make believe that they were more to me in writing than they might have been in reading—that is, my own stories in the making of them were very much what other people's stories (but these the best) were in the reading. I am no more interested in my own characters than I am in Jeanie Deans, and do not remember them half so well, nor do they come back to me with the same steady interest and friendship. Perhaps people will say this is why they never laid any special hold upon the minds of others, though they might be agreeable reading enough. But this does not mean that I was indifferent to the work as work, or did not beat it out with interest and pleasure. It pleases me at this present moment, I may confess, that I seem to have found unawares an image that quite expresses what I mean—*i.e.*, that I wrote as I read, with much the same sort of feeling. It seems to me that this is rather an original way of putting it (to disclose the privatest thought in my mind), and this gives me an absurd little sense of pleasure.

We left Paris in the summer—my little boys, the governess, Jane, and I. I did not want to go back to England till the end of the year, and we strayed about a little. The tutor aforesaid and his wife had taken a house in Normandy with the intention of having boarders, and there it occurred to me to go for a short time. Mr Story, who was in Paris, came down to visit me, I remember; and we went to see Bayeux and the tapestry, jogging along in a country shandrydan with a huge red umbrella. That fact and a wonderful thunderstorm there was—which he and I sat at an open window to watch, much to the annoyance and terror of our hosts, who would have liked to shut it out with bolted shutters—are about all I recollect. We escaped as soon as we could, and went to Avranches, to the little country town hotel, where the good people of the place came in to dine, and tied their dinner napkins round their half-finished bottles of wine; and we went to Mont St Michel, which delighted me, and where I had half a mind to take one of the many empty houses left by the prison officials when it ceased to be a prison. One imposing white house dominating the village I was told I could have for a hundred francs a-year! There would have been economy, and a certain amount of interest and picturesque surroundings, but the sea and the vast sands were very grey. We bivouacked in an almost empty house, containing little but what are called box-beds in Scotland, and a table and chair or two, which belonged to an old priest, very snuffy and shabby, who was called M. L'Aumônier, and had, I suppose, filled that office in the economy of the great prison, though I don't quite know what office it is. He took me to window after window to show me little shelves of garden which he had on the slopes of the rock—one here and another there, but each provided with certain conveniences, on which the good man insisted much. The first night there I was seized by a sudden panic to find that I had lodged myself and my helpless little party in the midst of a strange, unknown, and rather rough community—in a house which had not a key even to its outer door,—and sat up till daylight to watch over them. The light reassured me, and the thought of my big and dauntless Jane, who was worth two men, and who would have faced an army for her two little boys. Oh, my little boys! and the happiness of watching over them and all their ways and sayings, though I was sad enough then, thinking there was no sadder mother, longing for my Maggie wherever I went.

We spent a long time at St Adresse, near Havre, in a house which belonged to Queen Christina of Spain, where there was capital sea-bathing ; and the children, or at least Cyril, began to learn to swim, and enjoyed themselves in all the amusements of the sea-side. One half tragic experience we had. Setting out to row, I and my little man, only eight, with a recklessness which I shiver now to think of, we were caught by the current, and had not our plight been seen from the shore and a man sent after us, I don't know what might have happened. The current was well known, only not to me, newly arrived and, as it appeared, very imprudent. We had rowed a great deal on the Gairloch, and we were close inshore, and the shining sunlit water looked like burnished glass or gold, or both. How much would have been spared if that boat had drifted out to sea! many years' toil coming to so little, many years' misery and sorrow, though many happy too—and this long tragedy at the end! To have ended all together under that rippled sheet of gold, what an escape from all that came after! I feel a kind of envy now of the situation and of the possibility—but this is all so vain.

I suppose it must have been after St Adresse that we went to St Malo, where the delightful bay, crowded with rocky islets and downy white sails, delighted me. We found a small cabin of a house on the very edge of the cliff at Dinard, which was then a little village, very primitive and quiet, whence we crossed to St Malo in a small boat with a big sail,—always somewhat alarming to me, notwithstanding my rash boating. It was called the *bateau de poissage*, I remember, in the Norman-French that always sounded to me like Scotch. We had a noble Marie for our *bonne*, a woman with the finest thoughtful face, whom I had photographed in her beautiful cap, in spite of her protestations that it would have been much better to take her niece, a commonplace, pretty little girl. Probably they do not wear those caps now, in which they looked like medieval princesses, wandering after the procession of the *Fête Dieu*, which took place while we were there. But these are all very trivial recollections. I remember being extremely touched by the playing of the local band in the Dinard church, I suppose on this occasion. They played where the anthem would come in in the English service, and what they played was *Ah che la morte*, and other airs from the "Trovatore," which shocked me at first into the usual English sense of superiority, and then affected me greatly with the thought that it was absolutely the best thing they could do which they were offering to God, whether very worthy or not, and what could the finest genius do more? My other best recollection is of the country doctor, whom I called to see my dear little Cecco in some illness, just enough to make an anxious woman more anxious, and who laughed and prescribed the *galette* of the place, a kind of cracknel, and *confiture* and cider, the drink of the place. I could have hugged him for his laugh, which proved how little was the matter, and administered the cracknel and the jam, but not the cider, which was sour. So little a thing dwells on one's mind, but it was not little at that moment, when these infantile vicissitudes were the most important matters in life.

We had rather a wild, rather a wearisome, but in some ways an amusing, journey from St Malo to Boulogne. There was a boat direct from St Malo, which, if I had been a wise woman, I should have taken, and so got home quite cheaply. But I had a great dislike to the sea; and with some compunction for the expense and more pleasure in the adventure, — though adventure there was really none, except that the manner of the journey was by that time a little out of the way,—we set off by land. We started with that perfect ignorance of where we were going, and perfect confidence that everything would go well, which, I suppose, is peculiar to women (when they are not nervous and timorous). The carriage was packed with toys and books and all kinds of things for the children, and the progress through the air, the little exhilaration of the start, the glimpse of village interiors as we rattled past, the arrivals and departures, were quite enough amusement for me. I suppose Mademoiselle must have liked it too, for she threw herself completely into the frolic. I think we passed one night at Granville. I remember distinctly that we all lunched in the middle of the day at an unknown and nameless village, upon potatoes *en robe de chambre*, which Mademoiselle sagely advised as a thing we could be quite sure of, whereas other dishes might be doubtful; and the fragrant tray of fresh sponge biscuits, taken warm and sweet out of the oven while we were there, and added to our meal as dessert, made me feel that the capabilities of the place were greater than we thought. We spent a day or two in Dieppe, intending at first to take the boat there, but finally decided to continue our drive along the coast to Boulogne, and, though we did not deserve it, were rewarded at last by the smoothest of passages across the Channel—a thing which in those days I always dreaded. We found rooms in London in the Bayswater Road, opposite Kensington Gardens—a place I have always liked; and then I set to work to find a home for us, where there should be means of education for the boys. My mind was at first inclined for Harrow, but something, I forget what, induced me to come to Windsor, which captivated me at once. Either then or later I wrote a letter to Mr Warre, now the Head Master, then young and "rising," whom I found very agreeable, and who decided, but with some reluctance, that it might be possible to educate my sons at Eton in all respects like the other boys there, but sleeping at home; which possibility, combined with the beauty of the river and the castle, and the air of cheerful life about, decided me to settle here. And a house was found very quickly—not this in which I now sit, and where almost all the events of my later life have taken place, but one in the same Crescent, within two doors of me, smaller than this. We came into it in November, I think, 1865. I have been here ever since. The house was very bright, the sun on it almost from its rising to its setting, a pleasant little garden behind, and the Crescent garden—a piece of ground of considerable extent, which we called, I don't know why, the plantation, beautifully planted, and, considering its position, a wonderful little piece of landscape gardening,—of which we took possession by acclamation. Very few people used it in these days: the day of lawn-tennis was not yet, and I suppose most of the people were elderly, for we had it almost altogether to ourselves. I never knew till a long time after of how much importance it was in the first chapter of my boys' life, this bit of town garden with its fine trees and wild nooks and corners. Lately my Cecco has told me of so many things that were done there, "when we were small," as he always said. It lies under my windows now, but I can't trust myself to go into it.

Here we got to know gradually various people about. The Hawtreys, a family of old brothers and sisters, relatives of the old Provost Hawtrey of Eton, were in themselves a very characteristic household. They lived in a large red-brick house near the church, the centre of an enormous connection, married brothers

and sisters, nephews and nieces innumerable. The
Windsor portion of the family were known universally by their Christian names, Stephen and Anna,
Henry and Florence. They have all lived in my
ken to be very old people,—the two first having both
died over eighty, while the younger pair still survive,
still ascending towards the snows. It was a house
full of entertainment, of family gatherings, Christmas
festivities, in which the overwhelming atmosphere of
Hawtreyism pervaded everything. They were all
kind naturally, but anything so bland as John Hawtrey, who was an Eton master, or so effusively benignant as old Stephen, I never saw. They had all
kinds of parties continually going on,—dinner-parties,
garden-parties, musical-parties. In one of the last
a family quartette played what was rather new and
terrible to me, long sonatas and concerted pieces,
which filled my soul with dismay. It is a dreadful
confession to make, and proceeds from want of education and instruction, but I fear any appreciation of
music I have is purely literary. I love a song and a
"tune"; the humblest fiddler has sometimes given
me the greatest pleasure, and sometimes gone to my
heart; but music properly so called, the only music
that many of my friends would listen to, is to me a
wonder and a mystery. My mind wanders through
andantes and adagios, gaping, longing to understand.
Will no one tell me what it means? I want to find
the old unhappy far-off things or battles long ago,
which Wordsworth imagined in the Gaelic song.
I feel out of it, uneasy, thinking all the time what
a poor creature I must be. I remember the mother
of the sonata players approaching me with beaming
countenance on the occasion of one of those performances, expecting the compliment which I faltered
forth, doing my best not to look insincere. "And
I have that every evening of my life!" cried the
triumphant woman. "Good heavens! and you have
survived it all this time," was my internal comment.

I can see the kind glow on her face and the mother's
pride, and thought myself, I am glad to say, a very
poor creature to be left so helplessly behind, though
not without a rueful amusement too.

I had a little neighbour in one of the smaller Crescent houses, whom the children soon got to call Aunt
Nelly, and I "Little Nelly,"—I hardly know why,
unless for the too perfect reason that she was Nelly
and very little, which of course was much too simple
to be the true meaning of the name. She it was who,
dying in her sleep without so much as the movement
of a finger—little happy woman, always of the angel
kind—put the story, if story it can be called, of "The
Little Pilgrim" into my mind. Many simple people
here had a sort of grotesque notion that there was
something of her in it more than the suggestion, as
if, alas! it were possible to follow and describe the
ways of those who are gone. She was far from being
wise or clever, generally reputed rather a silly little
woman; but with a heart of gold, and a straight-
forward, simple, right judgment, which was always
to me like the clear shining of a tiny light. She *was*,
perhaps, a silly little woman, in fact, in some ways.
There are kinds of foolishness I like for my own part,
as there is also a kind of benignant gentle dulness
which always soothes me, and which I constantly
recommend as so good a relief from the intellectualism some of my friends love; but then they do love
the intellectual, and I don't—much. She was the
guardian, when I first knew her, of an old, old mother,
whose head and memory were gone, and of a brother
with a nervous disease—a poor man cast out of life
in the middle of his days, and feeling himself to the
bottom of his heart a cumberer of the soil. Her life
was spent in amusing and caring for these two in-
valids, playing cards for hours with them. My little
Cecco used to go in the evening, rather proud of
being wanted, seven or eight years old, in his little
velvet suit, to make the fourth at whist, and when he

was a man would speak of the long whist "which was Aunt Nelly's way." The invalid brother was rarely visible, but sometimes I found a bouquet of flowers laid on my balcony, which was low enough to be reached from outside, which he laid there, stealing unnoticed into the garden.

Both these poor people died after long years, and left my little Nelly free—to take other burdens on her shoulders, and save other wounded creatures of God. Once when I was in great straits, and very anxious and unhappy, I asked her to help me in praying for the great boon I desired. I am not of the kind who do that usually, and perhaps when the trouble had been softened away I forgot even that I had done it; but thinking of it all years after, in the great and deep joy of knowing that the change I desired had come to pass, though without knowing what had led to it, I suddenly remembered how in my trouble I had sought her help, and it seemed to me like a flash of light upon the road by which we had come, not knowing. I have never asked any one else to do that for me.

· Notwithstanding, she was the object of perpetual · banter in the house. There was almost always some current joke about what little Nelly had done or said, at which she herself was the first to laugh. How many of those foolish, dear, affectionate mockeries I remember! Not mockeries—the word is too harsh: the ring of the laughter, the shining of the young eyes, and the light in her own, as beautiful as the youngest eyes among them, worn and faded as she was, are as fresh as ever. I wonder sometimes if what has been ever dies! Should not I find them all round the old whist-table, and my Cecco, with his bright face and the great blue vein that showed on his temple, proud to be helping to amuse the old people, if I were but bold enough to push into the deserted house and look for them now? I have so often felt, with a bewildered dizziness, as if that might be.

Then there was another near neighbour, one whom I have seen to-day, who lives on as I do, lonely and forlorn, with all the elements in her then of a brilliant life,—clever, witty, pretty, a woman not to be passed over, and who, had her lot fallen otherwise, might have filled any position almost, and perhaps been a leader of society, had life been more auspicious to her. When I knew her first she lived in one of the most important houses in the place, with a delightful old mother in a delightful house and much apparent comfort. It might be because she was abandoned by her fine friends, or it might be that she found something sympathetic in me, who have always been a very good listener, and apt to admire and be interested in attractive people, but she fell into a great intimacy with me, and used to spend at least half of her time in my house. She had not the merry heart which goes all the way, the happy blood that Mrs Craven speaks of; and yet she had a certain version of the merry heart, and threw herself into all the little entertainments and pleasures which I gradually began to be drawn into, by reason of the household of girls I soon had. Cousin Annie, whom I did not know before, drifted towards me almost as soon as I came to Windsor, and as she was an orphan without a home, stayed with me for a number of years; and Sara and Fanny Tulloch paid me long visits; and my boys began to spring up and carried me along on the stream of their rising life. My neighbour threw herself into all we did, and we soon began to do a great deal. It makes me wonder, looking back, how, after the despair of my grief, which found so much utterance, I should have risen again into absolute gaiety thus, twice over. But so it was. I thought it was for the young people round me, and no doubt it was so, but equally without doubt my own life burst forth again with an obstinate elasticity which I could not keep down. The merry heart goes all the way. I worked very hard all the time, but could always spare a day or any amount of evenings to please the girls, still more to please the boys. For the children, after my Cyril went to Eton, we began to have theatricals, which grew into more and more importance, till we used to play Shakespeare and Molière in my little drawing-room, alternating with innocent versions of "Barbe Bleue," &c., but that in the earlier days. I never attempted any performance myself but once, that of Mrs Hardcastle in "She Stoops to Conquer." Of course the great inspiration of these performances was Mr Frank Tarver, an Eton master, an excellent amateur actor, who, as he very soon fell in love with Sara, made himself prime minister, or, at least, master of the revels, with great energy, and helped to keep up the circle of amusement. There were others, too, full of character, and as interesting in their way as if they had been great lights in the literary or any other world, whom I might describe, and who made up a very intelligent and light-hearted society; but as not one of them turned out remarkable in any way, I need not insist upon them. One, who was one of the first to break the circle, my young friend Captain Gun, an engineer officer stationed here, I may mention. He was the Tony to my Mrs Hardcastle,—a large plain young man, full of ability and force. Had he lived he would, no doubt, have come to something. He had the readiness and resource of a soldier, seeing in a moment in a way that seemed magic to me where there was any kind of danger. I remember in Romney lock, in the dusk of a summer night, a sudden incomprehensible movement of his which filled me with alarm for a moment, as he suddenly made a step out of our boat, which shivered with the motion, into another close by and dimly seen. He had perceived that it was in unskilful hands, and that the bow had caught in the side of the lock,—a dangerous position, which his sudden additional weight at once remedied. This to my ignorance was wonderful, though, of course, it was the simplest thing in the world; but the quick sight and the quick action were delightful to witness, as soon as one understood them.

Into the midst of this half-childish gaiety there came a very sudden and alarming interruption. My brother Frank had married at the same time as I myself did, and had lived a very humdrum but happy-ish life with a wife who suited him, and had now four children—a boy and three girls. He had been in rather delicate health for a year or two, and had fallen into rather a nervous condition, his hand shaking very much so that it was difficult for him to write, though he still could do his work. One morning very suddenly, and in the most painful and disagreeable way, I heard that he had got into great trouble about money, and was, in fact, a ruined man. It was the thunderbolt out of the clear sky, which is always so tremendous. I spent a day of misery, expecting him to come to me, not knowing what to expect, and fearing all sorts of things. A day or two after I went to look for him, and found him absent and his wife in great trouble. His health, from what I now heard, was altogether shattered; and it was that as much as anything else which had brought his affairs into the most hopeless muddle, from which there seemed no escape. They had not very much money at any time, but what they had had somehow slipped through his fingers. His wife and I did everything we could, but that was very little. He was a man without an expensive taste, the most innocent, the most domestic of men, but what he had had always slipped through his fingers, as I well knew. Poor dear Frank! how well I remembered the use he made of one of my mother's Scotch proverbs, to justify some new small expense following a bigger one which he would allow to be imprudent. "Well," he would say, half-coaxing, half-apologetic, "what's the use of eating the coo and worrying [choking] on her tail?" Alas! he had choked on the tail this time without remedy, and the only thing to be done was to wind up the affairs as well as possible. We neither of us had a word of blame on our lips or a thought of anger in our hearts. Frank and Nelly, the two elder children, came to me, and Jeanie with her two little girls (my two girls this many a year, and now the only comfort of my life) joined her husband in France. It was a terrible break in life, and affected me in many ways permanently; but after the shock of seeing that chasm opening at our feet, and all their life shattered to pieces, everything quieted down again. The children were well. Oh, magic of life that made everything go smooth! they had taken no harm. They had their lives before them, and unbounded possibilities of making everything right. I am not sure that I had not a sort of secret satisfaction in getting Frank, my nephew, into my hands, thinking, with that complacency with which we always look at our own doings, that I could now train him for something better than they had thought of. This was in 1868. My Cyril was twelve and at Eton, having his room at his tutor's, and living precisely like other Eton boys, though coming home to sleep, which was one of the greatest happinesses in my life. Frank was fourteen, a big strong boy. I planned to send him to Eton too, but coming home for his meals, which was much less expensive, as I could not afford the other for him, and it answered very well. He was always the best of boys, manful, and a steady worker. Cyril had begun to be by this time noted as one of the cleverest boys, far on for his age, and promising everything, besides the brightest, wittiest, most sparkling little fellow, as he always was. I used to make it my boast that both my boys received Frank as a true brother, and never would have allowed me, had I wished it, to give them any pleasure or advantage which he did not share. But it is not likely that such family details would be of interest to the public.

And yet, as a matter of fact, it is exactly those

family details that are interesting,—the human story
in all its chapters. I have often said, however, that
none of us with any of the strong sense of family
credit which used to be so general, but is not so, I
think, now, could ever really tell what were perhaps
the best and most creditable things in our own life,
since by the strange fate which attends us human
creatures, what is most creditable to one is often
least creditable to another. These things steal
out; they are divined in most cases, and then forgotten. This catastrophe was tremendous in appearance, and yet was more or less a good thing for the
children, whose prospects seemed to be utterly
ruined,—not for the parents. Poor Jeanie—not
strong enough, I suppose, to bear what fell upon
her—died most unexpectedly in her sleep, in a mild
attack of fever which excited no alarm. My brother
had been glad to get an appointment among the
employees of a railway that was being made, of all
places in the world, in Hungary, and went there with
his wife and the little girls. I forget how long they
were there,—only a very short time. The shock of
their downfall was over, they were more or less happy
to be together, and Frank and Nelly were happy
enough here. We had returned to all our little
gaieties again, our theatricals,—our boating, and the
rest,—without much thought on my part, I fear,
of the additional responsibility I had upon me of
another boy to educate and set out in the world. We
were all assembled, a merry party enough, one
summer evening, after an afternoon on the river, at a
late meal,—a sort of supper,—when a telegram was
put into my hand. I remember the look of the long
table and all the bright faces round it, the pretty
summer dishes, salad, and pink salmon, and orna-
mented sweet things, and many flowers, the men and
boys in their flannels, the girls in their light summer
dresses—everything light and bright. I have often
said that it was the only telegram I ever received

without a certain tremor of anxiety. Captain Gun, who was there, had been uncertain of his coming on this particular day, and a good many telegrams on that subject had been passing between us. I held the thing in my hand and looked across at him, and said, "This time it cannot be from you." Then I opened it with the laugh in my mouth, and this is what I read: "Jeanie is dead, and I am in despair." It was like a scene in a tragedy. They all saw the change in my face, but I dreaded to say anything, for there was her son sitting by, my good Frank, as gay as possible. He was only about fifteen, or perhaps sixteen. We managed to keep it from him till next morning, not to give him that shock in the midst of his pleasure; and somehow the supper got completed without any one knowing what had happened.

A very short time after my poor brother came home with the two little white-faced, forlorn children, with their big eyes. I never thought but that it must kill him, but it did not; though, when I met them at Victoria, I thought I never should have got him safely back, even to Windsor. He was completely shattered, like a man in a palsy, for a time scarcely able to stand or to speak, but not so overwhelmed with grief as I expected. Grief is the strangest thing, or rather it is very wonderful in how many different ways people take those blows, which from outside seem as if they must be final. Especially is it so in the closest of human connections, that between man and wife. People who have seemed to be all the world to each other are parted so, and the survivor, who is for the moment as my poor brother said "in despair," shows the most robust power of bearing it, and is so soon himself or herself again, that one, confounded and half-ashamed, feels that one is half-ridiculous to have expected anything different. Frank, poor fellow, had got over his sorrow on the long journey. He lived for about six years after, for a great part of the time in tolerable comfort, but, so far as work was concerned, was capable of no more. He settled down to a kind of quiet life, read his newspaper, took his walk, sat in his easy-chair in the dining-room or in his own room for the rest of the day, was pleased with Frank's progress and with Nelly's love for reading, and with his little girls, and so got through his life, I think, not unhappily. But he and I, who had been so much to each other once, were nothing to each other now. I sometimes thought he looked at me as a kind of stepmother to his children, and we no longer thought alike on almost any subject: he had drifted one way and I another. He did not even take very much interest in me, and I fear he often irritated me. Poor Frank! it was sometimes a great trial, and I often wonder how the life went on, on the whole, so well as it did.

Of course I had to face a prospect considerably changed by this great addition to my family. I had been obliged to work pretty hard before to meet all the too great expenses of the house. Now four people were added to it, very small two of them, but the others not inexpensive members of the house. I remember making a kind of pretence to myself that I had to think it over, to make a great decision, to give up what hopes I might have had of doing now my very best, and to set myself steadily to make as much money as I could, and do the best I could for the three boys. I think that in some pages of my old book I have put this down with a little half-sincere attempt at a heroical attitude. I don't think, however, that there was any reality in it. I never did nor could, of course, hesitate for a moment as to what had to be done. It had to be done, and that was enough, and there is no doubt that it was much more congenial to me to drive on and keep everything going, with a certain scorn of the increased work, and metaphorical toss of my head, as if it mattered! than it ever would have been to labour with an artist's fervour and concentration to produce a masterpiece. One can't be two things or serve two masters. Which was God and which was mammon in that individual case it would be hard to say, perhaps; for once in a way mammon, meaning the money which fed my flock, was in a kind of a poor way God, so far as the necessities of that crisis went. And the wonder was that we did it, I can't tell how, economising, I fear, very little, never knowing quite at the beginning of the year how the ends would come together at Christmas, always with troublesome debts and forestalling of money earned, so that I had generally eaten up the price of a book before it was printed, but always—thank God for it!—so far successfully that, though always owing somebody, I never owed anybody to any unreasonable amount or for any unreasonable extent of time, but managed to pay everything and do everything, to stint nothing, to give them all that was happy and pleasant and of good report through all those dear and blessed boyish years. I confess that it was not done in the noblest way, with those strong efforts of self-control and economy which some people can exercise. I could not do that, or at least did not, but I could work. And I did work, joyfully, with pleasure in it and in my life, sometimes with awful moments when I did not know how I should ever pass some dreadful corner, where the way seemed to end and the rocks to close in: but the corner was. always rounded, the road opened up again.

I recollect one of these moments especially, I forget the date: I always do forget dates, but the circumstances were these. We were a family of eight, children included, two boys at Eton, almost always guests in the house,—every kind of thing (in our modest way) going on, small dinner-parties, and a number of mild amusements, when it so happened that I came to a pause and found that every channel was closed and no place for any important work. I had always a lightly flowing stream of magazine articles, &c., and refused no work that was offered to me; but the course of life could not have been carried on on these, and a large sum was wanted at brief intervals to clear the way. I had, I think, a novel written, but did not know where I should find a place for it. Literary business arrangements were not organised then as now—there was no such thing as a literary agent. Serials in magazines were published in much less number, magazines themselves being not half so many (and a good thing too!). The consequence was that I seemed to be at a dead standstill. It was like nothing but what I have already said,—a mountainous road making a sharp turn round a corner, when it seems to disappear altogether, as if it ended there in the closing in of the cliffs. I was miserably anxious, not knowing where to turn or what to do, hoping every morning would bring me some proposal, waiting upon God, if I may use the word (I did the thing with the most complete faith,—what could I else?), for the opening up of that closed way. One evening I got a letter from a man whose name I did not know, asking if he could come to see me about a business matter. I forget whether he mentioned the name of the 'Graphic,' then just established,—I think not; at all events, there was nothing in the letter to make me think it of any importance. I replied, however (I didn't always reply so quickly), appointing the second day after to receive him. I had decided to go to London next day to see if I could persuade some one to take my novel and give a good price for it. I think it was to Mr George Smith I went, who was very kind and gracious, as was his wont, but would have nothing to say to me. I fancy I went somewhere else, but I had no success. I recollect coming home in a kind of despair, and being met at the door when it was opened to me by the murmur of the merry house, the cheerful voices, the overflowing home,—every corner full and warm as if it had a steady income and secure revenue at its back.   My brother, I remember, who I suppose had seen some cloud on my face before I left, came forward to meet me with some trivial question, hoping I had not felt cold or taken cold or something, which in the state of despair in which I was had a sort of exasperating effect upon me; but they were all dispersing over the house to get ready for dinner, and I escaped further notice.   No one thought anything more than that I was dull or cross for the rest of the evening.   I used to work very late then, always till two in the morning (it is past three at this moment, 18th, nay, 19th April 1895, but this is no longer usual with me).   I can't remember whether I worked that night, but I think it was one of the darkest nights (oh, no, no, that I should say so! they were all safe and well), at least a very dreadful moment, and I could not think what I should do.

Next morning came my visitor.   He came from the 'Graphic': he wanted a story, I think the first they had had.   He wanted it very soon, the first instalments within a week or two; and after a little talk and negotiation, he came to the conclusion that they would give me £1300.   The road did run round that corner after all.   Our Father in heaven had settled it all the time for the children; there had never been any doubt.   I was absolutely without hope or help.   I did not know where to turn, and here, in a moment, all was clear again—the road free in the sunshine, the cloud in a moment rolled away.

It was not, however, the story which I had finished at the time which I gave them (which did not seem suitable).   I began another instantly, and went on with it in instalments, I think.   It was the novel called 'Innocent,' and was not very good, so far as I can remember, though the idea was one that had pleased me,—the development by successive shocks of feeling of a girl of dormant intelligence.   I believe the trial scene in it was very badly managed—not unnatural, for I never was present at a trial, though that, of course, was no excuse. It was seldom that an incident so dramatic as this little episode I have described took place in my life; but it was checkered with similar, if lesser, crises. It was always a struggle to get safely through every year and make my ends meet. Indeed I fear they never did quite meet; there was always a tugging together, which cost me a great deal of work and much anxiety. The wonder was that the much was never too much. I always managed it somehow, thank God! very happy (and presuming a little on my privilege) when I saw the way tolerably clear before me, and knew at the beginning of the year where the year's income was to come from, but driving, ploughing on, when I was not at all sure of that all the same, and in some miraculous way getting through. If I had not had unbroken health, and a spirit almost criminally elastic, I could not have done it. I ought to have been worn out by work, and crushed by care, half a hundred times by all rules, but I never was so. Good day and ill day, they balanced each other, and I got on through year after year. This, I am afraid, sounds very much like a boast. (I was going to add, "but I don't mean it as such.") I am not very sure, however, that I don't mean it, or that my head might not be a little turned sometimes by a sense of the rashness and dare-devilness, if I may use such a word, of my own proceedings; and it was in its way an immoral, or at least an un-moral, mode of life, dashing forward in the face of all obstacles and taking up all burdens with a kind of levity, as if my strength and resource could never fail. If they had failed, I should have been left in the direst bankruptcy; and I had no right to reckon upon being always delivered at the critical moment. I should think any one who did so blamable now. I persuaded myself then that I could not help it, that no better way was practicable, and indeed did live by faith, whether it was or was not exercised in a legitimate way. I might say now that another woman doing the same thing was tempting Providence. To tempt Providence or to trust God, which was it? In my own case, naturally, I said the latter, and did not in the least deserve, in my temerity, to be led and constantly rescued as I was. I must add that I never had any help from outside. I never received so much as a legacy in my life. My publishers were good and kind in the way of making me advances, without which I could not have got on; but they were never — probably because of these advances, and of my constant need and inability, both by circumstances and nature, to struggle over prices — very lavish in payment. Still, I made on the whole a large income—and spent it, taking no thought of the morrow. Yes, taking a great deal of thought of the morrow in the way of constant work and constant undertaking of whatever kind of work came to my hand. But, indeed, I do not defend myself. It would have been better if I could have added the grace of thrift, which is said to be the inheritance of the Scot, to the faculty of work. I feel that I leave a very bad lesson behind me; but I am afraid that the immense relief of getting over a crisis gave a kind of reflected enjoyment to the trouble between, and that these alternations of anxiety and deliverance were more congenial than the steady monotony of self-denial, not to say that the still better kind of self-denial which should have made a truer artist than myself pursue the higher objects of art, instead of the mere necessities of living, was wanting too. I pay the penalty in that I shall not leave anything behind me that will live. What does it matter? Nothing at all now—never anything to speak of. At my most ambitious of times I would rather my children had remembered me as their mother than in any other way, and my friends as their friend. I never cared for anything else. And now that there are no children to whom to leave any memory, and the friends

drop day by day, what is the reputation of a cir-
culating library to me? Nothing, and less than
nothing—a thing the thought of which now makes
me angry, that any one should for a moment imagine
I cared for that, or that it made up for any loss. I
am perhaps angry, less reasonably, when well-inten-
tioned people tell me I have done good, or pious ones
console. me for being left behind by thoughts of the
good I must yet be intended to do. God help us
all! what is the good done by any such work as mine,
or even better than mine? "If any man build upon
this foundation . . . wood, hay, stubble; . . . if the
work shall be burned, he shall suffer loss: but he
himself shall be saved; yet so as by fire." An in-
finitude of pains and labour, and all to disappear like
the stubble and the hay. Yet who knows? The
little faculty may grow a bigger one in the more
genial land to come, where one will have no need to
think of the boiling of the daily pot. In the meantime it was good to have kept the pot boiling and
maintained the cheerful household fire so long, though
it is smouldering out in darkness now.

There is one thing, however, I have always
whimsically resented, and that is the contemptuous
compliments that for many years were the right
thing to address to me and to say of me, as to my
"industry." Now that I am old the world is a little
more respectful, and I have not heard so much about
my industry for some time. The delightful superiority of it in the mouth of people who had neither
industry nor anything else to boast of used to make
me very wroth, I avow,—wroth with a laugh and
rueful half sense of the justice of it in the abstract,
though not from those who spoke. The same kind
of feeling made me angry the other day even, comically, not seriously angry, at a bit of a young person
who complimented me on my 'Beleaguered City.'
Now, I am quite willing that people like Mr Hutton
should speak of the 'Beleaguered City' as of the one

little thing among my productions that is worth remembering (no, Mr Hutton does nothing of the kind—he is not that kind of person), but I felt inclined to say to the other, "The 'Beleaguered City,' indeed, my young woman! I should think something a good deal less than that might be good enough for you." By which it may perhaps be suspected that I don't always think such small beer of myself as I say, but this is a pure matter of comparison.

I need scarcely say that there was not much of what one might call a literary life in all this. I was very seldom in town, Windsor being near enough to permit of almost all that one wanted to do in town, except society, being done in a day, between two trains so to speak, which was the most convenient thing in the world, and the most impossible for any sort of social intercourse. Even a dinner-party, which could only be done at the cost of a visit, thus became much more out of the question than if I had lived at a greater distance, and thus been compelled to pass a week or two occasionally in London. Now and then I went to a luncheon-party or an afternoon gathering, both of which things I detested. Curiously enough, being fond on the whole of my fellow-creatures, I always disliked paying visits, and felt myself a fish out of water when I was not in my own house,—not to say that I was constantly wanted at home, and proud to feel that I was so. The work answered very well for a pretence to get me off engagements, but I could always have managed the work if I had liked the pleasure, or supposed pleasure. I need not speak, however, as if I had been a person in much request, which would be giving an entirely false view of myself. I never was so in the least. From the days when my Jewish friend complained that I did not do myself justice, with the aggrieved tone of a woman to whom I had thus done a great injustice by not doing anything to make myself agreeable or remarkable, being asked to her house for that purpose, I have always been a disappointment to my friends. I have no gift of talk, not much to say; and though I have always been an excellent listener, that only succeeds under auspicious circumstances.

I think I never met so many people as in the days of Mrs Duncan Stewart, that dear and bright old lady who used to fill her little rooms in Sloane Street with the most curious jumble of entertaining people and people who came to be entertained, the smartest (odious word!) of society, and all the luminaries of the moment, many writers, artists, &c., and a few mountebanks to make up. She herself was very worthy of a place in any picture-gallery. There is a very droll sketch of her by Mr Augustus Hare, which does no justice to the subject. She was an English and nineteenth-century shadow of the French ladies who take up so much space in the records of the eighteenth, and who were, indeed, I suppose, of no more personal consequence than she, were it not for the mention they have secured in so many records of a memoir-writing time, and the numbers of great people who circled round them. Mrs Stewart had known almost everybody in her day, which of itself is a wonderful attraction. She had at one time seen much of Disraeli—almost at one time run the risk of having her head turned by him. The loves (but this never came to be a love—on her side at least; "For, my dear," she used to say, "I had the great preservation of being in love with my husband") of a lady of eighty are always amusing and pathetic. Age takes all the doubtfulness out of them, and gives them a piquancy as of the loves of children. She had ancient suitors, worshippers of her old age, always about her. I believe she refused a proposal of marriage after she was seventy. She was at the time I knew her of the most picturesque appearance, with a delicate small face of the colour of ivory, fine features, except that always troublesome mouth,

which is imperfect in almost every face that is good
for anything, and those dim blue eyes which have a
charm of their own—half veiled and mystic. She
was one of those people who do not grow grey, and
she wore a peculiar head-dress—a kerchief of fine
muslin and lace falling upon her shoulders, and softly
veiling her small erect head. In the middle of the
flutter of general company about her, she had always
(as indeed every one has) a constant circle of intimates always the same, and sometimes not quite
worthy of the idol they surrounded. It seems a law
of nature that this should be so, and that every
remarkable person should have a little ring of commonplace satellites, who are apt to make the object
of their adoration a little absurd, out of pure love and
desire to do her or him honour, with perhaps the
leaven of a little hope to do themselves honour too,
by being known as her or his friends. This delightful old lady was very fond of seeing and knowing
everything. She went to every entertainment, grave
or gay, and was all agog to go to the Greek play at
Eton, where it came to entrance us from Oxford,
with a chorus *pour rire* of a dozen dreadfully recog-
nisable young Dons and scholars *affublés* in incon-
venient robes and beards; as well as to see Sarah
Bernhardt, or any and every novelty that turned up.
"La pièce m'interesse," she said, looking out upon
her parties with her dim eyes that saw everything,
and never so pleased as when the crowd fluttered
about her, and a little special court gathered round
her sofa. Some vile young journalist, I remember,
made a cruel sketch of her, which was published in a
cruel and wicked series then giving great piquancy to
the 'Saturday Review' (I think it was in the Girl of
the Period and Mature Siren time, which are all so
forgotten nowadays), for which I hope he has had his
deserts somewhere. Of course, nothing could be
easier than to travesty this sweet and bright old lady
into a spectre of society, clinging on to the last to

social dissipations, and incapable of being alone—and nothing more absolutely untrue. Her grandchild said of her after she was dead, in the hush of that pause in which the longing to know what they are doing, what they are thinking, who have left us, is overwhelming, "Oh, she will have no time to think of us, she will be so much interested in seeing everything." Even in the shock of loss it was impossible not to be consoled by the thought of that vivid curiosity and interest and enjoyment with which she would find a new sphere before her, with everything to be found out.

Whom did I meet at Mrs Stewart's? I forget; nobody, I suppose, of any great consequence. She had little boxes of rooms over a tailor's shop in Sloane Street, and there gave the most elaborate luncheons, all sorts of delicacies, to which a number of very fine people would crowd in, sitting at all the uneasy angles of a table with adjuncts to it, which completely filled the room. Her income, I believe, was as small as her rooms; and her pleasant way was to tell her daughter or some intimate friend she had so many people coming to lunch, and then to prepare her pretty head-dress and her careful little *mise en scène* to receive them, with no further thought of more substantial preparations. But the table groaned all the same, and there was every costly and delicate viand on it that was to be had, and heaps of flowers, thanks always to her daughter or her loving admirers. There used to be Lady Martin, seventy or thereabouts, with the consciousness of having been more admired than any woman of her day, which gives an ineffable air to an old beauty. Her husband, the excellent Sir Theodore, was so evidently and so constantly the first of all her admirers, that the group was always interesting and touching in its bygoneness yet perfect sincerity and good faith. There was the twinkle of Bon Gaultier in Sir Theodore's eye on other matters, but never where his wife was concerned. And a very frequent visitor was the kind, the gentle, the sympathetic Censor of Plays, dead only this year, Mr Pigott, a man to whom everybody's heart went out, I don't know exactly why or how, except from an intuition of friendship, a sort of instinct. He was always interested, always kind,— a sort of atmosphere of humanity and warm feeling and sympathy about him, his little round form and round head radiating warmth and kindliness. He is the only man I have ever met, I think, from whom I never heard an unkind word of any one. This, to tell the sad truth, is apt to make conversation a little insipid; but he had the most extensive acquaintance both with people and things, and had many a happy turn of expression and *mot* of social wisdom which preserved him from that worst of faults: he was never dull, though always kind, which is almost a paradox. I have my own way of dividing people, as I suppose most of us have. There are those whom I can talk to, and those whom I can't. With the first no subject is needed, the conversation goes on of itself; with the other all the finest subjects in the world produce no result. (I remember as I write one story of Mr Pigott which slightly, but very slightly, contradicts this statement that he never said an un-kind word. We were talking once of the son-in-law of a friend of ours, who had most gratuitously and unnecessarily appeared against her in a trial in which she was unhappily involved, to prove (as if any one could prove such a thing) that certain anonymous letters were written by her. We were discussing his conduct with indignation, when Mr Pigott looked up with a smile,—" Look in his face and you'll forgive him all," he said. It was true that the man was a fool, and bore it on his face.)

It was with Mrs Stewart that I first saw Tennyson. She had, I suppose, asked leave to take me there with her to luncheon, and I was of course glad to go, though a little unwilling, as my manner was. I for-get where it was—an ordinary London house, where they were living for the season. Mrs Tennyson lay upon her sofa, as she did always—though able to be taken to the luncheon-table by her excellent son Hallam, whom I knew a little, and who was always kind and pleasant. I have always thought that Tennyson's appearance was too emphatically that of a poet, especially in his photographs: the fine frenzy, the careless picturesqueness, were almost too much. He looked the part too well; but in reality there was a roughness and acrid gloom about the man which saved him from his over romantic appearance. He paid no attention to me, as was very natural. The conversation turned somehow upon his little play of "The Falcon"—now more forgotten, I think, than any of his others, though it seemed to me much the most effective of them. I said something about its beauty, and that I thought it just the kind of entertainment which a gracious prince might offer to his guests; and he replied, with a sort of indignant sense of grievance, "And they tell me people won't go to see it." I am afraid, however, that I did not attract the poet in any way, to Mrs Stewart's great disappointment and annoyance. She was eager to point out to me that he was much occupied by a very old lady—a fair, little, white-haired woman, nearly eighty, the mother of Mr Tom Hughes (Tom Brown), who was just then going out to America to the settlement in the backwoods which was called Rugby, in Tennessee, where the young Hughes were, and which was going to be the most perfect colony on the face of the earth, filled with nothing but the cardinal virtues. I think the old lady died there, and I know the settlement went sadly to pieces and ruined many hopes. However, feeling I had not been entirely a success,—a feeling very habitual to me,—I was glad of Mrs Stewart's sign of departure, and went up to Mrs Tennyson on the sofa, to which she had returned, to take my leave. I am never good at parting politenesses, and I daresay was very *gauche* in saying that it was so kind of her to ask me; while she graciously responded that she was delighted to have seen me, &c., according to the established ritual in such cases. Tennyson was standing by, towering over us with his ragged beard and his saturnine look. He eyed us, while these pretty speeches were being made, with cynical eyes. " What liars you women are ! " he said. There could not have been anything more true; but, to be sure, it was not so civil as it was true. I never saw him again till that recent occasion when my Cecco and I went to Farringford when he was Lord Tennyson, and very old and infirm, and his wife was a shrunken old, old lady, laid upon a sofa from which she never moved, the flood of life flowing past her but never touching her,—a pathetic sight. It was after Lionel's death, and after my Cyril's death, and I sat by her and cried; but she seemed in her old age as if she could weep no more. That time Lord Tennyson was delightful—kind and friendly and full of stories, talking a great deal, and in the best of humours. He read the " Funeral Ode " to us afterwards, and one or two shorter poems ("Blow, bugles, blow "; and I was so glad and thankful that Cecco should see him so, and have such a bright recollection of him to carry through his life. Alas! alas! It had always been a regret that he had never seen Carlyle—so little as it matters now !

It is rather a fictitious sort of thing recalling those semi-professional recollections. It is by way of a kind of apology for knowing so few notable people. I met Mr Fawcett once, the blind politician, a huge mild man, cheerful in talk and amiable in countenance, whom somebody (not me, I am afraid) overheard saying to his wife when she came back to him from another room, to take—the small smiling woman she was—his colossal person in charge, " Oh, Milly, your step is like music." He spoke to me very kindly, magnifying my work, though I don't remember how, except the pleasant impression. At the same party was Sir Charles Dilke, who, on being introduced to me, began at once to speak of *his* books and of his publishers, as if he and not I were the literary person. The same thing happened with a great lady I afterwards met in the same house,—a Roman Catholic lady, and a very great personage. There had been several invitations given to her at one time and another by the mistress of the house, but they all failed somehow, and at last the one she could accept fell on a Friday. The great lady took the trouble to write the day before to remind my friend that it *was* Friday, and consequently to her a fast day. This put C. R. on her mettle, as any one who knows her will understand, and we were served with the most exquisite and luxurious meal, I don't know how many *maigre* dishes—fish, eggs, and vegetables, all beautifully cooked and seductive to the last degree, about as little like fasting as the imagination could conceive. I like fish and vegetables better than any other kind of food, and, beguiled by the variety, followed Lady ——'s example and kept up with her as long as I could. But it was a vain attempt, and I had to sit and look on for some time while she travelled valiantly through every dish. She, too, chose as the theme of her conversation her own books, their success or rather their relative successes, and the trouble she had with her publishers, and all the rest, while I sat with rueful amusement listening, feeling my little *rôle* taken from me. The worst was, I had never heard she had written anything, and was in mortal terror of betraying my ignorance! What with her literature, and her beautiful appetite, and our beautiful meal, the occasion was delightful. There were some actor-gentlemen of the party,—I know not if the great lady had a liking for actors, but there they were, furtively regaled with beef after the lighter quips and fancies of the feast, and rather ignored in consequence by us finer people who had fasted on about twenty of the daintiest dishes in the world.

I

The year 1875 was an era in my life—a great many things happened in that year. Frank, my good Frank, my nephew, who had grown the most trustworthy and satisfactory boy in the world, loving home, fond of amusement and diversion, but only in the right ways,—such a one as is a stand-by and tower of strength in a family,—completed his work at Cooper's Hill very well, taking a high place, and so having the right to choose what part of India he would go to. Things had so developed in the family that this event seemed an occasion for various other changes, especially as at the same time Cyril was to go to Oxford. My brother had been getting feeble and less easy to take care of, and I was anxious that he should live in a doctor's house and be watched and cared for, as his state seemed to demand; and that the little girls, whose education ought to be seriously thought of, should go to Germany at the same time. I was trying to make Frank's last summer at home pleasant, and wanted him within the limitations of our small ways to see and do everything possible. There is an incident in one of my own books, in ' Kirsteen,' which is a sort of illustration of my feeling about him. It was not my own invention, but told me as the family custom in the large, poor, proud family which formed the model of the family in that book,—the bottle of champagne solemnly produced and drunk by the whole party on the night before the boy went away. I wanted Frank to have his bottle of champagne. I had settled to take them all to Switzerland for one thing, and I took them up to an opera for another, and to stay a night or two in London, and to see everything they could see in the small amount of time. There was a match going on at Lord's, I think, which filled the morning, and then we were to dine at Miss Blackwood's, and stay in the same house in Half Moon Street where she was. All was very lively and pleasant for the boys, who went up in the morning all so bright and gay, with their little bows of blue ribbon, and button-holes with a bit of forget-me-not, to serve the same purpose. How often have I come out with them to the door, seeing them off, so spruce, in the bright morning (surely the days were always bright when they went up for that Eton and Harrow match), so full of pleasure. I found one of these little blue bows in my Cyril's room after— God bless him!—and it lies with other treasures. I can see them now setting out, the little hall full of the little bustle, and I half scolding, telling them they were sure to be late, and so proud—the three of them —all well, not a cloud, the most hopeful youths, Frank tall and strong, my Cyril with his beautiful face, my Cecco only a boy and little, straining to keep up with them, all dressed in their best, with that keen regard to the fashion which I laughed at and loved,—but what did I not love in them? They were my all in this world. I was always anxious; but there was not a cloud upon the skies, and what had I to fear?

Next morning we were called back by a telegram. My brother had been taken ill, and the little scheme of pleasure was broken up. I found him very ill, scarcely conscious, when I got home, and in that state he remained, with a few lightenings, till he died.

Cyril left Eton at the end of that half, a little while after. When he went down to see if the lists were out before we left home, the man at Drake's told him, smiling, that he could not tell him the names, but he could tell him this, that in the first three, two were Oppidans. This was very rare, and there was little doubt that he was one of them. He and Frank came rushing up with this exciting news to tell me. I have had great trouble, but also I have had many joys. I forget who the Colleger was who was first,— I think it was Ryle, or perhaps Harmer, now Bishop; then Farrar, Oliphant. These two went to Balliol, both with scholarships from Eton, Farrar also with a

Balliol scholarship, which Cyril ought to have got too, but did not.   Both of them now are, I hope and believe, fulfilling their lives in a better place than this, Farrar very young.   He was more regular, more dutiful; he had not the wayward touch in him, the careless heart.   He did far better after.   At that time there was no better possible,—it was all triumph and anticipation of every good.   Eton is very dear, very bright to me in all its recollections.   No brighter being than my Cyril ever came from it, a boy un-harmed in every way, handsome, winning, clever, gay, the most light-hearted, the most generous in feeling, full of understanding and of tenderness, nothing about him commonplace or dull, looking as if he would not subdue but win the whole world.   I used to think that if one could desire to have another personality than one's own, his would have been the thing to dream of at that bright moment.   And I used to apply to him the description of the young squire in Chaucer,—

> "Singing he was, or flyting, all the day,
> He was as fresh as is the month of May."

There was no prouder woman in the world than I was with the three.   Frank was twenty-two, Cyril nineteen, Cecco sixteen—he doing so well too, with his strange little ways and shyness and close clinging always to his mother.   It is just twenty years ago.   I think often if all had gone well, as might then have been so confidently expected,—had Frank been a prosperous man in India, perhaps sending home his children to be educated, and Cyril been a rising lawyer as was hoped, and Cecco, if delicate, still able with care to keep on,—it would all have been so natural, not anything wonderful, just the common-place of life for which other fathers and mothers would scarcely pause to give special thanks, it being all so usual, exactly what might have been expected.   And ah, the difference to me! But, thank God! we did not know what was coming in these days.

We went to Interlaken, Cecco and I and our dear "little Nelly." The older boys took the little girls to their German school at Arolsen, and joined us after, coming round by the Lake of Constance. We found Annie Thackeray, attended by Miss Huth, a gentle little soul, very much like my little Nelly, and making great friends with her at Interlaken; and here it was that Annie and I became fast friends. There never was any one more fascinating or a more delightful companion, so pleased to please, so ready to see the best of you—a little, perhaps, too ready to perceive a best that might not be in you, yet with a keen observation underneath that was—though if the report was unfavourable would scarcely permit itself to be—critical. She was always more effusive than myself, delightfully flattering, appreciating. I used to say that if you wanted the moon very much, she would eagerly, and for a moment quite seriously, think how she could help to get it for you, scorning the bounds of the possible. We went to Grindelwald together and were in the same hotel—the old Bear in its homely days—for about a fortnight, and grew intimate. She was joined there by the Leslie Stephens, meaning her sister Minnie and Minnie's husband. It was Mrs Stephen's last summer in this world, but we did not know that either. She was not strong, but there were reasons for that, and no sort of alarm about her. Little Minnie, her one little girl, was the baby of the party—a little, fragile, quaint thing, whom I remember standing by the great St Bernard, Sultan, with her hands in his deep fur, a curious little picture. She was full of quaint sayings and wondering looks, looking on at the boys and asking solemnly, "What are they ninking about?" with the gravest observation, and defending her little basket of cakes from Cyril's pretended attacks with a serious discrimination of him as the greedy boy, which became one of our little jokes. It takes but a small matter to make a joke when all is well and one's heart inclined that way. I made acquaintance with Mr Leslie Stephen at that time,— a man with whom I had had a slight passage of arms by letters about some literary work, he being the editor of the 'Cornhill,' a prosperous magazine in those days. I fell into a chance talking with him one evening in front of the Bear, when the sky was growing dim over the Wetterhorn, and the shadows of the mountains drawing down as they do when night is coming on. I recollect we walked up and down and talked, I have not the smallest remembrance what about. But the end of it was that when I went in we had become friends, or so it was at least on my side.

Leslie Stephen was kind to the boys, taking them for walks with him up among the mountains; and he was so far kind to me that he took two of my stories for the 'Cornhill,' which meant in each case the bulk of a year's income.

This expedition was altogether very successful and delightful, the last time the three boys were to spend together, for many years, we thought,—for ever in this world, as it turned out. One thing happened in it on which I look back with a mixture of tenderness and amusement. It was the coming to life of the two who were then called the little girls. They left home with no apparent feeling at all, and much comment among us at the absence of it. But when they were left in Germany among strange-speaking people, among new ways, in such a strange place, the two little hearts gushed out all at once. They wrote to me the most pathetic, imploring letters. "Oh, come and take us home; oh come, come and take us home. We will be as good as angels," said Madge, "if you will only come and take us home." It was rather hard work refusing. We were in Interlaken, I think, when these letters came, and we made up a basket of all the toys and pictures and cakes that would carry, to console them. And they soon got over their first home-sickness. And they never relapsed into those chills and mists of their childhood, but have always been since my true children, the unquestioned daughters of the house, and with no further cloud upon the completeness of their adoption—they of me, as well as I of them. The first is often the more difficult of the two.

With that year began a new life, one of which I cannot speak much. That was the burden and heat of the day : my anxieties were sometimes almost more than I could bear. I had gone through many trials, as I thought, and God knows many of them had been hard enough, but then I knew to the depths of my heart what the yoke was and how heavy. Many times I have woke in the morning feeling in myself that image of Shelley's " Prometheus," which in my youth I had vexed my husband by not appreciating, except in what seemed to me the picture rather than the poem, the man chained to the rock, with the vultures swooping down upon him. Their cruel beaks I seemed to feel in my heart the moment I awoke. Ah me, alas! pain ever, for ever, God alone knows what was the anguish of these years. And yet now I think of *ces beaux jours quand j'étais si malheur-euse,* the moments of relief were so great and so sweet that they seemed compensation for the pain,—I remembered no more the anguish. Lately in my many sad musings it has been brought very clearly before my mind how often all the horrible tension, the dread, the anxiety which there are no words strong enough to describe,—which devoured me, but which I had to conceal often behind a smiling face,—would yield in a moment, in the twinkling of an eye, at the sound of a voice, at the first look, into an ineffable ease and the overwhelming happiness of relief from pain, which is, I think, our highest human sensation, higher and more exquisite than any positive enjoyment in this world. It used to sweep over me like a wave, sometimes when I opened a door, sometimes in a letter,—in all simple ways. I cannot explain, but if this should ever come to the eye of any woman in the passion and agony of motherhood, she will more or less understand. I was thinking lately, or rather, as sometimes happens, there was suddenly presented to my mind, like a suggestion from some one else, the recollection of these ineffable happinesses, and it seemed to me that it meant that which would be when one pushed through that last door and was met—oh, by what, by whom?—by instant relief. The wave of sudden ease and warmth and peace and joy. I felt, to tell the truth, that it was one of them who brought that to my mind, and I said to myself, " I will not want any explanation, I will not ask any question,—the first touch, the first look, will be enough, as of old, yet better than of old."

I do injustice to those whom I love above all things by speaking thus, and yet what can I say? My dearest, bright, delightful boy missed somehow his footing, how can I tell how? I often think that I had to do with it, as well as what people call inherited tendencies, and, alas! the perversity of youth, which he never outgrew. He had done everything too easily in the beginning of his boyish career, by natural impulse and that kind of genius which is so often deceptive in youth, and when he came to that stage in which hard work was necessary against the competition of the hard working, he could not believe how much more effort was necessary. Notwithstanding all distractions he took a second-class at Oxford, —a great disappointment, yet not disgraceful after all. And I will not say that, except at the first keen moment of pain, I was in any way bitterly disappointed. *Tout peut se réparer.* I always felt so to the end, and perhaps he thought I took it lightly, and that it did not so much matter. Then it was one of my foolish ways to take my own work very lightly, and not to let them know how hard pressed I was sometimes, so that he never, I am sure, was convinced how serious it was in that way, and certainly never was convinced that he could not, when the moment came, right himself and recover lost way. But only the moment, God bless him! did not come till God took it in His own hands. Another theory I have thought of with many tears lately. I had another foolish way of laughing at the superior people, the people who took themselves too seriously,—the boys of pretension, and all the strong intellectualisms. This gave him, perhaps, or helped him to form, a prejudice against the good and reading men, who have so many affectations, poor boys, and led him towards those so often inferior, all inferior to himself, who had the naturalness along with the folly of youth. Why should I try to explain? He went out of the world, leaving a love-song or two behind him and the little volume of " De Musset," of which much was so well done, and yet some so badly done, and nothing more to show for his life. And I to watch it all going on day by day and year by year!

My Cecco took the first steps in the same way; but, thanks be to God, soon righted himself and overcame —not in time to save his career at Oxford, but so as to be all that I had hoped,—always my very own, my dearest companion, choosing me before all others. What a companion he was, everybody who knew us knows: full of knowledge, full of humour—a most accomplished man, though to me always a boy. He did not make friends easily, and he had few; but those whom he had were very fond of him, and all our immediate surroundings looked up to him with an affectionate admiration which I cannot describe. " I don't know, but I will ask Cecco," was what we all said. He had not much more than emerged from the desert of temptation and trial, bringing balm and healing to me, when he fell ill. When his illness first was declared, it seemed to me that my misery was more than I could bear. I remember that we all went to the Holy Communion together the Sunday before we left for Pau, and that as I went up to kneel at the altar I was so nearly overcome, that Cyril put his hand on my arm and gripped it almost roughly to recall me to myself. And then the whole world seemed to come back again into the sun after a time ; he got so much better, and the warm summer of the Queen's Jubilee year seemed to complete what Pau had begun. And he passed his examination for the British Museum, coming out first, and his life seemed now to be ordered in a safe place—in the work he loved. Alas ! Then Sir Andrew Clark would not pass him, but other doctors gave the best of hopes. And he did a great deal of good work, and finally went to the Royal Library here ; and we had many blinks of happiness, both in the winter on the Riviera and at home. I cannot tell what he was to me—consulting me about everything, desiring to have me with him, to walk with me and talk to me, only put out of humour when I was drawn away or occupied by other things. When he was absent he wrote to me every day. I never went out but he was there to give me his arm. I seem to feel it now—the dear, thin, but firm arm. In the last four years after Cyril was taken from us, we were nearer and nearer. I can hear myself saying "Cecco and I." It was the constant phrase. But all through he was getting weaker ; and I knew it, and tried not to know.

And now here I am all alone.

I cannot write any more.

END OF AUTOBIOGRAPHY.

LETTERS.

———

AMONG the considerable number of letters from different correspondents which Mrs Oliphant left behind her, the earliest—or at any rate the earliest of any general interest — is from the redoubtable Francis Jeffrey. He was at the very end of his long and brilliant literary career when there came to him an offering—the first work of a young and unknown writer—which seems to have touched the springs of kindness and sympathy in a way very charming and attractive.[1] The letter of the old critic was, naturally, most highly valued by the neophyte. She seems never to have lost a sense of the pleasure it gave her; and Jeffrey's death, shortly after she received it, made it even more of a relic. Here is the missive, sent to her through her publisher :—

1850.

To the Author of 'Passages in the Life of Margaret Maitland.'

EDINBURGH, *5th January* 1850.

I was captivated by 'Margaret Maitland' before the author came to *bribe* me by the gift of a copy

[1] Passages in the Life of Mrs Margaret Maitland. Colburn: London, 1849.

and a too flattering letter—which I am now taking
the chance of answering—though not trusted either
with the name or address of the person to whom I
must express my gratitude and admiration! Nothing
half so true or so touching (in the delineation of Scottish character) has appeared since Galt published his
'Annals of the Parish'—and this is purer and deeper
than Galt, and even more absolutely and simply true.
It would have been better though and made a stronger
impression if it had copied Galt's brevity, and is sen-
sibly injured by the indifferent matter which has been
admitted to bring it up to the standard of three volumes. All about the Lectures and Jo Whang, and
almost all about Reuben and the ladies at the Castle,
is worse than superfluous; and even the youthful Poet
and his allegory, though the creation of no ordinary
mind, is out of place and *de trop*.

The charm is in Grace and Margaret Maitland,
and they and their immediate connections ought to
have had the scene mostly to themselves. It is debased and polluted by the intrusion of so many
ordinary characters. The conception of Grace, so
original and yet so true to nature and to Scottish
nature, is far beyond anything that Galt could reach ;
and the sweet thoughtfulness and pure, gracious, idio-
matic Scotch of Margaret, with her subdued sensi-
bilities and genial sympathy with all innocent enjoy-
ments, her ardent but indulgent piety, and the modest
dignity of her sentiments and deportment, make a
picture that does equal credit to the class from which
it is taken and to the right feeling and power of observation of the painter. Claud perhaps is scarcely
made thoroughly deserving of Grace, though it certainly must not have been easy to finish a *male*
character either so highly or so softly as these two
delightful females—and Mary, especially in the later
scenes, is nearly as good as they are.

When I first read the book I settled it with myself
that it was the work of a *woman*—and though there

are *pronouns* in the letter of the author now before
me which seem to exclude that supposition, I am so
unwilling to be disabused of this first impression that
I still venture to hope that it was not erroneous, and
that these words were introduced only to preserve
the *incognito* which the author (though I am sure I
cannot guess for what reason) seems still anxious to
maintain.

I have no wish certainly, as I have no right, to
violate the *incognito*, but write now merely to return
my humble and cordial thanks for the honour the
author has done me, and to express the deep and
most pleasing sense I have of the great merit of his
(if it must be *his*) *personnel*, and with all good wishes
transcribe myself the said author's very grateful and
sincere humble servant,   F. JEFFREY.

After the date of this letter there is a gap of about
two years, and then begins, though with many breaks,
especially in the earlier portion, the long series of
those written by Mrs Oliphant to the Blackwoods—
chiefly to Mr John Blackwood, but also to Mr William
Blackwood, the present head of the house; to Miss
Isabella Blackwood, with whom she maintained a very
long and intimate friendship; and to some of the
younger members of the family. It may be permitted
here to insert the account given by Mr John Blackwood himself, and noted down at the time by one of
his hearers, of Mrs Oliphant's very first introduction
to the pages of 'Maga.' On the 25th anniversary of
that introduction Mr Blackwood and many of his old
contributors were invited to spend a lovely summer
day on Magna Charta Island, within a few miles of
her house at Windsor, and to lunch on the spot where
King John met his barons. Mr Blackwood began his
short after-luncheon speech by a humorous parallel

between the earlier sovereign and himself—the barons of Magna Charta and the bold barons of Blackwood; then, falling into a more serious tone, passed on to relate the commencement of his acquaintance with his hostess. He described the young woman new to literature and shy, but with the same bright eyes full of intelligence as in later years. "She talked to me," he said, "among other things, about Thackeray and Dickens, and I thought I had never heard anything better said. I asked her to write it down, and she did so; and that was the beginning of her work for the Magazine."

'Katie Stewart' was the first book of Mrs Oliphant's published by the Blackwoods, and, as she has herself recorded elsewhere, the family adopted a fashion of speaking of her by the name of her heroine.

1852.

To Mr John Blackwood.   BIRKENHEAD, *4th February.*

I am conscious that there is rather too much Scotch in particularly the first chapters of 'Katie Stewart'; but considering the time and the rank of the characters, I think any alteration in this point would make the book less true. I think I mentioned before that there is no fiction in the history, except indeed in the introduction of some of the subordinate characters; the incidents—all of them—are simply and strictly true: this, however, I am aware is quite a doubtful advantage, since it is somewhat difficult to be at once true in fact and true to nature—but Katie Stewart and Lady Anne Erskine were both of them real existences.

BIRKENHEAD, *26th April.*

This is the last week I shall spend in this place, and there are now very few days to spare. Do you still intend that the first number of my story should appear in the Magazine for May?

This is the last letter signed M. O. Wilson. The proofs of 'Katie Stewart' were delivered to Mrs Oliphant on her wedding-day.

HARRINGTON SQUARE, LONDON, 29*th May.*

I am sorry that the proof of 'Katie Stewart' should have been so long detained, and also that your remittance was not, I believe, properly acknowledged. It did not arrive until after I had left Birkenhead at a time when there was much commotion and business in the household, and I trust you will excuse the omission on these grounds. I think I have done as much to prune the Scotch as was practicable without a complete change in many of the earlier scenes. I am, like my heroine, not much of a Jacobite; and as I do not wish to claim loftier sentiments than she possessed for Katie Stewart, I must, I think, suffer her opinion of the Chevalier to remain as it is. I think it accords better with the character than anything of that imaginative poetic loyalty which seems to have belonged by some strange right of inheritance to those unhappy Stuarts. As to the Chevalier himself, my opinion of his face is formed from a youthful portrait taken before the vices of his later life could at all affect him. It may be that I judge wrongly of its expression—still I do judge so; it is an honest opinion, and this also I think must stand as it is. . . . I am obliged by your kind interest in Lady Anne, and should willingly give up the thin shoulders and the long arms; but then these are fully balanced by good qualities which Katie Stewart does not profess to possess, and for the sake of contrast I must be content to do the good Lady Anne even a little injustice. She is loftier in many respects than her humble companion, and for the sake of due individuality Lady Anne must preserve her angles.

The following letter, written by Mrs Wilson, Mrs Oliphant's much-beloved mother, to her brother, is interesting as showing how that vivacious old lady flung herself into her daughter's interests and enjoyed her successes :—

August 22, 1852.

'Katie Stewart' seems to have made a great sensation. Maggie has had two letters lately from Mr Blackwood, both of them exceedingly kind; the first saying that he had not said to any person who the author was, but that Sir Ralph Anstruther had written asking if he might know, whereat I was very proud, as it was a testimony to the truthfulness of my memory, his own grandmother being the Lady Janet. The reason Mr Blackwood gave for not saying who the author was, was that it might be good for her to have an anonymous reputation,—honest man, he little knew of 'John Drayton' and his neighbour,[1] —and that the other contributors were Professor Wilson, Sir A. Alison, Sir E. Bulwer, and Samuel Warren, and he hopes she is pleased with her company. His next is still more gratifying : he says Fife is in a ferment,—that is, not our Fife but literary Fife,—and the authorship is divided between Sir Ralph Anstruther and Lord Lindsay.

1856.

To Mr Blackwood.   7 ULSTER PLACE, *Friday.*

About Macaulay, if you can give me a very late day I will try and be ready with *a bit of him* for the June number. Macaulay seems to me the historian

[1] Novels published anonymously for the benefit of her brother William, which some ingenious critics have supposed to be written by him.

of sophistication, a man who writes only and always for "society," and knows as little of any primitive existence as a New Zealander could know of Mayfair. Everybody admires him, of course, but nobody believes in him—at least, so far as my experience goes.

1858.

We have quite made up our minds about going abroad, and are working towards that end now,—a troublesome operation enough, as it will be a temporary breaking up of our household.

I enclose the proof: all my superlatives apply to Irving himself rather than to his genius. I knew nothing whatever of him till his 'Last Days' fell by chance into my hands. Try the 'Orations' and you will come over to my opinion: it is Irvingism which has smothered them, but Irvingism has very little in common with Irving.

I think it is rather a feather in my cap to have produced a MS. undecipherable even to you: printers fortunately can read everything,[1] but I did not know the Christopher was worse than usual. We shall get away, I trust, in about three weeks. We should be glad of some kind of introduction to the English Minister at Florence,—could you help us in that? I daresay we could manage it otherwise, but you are *in* and influential.

I have had some correspondence with Mr Drummond, and almost think we shall run down to Albury one day next week to see him. A dear old friend and

---

[1] On the 19th of October 1872 Mrs Oliphant had seen reason to doubt the omniscience of printers. She writes to Mr Blackwood : " You seem to have some wicked wag in the printing office whose performances are most bewildering. Fancy printing ' Troplemus' instead of ' hopelessness ' ! There is something in the interpolation of an unknown name spelt with a big capital that takes one quite aback. One feels it ought to be some classic personage worthy of veneration."

K

relation of ours, who is the sister of the late Mrs Irving, is very anxious that I should undertake a life of Edward Irving: she has all the materials within her power. However, this is far in the future. But it makes me more disposed to find out what Mr Drummond has to say on the subject.

We hope to get away next Saturday, Mr Oliphant having now got all his work completed and nothing but arrangements to make.

We spent Wednesday and the morning of the next day with Mr Drummond. He is an interesting old man—I have no doubt, as you say, a very good type of an English country gentleman, and almost *too* tempting a study for a novel-writer. To listen seriously while a man of indisputable mind and knowledge of the world talks with the most serious good faith of people possessed with devils, and the manner of exorcising familiar spirits, is no small exercise of one's self-control, and a very piquant variation upon ordinary life. I am afraid I am committed to the Life of Irving, which I think a noble subject, but I shall not think of entering upon it till we return.

Mr Drummond lives rather in the grand style, his son-in-law and daughter, Lord and Lady Lovaine, sharing his household. He seems one of those happy men who are interested about everything, and ready to speculate upon any subject from an election up to the greatest of spiritual mysteries. These last formed the bulk of my conversations with him, and his explanations were more odd than I can describe. He smiles at the mere idea of anything less than perfect belief of the Spiritual Utterances, which still, it appears, guide the Church which bears the name of Irving, but which has gone far beyond anything in *his* intentions—and assumes the reality of these with a confidence which one can only wonder at, though, I confess, under strong temptations to smile. He is evidently full of speculation of the oddest character, supported partly on very good sense and good reason, and partly by the most delightful *non sequitur* which takes away one's breath. He was extremely kind, as were his daughters. We spared the time with great difficulty, but I was glad we had done so.

We will get away, I trust, some day next week, though I cannot exactly say which. Mr Oliphant has been and continues very indifferent in health, but we have great hopes from the doctor that he wants chiefly rest and change.

1859.

To Mr Blackwood.   VIA MAGGIO, FLORENCE.

We are very curious and interested about 'Adam Bede,' which we see advertised and criticised in the 'Athenæum.' We shall be having a parcel sent out to us shortly,—might I ask for a copy?—which if you will kindly send along with my copy of the Magazine to my brother, would be forwarded to me here, and would be a great gratification, as English books are not plentiful.

. . . I am sure you must be very much gratified by the extraordinary success of 'Adam Bede.' I have never yet had an opportunity of getting the book sent out, so I am still ignorant of it, but the flutter of curiosity in the newspapers is sufficiently exciting. I don't want to pry into the secret, but pray tell me one thing: I cannot believe that the author of the 'Scenes of Clerical Life' is a woman—is that extraordinary guess correct? I shall feel quite satisfied if you say no.

The time of deep sorrow and struggle which followed the writing of this letter is described in the Autobiography, and need not be recapitulated here. Mr Oliphant died in Rome; and six weeks later the baby son who, as he grew up, always retained his baby

name, " Cecco," was born.   It is hard to imagine anything more desolate than the young widow's position
at this time, yet her letters show how bravely she kept
up her heart, and how indefatigably she worked for
the three little ones dependent on her.   Perhaps one
secret of her amazing power of work was that she
never lost interest in the lives and work of other
people.

1860.

To Mr Blackwood.   BIRKENHEAD, *6th March.*
I should like very much to put in a claim beforehand for the new book by the author of ' Adam Bede.'
I wish very much you would tell me whether this mysterious personage is a woman.   I shall feel very much
humiliated if it is so, seeing I have staked my critical
credit on the other side, and I fear shall scarcely believe it even if you tell me ; but my curiosity is great.
Thank you very much for the Magazine—I am charmed
with ' St Stephen's.'   It is Sir Edward's, of course.

23rd March.
Many thanks for your kind exertions in the matter
of Hampton Court.   I am sorry her Majesty does not
think it worth while to exert her royal bounty on my
behalf; but I had not placed my hopes very high.
Indeed I wanted more a bond which should oblige me
to fix some definite place to live in than the place itself.   I feel my entire freedom of choice in this particular a very forlorn liberty, and, always accustomed to
consult another will, would be thankful now, when I
have but my own to think of, to have an obligation
or necessity, anything almost which would fix me to
one place, without giving to my indolence and lassi-
tude the pain of choice.   I am very much obliged not
the less by the kind trouble you have taken on my
behalf.

The article I trust you will let me postpone till next month. I have been falling out of one cold into another since ever I arrived here. The change of climate is very perceptible, and this is one of the windiest corners in all England; so that I think I have gone through almost all the varieties of cold and influenza, and may now hope for a little exemption.

July.

I send you enclosed the first chapter of 'Montalembert.' I think it very likely you won't like the execution, and pray don't hesitate in the least to say so, for I am not vain of my French.

1861.

To Mr Blackwood. FETTES ROW, EDINBURGH.

It would be affectation to say that I was not much disappointed and mortified by receiving your packet last night. I should be glad to console my *amour propre* by thinking that the stronger fare to which you are accustomed has given you a distaste for my womanish style. One finds it always odd somehow to account for being stupid in one's own person. But at all events I am not sulky. Greater people than me have had a run of failures, and I shall still hope to recover myself. I write now to ask you whether it is any use to send you a revised version of the other condemned article. It would be, of course, a great salve and solace to my wounded soul, and if you are disposed to keep a corner open for me I would send it up to-night. But if not, it is a pity to give you the pain of rejecting another effort, which I am glad and obliged to be able to think *is* a pain to you.

This is the moment already alluded to when Mrs Oliphant's work came to a kind of standstill. Worn out by sorrow and physical suffering, it is little short of miraculous that she was able to gather up her forces again, and with admirable success. She has told the story of these days in her Autobiography, and, briefly, in 'Annals of a Publishing House.'

WILLOWBURN, ROSENEATH.

I am very glad, though I confess a little surprised, to find you speak so favourably of the little story[1] which I now return corrected. I had my fears about it when I sent it to you. I cannot tell you how much gratified and affected I am by what you kindly say of my writing. I take it as one of the most valuable compensations for a lot more laborious and heavily burdened than that of most of my neighbours, that Providence has given me friends who judge my endeavours so kindly: I should be forlorn enough else. But you were quite right in winter; and if I do better now, I reckon it greatly to the account of your own family and my friends here who have taken the pains to shake me out of my shell. Though I retire into that tub again for the winter, I hope the brighter influences may not forsake me.

Many thanks for your charming long letter. I return Buckle, and have done according to your orders, though it was not without compunction I interfered with your sentences, about which you appear quite too humble. You know I don't agree with you about Carlyle, and am delighted to think I have the means of raising him in your estimation by telling you that he seems to have loved and honoured Edward Irving more than any other human creature. I don't know that I have ever been more gratified in my life than by your praise of this bit of biography. I feel quite exhilarated and set up in consequence, your previous truculencies having inspired me with the profoundest confidence in your judgment. The worst of it is that I feel a certain awe upon me in proceeding,

----

[1] "The Rector," 'Maga,' September 1861.

with dreadful doubts of keeping up to the mark, and
the profoundest alarm lest I should lose the ground
I have gained. . . . I see a book mentioned in the
papers which I should like very well, if agreeable to
you, to take up if it proved practicable.   It is 'Recollections of Welby Pugin,' the famous architect.   If
you could let me do it I should be pleased.   He was
a great friend of my husband's.

WILLOWBURN, ROSENEATH.

Your note of this morning put me in great spirits:
I am more pleased than I can tell you that you approve of Irving.   I have been in great doubt and tre-
pidation, and am still alarmed lest further reading
may change your opinion, but in the meantime thank
you very much. . . . We all continue to enjoy the
freedom of our primitive existence exceedingly, and
have (for the West Country) wonderful weather.   We
had a most delightful excursion up Loch Long to
Loch Lomond the other day.

I have got what I suppose must be a curiosity of
littleness in the shape of a house at Ealing near London, to which I am going with some regrets and
doubts of my own wisdom—a quality of which I am
never too confident.

Would you please to send me the manuscript of
Irving?   The London people would like to have it
and put it in hand.   I am getting on, I hope, with
some success in the more difficult and delicate part of
the Life, which I should be very glad to submit to
you also.   It is harder work than the first, and I
trust you will sympathise with me in the terrible
amount of sermons which I have to read and remember.   If Irving had been an ordinary preacher I must
have succumbed long ere now.

To Miss Blackwood.

MY DEAR DONNA ISABELLA,—Are you really going
to Ross - shire? and if so, could we not meet and

do Loch Katrine? on which my Cockney soul is still set. I should really like, having had my appetite whetted by the glorious three days, to see the Trossachs, which would be done with only a single night's absence from home — especially in your charming society. . . . Yesterday I plodded through the wet to hear Dr Robert Lee preach, and did not in the least like him — a galvanic cast - iron man, quite unworthy of a mile's walk through the rain. All the children are well.

To-day Mrs Tulloch and I have had a little maternal picnic with all our chicks at the head of the loch. We had the servants with us, but nobody else, and had a great success, the children enjoying themselves to the top of their bent. The day has been glorious—staying indoors was quite impracticable, so I took my work outside, the first time for many weeks. I scarcely think I ever saw the Gareloch look so beautiful, but it begins to get cold, and notwithstanding all its attractions the wandering impulse is once more upon me, and I long to be off again, though only to the prim retirement of Ealing. I shall look forward to your visit even more pleasantly than you kindly say you do. It will be something to think of during the winter, which I expect I shall spend dolefully enough. . . . I can't get on with my work just now, after having been packed up and made uncomfortable by my domestic tyrant, Jane, and miss my Maggie mightily; so that I am extremely useless and good for nothing, and a little friendly abuse would do me good. Many thanks for your former letter. You are very right about the blessing of a spirit that rebounds. What should I do else? with all my toils and necessities.

You have all spoiled me for stupid society, do you know? I had an experiment the other day, being obliged to visit some people in Greenock, and the

fatigued condition in which I came home is something indescribable.   How am I to endure Ealing?
I begin to be appalled when I think of it.   In ordinary
circumstances I am stupid enough for anything in my
own person, but your exhilarating and stimulating
society makes dulness dreadful.   I feel a premonition
of the forlorn sensations that will steal over me, of the
fond thoughts which will revert even to Fettes Row.
Ah me!   Why are you all so bright and all the London side of the question so stupid?   When I get into
my doll's house I hope your thoughts will dwell upon
me sympathetically sometimes.   It will be hard
enough, even without any considerations of society,
settling down among the familiar things under circumstances so different.   Just now, as for the last
two years, always moving about and changing from
one place to another, everything has seemed exceptional.   I shall seem to be setting out anew upon the
dread reality when I get settled.   However, I must
comfort myself with the economies which you don't
believe in.

To Mr Blackwood.

I am very sorry to hear of your accident, which certainly, however, must have been a trick of Apollo—
isn't he the patron of your trade?—in the interests of
literature.   I will give your message to Mr Story, who
is at present suffering all those qualms of fear and
hope and suspense common to literary aspirants, and
regarding you, I suppose, as I remember doing, as a
mysterious fate whose decisions are as absolute as
they are inscrutable.   The pangs you inflict upon poor
authors ought to overshadow your dreams; only I
fear our sighs and sorrows awake but little emotion
in the flinty editorial bosom.

To Miss Blackwood.   *Sunday Evening.*

Though it is again Sunday evening I don't write in
the perfect state of quietness which the words suggest.

My circumstances are as follows: Tiddy is seated behind me, or rather on the arm of the easy-chair which I occupy, and is driving it for a cab, so if you see any sudden jerks in this letter you will know the cause. The table is heaped with picture-books, and Maggie, rather sentimental with a bad cold, is reading Mrs Jameson's Legends of the Saints, so there you have a peep of our interior.

Thank you very much for your letter. Why don't you tell me the plans you have in your mind for the termination of my story? Now that you have read a little more of it, you will see that I want to represent one of my women as a *fool*, which character, I think, wants elucidating, and has not received its due weight in the world of fiction. As for your question about whether I think a woman sure to dislike one of her own sex who comes out when she cannot, I answer most decidedly no. There are many women who, obliged to be inactive themselves, follow the labours of other women with such generous sympathy and admiration as makes me feel very small when I think of it. To be perfectly candid, I don't think I could do it, otherwise than very imperfectly, myself. I imagine I should find it very hard to play second for any length of time, or in the estimation of anybody I much cared for; but I do believe there are many women who can do that most magnanimous of acts, and I honour them accordingly. But recollect my secondary character in the present instance is a *fool*. I am charmed to have your criticism. Without being sentimental in the least on this subject, I have nobody belonging to me now to do me that good office, and you could not possibly do me a greater kindness than by pulling me up whenever you dislike my work and giving me the benefit of your freest criticism. I mean every word of what I say. Sometimes I find it totally impossible to form any opinion of what I have done, and send it off in hopeless perplexity, not knowing whether it is good or bad; so speak out, I beg of you, *Isabella mia*, and be quite sure that you will always do me a service by so doing. You shall have an early copy of the new novel, which I know you will cut to pieces. I have tried my hand in it at a *wicked woman,* and the reason why, as you say, I give softness to men rather than to women, is simply because the men of a woman's writing are always shadowy individuals, and it is only members of our own sex that we can fully bring out, bad and good. Even George Eliot is feeble in her men, and I recognise the disadvantage under which we all work in this respect. Sometimes we don't know sufficiently to make the outline sharp and clear; sometimes we know well enough, but dare not betray our knowledge one way or other: the result is that the men in a woman's book are always washed in, in secondary colours. The same want of anatomical knowledge and precision must, I imagine, preclude a woman from ever being a great painter; and if one does make the necessary study, one loses more than one gains. Here is a scientific lecture for you! Did not you call me a blue-stocking, and am I not proving my title to be called so?

To Mr Blackwood.   *November* 4, 1861.

I send you with this the third part of the ' Doctor's Family.' One number more will conclude it. But I should like to go on with a succession of others under the main title of ' Chronicles of Carlingford,' if it so pleases you. . . . My cares, as you can easily understand, came up by express before me, and were waiting my arrival. However, they were not such as appalled me, only the certainty of having a little reserve on which I could draw would be a comfort. If you will think this over and let me know I shall be very glad. I should continue to send you the said stories part by part only; for I think it seems to succeed better that what is read bit by bit should be written in the same way. One looks more carefully to one's points, and by dint of requiring to keep up

one's own interest, has a better chance of keeping up
one's reader's.   Your approbation lately has given me
great encouragement : a person in my position feels
afraid to say much on the subject of her own cares
and prospects, lest it should look like an appeal for
sympathy; but at the same time it was cheerless work
last winter, when necessity and failure came in such
forlorn conjunction.   Notwithstanding, fortunately, I
could not help being hopeful if I tried; and indeed I
suppose the over-exuberance of that quality must
have wanted all the heavy weight I have had to keep
me steady.   However, this has nothing to do with
the matter in hand. . . . I should like to send you
perhaps three more stories of equal length with the
' Doctor's Family,' and fill up with shorter ones if you
approve.

I enclose proof of 'Pugin.'   Just one word in reference to your note about his being sent to Bed-
lam.   He was actually sent, as pauper lunatics are,
by what extraordinary chance or device of Satan
nobody knows.   Ferrey in the Life admits without
apparently being in the least able to explain the fact;
and all the little world which knew Pugin is entirely
aware of it.   He was removed only when a commotion was made about it in the papers, and Lord John
Russell wrote to the 'Times' offering £10 to a sub-
scription in his favour, and nobody has ever attempted
to explain the mystery.

May I get Ruskin's late volumes of 'Modern
Painters' from Mr Langford?   I have got the 'Life
of Turner,' but I believe the last of these volumes is
much occupied with that strange, shabby divinity.   I
suppose it does not much matter in choosing a god
what sort of creature it is you choose, as persistent
worship seems always to gain a certain amount of
credit for the object of it.

I heard something about your friend George Eliot
the other day from my friend Mrs Carlyle (wife of

that great Tom whom you have set your heart so
entirely against).   Her opinion, I am sure, will amuse
you.   She says "Mrs Lewes" has mistaken her *rôle*
—that nature intended her to be the properest of
women, and that her present equivocal position is
the most extraordinary blunder and contradiction
possible.

I am rather anxious at present about my youngest
little boy, who has hurt the bone of his arm by a fall,
and is quite crippled by it.

1862.

To Miss Blackwood.

I was plunged into dismay by your last letter.
What is to become of my small family if you de-
moralise their mother?   Maggie is improving, and
makes a nice little companion, and on the whole I
find life very endurable in their society. . . . I don't
yet know exactly when the book of the season, as you
so flatteringly call it, is to be out; but I have been
half killed with proofs, and am just about finishing.   I
don't expect you to like it.   However, there is no use
anticipating evil.   I do believe I have done my best,
and the issue will most likely be more critical and
important to me and my bairnies than anything I
have ever done.   For their sakes I regard with a
little awe and trembling this new step into the world.
When by any chance I look gravely forward, which
happily for me is a thing my temperament does not
much oblige me to, the prospect sometimes appals me
more than is quite consistent with all these absurd
letters, laughters, &c.   But I don't suppose I could
have existed, much less made progress, but for the
buoyancy with which I have been mercifully endowed
beforehand.   But in every way this Irving publication
is an important one for me.   I am obliged to write in
haste, and as Checchino is with me and hammering

with all his might, I trust you will put down any little incoherencies in this epistle to his small score.

The weather already begins to brighten delightfully, and I have made my own room, which is very sunny and cheerful, my study.   I begin to like this little place: it is intensely tame, of course, but has a kind of village aspect and a wealth of those green lanes which do not seem practicable out of England, when one has any time to walk. . . . What preposterous thing do you imagine I am doing in the midst of my serious labours?   Writing a little drawing-room play, founded upon a most ludicrous real incident, and called " The Three Miss Smiths."

Thank you very much for liking the Pugin paper. I am not badly pleased with it myself.   I begin to think biography is my forte!   It is very pleasant work, at least. . . . I am just about to launch into the life of Turner the painter—old beast—in which I hope I shall give you equal satisfaction. . . . I have just finished the ' Doctor's Family,' and don't at all like the termination.   Sometimes one's fancies will not do what one requires of them, and when that happens it is excessively disheartening and un-pleasant.

A very affectionate young lady friend is distressing. I get alarmed when I throw myself back in my chair and take a moment's rest, lest I should have sudden arms thrown round me, and be kissed and embraced without any warning.   All very well, you know, when there is any occasion, but to have a caress always impending over you is highly alarming and not comfortable.

I have been in the most dreadful pressure of work finishing my Irving book, and now I am snowed up with proofs.   I must say in confidence that I should be much disappointed if this book does not make some little commotion.   There never was such a hero—such a princely, magnanimous, simple heart.

To Mr Blackwood.

Much exhilarated by your favourable judgment. I had almost written you yesterday a note at which you would have laughed, being a protestation called forth by an article in the 'Saturday Review.' That discriminating critic, as you will most likely have seen, announces that the 'Chronicles of Carlingford' can be written by nobody but George Eliot—a high compliment to me, no doubt; but women, you know, according to the best authorities, never admire each other, and I mean to protest that the faintest idea of imitating or attempting to rival the author of 'Adam Bede' never entered my mind. I hope you don't think so. This protest is made for my private satisfaction, and because I should not like you to think me guilty of imitation or of any intention that way. Critics as a race are donkeys, and may say what they please.

I must say I think the 'Woman in White' a marvel of workmanship. I found it bear a second reading very well, and indeed it was having it thrown in my way for a second time which attracted so strongly my technical admiration. . . . Dickens is not a favourite of mine; I think it would go against the grain to applaud him highly in his present phase.[1] I had the pleasure of dining at Mr Warren's the other day in humble attendance upon your sister. He came out famously, showed me the manuscript of 'Ten Thousand a-Year,' and was as amusing as possible. Such simple-minded and effusive vanity is charming at first sight. We are going to look up old David Roberts, whom I know a little, after Miss Blackwood returns from Brighton.

From Mrs Carlyle to Mrs Oliphant.

5 CHEYNE ROW, CHELSEA.

DARLING WOMAN, — Already *the* Exhibition has borne me the fruit of *one* Scotch cousin, who will be

---

[1] After the publication of 'Great Expectations.'

coming and going all this week, and I have other things laid on my arms, like the baby in the omnibus! And on the whole I fear I must put off my visit to you till the week following. But if you will name any day of *that*, I shall take care that no pigs run through it, *D.V.*

I do long to see you to tell you, not what *I* think of your book but what Mr C. thinks, which is much more to the purpose! I never heard him praise a *woman's* book, hardly any man's, as cordially as he praises this of yours! You are "worth whole cart-loads of Mulocks, and Brontës, and THINGS of that sort." "You are full of geniality and genius even"! "Nothing has so taken him by the heart for years as this biography"! You are really "a fine, clear, loyal, sympathetic female being." The only fault he finds in you is *a certain dimness about dates and arrangements of time !*—in short, I never heard so much praise out of his head at one rush! and I am so glad!

For me, I am not in a state to express an opinion yet, having read only here a little and there a little, in whichever volume Mr C. was not occupied with, and admit "a pressure of things"!—all the worse for being trivial things. But to-morrow I shall begin at the beginning. Mr C. got to the end last night, and the last part was the best of all, he says; and that he is "very glad—very glad indeed that such a bio-graphy of Edward Irving exists." Now tell me a day next week, if you are to be at home and leisure, and believe that I love you very much, and try to love me a little.   J. W. CARLYLE.

To Mr Blackwood.   EALING.

MY DEAR MR BLACKWOOD,—I am perfectly charmed to hear that you continue to like 'Salem.' I am afraid the machinery I have set in motion is rather extensive for the short limits I had intended. The second part should have reached you before now but for my baby's illness, but I hope the little fellow is mending, and that I shall be able to send it off in a day or two. . . .

I am delighted with your approbation. I mean to make what one of the poor London painters despised by the Academy calls an 'it if I can with this story. Did you go to Osborne? The Prince Consort paper is beautifully got up, and a credit to us all who have the honour of being included under the mantle of 'Maga.' I am proud of having my own verses appended to anything so graceful and fine.[1]

I am the most mild and placable of women and authors, but at the same time your report of Lewes's criticism on my paper strikes me, now I think of it, as mighty impertinent. I don't take offence, but I think I have as much right to the due consideration of my standing and *age* in literature as if I were asserting myself in society, or even had done something equivocal to pique the curiosity of the world. I have never taken much credit to myself nor cared overmuch for it, but I know I have done as much honest work in my day as most people of my years; and patronising approbation of the kind you told me of does not quite suit me.

I am, as you may imagine, delighted with your letter and verdict upon 'Salem.' After all you have kindly said on the subject I get so nervous, and am haunted with such a conviction that this luck is much too good to last, that I bewilder myself and fall into panics over every chapter. I suspect some kind fairy has thrown glamour in your eyes.

I have just been expressing my congratulations to Mr William. I hope to do so, if I live so long, on the still more auspicious occasion when the " little Editor," who, I have a conviction, was specially born for the Magazine, takes up the old ensign, till which time all glory and prosperity to the flag which has braved for how many? years the battle and the breeze.

---

[1] "The Nation's Prayer," 'Maga,' January 1862.

I hope by that time I shall have a cadet too, able to do better work than his mother.[1]

I spent last evening with Thomas Carlyle, whom I am sorry you don't like, but whom I do like heartily and more than ever. He has added to all his great qualities a crowning touch of genius—he likes my book! and has spoken of it in terms so entirely gratifying that for the space of a night and day I *was* uplifted, and lost my head. He was at home and alone, with his clever and original wife, and I never was more delighted with any man. I am ready henceforth to stand up for all those peculiarities which other people think defects, and to do battle for him whenever I hear him assailed.

You have given me too much money for my little paper. I am very glad it pleases you, but you have been too liberal, and I feel uncomfortable with over-pay.

How delightful are Sir Edward's [Lytton's] Essays. One seems to see his own special creation, the accomplished man of the world, not entirely worldly, a quintessence of social wisdom and experience, sweetened by imagination. I don't know whether he is actually such a man himself. I suspect not by a long way so good as Alban Morley and the others, of whom the Essays seem to me a kind of embodiment over again.

To Mr William Blackwood.

Let me congratulate you on the pleasant news Mr John sends me, that you have become one of the actual pillars of the house. I trust it may go on prospering to the highest height of the good wishes of "our connection," which I am sure have no bounds but possibility, and that the young generation may be as kind, genial, and strong as their predecessors—like a woman I put the softer qualities first.

---

[1] The "little Editor" died in 1881. Cyril Oliphant died in 1890.

1863.

To Mr Blackwood.

I am very glad you like "David Elginbrod," and my anxiety to get the article admission I may explain by telling you that it was at my urgent recommendation (having read the MS. and made such humble suggestions towards its improvement as my knowledge of the literary susceptibility made possible) that Mr Blackett published it; and that the author is not only a man of genius but a man burdened with ever so many children, and, what is perhaps worse, a troublesome conscientiousness; so please, if you are persuadable, let me have my way this time, and I will assault or congratulate, haul down or set up, anybody your honour pleases hereafter.

I am delighted with Kinglake:[1] has he steered quite clear of action for libel, or is it not within the bounds of possibility that you may be defendants in an imperial plea? Such a concentration of suave hatred, malice, and uncharitableness surely never was. The narrative is perfectly delightful. It reminds me more of the oral narrative of a perfect speaker, perfectly master of his subject, than anything I ever saw in print.

St Andrews, *18th May.*

I am very much comforted and exhilarated by your favourable opinion of his Reverence.[2] He is a favourite of mine, and I mean to bestow the very greatest care upon him; but I think, if it suits you, I should rather like the first part to appear next month. Though I am not sure that I approve of it in theory, it seems to suit me in practice, and the publication and the talk stimulates and keeps me up. Very likely this is because I have nobody at home nowadays to talk it over with; but I think it is for the advantage of the

---

[1] 'The Crimean War.'   [2] 'The Perpetual Curate.'

work to be written just as it is published; and I see my way, and am not afraid that you will tread too closely upon my heels. I think I have materials in my hands for a little exhibition of all the three parties in the Church. I mean my curate's brother to go over to Rome, and we will not be neglectful of the claims of Exeter Hall. As to his own position, a perpetual curacy *is* independent, but it is because Mr Wentworth is working *in the parish* with which he has nothing to do, and which it is in reality high treason for any one, even the bishop, to interfere with, that he comes under the rector's displeasure. So good an Anglican would never have taken such a step but for the sanction of the late rector, which I think may be held to justify Mr Wentworth for carrying on his work until he is absolutely interdicted by the new incumbent.

It is rather hard to be interdicted from other work —you must let me do a little now and then, for the disease has got to be chronic with me, and I must work or die; not to speak of the daily—nay, hourly— necessity of bread and butter, and the determined disinclination of my small steeds to wait till the grass grows. I wish they would with all my heart: it would simplify matters greatly.

In the autumn of this year, 1863, Mrs Oliphant went with her two friends, Mrs Tulloch and Mrs Macpherson, to Rome. The earlier part of the winter there must have been very cheerful. Mrs Tulloch had taken with her the two eldest of her daughters, girls a little older than Maggie Oliphant, while Mrs Oliphant had her three children, all well and bright. The two mothers shared a house, as Mrs Oliphant has told us in her Autobiography; and it was there that the eleven-years-old girl—her mother's one daughter and most beloved little companion—was suddenly struck down. After only a very few days of illness she was laid beside her father in the English cemetery.

No wonder that at this time there is a gap in the long series of Mrs Oliphant's correspondence. She probably wrote no letters that could possibly be avoided, until in the spring of 1864 she had removed with her little boys, and the two girls, who had been her child's beloved companions, to Capri.

1864.

To Miss Blackwood.　　　HOTEL QUISISANA, CAPRI, *May* 15.

It is not because I am careless or don't appreciate your kindness in writing to me that I have been so slow to answer your letters.　There are some exercises of patience and self-denial that are possible, and some that are beyond my powers.　I have managed to regain possession of myself in the presence of other people, and no longer obtrude my sorrows on the strangers I meet; but when I am by myself and begin to write I am no longer capable of keeping on the veil.　When my mind is full of one subject I cannot keep from expressing it, and I know that the monotonous voice of grief grows soon tiresome even to one's dearest friends.　We have been here about six weeks, and I am better than I was; if not more resigned as people say, at least more accustomed to the impossible life to which God has seen fit, He alone knows for what mysterious reason, to ordain me.　The very possibility of becoming accustomed to it is one of its bitterest aggravations.　One feels as if, having survived such a blow, one could survive anything and everything, and that the worthless life would still hold out although all that made it worth having was withdrawn.　I sicken at it every morning when it comes back, but nevertheless I go on with how much more trembling and how much less hope, not to speak of the sharp pangs of present grief, I cannot describe to you. You will understand by this why I hated to write letters, for whatever I start from I come back unawares to the same point.

Though I am reluctant to form any plans, I don't think I will leave the Continent till after next winter. We are going to Switzerland now, and afterwards may perhaps stay in Paris; but that I make no arrangement about as yet. This island is very lovely, very quiet, and has a softening influence which I am very glad to feel. It lies just at the entrance of the bay, looking towards Vesuvius, and the white line of towns which mark the coast, Naples being the centre; on the one side the noble hills above Sorrento, and the point which rounds off into the Bay of Salerno; on the other the line of islands drawn out seaward and terminating in Ischia, which forms the other arm of the Bay of Naples. I don't suppose there is anything more lovely on earth; and we have it in all lights always varying. When we came the mountains were covered with snow; now they have dressed themselves in inexpressible colours, with the soft foreground of olives and young vines that belong to Capri itself, and a sea which is always blue, of a blueness which does not seem to be adequately described by the mere name of the colour. I doubt if you would care for Capri, however, for there is not a carriage of any description on the island, and you must either walk or ride. We go everywhere on ponies, and have got to feel at home in the place.

To Mr Blackwood.   108 CHAMPS ELYSÉES.

I have meant to write ever since I got your last letter to say that I could not send you any miscellaneous paper this month—at least, in case you expected to hear from me—as I am busy with a book

which has been for a long time, so long that I am
ashamed of my delay, promised to my kind and
excellent friend Mr Blackett.[1]

Thank you for sending me the 'Times' with the
review. It is very gracious and good, and its praise
of my freshness after twenty years' work went to my
heart, though the date is slightly extended. I don't
know whether I am alone in thinking so, or if the
opinion is general, but it seems to me that the writing
of the 'Times' just now is wonderfully bad. Not
having seen it for a long time, it came upon me
with something of the force of a surprise. There
was in the same paper which reviewed the "Perpetual" another critique of Lady Strangford's book,
which, I think, was as vulgar and stupid a piece of
writing as I remember to have seen.

CHAMPS ELYSÉES, *December '64.*

I cannot say much of myself, except that I keep
on living and working without having much interest
in either; but my little boys are well, which is the
summit of all blessing. I don't know what a poor
soul such as I am can say to you, to whom I am
bound by so many years of kindness and good offices,
at this season of good wishes, except that I wish you
everything that is prosperous and happy, and that
God may bless your house and keep your children
safe.

1865.

To Mrs Tulloch.　　　　CHAMPS ELYSÉES, *Jan.* 22.

MY DEAREST PADRONA,—Many happy years to you,
my dear and sweet sister. Your birthday last year
was about the last day of my happiness. I had little
thought of ever looking back upon it as the end of
the brightest period of my life, but it must be that

---

[1] 'Agnes.'

God knows best.   He has given me a painful and troubled passage through life, but to you the years are still pleasant and full of hope, and you know I wish you all that is best and most blessed in the world.   I am not capable of much just at this time, as you will understand; but perhaps I may have more courage after this week is over.   I think of going away to the country for a day or two, to fight it out by myself.   Think of me a little when you say your prayers.   It is hard to go out in the streets, to look out of the window, and see the other women with their daughters.   God knows it is an unworthy feeling, but it makes me shrink from going out or facing the world. . . .

As for the little boys, they have got on astonishingly.   I cannot quite support Cecco's own opinion of his proficiency, but he really commences to read French, and when he picks up an English book spells out the words after the pronunciation, which Mademoiselle has taught him in the funniest way. . . . I have grown an old woman all at once, reluctant to move and impatient of having my routine disturbed, and the arrival of a visitor intent upon amusement is a kind of horror.

To Mr Blackwood.

I send you with this the second number of 'Miss Marjoribanks,' which I hope you will like.   I am not quite sure myself that there is enough progress made, and I am afraid I am getting into a habit of over-minuteness.   Thank you for your letter and the cheque.   Happily the air here seems to agree very well with my boys, who can bear the cold much better than the heat, and the little one, Cecco, begins now and then to get a little hazy in his English, and finds French come handier.   I was at St Germains for a few days in the end of last month, and was so impressed by it that perhaps I may send you a little paper about it one day or another.   I am not in the

least disposed to be a Jacobite, and Dundee and Cul-
loden and Professor Aytoun sort of thing have very
little effect upon me.   But there was something wonderfully touching in that long silent terrace and the
thought of all the weary days and miserable hopes and
disappointments that must have passed without any
record—that and the other terrace at Frascati where
poor Prince Charlie lies.   I was sad enough myself
at both places, and no one, being Scotch, could be
unmoved by their associations.   I got some time ago
a most gracious letter from M. de Montalembert,
whom I took courage to remind that I had brought
a letter to him last year.   He writes from La Roche
en Bressy with that graceful French politeness which
is quite excessive and uncalled for, and at the same
time quite delightful.   He is to be in Paris after
March, and is coming to see me.

March 8.

Don't frighten me, please, about 'Miss Marjoribanks.'   I will do the very best I can to content you,
but you make me nervous when you talk about the
first rank of novelists, &c.: nobody in the world cares
whether I am in the first or sixth.   I mean I have no
one left who cares, and the world can do absolutely
nothing for me except giving me a little more money,
which, Heaven knows, I spend easily enough as it is.
But all the same, I will do my best, only please recognise the difference a little between a man who can
take the good of his reputation, if he has any, and a
poor soul who is concerned about nothing except the
most domestic and limited concerns.

The difference in my books is natural enough when
you reflect that the first one was written when I was
twenty, and the others were the work of a troubled
life not much at leisure.   It is only to be expected
that one should do a little better when one has come
to one's strength.   As for your courteous critic's remarks (but it is incredible that a 'Saturday Reviewer'
should write such a pretty hand), I am quite con-

scious of the "to be sures" and the "naturallys,"
but then a faultless style is like a faultless person,
highly exasperating; and if one didn't leave these
little things to be taken hold of, perhaps one might
fare worse.

April 12.

I am quite delighted with Montalembert. There
is a kind of cream of graciousness and cordiality about
him which smooths one down all over. I dined there,
much, I confess, to my panic, for I don't feel sufficiently sure of my French to be quite comfortable in
society: however, they were all very kind. Montalembert gave me the first half-dozen sheets of his
third volume, which is now going through the press,
to let me see, as he said, what it was like. What do
you think about it?

To Mrs Tulloch.　　　　　　AVRANCHES, *May* 28.

MY DEAREST PADRONA,—I was very glad to get
your letter and that of Fanny. They were a great
pleasure to me in this cold, raw country, which is not
particularly pretty nor inviting. To be sure there
is far in the distance a margin of sea with Mont St
Michel, a greyish rock with a castle and very fine
chapel on it stuck in the middle of a vast extent of
sand, and looking at a distance not at all unlike a
great pie (don't be shocked by the comparison) set
out on a brown uncovered table. In the course of
next week we will go on to St Malo again for a few
days, where we will be for half our time surrounded by
sea; and then to Dinan in Brittany, where please address to me. . . .

I am thinking of staying here longer than I first
intended, to wait for a great popular *fête*, or feet, as
Jane calls it, in Brittany, which may do service in
the book Mr Blackett has engaged me, without any
great will of my own, to write. . . .

You ask when shall we meet? In my own house,
I hope, if I get a house at Harrow or elsewhere. It

is not dislike of St Andrews that would keep me from going to it—I need not explain what the other reasons are. You know I love you and all yours, and therefore you will think no harm of it, and indeed will anticipate what I say, that there are comparisons that I cannot bear. I have to put force upon myself when I go into the streets, and especially to church, and wonder and ask myself if it was that God found me unworthy of bringing up a woman. It was her birthday the day after we came here — twelve she would have been, and how different my life! You must come and see me, *Padrona mia*, and let it be understood that you have a house in England always happy to receive you whenever you can come. Tell S. that Mr Ruffini on his last visit presented me with Leopardi, to my great content—that I might have a pleasant association with him, said the courtly Dr Antonio. You will be quite charmed with him.

DINARD, *June* 14.

In place of going to Dinan, which is English, we have settled here on the bay of St Malo in a pleasant village which struck my fancy. The sea is lovely, and broken by no end of bristling rocks and fortifications, with clouds of white-sailed boats floating about perpetually. You know I have a weakness for seeing my fellow-creatures, or at least the signs of them. I have got a tiny little house perched on the very edge of the rocks, so near that when the tide is full one can imagine oneself in a boat, for the rocks are steep and go sheer down into the water. It is very tranquil and sweet, and I think will do us all good, though Cecco has been for the moment a little upset by the change—not, however, in his old feverish way. I have got all your letters sent on from Dinan; they do me no end of good. I began to get persuaded that I had no such thing as a friend in the world, that nobody cared for anybody, and that to expect sympathy or

friendship was folly.   Your letter, which is like yourself, heals me again.   I think you must have been intended by Providence to be my better half and not
the Principal's, which is a sentiment he may laugh at
with safety under the circumstances.   Please tell him
with my love that I am taking Strahan's proposal
into serious consideration.   It was very kind of him to
be the medium of conveying it, and it is an extremely
good proposal, and one I would jump at but for the
idea that it might perhaps hurt me with the Blackwoods, who are, you know, my great dependence.
. . . You speak of my being alone here, but I am no
more alone here, you know, than it is my lot to be
anywhere, and I am not sure that one does not feel
one's loneliness more when settled down at home than
when wandering as I am doing.   Here I can cheat
myself into the idea that there are some people who
will be glad to see me when I go back ; but then when
one has gone back, and when the old life, as it was
and yet so different, is resumed once for all, it is then
that the hardest part of it comes.   That is no reason
why one should not go back and settle to one's duties,
which I mean to do if all is well in a month or two,
and accept as best I may my position as shadow in
the landscape.   The Blacketts are looking for a house
for me, but as I should not like to take one definitely
without seeing it, I think most likely in September I
will return to London.

To Mr Blackwood.   *June* 23.

I send you with this a paper upon the Italian Leopardi, which I hope very much you may like.   I am
so destitute of anybody to speak to here, on literary
subjects, that I cannot feel sure whether my author
will impress you as he does me, or whether I have
done him anything like justice.   The paper is very
long, I am afraid.

It is hard that a poor woman should have to decide
as well as to work for herself; it is the more difficult

business of the two.   How can I possibly tell whether
'Miss Marjoribanks' will be a great success or not?
I am working at her with all my might and power;
but you know yourself that if I happen to have a
favourite bit for which I have a kind of natural weakness, it is always precisely on that bit that you snub
me, so that I am the worst judge in the world as far
as that goes.   At the same time, I never would for an
instant dream of giving a story by the author of the
Carlingford Series to any periodical whatever on any
terms, unless indeed you were first to throw me over-
board.   I have decided to tell the 'Good Words'
people that they may have a novel by Mrs Oliphant
or the author of 'Margaret Maitland' if they wish it.
The other I should never have thought of under any
circumstances.

I am sure your week at Ascot must have been very
pleasant.   I told a coachman I had in Normandy of
the victory of the French horse at the Derby, and the
grin of intense satisfaction that came over his face
was something beautiful to behold.

To Mrs Tulloch.   ST ADRESSE, HAVRE, *September* 1.

I suppose you are all still enjoying your woodland
walks and mountain rides, while I am lingering out
here the end of my wanderings.   I should be half disposed to envy you being where you are if I had not
occasion to envy you so many other things that it is
not worth while beginning with that.   There is nothing attractive here to speak of except the sea, which
is in a rage half its time, and knocks one down with
mighty tawny waves, stronger and more violent than
I ever saw anywhere.   Tiddy has learned to swim,
and performs very triumphantly when it is calm—
which is not often; and Cecco is full of plans to attain
the same proficiency, but I don't expect he will succeed this year.   I have promised him that he is to
write his name in this letter to let you see how far he
has got.   It is an accomplishment he is very proud

of. They are both very well, thank God, though Cecco has amused himself by having the chicken-pox. We have got a very pretty house, which belongs to Queen Christina of Spain, who lives here in summer. There is a pretty little garden and a nice view of the sea, and the internal arrangements are so satisfactory that I should be very glad to take it up and transplant it bodily to Harrow or Eton. I am beginning now to turn my thoughts to the latter place. Houses are not to be had at Harrow, and if I could satisfy myself that Eton was equally good for the boys, it would be much more interesting to me than the other. I begin to weary much to be settled, even though being settled will make very little difference one way or the other: indeed I think the sense of being abroad and away is rather a kind of ease, and permits one to cherish the delusion that there is something better at home—if one was but at home,—whereas there is nothing better anywhere, and the only thing one has before one is to learn to be content.

To Mr Blackwood. *September* 20.

I send you with this the next number of 'Miss Marjoribanks.' . . . As for what you say of hardness of tone, I am afraid it was scarcely to be avoided. I hate myself the cold-blooded school of novel-writing, in which one works out a character without the slightest regard to whether it is good or bad, or whether it touches or revolts one's sympathies. But at the same time I have a weakness for Lucilla, and to bring a sudden change upon her character and break her down into tenderness would be like one of Dickens's maudlin repentances, when he makes Mr Dombey *trinquer* with Captain Cuttle. Miss M. must be one and indivisible, and I feel pretty sure that my plan is right. It is the middle of a story that is always the trying bit — the two ends can generally take care of themselves.

To Mrs Tulloch.

CARISSIMA PADRONA MIA,—I was very glad to get your letter. I got it just after returning from a ramble on the banks of the Seine, with which I have been diversifying a little my quiet life. The country is nothing particular, but the lovely Gothic churches everywhere are quite wonderful. In a little bit of an insignificant town or village you come suddenly, without any warning, upon a grey, glorious, sometimes mouldered, old church of (what Mr Ruskin would call debased) Flamboyant Gothic, all clad in solemn stony lace and embroidery, which nobody ever said a word about or ever heard of, unknown to Murray and unfrequented by tourists. We were three days gone and saw no end of such, and the lovely ruins of the Abbey of Jumièges. Do you remember when you were at Ealing that time when the Principal was so ill, I took a great fancy for a semi-pedestrian tour on the banks of the Seine if you would or could have gone? Ah me! If I had but contented myself with that and not gone to seek sorrow farther off. This is the last week we shall be here. I think of leaving on Friday, as Jane and the boxes are going direct from Havre, and I have still Rouen to take a glimpse of and to get to Boulogne, where there is a shorter passage across the Channel. If all is well we shall probably be in London on Monday the 25th.

To Mr Blackwood.   15 BAYSWATER TERRACE, *Sept.* 29.

I write simply to tell you that I have got here safe and sound, and have established myself for a few weeks *en attendant* a more definite settlement. We had on the whole an agreeable journey across country and finally by Boulogne here. London looks wonderfully well even after Paris, and I think can bear the comparison, and I find my simple-minded Swiss governess, who evidently laboured under the idea that

les Anglais went abroad because they had no inducement to stay at home, quite overwhelmed with great
astonishment to find that the island is wonderfully
habitable on the whole.

I have been in communication with Mr Collins, to
whom I narrated in my innocence that Tiddy had
had six months of Latin, and who takes me up in a
note I received on coming here, chuckling much over
my womanish idea that six months' Latin was a sufficient preparation for Eton. I had no such idea, of
course, but I think it is best to tell you the joke myself, as naturally you will hear it some time and have
a laugh at my simplicity. I have made no decision
as yet as to my final abode, as Mr Collins says
decidedly Eton instead of Harrow, and a friend of
mine here in whose judgment I have much confidence
says with equal decision Harrow instead of Eton. I
find myself a little in the position of the old man with
the ass, being, as you and all my friends know, one of
the most pliant and advisable of women. . . . It is
easy to laugh, but it is horribly hard work coming
back here, and I am very little disposed in reality to
be amused or amusing. Let me hear from you,
please.

The question which Mrs Oliphant had so anxiously
debated as to the respective advantages of Harrow
and Eton was finally settled in favour of the latter;
and a very pretty cheerful little house, No. 6 Clarence
Crescent, Windsor, was taken. Six years—on the
whole, very happy ones—were spent here, and the
following twenty, much checkered, in a larger house
close by. This second house she bought, but during
the last year of her life it was let.

1866.

To Mrs Tulloch.   15 BAYSWATER TERRACE, W.

MY DEAREST PADRONA,—I have had a copy of
'Agnes' addressed to you for a week, but have not
sent it away. I hope you will like it, though I feel
that it is dull and long-winded; but then when one is
so happy as to have a *padrona*, one knows that one has
an indulgent critic. I have been in a very bad way,
padrona mia, since ever I came here. I suppose this
translating work, though it is very hard work, is not
engrossing enough; and while I am writing about S.
Columba mechanically, I am going over and over all
the details of those four days that made such a terrible
change in my life. I begin to understand better the
Principal's illness, for now and then my mind fixes on
one point till I get almost to feel as if it was I who
had sacrificed my child. I feel thankful now that I
did not come to England sooner. It is bad enough
now. Life to me seems to be so very little worth the
pains that I have to take to keep it going. I can say
this to you, dear, to relieve my heart, but of course
at the same time I am going on and making my
arrangements all the same as if I loved it, as one
must do.

I have taken a very pretty little house at Windsor:
it is about a mile from Eton, which is a drawback, as
the boys have to be there so early.

I spent an evening last week all alone with Thomas
Carlyle and his wife. She has had a dreadful illness
and looks like a weird shadow, not quite canny, but
nothing could be kinder or nicer than both of them.
She has to drive three hours every day, and has got a
little brougham in which she performs that penance,
making the best of it by driving her friends about.
As for True Thomas himself, he expounded the

Schleswig-Holstein business to me from a few hundred years before the beginning of it, to his wife's intense horror.   But notwithstanding this dull choice of
a subject his talk is delightful.

To Miss Blackwood.

I have had a good deal of trouble to find a house,
but have finally taken one at Windsor from which
Tiddy, and Cecco when he is old enough, can go to
Eton.   The children are very well, I am glad to say,
and Tiddy is full of excitement about the long trousers
and tall hats of Eton, the most frightful boy's dress
that ever was invented. He will have to be at school
at half-past seven in the morning, poor little soul!

To Rev. Dr Story.   WINDSOR.

. . . I have had a little visit from Mrs Carlyle, who
is looking very feeble and picturesque, and as amusing
as ever, and naturally has been taking away everybody's character, or perhaps I ought to say throwing
light upon the domestic relations of the distinguished
people of the period.   I was remarking upon the eccen-
tricity of the said relations, and could not but say
that Mr Carlyle seemed the only virtuous philosopher
we had.   Upon which his wife answered, " My dear,
if Mr Carlyle's digestion had been stronger, there is
no saying what he might have been!"

To Mr Blackwood.   WINDSOR, 17*th May.*

As for 'Miss Marjoribanks,' I am a little disgusted
with her, and with novels in general—with the latter
so greatly that I have been contemplating an indignant address to all who are worth their salt in the
trade, praying them to give it up and take to some
more honest mode of livelihood.   Let us take people's
lives, or anything that is worth the trouble.   I have
a great mind to come down upon the miserable mass
of novels that make one ashamed of one's trade.

WINDSOR.

Most unreasonable and exacting of editors, what would you have ?   Was it not only the other day that you were abusing me for Lucilla's want of heart, and now, when the poor soul finds herself guilty of caring for somebody, you think she has too much !   It is the sad fate of gifted women in general never to be appreciated.   For my own part, I think my poor dear heroine always had a very good heart, and though it was silly of her to like Tom, still we never set up for inhuman consistency, neither Lucilla nor I.   The last part shall come on Monday, and I hope Tom will give you satisfaction, and you will find that Miss M. has not done so badly for herself after all.

I have got two copies of ' Felix Holt '—the last sent me by Mr Langford.   It leaves an impression on my mind as of "Hamlet" played by six sets of grave-diggers.   Of course it will be a successful book, but I think chiefly because 'Adam Bede' and 'Silas Marner' went before it.   Now that I have read it, I have given up the idea of reviewing it.

WINDSOR, 30th June.

I hope you don't think me so utterly stupid as to have any doubt about the perfection of George Eliot's writing : I don't suppose she could express hersel. otherwise than exquisitely if she were to try, and there are a thousand tones of expression which nobody else could have hit upon, and which give one a positive thrill of pleasure to read them.   All that is pretty well implied in her name, but I am mightily disappointed in the book all the same.   One feels as if a great contempt had seized her for the public and her critics (quite legitimate in some respects, I think), and she had concluded that it was not worth her while to put forth her strength,—that this would please them just as well as if it was twenty times better.   And I think the praise of the ' Saturday Re-

view' and the 'Times'—evidently both much dissatis-
fied with the book, and neither daring to say so, except in the most timid way—proves this conclusively.
Perhaps it is the height of literary triumph to strike
criticism with awe—I think it is, and a very comical
effect.

This year Mrs Oliphant went back to Roseneath,
where she had spent so many happy days with her
children.   In the church there she put a memorial
window, a tribute to her little daughter.

To Mr Blackwood.   THE MANSE, ROSENEATH, *August* 16.
    I send you a little paper I have just finished about
Stuart Mill and his mad notion of the franchise for
women.   I daresay there are repetitions in it, but
that (if you like it) I could remedy in proof; and
probably you will think it too respectful to Mr Mill,
but I can't for my part find any satisfaction in simply
jeering at a man who may do a foolish thing in his
life but yet is a great philosopher.   I shall be glad if
you like it.

1867.

To Miss Blackwood.   . *4th Feb.*
    MY DEAR ISABELLA,—I think you took me up as
meaning more than I did mean in what I said in my
last letter.   I never dreamt for a moment that you
did not sympathise with me in my grief, but there
are *moods* which are as much a part of grief as sorrow
itself, and in which nobody can or ought to be expected to sympathise, which made me say that I was
pitched upon a different key.   The fact is, that people
are sometimes in discord with everything—with common life and the will of God as well as with the more
natural thoughts and feelings of their friends.   I was

still in that condition when I was in Paris, Heaven
knows, often enough, and—especially in the anniversary which has just passed—I am so still.

Sad as this letter is, and most genuine in its sadness, the time when it was written is that of the beginning of several very happy years. Eton, where
Cyril was now settled, was becoming an immense
source of interest. Numbers of small boys came
about the house, and there was always something
going on for them or their elders.

WINDSOR, 25th Feb.

. . . You talk of theatricals, and, oddly enough, I
am up to the eyes in preparation for a very mild kind
of theatricals now—charades. I had meant to have
a party of little Etonians before I left home, and to
amuse them with a little performance of this kind;
but I had forgotten that *Lent* was coming on, and as
my right-hand man is a clergyman, I have been
obliged to hurry matters on, and it is to come off
next Saturday. I have written a small skeleton
drama for one of the charades, with one great scene,
a trial, which promises to be rather successful. You
shall have the reversion of it if you like. The word
is *schoolfellow*, and there is a quarrel between two
heroes about a pretty girl, and a row, which ends
in one of them being brought to trial. I was in
hopes I might have been able to have had this at the
time when Emma came next month, but that is now
impossible. . . .

I shall be rather dissipated this week, as I am going
up to the House of Commons on Thursday evening
in hopes of hearing a debate on the Reform business,
unless indeed your friend Disraeli makes too great a
mess of it to-morrow for further proceedings. This
sober kind of dissipation is the only one I have been

guilty of since I came back to Windsor, where we have been living like hermits.

This letter refers to an article in 'Blackwood' entitled "Elizabeth and Mary."

To Mr Blackwood.   WINDSOR, 15*th March.*

I think it best since receiving your letter to send you my MS. No. 1 at once, without waiting for the other. I hope you will like it—it has given me no end of trouble: in short, I have felt that I would gladly strangle both the ladies in question with my own hands, simply to get rid of them. I wonder how history-writers survive it. I trust the admiration which Mary has extorted from me will reconcile me sufficiently with 'Maga's' chivalrous creed in respect to her. All the same, I think you are all doing that wonderful woman the greatest injury by setting her up as innocent. Mary innocent! You might as well say at once that she was a fool, which comes to much about the same thing. It is ticklish work saying so in public, yet there does seem to be a kind of glorious human creature that is incomplete without crime—witness your Davids and Marys. The way in which she shakes it all off her—love, murder, Bothwell, and all,—takes as it were a bath of tranquillity at Lochleven and comes out fresh, innocent, and indomitable,—is, I think, one of the most marvellous things in history. . . .
We have dreadful weather—snow for three days, and everything looking miserable. Have you a Correspondent in Paris for the Exhibition, or do you mean to give me that post? I shall be going there in the end of this month—a doleful prospect enough.

To Mr Blackwood.   PARIS, 3*rd May.*

MY DEAR MR BLACKWOOD,—I can't do it. I have been labouring on it at every spare moment for some

time back, and only getting deeper and deeper into
the mud.   I am very sorry if it will disappoint you,
but the fact is, I detest Exhibitions.   Even the pictures are not striking, and how, I appeal to your
feelings, can one write about cotton or flannel, or
machinery, or manures, as 'Galignani' does to-day?
If you would make a vigorous crusade against the
wretched rubbish of exhibitions, then I will with all
my heart write you a paper descriptive of these
miseries—shall I ?—in prose or verse, as you will.   I
feel equal to that.   I confess I envy you men your
power of swearing at such prodigious humbug.   There
is my MS. lying before me, ever so many sheets, as
bad as its subject, mere loss of time and unutterable
weariness, when I might have been getting on with
my legitimate work.   It would be a kind of satisfaction to my mind in my present state of feeling to go
down to the Champs de Mars and break a lot of
windows, but I fear that is a gratification impossible
to anything but a boy.

HOTEL ROYAL, BERLIN, 13*th May*.
. . . I am much afflicted in my mind about the
'Monks.'   I can work thirteen hours a-day at home,
but I can't do that abroad upon the world in this
way, cultivating the German clergy and other strange
species.

I am getting on with my notes, but I will be unable
to make any use of them till I get home.   The dreadful responsibility of paying bills and getting railway
tickets in an unknown tongue comes in the way of
other mental work.   I begin to think, however, with
modest satisfaction, that I must speak better German
than the Germans themselves, for they understand
me, but I don't understand them!

PRAGUE, 25*th May*.
. . . I am here for three-quarters of a day, and am
just going to look for Nina Balatka's bridge, &c.—a

pilgrimage which Mr Trollope (I beg your pardon, I forgot he was anonymous) should take as a compliment from a veteran novel-reader like myself. . . .

Did anybody ever go up the Elbe before me, I wonder? I don't remember any record of its beauties. It is a glorious river—worth twenty Rhines, so far as natural beauty is concerned.

WINDSOR, *Aug.* 8.

I have been—to make a jump—thinking over my biographical scheme, and I think George the Second's would be a good period—fresh ground; and there is Queen Caroline, Duke John of Argyle, Prince Charlie, and quantities of interesting people,—an age that has not been touched by any recent historian, except, by the way, Carlyle in his Frederick, but only very slightly there. I think I could throw myself into it, and make a collection of sketches worth paper and print. Tell me what you think.

The admirable 'Historical Sketches of the Reign of George II.,' after appearing in 'Maga,' went through three editions—1869, 1870, and 1875.

To Mrs Tulloch.   *Nov.* 26.

PADRONA CARISSIMA,—I daresay you must be thinking everything that is dreadful of me, but I have been so harassed and bothered that I have never had a moment for anything. Our theatricals (an awful business to take in hand) went off very successfully at last, but took no end of trouble. . . . Cecco made his appearance as a little herald in a tabard with Bluebeard's arms, and was greatly appreciated by the audience, as was also Mr Tids, whose health was drunk afterwards. . . .

My time is constantly liable to be broken in upon, and I get grumbly and cross and ill-natured. I wish you would come and be my wife, as is your duty— and behave yourself as such: the Principal might give me half a quarter of you, but men are such selfish wretches. . . .

I have been hearing pretty regularly from Rome during these stirring times; they are all well, though they were rather frightened at one time. William says in his last letter that Robert and he had visited the battlefield of Mentana, and he encloses a bit of a love-letter he picked up on it, signed "tua, per sempre, amanti, Colomba." Poor Colomba! I wonder if her Luigi was killed or taken prisoner, or only ran away!

1868.

To Mr Blackwood. WINDSOR.

. . . It is very disheartening that the writers who talk about all the rubbish that is published should let the best efforts of one's life fall flat without a word. I don't understand it, unless it is that under the present system only those who have connections in the critical world get any notice. One must bear it, of course, along with one's other burdens. I hope at least that this silence will not occasion any loss to you.

I have been stimulated by the sight of a printed letter addressed by Ruskin to his friends, to carry out an idea of reviewing his late brief productions. Shall I do it? The letter itself would throw you into fits of laughter. He is "about to enter on some work which cannot be well done except without interruption," he says, and therefore begs his friends "to think of me as if actually absent from England, and not to be displeased though I must decline all correspondence"! Shouldn't you like to follow such a splendid example? It is positively sublime.

I am extremely glad you like the historical papers. With modesty so do I! Poor Chesterfield!—one's heart aches for the disappointed man.

WINDSOR.

I was very sorry not to be able to write to you before
you left town, but I have been quite ill since I got
your letter, and kept in a flutter with the Court ladies
who are arranging my visit to the Queen.   That great
event is to take place this afternoon, the plenipo-
tentiaries on both sides having settled all the preliminaries.   I don't know whether I feel most like the
Queen of Sheba or the Pig-faced lady!

ST ANDREWS, Sept. 18.

. . . I have at the present moment two families
to support, which is not easy to be done when one
has nothing but one's head and hands.   The additional
and unexpected burden has made me stagger a little,
but I hope it will come round all right. . . .

The pension of £100 granted to Mrs Oliphant at
this time came to her as a most pleasant surprise.
She speaks of it in the following letter

To Mrs Tulloch.   WINDSOR, 3rd October.

. . . I am so unused to pieces of luck that I find
myself wondering on what principle this is—or is there
no principle (except Him of St Andrews) but only
royal grace and favour involved?   I enclose the necessary certificate, which looks formal enough for
anything.   It is very nice to get a hundred totally
unexpected pounds.   I don't think it ever happened
to me before.   Curiosity, however, mingles with my
rapture.   Are pensions of this kind generally paid in
the lump once a-year?   It is very good of the Queen
—if she has anything to do with it, which you will say
is a doubt of the profanest kind.

To Principal Tulloch.   WINDSOR.

MY DEAR PRINCIPAL,—They tell me, or rather Mr
Blackett tells me, that I am indebted to you for £100

a-year. I was quite taken by surprise by the announcement, though Mr Blackett spoke to me some time since
to know whether I would accept such a thing or not,
but I thought it was a business to be done by him and
not by you. A thousand thanks for your kindness
and delicacy, and the way in which you have done this.
The money is nothing to the kind care and thoughtfulness, which is worth it a hundred times over. Many
thanks. I shall always consider it is a gift from you
—that you have given me a house, or, as Mr Blackett
puts it, three thousand pounds in the Funds, which is
excessively pleasant ; but I am sure you who know me
will believe me when I say that I like your kindness
and brotherly thought for me much more than I care
for the 100 pounds.

1869.

To Mr Blackwood. WINDSOR, 3rd *February.*

 . . . I have been and still am extremely busy, so
busy that anything which I possibly can put off I do.
I am working at Richardson now, and will send you
the paper by the end of the week. I suppose I ought
to be ashamed to confess that, tedious as he often is,
I feel less difficulty in getting through him than in
reading Fielding, and that as a matter of taste I actually prefer Lovelace to Tom Jones! I suppose that
is one of the differences between men and women which
even Ladies' Colleges will not set to rights. Pray
don't tell of me ; if I betray my sentiments in public
they shall be laid upon the heavily burdened shoulders
of what Clarissa would call " my sex," and your contributor shall sneer at them as in duty bound.

WINDSOR.

 I enclose proof of ' John,' of which Mr William has
just sent me a reminder, and am working at Froude,
with some difficulty I confess, having so lately said my

say about Mary; and the article will not be a long one,
but I hope to be able to send it off to you on Saturday
(to-morrow), and I trust you will find it do.   This is
a long month!   We are all in a state of excitement
about Tids, who has gone and won the Prince Consort's
prize for French,[1] quite promiscuous, neither himself
nor anybody else having the least idea that he could
possibly succeed, as he is the very youngest of the
competitors, and only went in at the last moment with
ten days to do the preparation in, which all the others
have been busy with for at least half a year.   It is his
first appearance as public prizeman, and naturally we
are all somewhat elated.

The following letter from Tennyson refers to a request made by Mrs Oliphant that he would permit
the publication of some stanzas of "In Memoriam,"
very beautifully set as a part song by Mr Bridge, then
organist of Holy Trinity, Windsor, and now Sir F.
Bridge of Westminster.

From Lord Tennyson to Mrs Oliphant.

BLACKDOWN, HASLEMERE, *October* 18.

MADAM,—I forwarded your request to Mr Strachan,
because to him properly belongs the right over my
published poems.   What he says of my objection to
having any part of "In Memoriam" published to music
is perfectly correct.   Those portions which you have
seen so published have been granted to the solicita-
tions of friends not to be refused, as this is now granted
to Mr Carlyle's, and would, I have no doubt, have
been granted to your own, had I had the privilege of
your friendship.   Pardon my seeming discourtesy, and
believe me, your faithful servant,   A. TENNYSON.

----

[1] The Prince Consort's French prize was won by both the Oliphants.
Cyril was just over twelve at this time.

1870.

To Mr Blackwood.   WINDSOR, *2nd February.*

. . . You would not care (would you?) to send me as your own commissioner to report upon the state of Italy?   I am doing a Life of S. Francis of Assisi for Macmillan's Sunday Library, and I wish some benevolent person would send me out to Umbria. I should not mind taking a situation as courier at £100 a-month to a party of inexperienced tourists. Recommend me, please!   My acquirements are mild French and a little Italian, and a capacity for getting up any given subject so as to be able to filter it into the millionaire mind, and I would not mind dedicating the book to my patron or patroness! Do find me a place.

WINDSOR.

The 'Edinburgh Review,' in the person of Mr Reeve, is coming to see me to-morrow.   Do you think he will eat me?   I feel very nervous.   If you should never hear anything more of me you will know how to account for it. . . .

I hope your nephew is better.   I am in the doctor's hands myself, and ordered not to work ! ! !

WINDSOR.

The question I am going to ask you is not one I had any idea of asking you yesterday, nor will your answer in the negative at all disappoint me.   Do you care for having a story from me, a full-sized story, during next year?   I have (*ça va sans dire*) something planned, though not written as yet, three-volume size.   And yesterday an American publisher called upon me, offering me some money for the advance sheets of my next serial story.   He offered me the appalling sum of two hundred pounds! and my head is a little turned with the intense novelty of the notion; therefore I write to ask you whether you would be disposed to have my story, and aid me in spoiling the Egyptians. My Yankee friend wants something beginning in January. Tell me, please, whether you are disengaged, and if you have room for anything of mine; but pray don't have any feeling on the subject if your answer is No, for I shall not be disappointed—except of the undercurrent of delight of getting some money out of those trans-atlantic robbers. My visitor was so flattering about my popularity in America that I felt mightily disposed to fling a sofa cushion at his head, or else to impound him, and hold him to ransom, which perhaps would have been the better way.

WINDSOR.

With this I send proofs of both 'John' and the t'other papers, feeling rather spiteful at myself, and a little at you in respect to the former. I wanted to cut the half of it out, and I have not done it, lacking encouragement. And I am wounded to the depths of my soul by one word in your criticism—Cuddling! Good heavens, that I should have lived to hear such a word spoken of my heroine! It is a sign that I should abandon novel-writing and take to plain sewing, for the rest of my life, I suppose.

I am up to my eyes in the 'Acta Sanctorum' at present, and unless you would like a review of one or two volumes of that elegant and light work, I don't think I shall attempt anything further this month. Tiddy is going down to St Andrews with the bridegroom in about ten days. In respect to the war, the said bridegroom is like you golfers. I asked him just at the moment of greatest excitement whether there was any news, and he answered me complacently, Yes, he had got a letter by the midday post! Our interest here, however, has been much enhanced by the excitement of my friend Mrs Macdonald. who has gone to France to join her daughter. I had a great mind to have gone over to Paris with her, and sent you a paper to pay my expenses withal.

Mrs Macdonald, who was a very near neighbour of Mrs Oliphant, was the mother of Madame Canrobert, and of course all the events of the Franco-German war became more vividly interesting as they affected these two ladies.

WINDSOR, *18th August.*

I am very glad you liked the Piccadilly paper. I feel rather strongly on the subject myself, and consequently (I suppose) thought it rather bad. I have made most of the corrections you suggest. Mr Oliphant told me he had the intention of returning to his original work, and I rejoiced like you; but what if he should fall into an ordinary man of the world again, and like to hear his book praised, and himself applauded like the rest of us? In that case would you not rather have had him stay away? It is so difficult to know what is the right way. It is all very well for Mr Stopford Brooke (his letter is very good and clear, and I have quoted from it), but I had rather, for my part, having a high esteem for Mr Oliphant and great admiration of his powers, that he went in for any amount of extravagance and enthusiasm than that he fell back into your banal world, and contented himself like other people. I do not agree with you in thinking that he has begun to find out the weakness of his system, and I trust he will not find it out. When he does it will kill him, either body or soul—or such at least is my conviction.

This war is too frightful. I cannot say I sympathise really with either party, but I know much more of the French than of the Germans, and, right or wrong, one's heart goes with the losing side.

WINDSOR, 21st October.

You put me into rather a whimsical puzzle by your letter. You say you like my paper, and then object to almost everything in it. If you remember, my object in beginning these criticisms was to speak the truth and shame the newspapers—praising and blaming without fear or favour. Of course when my opinion is opposed to yours, it is but right and natural that mine should go to the wall; but I cannot stultify myself and deny my judgment, you know, with my own hand. I can hold my tongue, but if I do speak it must be according to my own judgment. What is to be done? I will strike out as far as my own judgment will permit me, but I can't do any more. Of course the final excision of it, even of the entire paper, remains always in your hands.

WINDSOR, 2nd November.

. . . I am glad Mr Oliphant is out of town, for I had been half disappointed not to hear anything of him. I have just had a letter this morning from a lady who is a medium, and who invites me to inspect a drawing made by her under spiritual guidance of my own " crown of glory in water-colours." What do you suppose it can be? I have the Scriptural requisite for a crown of glory in the shape of grey hair, but you don't suppose she can have a hair-wash to recommend? It is very funny.

1871.

To Mr Blackwood.   WINDSOR, 18th March.

Mr Blackett's sudden death without any arrangement for the care of his family has impressed me so much that I am very anxious to set my affairs in order, and I write to ask you whether you would kindly consent to be my executor and a kind of guardian to my boys in case of my death before they are grown up? I have asked Principal Tulloch to accept the same charge. . . . Should my death take place while the boys are still under age I have no doubt my pension would be continued to them, so that I think there would be enough properly managed to bring them up, especially as they both show promise of being able to help themselves in the way of scholarships, &c.

4th April.

. . . I will make any reasonable sacrifice to please you, but one of the passages you have marked I cannot see my way to leave out. It seems to me the very secret of all Cowper's weakness, and one which it is for the good of everybody, and especially of religious people, to have fully indicated; and besides I take pains to say their Calvinism is not to blame, and that a Jesuit director would or might do the same as Newton did. So much of Cowper's life is involved in this, that to take it out would be to omit the chief explanation of many of its mysteries. I will try if I can soften it, but even that I doubt.

4th May.

If your old contributors had to yield the *pas* to such writers only as the author of the ' Battle of Dorking ' we should have little to complain of. It is wonderfully fine and powerful. Is it Laurence Oliphant? I can't think of anybody else with such a power of realism and wonderful command of the subject. It is vivid as Defoe. I had it read to me last night, and I have done nothing but dream of invasion all the night through. The effect is almost too vivid. I hope you will make a separate publication of it. It ought to have a very great effect, unless, indeed, the public which consumed by the hundred thousand all that flat rubbish about ' Dame Europa ' should be unable to understand this infinitely higher effort. I hope I have guessed rightly, and that it is my interesting namesake who has written it. If it is so, I wish you would convey to him the expression of my unbounded admiration, not to say emotion, in reading it. But how do you come to suffer such reflections on your friends the Prussians?

WINDSOR, 18th November.

. . . I am glad to hear you are going to Paris. I am sure a little rest and change will do you good. I shall stay a day or two there, I think, as I come back,— about the 20th of December,— and should like much to see Mr Oliphant. I thought of trying to do so, and to speak to him about the Continental series of books I once talked to you of. I don't know whether you have dismissed the idea, but I have not, and he looks as if he might be a likely man.

. . . I had the most comical account of Mr Oliphant's colony the other day from Miss S. She said they held "community of wives and children"—or at least she knew the children were in common, and she supposed he had not mentioned the wives because of her presence! Don't tell him.

A terrible winter visit to the Château of La Roche en Bressy—the country seat of the Montalemberts—was undertaken at this time for the purpose of obtaining materials for Comte de Montalembert's biography. Mrs Oliphant took her little Cecco with her for company, and had great need of the solace, for she hated to be out of her own house (except with one or two beloved friends), and she felt that her time and labour were being wasted. Some of the following letters are to the cousin who for several years was her inmate and housekeeper.

To Cousin Annie.   LA ROCHE EN BRESSY, *Dec.* 1.

. . . Nothing can well be less comfortable or more
dreary than my life here, and but for the absolute
duty I should have left La Roche before now.   It
has been raining more or less for three days.   Yesterday and the day before Cecco and I (the only people
in the house who thought of such a thing) ventured
out a little, wading through the snow.   This morning
it is worse than ever, snowing fast, and nothing but a
sheet of white visible from the windows.   To crown
all other *désagréments*, Lina [her maid], who was to
have left for Switzerland to-day, is laid up, having
had two of her attacks in succession.   My materials
come to me very slowly.

The course of life here is odd enough.   I don't
know that it would suit you badly, but I can't say
I like it.   We leave our rooms at midday only for the
déjeuner.   After that, unless there are visitors, all disperse again to their rooms, meeting only at dinner,
which is at half-past six.   We then go to the drawing-
room till ten.   So that the social life of the household
is entirely confined to the three hours and a half in
the evening.   Sometimes, as this is an exceptional
moment, and the family are all employed more or
less upon M. de Montalembert's papers, they all go
to the library for an hour or two after the *déjeuner;*
but this is evidently an accidental matter, and the
natural way is what I have said.   Of course they visit
each other in their rooms, I suppose.   Sometimes I
feel as if this leisurely reading of a dozen pages or so
of a journal might go on for ever and ever, and I
grow intensely impatient, knowing how little time I
have to give.   But the idea of a life like mine of
course could never enter into the heads of these good
people, who are kind as kind can be, but evidently
think my work is entirely a work of predilection, and
that I can spend upon it as much time as pleases
me—Alas !

To Mr Blackwood.   LA ROCHE EN BRESSY, *Dec. 2.*

The *vie de château* is the coldest *vie* I ever had any-thing to do with. The journey was terrible, *five hours* driving after the railway; but the château might be (must be, I sometimes think) in Siberia instead of the Côte d'Or. I never in my life felt such cold. Every-thing is stone and ice. I inhabit a vast tapestried chamber, and have a section of a tower for my dressing-room, in the midst of which grandeur I shiver. I tremble too with impatience to find myself in the midst of masses of papers which would make my work most interesting and easy, but which I am not permitted to have access to. Montalembert, it appears, kept a journal from his twelfth year to the end of his life, and I am tantalised with the sight of these volumes, which Madame de M. reads to me for a couple of hours in the afternoon. We have been at it a week, and have got to his eighteenth year! Imagine my feelings. I have, however, raised a standard of rebellion, and declared that I cannot give more than next week entire, which begins to quicken the movements of my most kind hostess. It is very difficult, however, to intimate delicately to people whom any part of his life interests that all the details are not equally interesting to me. They are all extremely complimentary about the little paper in the Magazine, and I have been congratulated on all sides on having so thoroughly understood Montalem-bert's character, which is satisfactory so far, though I have had such hours of explanation about his attitude in regard to the Infallibility question, that I wish the Pope at Jericho a hundred times in a day. The posi-tion is comical, and I think some time or other I must write a paper on the tribulations of a historian in search of information.

Letter from Cecco (aged eleven years).

HÔTEL MIRABEAU, PARIS, 14*th Dec.*

MY DEAR COUSIN ANNIE,—The principal reason why I have not written to you is that I have been working at the Montalembert genealogical-tree trying to get it done.   I hope everybody at home is all right.   I received all the letters on Wednesday. Last Friday at La Roche we drove to a stone cross in the woods (all of which nearly were planted by M. de Montalembert), which was also erected by him.   The drive was cold and miserable enough for me as I sat on the box.   I got some stamps and seals the other day from Mdlle. Le Duc; most of them I had got already, but there were some Belgian new issue which I had not got.   We have no proper coachman here.   A labourer called La Motte generally drives us, but not always, Sylvain the *régisseur* sometimes taking his place.   On Tuesday, my birthday, we left for Semur.[1]   It was a very pretty road, but Semur, we found, was much prettier. The whole town slopes up to the middle, where stands the cathedral, which is very large and beautiful both outside and inside, though all the images had been torn from their niches in the front of the church. There were also four curious old towers at the gate. The rampart has within it another rampart of trees, which looks very pretty.   A pretty broad stream runs through the town, and the view from the bridge is very pretty.   The gardens, one above the other, only separated by little walls on the left, and to the right a dark pine-wood with a path quite white with snow leading up to it, which made a very pretty contrast. We arrived at Paris at half-past ten, but could not get into our cab before eleven.   The roads were covered with snow, not white but brown, and it was about twelve when we reached the Mirabeau.   Here

[1] Semur is the scene of " A Beleaguered City."

we got apartments looking on the court, which we didn't want them to be. I was out buying presents this morning in the Rue de Rivoli. Mama was this afternoon at Versailles, and is now at Lady Oliphant's at dinner.

I can't think of anything else to tell just now, so with love to Tiddy and Frank, I remain, your affectionate cousin.

1872.

To Mr Blackwood.   WINDSOR, *2nd February.*

. . . My idea in coupling Southey and Keats was —their absolute unsuitability. They are the very opposite poles, and as one has a sort of artificial connection with the Byronic school, so has the other with the Lake school; so that I thought I might treat them together as hangers-on of these two real fountains of poetry. I am very much afraid that you and I will come to blows about Byron. I did not read him young as most people do, and accordingly have never worshipped him, and he is to me a gigantic sham in everything but poetry. Of course I shall keep clear of the mud in which he is embedded, and especially of the last mud thrown by Mrs Stowe, and will endeavour to do him poetically all the justice possible. I should like to take in Campbell. He and Moore might come very well together, but Moore is nothing in my opinion, and never would have been anything but for the lovely music he is identified with. Crabbe, too, I should like to take up. I enclose a little note of the poets done and proposed. Please make what corrections you like.

When you have time, pray look at my story, and tell me if you like the beginning, for "my barmy noddle's working prime," and if you don't like that I want to write to you about something else.

Windsor, 28th February.

. . . I did not go to London yesterday. . . . We had grand doings here, however. There is a curious sort of a man called Richardson Gardiner, who has contested the borough more than once on the Conservative side (don't be angry, he was a red-hot Radical first, but found, I suppose, that that did not answer), and whose efforts to keep himself before the public are very funny. He heard, it is said, a report, which was false, that the member for Windsor meant to roast an ox whole on the Thanksgiving Day, and he accordingly sent orders to roast *three* oxen, which was done yesterday in presence of a delighted crowd. There was a large bonfire in addition, and fireworks and illuminations, in which delights Jack shared with my boys. I must wind up this long history, however, by telling you a capital remark of a poor woman who is to benefit by the beef. In answer to some suggestion that such a benefactor of the people should be returned at next election — " No, no," said this philosopher; " let's keep him out : if he were elected he would be just as useless as Roger [our member], and we'd get nothing out of him ! "

Windsor, 30th March.

As you have been my very kind friend always, let me tell you once more exactly what my position is. I have four people, an entire family, three of them requiring education, absolutely on my hands to provide for. My only chance of ever escaping from this burden is to train and push on my nephew into a position in which he can take this weight upon himself. This process of course involves a great additional expense, and I cannot let my own boys suffer for what I am obliged to do for him. For the next three years, during which I shall have all three at work, I can look forward to nothing but a fight *à outrance* for money: however it is to be

honestly come by. I don't care how much or how
hard I work, and fortunately my sanguine temperament and excellent health save me from the gnawing
of anxiety which would kill many people. At the end
of these three years Frank, I hope, will have a capital
position, and be able to relieve me to a considerable
extent, and Tiddy will have reached the age to which
scholarships are possible, and according to all human
probability will be able to do much of what remains
to his education for himself. Now, perhaps, it would
be wiser, with this tremendous struggle before me,
to retire from my pretty house and pleasant surroundings and go to some cheap village where I could live
at less expense. I hold myself ready to do this
should the necessity absolutely arise; but you will
easily understand that while still in the full tide of
middle life I shrink from such a sacrifice, and would
rather work to the utmost of my powers than with-
draw from all that makes existence agreeable: at the
same time, I hold myself ready to make the sacrifice
should it prove absolutely necessary. My life is
insured, and I trust I will always, as long as I live,
be able to do something small or great, so that I
think I am justified, as long as strength and work
hold out, to pursue the career I have marked out for
myself. I never can save money, but if I can rear
three men who may be good for something in the
world, I shall not have lived for nothing. Twelve
years ago I began my solitary life a thousand pounds
in debt. I don't think in all my life since I began my
independent career that I have ever got five pounds I
did not work for.

Madame de Montalembert paid two visits to Mrs
Oliphant at this date, and devoted much time and
energy to getting some changes made in the life of
her husband, then just ready for the press. By sheer
persistence, aided by a very hot summer, and all the

inconveniences of a change of residence, she triumph-antly carried her point, and left her hostess vanquished and exhausted.[1]

To Mr William Blackwood.   WINDSOR, 18*th June.*

Thanks for your letter : it will answer the purpose admirably. I send off by post to-day 100 pages for press, which will clinch the matter. But alas, pity me! the Countess has just written to say that she is coming down here again to-day to read over the second volume with me. I hope I shall be alive at the end of the reading, but what with the hot weather, and a most eloquent and energetic member of the noble house of De Mérode, I don't know what is to become of me. . . .

What with my flitting and this invasion of the—not Goths, but delightfullest and troublesomest Gauls, I am rather hardly called upon just now.

WINDSOR, 17*th July.*

. . . Heaven be praised, indeed, that this terrible book is now out of hands! If the public are as much pleased as his friends are, we shall have nothing to complain of.

WINDSOR, 22*nd October.*

. . . I have begun, partly to amuse myself, and on a sudden impulse, a new series of the 'Chronicles of Carlingford' to be called 'Phœbe Junior,' and to embody the history of the highly intellectual and much-advanced family of the late Miss Phœbe Tozer. I don't know whether you will have any interest in this or not, but you have a right to be told of it at least.

---

[1] A recent reviewer has said that Mrs Oliphant knew of Montalembert only what his family chose to tell her. This is far from the truth. The 'Life' as originally written contained much interesting matter, the result of independent investigation, which was unfortunately struck out to satisfy Madame de M.'s persistent entreaties.

1873.

To Mr Blackwood.   WINDSOR, *21st January.*

. . . I am a good deal amused and rather flattered
in my *amour propre* by the revelations of the ' Times '
this morning about Lord Lytton.   His name had
occurred to me in connection with the ' Coming
Race,' but I dismissed the idea as impossible.   The
second number of the ' Parisians ' I was convinced
came somehow from him, but circumstances seemed
so much against it that I propounded to my friends
the notion that the author must be Mrs Lytton,
which might account for the unquestionable Bul-
werism of the book.   I feel quite pleased that I was
so close on the heels of the mystery.   I hope it is
true that the story is finished.

WINDSOR, *6th February.*

. . . I enclose Mr Kinglake's letter.   Thanks for
sending it to me.   Your other correspondent is hyper-
critical.   That I should extract the only amusing
thing out of a slight and dull book may, I think, be
easily pardoned me.   As for the Hares, I refrained
from saying anything about the sonship, which was
no sonship, simply because it seemed to take away
the only excuse for the mawkish worship of the book;
and seeing I expressed my opinion of it fully, I did
not think it necessary to dwell upon this detail.
The book was (before I opened it) more interesting
than usual to me, from the fact that I knew Mrs
Julius Hare very well.   But your correspondent's
opinion, even had I had the advantage of knowing
it before I wrote my paper, is not mine, and I can
only review books at all on the condition that I
express my own feelings in respect to them.   I read
every word of both the books mentioned, to my pain
and sorrow. . . . The tremendous applause which

has greeted this performance is a good specimen of
the sort of thing which I am anxious to struggle
against—the fictitious reputation got up by men who
happen to be "remembered at the Universities," and
who have many connections among literary men.

WINDSOR, 13th *May.*

What a terrible question you ask me about the
sequence of my books! Thank Heaven, I don't remember much one year what I wrote the year before,
which is a special dispensation of Providence, I think,
in my behalf; for how could I write another word
more if my conscience was oppressed with a recollection of all the rubbish I have poured upon the
world? 'Katie Stewart'[1] was, I think, the third—
the proofs of it came to me, I remember, on the
morning of my wedding-day; and there was a book
called 'Merkland,' of which I have a faint recollection, between. The Carlingford books were begun in
the year '60 or '61, when I was very low in spirit and
hope, and after you had snubbed me very much, as
you have been doing lately! Please don't let anybody upbraid me with writing too much until the
year 1876, if we live to see it, by which time I hope
the bulk of the schooling will be over, and I will
not mind it.

I am sorry that Browning's last appearance is not
worthy of him. The only amends Miss Thackeray
can make him for seducing him to choose such an
absurd title for a book[2] is to marry him, it seems
to me.

WINDSOR, 5th *June.*

By that curious chance which seems to rule over
accidents, the Magazine never arrived this month,
and I have only seen it for the first time this morn-

---

[1] 'Katie Stewart' seems to have been really the fifth book, the order
being: 'Mrs Margaret Maitland,' 'Caleb Field,' 'Merkland,' 'Adam
Græme of Mossgray,' 'Katie Stewart.'

[2] 'Red Cotton Nightcap Country.'

ing, having written to Mr Langford to ask for a copy.
A thousand thanks for the friendly thought which
suggested the review.   The article itself is excellent
and full of good feeling, but let me thank you first
for thinking of it.   I have not had too many en-
couragements of the kind.   Your contributor says
so much that is most flattering and delightful to
me, that I am sure he could have said much that
would have been valuable also in the way of criticism had he chosen; but probably I should not
have liked that so much!   I am very much gratified
by his notice of my earlier books, sad stuff though
many of them seem to me now, and by his appreciation of some special characters which have not caught
the public eye perhaps so much as I thought they
might have done, and especially by his notice of the
'Son of the Soil,' which was written at the most
sorrowful moment of my life, when I was wading
very deep in grief and doubt and all the discourage-
ment which grief brings.   I do not venture to guess
who the author is, but I should be very glad to know.
Certain geographical deficiencies prove his confession
that he is not Scotch.   Will you tell me to whom I
am indebted for so kind an appreciation of my work?
Anyhow, I am heartily grateful to him (I suppose it
is *him?*) and you.

Windsor, 26th November.

. . . I have entirely given up the notion of writing
a story at present for the 'Graphic.'   .   .   .

Tids has just come back from Oxford, where he
was trying for the Balliol scholarship (though without the least idea of getting it, as he has still two
years at Eton).   I hear that he passed a very creditable examination, and that his English essay was the
second in order of merit.   I am sure you will sympathise with me in my special pleasure in this respect.
I had not had much confidence in his literary powers.

1874.

To Mr Blackwood.   Windsor, *9th Febry.*

Thanks for letting me read Lord Lytton's letter. I see no reason why he should not know who his reviewer is, except that I think one usually thinks much less of the praise when one is aware of the identity of the writer. However, as it is an object worth considering, to connect the name which my boys, I hope, will make something of, with here and there a favourable prepossession, I have no objection to your telling him. In cases where the prepossession will be unfavourable, it is always known!

I am not doing anything for this month but 'Valentine,' which I am anxious to get on with. I wish I could have the advantage of reading this out to you: even the mere fact of hearing how it reads is such an advantage to a writer, and it is one of the drawbacks of getting old that domestic criticism becomes impossible—at least to a person in my position. I am going to Florence in the Easter holidays to revive my impressions of the place for a book to be published with illustrations which Mr Macmillan has asked me to do. I shall take Tids with me, but the trip will be a very rapid one, as we shall only have about three weeks. Should you care to have one or two articles about the subjects which I am going to study? Dante, Michael Angelo, and Savonarola are my three chief points, and I should not like to lose any of my material.

What a curious change in the political world! I hope Mr Disraeli, who I suppose must come in, will be able to work with everybody, and will have a good majority. I have no great sympathy with your side, but the Emperor Gladstone has been getting really too much.

WINDSOR, 12*th March*.

. . . I meant my Val to be the least good of the two lads, but I am getting to like him! The other must turn out to be the eldest. I will revise it all carefully, and if I can find anything to shorten will do so. I want to have an election for the county with Valentine, grown up, as candidate, which should bring up all the floating stories about him, and give the other side a chance of saying their worst; but the boyhood is perhaps too attractive to me, surrounded as I am by boys.

I shall send you my paper on Saturday. The books I have taken are Mrs Somerville (with which I am enchanted, and which recalls to me my mother and even my own recluse childhood in the most delightful way), Ampère's pretty touching story, and I think the letters of Merimée ('À une Inconnue'), on which you can conclude when you see them. The Merimée letters are absolutely spotless so far as morals go, and very pretty in many parts. I suppose the *Inconnue* must be *Connue*; but there is sufficient mystery to permit the critic to deal with it as an entirely dark matter, and there is much that is very charming, humorous, and tender in the letters themselves. If you do not like what I say about them, you can cut it out. Dr Guthrie I meant to treat as the most rampant specimen of the good-natured complacent Philistine I have met with for a long time. The smug self-content of the book is simply odious to me, and gives a very miserable exhibition of what his public like and esteem as the best. Must I not be permitted to say so? On this question too you must decide when you get the paper. I don't mind doing it, even if you don't publish it at all, for it serves the purpose of one of those little walks an artist takes away from his picture which he is in the act of painting—letting me see my more important work from a little distance.

WINDSOR, 24th July.

. . . About the Classics. I think the most effective review of them would be done from the unlearned point of view, without any pretence of knowing better —in short, as one of the English readers for whom they are intended: don't you think so? You might put an editorial note to say that this was done on purpose.

We have been roasted and baked and grilled here to such an extent that the coolness of St Andrews is very tempting. Fortunately even here the heat has moderated. The Lord Mayor's dinner was amusing. I sat next Matthew Arnold, with whom I struck up an acquaintance, and liked him better in his own person than in his books. He, Anthony Trollope, Mr Hughes, Charles Reade, and myself were the sole representatives of literature (barring the press) that I could see; but oh! my ladies of the Opera, how fine they were! The dinner was bad! fancy that in the Mansion House! I offered Tiddy 5s. for a copy of verses on the occasion (he was with me), but the monkey thinks the price too small, and wants to know first how much I get for mine!

To Miss Blackwood. WINDSOR, 22nd Sept.

. . . Tids has attained the dignity of sixth form, and thinks no small-beer of himself, and Cecco is already an old and experienced Etonian. I am sure you will be pleased to know also that my nephew Frank has done admirably, gained himself a scholarship at his college, and quite justified me in my expenditure for him, which is a great comfort.

To Mr Blackwood. WINDSOR, 19th October.

I have, I trust, done what you want in respect to the paper enclosed. I agree with you that Mr Collins's volumes are very good, but I don't agree with

you about Mr Trollope, whose 'Cæsar' I cannot read
without laughing — it is so like Johnny Eames.   I
hope your supplementary series will include Lucretius.
The two little bits from Virgil in this paper are
Tiddy's, as were the Greek quotations in my last, so
I can scarcely put a name to them.   They are his
first appearance in print.

To Miss Blackwood.   WINDSOR, 26*th December.* :
   . . . Tiddy, I am sorry to say, was not successful in
the Balliol examination.   I said all along that I did
not hope it, as he was a year under age; but I suppose I must have hoped all the same, for I was considerably disappointed.   He was mentioned as having
distinguished himself in the examination, but did not
get anything.   However, I hope he will get either a
scholarship somewhere else or an exhibition at Balliol
next year.   He will be just a fortnight too old next
November to try for the scholarship there again,
which is very annoying.   The others have been getting on very well. . . .
   As this is Frank's last Christmas at home, we are
doing all we can to make it a merry one for him.
Next year I expect everything to be changed.   The
little girls are going to a school we have found for
them in Germany, and my brother will also leave me
for a time at least.   And Frank goes to India and
Tids to Oxford, and I mean to let my house and try
six months' utter retrenchment in a lodging at Eton.
But all this, I think, I told you before.

1875.

To Mr Blackwood.   WINDSOR, 15*th February.*
   . . . I am much gratified by the kind messages
from Mr Kinglake.   It is a great pleasure to think
that my work is liked by any one so well able to

Windsor 1874.

judge.   Pray tell him that I have been an admirer of his for—Heaven knows how long!—since the days when I was shocked and delighted by 'Eothen.'   I remember being very much amused by the opening out of two old neighbours of mine at Ealing, after a discussion of his first volume.   In the enthusiasm created by it one of them, an old Peninsular officer, instructed me carefully how to make a pontoon bridge and get my (!) troops over it; while the other, Admiral Collinson, burst forth into naval experiences.

WINDSOR, 19*th March.*

. . . My nerves were a good deal upset with illness, which reacted, I suppose, upon my work.   By the bye, adversity has brought me acquainted with such a swarm of ridiculous novels that I feel a great desire to let loose my opinion on the subject.   The badness, the silliness, the utter futility of them is something quite appalling, and really ought not to be put up with.   Next month perhaps I might be allowed a massacre of these not innocents, for they seem to have got the length of a positive plague.

I enclose Mr Kinglake's letter; very many thanks for letting me see it.   I am much flattered by his good opinion.

We are beginning to get better weather here, so I hope it may soon reach you.   My unwellness is not in the least, I believe, of a kind to touch life, and is therefore not interesting, but it is very worrying and uncomfortable.

This illness was an extremely painful form of neuralgia, which returned once or twice, but seems to have made no serious attack upon Mrs Oliphant's wonderfully sound and vigorous constitution.   She could endure the most amazing amount of fatigue, except in walking, which was for many years painful and laborious to her.

WINDSOR, 16*th July*.

My anxieties have come to an end in the saddest way. My poor brother died on Wednesday night. Notwithstanding the inevitable severance which long years and difference of sentiment makes, I feel the natural pang of the parting more than I expected, and am almost glad that it is so. However (and that is saddest of all), there is no feeling possible but that it is best that his shattered life should have ended now, while still his children are with him, and all the last pious offices can be paid him by his son's hands. I am writing out of the gloom of the shut-up house, which is so trying to the nerves. The funeral takes place to-morrow.

To Miss Blackwood.   WINDSOR, *July* 20.

. . . All has been got over quietly. I am so much more affected in every way by the event than I had expected, that I am going away for a day or two in the hopes of coming back to my work more fit for it than I feel now. One cannot but feel that the best thing that could have happened was that my poor Frank should have been taken away before his children left him, and yet I feel the loss as much, perhaps more, than I should have done had his life been brighter and more valuable. It seems altogether so sad, and saddest of all in that it is the best that could have happened. He who was never out of one room seems now to pervade all the house, and with remorse I miss him dead of whom I was so often impatient when he was living.

To Mr Blackwood.   WINDSOR, *July* 27.

My nephew has finished his studies at Cooper's Hill, taking a first-class. He has chosen the Punjaub, as it is the privilege of the highest placed students to choose their district, and goes out in October. Nothing could be more satisfactory than his career at Cooper's Hill, and I trust he will do no less well in the future. Thus one of my anxieties is disposed of. Death has taken away another, and I trust my life may be less burdened in the future; but in the meantime this is a somewhat tremendous moment.

To Miss Blackwood.   GRINDELWALD, 24*th August.*

I intended to have written to you long ago, but you know how little time one seems to have in a strange place, and I have been working more or less all the time. . . .

We have been getting along very pleasantly on the whole. We came straight through to Interlaken—that is, Cecco and I—and were there joined by Tiddy and Frank, who had taken the little girls to their school in Germany, and came round by Constance and Zurich to meet us. . . .

We have met with Miss Thackeray and her sister, and have seen a great deal of them for the last ten days; and now the sister's husband, Mr Leslie Stephen, a great Alpine man, has just arrived, and the boys are going off with him to the ice to-morrow, to their great satisfaction, though I feel a little nervous. They have already been up a big hill on their own account and walking a great deal, and are enjoying their expedition thoroughly. We had glorious weather at Interlaken, only very hot, but up here among the mountains it is rather stormy and wet. On Saturday we are going to Mürren for a few days, where I intended to have gone long ago, and then to Chamouni, and then by Geneva and Paris, home, where, notwithstanding all the glories of Switzerland, I shall be glad to be.

To Mr Blackwood.   WINDSOR, 27*th September.*

. . . My engineer boy leaves on the 24th October for the Punjaub. I should be very much obliged, if you know anybody thereabouts (!), if you would kindly give him a word of introduction. He is a very good boy, and will do no one any discredit, I feel sure.

How about Jack? Does he go to Christ Church this term? I shall go with Tids to settle him, and if I can be of any use to Jack at the same time I should be very glad. I suppose they are the better of a little aid in settling their small domesticities. One's heart quakes a little launching them off into the world—at least the feminine heart does. I suppose you men who have gone through it and know the dangers take it more easily than we do, to whom it is all terrible in the mystery of the unknown. Alas that they can't remain children always! I don't know whether you feel as I do the inherent absurdity of the idea that we should be getting old and *they* should be getting men. It feels preposterous, and rather a bad joke sometimes.

To Miss Blackwood. WINDSOR, *October.*

. . . I have been so very much occupied that I have had no time to do or think of anything except the boys and their manifold preparations. I went to Oxford with Tiddy on Friday, and left him on Saturday settled in very nice rooms at Balliol, and amidst so many friends that I don't think he will feel the separation much, though I do. Two of his chief cronies, Farrer and Brodrick, both of whom you met here and heard at the Speeches on the 4th of June, are in the same quadrangle with him.[1] He has got a charming, big, lofty sitting-room on the first floor, with a bedroom opening from it. I had a party of youths to luncheon before I left, all his intimates, and he is surrounded by acquaintances. I hope he will be a good boy and

[1] Of these two young men one died young, and the other is now (1899) Under-Secretary for War.

work well. One cannot but have many tremors at thus launching one's child into life. Frank's launch is a more thorough one, it is true, but he has got over the first probation. Tids' trials are all to come. His scholarship is called the Bryant. It is about £50 a-year for three years. I hope he will get something else before long. Frank is to sail on Saturday in the Crocodile from Portsmouth. When you are writing to your nephew George will you recommend him in case they should come across each other ?

WINDSOR, *2nd December.*

I am sure you will be grieved to hear of Mrs Leslie Stephen's death, Thackeray's youngest daughter, with which I was brought most sadly into connection by the fact that her sister was staying with me at the time. I think I told you that we had met and seen a great deal of them in Switzerland. Mrs Stephen was in a delicate state, . . . and Miss Thackeray, whose perfect devotion and almost subjection to her I never saw equalled, had made up her mind with some doubt to be absent from her for one evening to come to me, partly to see me, partly to do honour to poor Mr Oscar Browning. . . . She was telegraphed for next morning, and hurried to London, . . . but her sister was dead before she got there. I had asked one or two people to dinner to meet her, and you may imagine the ghastly effect of a vacant place so caused. The final news came just as we were sitting down to dinner. I cannot get over the heart-breaking effect of it.

WINDSOR, *13th December.*

. . . I have not enjoyed Tids' absence at all, as you may well suppose ; indeed the three months seem to have flitted over in a kind of a dream, not even good for work, though the loneliness and quiet ought to have been of use for so much as that, at least ; but now the holidays are close at hand and

my boy will be back on Wednesday. I have the best
accounts of him: he seems to have got nice friends,
and even my ferocious anxieties which feed upon
nothing have been kept under. Cecco has been
very good and comfortable in his brother's absence,
his only fault being that he is too fond of home,
and prefers my society to that of other boys, which
I don't think quite good for him.

To Mr Blackwood.   WINDSOR, *Christmas.*

Let me wish you all the good that can be put into
a wish for this time and all times. Thank Heaven,
so long as the children are about, Merry Christ-
mases and Happy New Years are still possible, and
don't hurt instead of giving pleasure. Though we
are growing old, I suppose, the sensation is still
half amusing and not very severe. God bless you
and yours not only for the New Year but at all
times and seasons. Pray give my affectionate good
wishes to Mrs Blackwood, Mary, and Jack. I suppose the latter hero will be an Oxford man next year,
like my own freshman, who has come back after his
first term, I am glad to say (though my heart has
been in my mouth all the time), rather improved in
homeliness, kindness, and simplicity than otherwise.
I got a very good account of him, but he did not
get an exhibition at Balliol as I hoped. He was one
out, I believe, only, which is rather aggravating.
He seems to have formed a friendship with a young
brother (he thinks) of Major Lockhart. By the bye,
how good and clever his (Major Lockhart's) verses
are which you sent me. . . .

1876.

To Mr Blackwood.   WINDSOR, *4th January.*

. . . Just before your letter came I had been reading an old letter of my dear mother's written in 1852,

recounting with great delight and pride your complimentary letters to me about 'Katie Stewart,' and blowing her own little trumpet, dear soul, over her "little Maggie"! It was sent back to me by a relation by the same post which brought yours. And this reminds me to thank you very much indeed for what you say about 'Whiteladies.' I thought the book was not bad, but as no critic except the singularly stupid one who "does for" the 'Times' has even noticed it, I had begun to feel that I must be mistaken. Dreadful penalty of too much writing, but I am glad indeed that you approve of it.

WINDSOR, 10th February.

. . . I had heard of Mr Oliphant's arrival. He came over from New York in the same ship with my friend Mrs M.'s son. Has he fallen into telegraphy[1] and prosperity, and abandoned the wilder side of life and opinion? I should like to see him. I am glad to tell you that Miss Thackeray liked the little paper on her father. I had a note from her about it.

To Mr Frank Wilson.　　　　　WINDSOR, 1st March.

. . . There is not much news to give you. I am better (I think I grumbled last week), and working through the mountain of work under which, however, I still groan. Did I tell you that I have brought a hornet's nest about my ears by describing the Military Knights in my new story? I am very sorry to have vexed the old men, though of course I had not the least intention of doing so, and did not expect the sketch to be so readily recognised. You will see I have kept the Castle out altogether, which I thought would mystify the people. However, I have been too close. . . . Do you ever come

---

[1] Mr Laurence Oliphant had been occupied with the affairs of the United States Cable Company.

in contact with the Mussulman population, and what do you think of them?   There is a novel not very long published by a Mr Allardyce called the 'City of Sunshine,' entirely about Indian (not Anglo-Indian) life, which gives a very fine picture of an old Mohammedan officer in the old sepoy army.   It is a very clever book.   I don't know if it would interest you, who have the real thing under your eyes, as much as it interests us, or I would put it into the next box that is sent.

WINDSOR, 24th March.

. . . We have had the most villainous winter, which is dying hard, and yielding most unwillingly to such a burst of sunshine as we are rejoicing in now.   Tids, who came home on Wednesday night, is sitting on the steps of the greenhouse working at Homer and Philology (he says), and even across my desk while I write there is a glimmer—nay, a blaze —of sun.   And the greenhouse is full of hyacinths mixed (alas!) with a little tobacco!   Don't you see it all?   I wish I could have a photograph or a picture or something to give an idea of your surroundings, your tent and your canal and your dusky people : I wish it could be done, but I suppose you will very soon be going to the hills now, or at least when you get this letter.

The events since I wrote to you last have been the visits of cousin Annie and Mr Ralston. . . . Mr Ralston has developed into quite a new man.   He startled me from the first by his jocosity and a new strain of self-importance.   But the "lecture" (!) so-called, which he had come on purpose to give to the Eton boys (I think I told you), was a string of most amusing but very absurd stories, as funny as you can imagine, and keeping the audience in fits of laughter, told with the broadest yet the deepest comicality, but as little like a dignified lecturer·as you can imagine.   Dr Balston was in the chair, and he, I understand, was considerably shocked, and declared that he had never been at a literary society meeting before, and that he would not have known that the entertainment had anything to do with literature had he not been told. "Who is your low comedian?" somebody asked Mr Hale. So you see our friend produced a sensation. The 'Chronicle,' however, is most complimentary to him, and promises him an enthusiastic reception when he comes again, and he himself was delighted with the cheers and laughter.

To Mr Blackwood.   WINDSOR, 11*th April.*

I have begun Macaulay, and you shall have him in the end of the week, if possible. I think the fact of the very foolish, bitter, and useless remarks about 'Maga' and Professor Wilson makes it highly expedient that the book should be reviewed in a loftier and more generous spirit, with one very distinct and dignified notice of the equal injustice and bad taste of this reference, which I shall try to make as pointed as possible.

WINDSOR, 20*th April.*

. . . I have not seen the 'Edinburgh,' but will get hold of it as soon as possible. How very good of Mr Kinglake to interest himself about the poor little reputation which, alas! "thae muving things ca'ed weans" have forced me to be so careless of. Will you tell him how very much more I feel .gratified and honoured by such kind interest, as coming from him, a critic whose personal approval is better than vulgar praise? But no praise will do for me what was done for Thackeray, and reason good. I think, though, if ever the time comes that I can lie on my oars, after the boys are out in the world, or when the time comes which there is no doubt about, when I shall be out of the world, that I will get a little credit—but not much now, there is so much of me! But please say to Mr Kinglake all my gratitude for

such true friendliness, which I feel to the bottom of
my heart.

To Mr F. Wilson.   WINDSOR, *5th May.*
. . . The systematic way in which Mr Trollope
grinds out his work is very funny. It must have
answered, however, for he seems extremely comfortable; keeps a homely brougham, rides in the Park,
&c. I envy and admire, and wonder if daily bread
is all I shall ever be able to manage, and whether I
shall have to go on in the same treadmill all my life,
—I suppose so.

My new story begins in the 'Cornhill' next month.
I saw Miss Thackeray and Leslie Stephen for a few
minutes the other day—she looking very much herself, he looking very miserable. I asked them to
come here, while their things are removed from one
house to another. . . .

To Mr Blackwood.   WINDSOR, *7th June.*
. . . I was charmed with Mr Kinglake, and ex-
tremely glad to make his acquaintance. By the way,
I congratulate you on your new contributor. Of
course you will tell fibs about him, and declare the
'Woman - Hater'[1] to be by nobody in particular.
There is no one I admire so much. There is a swing
of easy power about him which is beyond praise.

This and several of the following letters refer to the
Foreign Classics Series, which Mrs Oliphant edited.

To Mr Blackwood.
          GOLF PLACE, ST ANDREWS, *20th September.*
Thanks for letting me see the letter to Mr Reeve.
I perfectly agree with what you say: he is not a man
to be affronted, but neither is his aid of any special

---

[1] The 'Woman-Hater' was the last, or almost the last, novel written
by Charles Reade.

importance. I think, however, that he might make a sufficiently interesting volume.

Mr Collins's list is very like mine—indeed, of course every list of the kind must be like every other. Do you incline to let him try his hand at Camoens? People who are learned in Portuguese are not common. I have been arranging what seemed to me a very feasible succession to begin with, if we can keep our men to time. I have bound over the Principal to be ready if called upon with Pascal. Have you mentioned Rabelais to Colonel Hamley? Shall I write to him about it? You will see that I have put myself down for a couple of volumes in the first year. This is simply because I can be sure of my own punctuality, and of course the arrangement is merely as a convenience to settle some order of starting. I shall set to work to get my German brushed up when I get home. It is not good for much at present. If Mr Lewes will do Goethe that will be admirable, and we should secure it as soon as we can. The series should be made as interesting and important as possible at the beginning. Shall I draw out a prospectus?

By the way, I know Mr Reeve tolerably well, and have written two or three papers for him, though I almost forget what they were about.

WINDSOR, 4th November.

I enclose you a small story of a ghostly description, which pray put in the Magazine if it happens to suit you; but if not, send it back to me, as I should like to have it published for Christmas. It was called forth by a discussion of the Glamis Castle mystery which I was a party to the other night, and is intended for a possible solution of that. I cannot remember whether there is a Lord Gowrie; if there is, of course the name must be changed. I should be pleased if you liked it.

Colonel Hamley will not reply to me about Voltaire.

In case he does not do it, as Rabelais seems for the moment out of the question, have you any more French-reading authors in your pocket to supply this volume, as I don't know whether you care for my independent researches? Have you heard from Mr Martin?

I am amused at the novel crusade Mr Reade has beguiled you into. I heartily agree with him, but I should not have thought you would do so.

The story mentioned above is called "The Secret Chamber." Whatever it did afterwards, it certainly had a success when it was read, as Mrs Oliphant's stories occasionally were, in the family circle. The reading had been begun rather late, and midnight passed as the climax was approaching. The reader, her nerves all excited and tense, came to the place where the old sword in the haunted room suddenly fell with a crash. At that very moment outside the closed door of the drawing-room something fell!— something that crashed and shivered! Every one started up, the door was flung open, but the long passage outside was dark and silent. The servants had gone to bed, and the lights were out. There was nothing to be seen, nothing to be heard. What had fallen? Was it an echo of the ghostly sword as it fell that we had heard? Half an hour later the mystery was cleared. The reader of the story, going cautiously in the dark towards bed, trod on the broken glass of a fallen picture!

To Mr Blackwood. WINDSOR, *28th November.*

When I heard from you that Mr Martin would not undertake Goethe, I asked Mr Kinglake, with whom I have been having some correspondence lately, whether he thought Mr Hayward would undertake it. He thought not, but said he would speak to him about it, without committing us in the least. Then he wrote to me that he thought Mr Hayward seemed disposed for it, and asked all the details as to time of publication, remuneration, &c., and last night I got the enclosed letter from him, which I think it best to submit to you as it stands. Of course I say nothing about the money. I am rather aspiring myself to make the series an amateur one (in the right sense of the word)—books done for the love of the subject.

Mr Hayward is a very big " swell," and I confess I should be proud of him. . . .

Mr Kinglake's hint about writing to Mr Hayward in very *appreciative* terms is amusing. If you don't know him personally (as, however, I have no doubt you do), perhaps it would be better that I should do this. The necessary admiration and enthusiasm might come easier to me than to you !

N.B.—I am not at all sure that I ever read a word of his writings.

WINDSOR, *8th December.*

I send you to-day a copy of my book, the ' Makers of Florence ': you will see a good deal about Dante in it ; and pray look at the translation in a footnote beginning on page 7, which is a specimen of the translations I am doing. The book is too pretty (I don't mean my part of it) for business purposes, so I hope Mrs Blackwood will accept it. I have put her name in it.

WINDSOR, *26th December.*

I respond with the most hearty goodwill to your good wishes. I trust Mrs Blackwood and you will find the years more and more happy as the life of the young generation develops and is enriched : after all, it is upon them that all our hopes depend as we get past the time of personal hope. . . . My boys are very well and all that I could wish them, though

Cyril disappointed me (and himself) horribly by getting only a second-class in Mods. We felt terribly cast down for a while, but the Master of Balliol cheered me up again, which was a wonder, as he is not too genial generally on the subject.

1877.

To Mr Blackwood.   WINDSOR, *8th March.*

I entirely agree with you in respect to Miss Martineau. The curious limited folly of her apparent common - sense struck me in St Andrews, and I thought it would make a good article. The autobiography seems much worse than could have been expected. How such a commonplace mind could have attained the literary position she did fills me with amazement. How did she manage it? I can only look and wonder. I will send the paper rather late, I fear, but I think it is worth while doing it.

GRANVILLE HOTEL, RAMSGATE, *March.*

. . . Why—how—did Miss Martineau get such a reputation? There is nothing so puzzling. I wanted to have put in a word or two about some curious comments of hers on public-school life as illustrated by Tom Brown, and the enormous depravities and low vices caused by—the boys breakfasting alone, and cooking sausages for themselves! which I got in St Andrews, when I first contemplated this paper; but I have not the book, and the article, I fear, is already too long.

WINDSOR, *19th April.*

I send the concluding chapter of the ' Divine Comedy.' I am very sorry to have been so long with it, but the work has been serious. It has given me a great deal of trouble. One's brain needs to be very clear to follow all the theological arguments that go on in heaven.   One hopes it is less doctrinal now up there, or one would certainly prefer the sunny hillside low down in Purgatory!   There is only a short chapter now on the Prose works (with a little about the Canzoniere) to complete the book, which is a very good pennyworth, so far as labour goes.   I will slip over the prose as lightly as possible: with a bad cold, and a considerable degree of unwellness otherwise, and various domestic cares, the Convito, &c., are far from easy reading—and this east wind! . . .

In June of this year Mrs Oliphant celebrated the twenty - fifth anniversary of her connection with 'Maga.'   Mr John Blackwood was, of course, the guest of the day; but there were many notable and interesting people present, few indeed of whom now survive.

To Mr Blackwood.   WINDSOR, *June.*
The day I had decided on for my party was the 16th [of June], that being Saturday and the most convenient day; but the 19th or 23rd would do equally well.   Pray, as you will be the special guest, choose which you prefer, and let me know: if you would send me word by return of post it would be kind, as I must ask my people, and had forgotten how time is running on.
I propose to hold the solemnity at Magna Charta, a charming little house on the banks of the river which a friend of mine sometimes lends me.

From A. W. Kinglake to Mrs Oliphant.
                    28 HYDE PARK PLACE, MARBLE ARCH, W.,
                              June 20, 1877.
DEAR MRS OLIPHANT,—Your *fête* of yesterday was a charming one, and for once a fulfilment of what one imagined it *might* be if all should go well.   You reigned

so brightly over your guests that everybody seemed
pleased.

And this morning I receive the Dante. I had
learnt accidentally from Mr Langford that you had
kindly directed that a copy of the volume should be
sent me, and am greatly pleased.

But there is yet another blessing that yesterday
brought me. When I came back to London last
evening, I went to one of my clubs to have some tea,
and look — with but little hope — for a novel really
attractive to me after having finished 'Mrs Arthur,'
and then — a happy surprise, for I had never been
prepared for it by any advertisement—I found awaiting me 'Carità'! As far as I have gone I like it
immensely.

With my kind regards to your guest (Miss Blackwood) and to your sons—both such nice young fellows
—believe me, dear Mrs Oliphant, very truly yours,

A. W. KINGLAKE.

To Mr Frank Wilson.   WINDSOR, *20th July.*

. . . Don't suppose for a moment (I am answering
your last letter, which perhaps you have forgotten all
about by this time) that we think, from our experience, Anglo-Indians to be bores. Your letters would
be interesting even if everything about you was not
so interesting as it is at home. I find your letters
always *you*, which is the very best thing letters can
be. At the same time, I can understand the temptation of getting gossipy and grumbly among yourselves.
But it really is the same everywhere. All society is
made up of small circles, and talks its own special
small - talk. I at least have never found yet the
bigger kind that some people talk grand about ; and
yours, though it may be flat to you, is piquant and
strange to us. . . .

Tids is by way of working tolerably hard. He also
does a tolerable amount of cricket, and it is very
pleasant to have him at home. You say I used to

say you had no energy: I suppose we elder people are inclined to think so with all boys. I can only hope Tiddy will take heart o' grace as you have done as soon as he gets real work in hand, though I don't think (this in my own defence!) that I said you were without energy the last year or two before you went away.

Cecco's first "summer examination" is just coming on, and I am rather anxious about it. He will be dreadfully disappointed if he does not get into sixth form next half, and that of course depends entirely on the number of boys who leave. . . . The children go away next Saturday, the 28th, and we follow a week later; so that the summer, we may calculate, is now about over. And it has been, on the whole, a coldish one, though with breaks of hot weather.

To Miss Walker.　　　　　　　　　　　St Andrews.

. . . I am deep in De Quincey, on whom I am doing a paper. Please do the proof as soon as you possibly can. The boys are very busy, as you may suppose, what with work (of which a little does get done), golf, and lawn-tennis. Tids especially is much in request, as it seems he is really a very good lawn-tennis player. Cecco seems going into literature in a funny kind of subterranean way. He showed me a rather impassioned speech out of a tragedy, which he seems to be doing in fragments, and I came upon a bit of a story the other day in his beautiful hand-writing, neither of them bad at all.

St Andrews.

. . . Did I tell you that the boys were getting up a ball—a bachelors' ball (save the mark! Cecco being one of the bachelors). You will hear all about it from Cecco. We have been hearing the Principal preach this morning, a fine, eloquent, striking, inconclusive sermon, preached with a good deal of emotion. He must take a great deal out of himself in preaching.

To Mr Frank Wilson.   St Andrews, *Sept. 25th.*

. . . I am very glad to have had so many more of your letters lately, though sorry to see that you have had an attack of fever. . . .

I should like very much to have some photograph of your works. Couldn't you make the man do your house and surroundings? I should so very much like to know your scenery, so to speak, and be able to picture you and the things and people about you to myself.

WINDSOR, *12th October.*

. . . Here we are at home again, and a great contrast it is to St Andrews. The trees in the Crescent are growing so tall and so thick that there seems no sky at all after the great vault that is over the Links, and which every year I continue making the most futile attempts to draw. " Your hills, mamma," the boys said derisively as we went past Leuchars. I wish that you, who can draw, would only be as persevering. If you would do a little scratch from your window at your various " cholsies " (isn't that the word?) it would be such a pleasure to me, and help me to realise your surroundings, which it is so very difficult to do,—do, there's a good boy. . . .

I suspect that what you say about having lost or not sufficiently used your time at Cooper's Hill is what every one feels when formal education is over. But education never stops, and perhaps if we did not always feel " how much more I might have done," we would be intolerable prigs or cease to be human creatures at all. I feel as if I were only beginning to get into the heart of work and see what may be made of it now, and the mere learning of that will have cost, no doubt, on the other side, perhaps more than it is worth—limitations and formalities and want of spontaneousness. I can perfectly understand your interest in *mile 10.* I have always thought that to *make,* to bring order and meaning and use out of nothing, must be the most delightful sensation in the world.   My first hero was to have built a light-house. . . .

To Mr Blackwood.   WINDSOR, 16*th November*.

. . . This is Cyril's twenty-first birthday, a great family event.   We are to keep it to-morrow, when he is coming home with two nights' leave, graciously granted by the Master.   How these children spring out of nothing!   Jack will be following his example in a month or two; but Jack has more to come of age for than my poor Tids, who is "lord of his presence and no land beside."   He is a very good sweet-hearted boy, and very tender to me, but I can't help feeling doubtful whether he has enough of the sterner stuff in him to get success in those thorny ways of law (not to say life) which he is bound for.   I am going to enter him directly at the Inner Temple.   If all these boys of ours had but ten thousand a-year what delightful fellows they would be!   I fear that is what our modern education trains them for, more than anything else.

To F. R. Oliphant (when at Oxford for his matriculation).

WINDSOR, *November* 24.

MY DEAREST CECCO,—You can't think how miserable and empty the house looks, and how hard it is to realise that you are not coming in late or early. I don't at all like this first experiment in loneliness. When you are both at Oxford I shall either have to go there too or hang myself, which latter experiment would be uncomfortable.   I hope I may hear from you to-morrow how you have got on these two days. I am anxious to know all about it, and I hope you will be more explicit in your descriptions than Tids is; indeed, I trust you will adopt rather the Frankian than the Tiddy-ish style of literature, for though a clever and entertaining letter is very nice, it is better to know really what you are about day by day, respecting which Mr Tids leaves one much in the dark. I hope you have been getting a little pleasure out of your first flight from home as well as doing well in the examination. Was the Master gracious to you?

If you have not written to-day be sure you do so to-morrow, and make Tiddy also do so. I want to hear all about you both to keep me going, which otherwise would be dismal work. I don't know that anything has been going on since you went away, except the dinner-party at the Ritchies' which I told Tids about. Captain Maurice, who is a neighbour of ours now in Park Street, and who went with us, is rather an acquisition. He is the author of one of the clever military essays, the one (if you remember the story) that was pitched in at Colonel Hamley's door (he being the judge) just as the clock was striking the very limits of the hour allowed for "showing up" (*à la* Tiddy), and which got the first prize.

I wonder what you two will do with yourselves to-morrow. I trust it will not be a hopeless day like this. God bless you, my dearest boy, and my Tids too. Be sure you both write.—Your loving mother,

M. O. W. O.

The next letter is addressed to Mrs Richmond Ritchie, who had only very recently ceased to be Miss Thackeray.

To Mrs Richmond Ritchie.　　　　　　　　*14th December.*

Here is your autograph, my dear Annie. I have never done such a thing for anybody before, but I am delighted to have a word from you (even though you have so cunningly disguised your new initials that I protest I don't know what the last one is!) and to hear something about you. *My* holidays have begun

—that is, I have got Cyril home, and Cecco's labours will soon be over, and that, you know, is my special argument for happiness. We must manage to get up to town early in the year, and get a glimpse of you among other pleasant things. I am glad the darkest of the dark winter days is over for you, dear, and that you have now support and solace by your side to counteract all the heaviness of recollection.

The new will never quite push out the old, but happiness is certainly the one elixir of life.

We have been having Mr Ruskin here again havering in his usual celestial way, and we are planning theatricals with Mrs Cornish in the part of Portia, which I think is altogether suitable to her. Won't you come and see her? I am busy as usual spinning continual webs that never come to much. I am very glad to see that you have begun again. I always feel you to be of the party with your pretty Felicias, and keep looking for you round the corner of every sentence.

God bless you, my dear, in all ways. I suppose I may, notwithstanding his dignified position as the head of a house, send my love to Richmond.

To Mr Frank Wilson. WINDSOR, 28*th December.*

I have not written to you now for two or three mails, and here we are in the midst of the holidays, Christmas over, and the end of the year close at hand. I have been a little gloomy in myself, thinking how noiselessly and certainly these passing year bring one towards the end; but I need not trouble you with these fancies, which I hope will not come to anything except passing clouds, which at my age are rather desirable than otherwise, for it does not seem a good thing to get too much into the habit of living, as one is tempted to do, more as one gets old than when one is young. Christmas will be entirely out of everybody's thoughts and 1878 well begun before you get this, so I need not say very much about it, but wish you a very happy year, my dear boy, and a good one. . . .

What a comfort, my dear Frank, that you have found the career that suits you, and are doing well in it and liking it. Nothing gives me so much consolation.

1878.

To Mr Frank Wilson.   WINDSOR, 18*th January.*

. . . Last week we were in London, which was the cause of failure in writing then, where we have spent a week. It is the time of theatres, as you know, and we went at that branch of pleasuring systematically, going to four plays, one the most idiotic performance I ever saw. Our stay in town, however, was distinguished this time by a perfectly novel feature. I told you of an old Mrs Stewart, a wonderful old lady of seventy-four, who has twice paid us a visit here. We got lodgings through her means close to her house, and she had a succession of luncheon-parties for my gratification and exhibition. The lionising process, you know, is not one that I encourage. I saw, however, a good many people, and I suppose even where there is the least possible enjoyment in it that is more or less an advantage. . . .

Dr Bridge gave us a rather peculiar performance at the Abbey one of the evenings we were in town. We dined with him at his quaint little house in the cloisters, and after dinner went into the choir, while he played to us. The Abbey was all dark except the light in the organ-loft and a solitary lantern, and the effect was very fine. He played an old " Ave Maria," and made great use of the stop which is called the *vox humana.* It was most dramatic and picturesque, the organ sounding exactly like the singing of monks far off in an unseen chapel. He took us afterwards about the church with a lantern; and to look down from a high chantry, down the long nave, with only the light from the organ-loft in the centre to show it, was very wonderful.

Now we are back again at home, to my great satisfaction. I know nothing more fatiguing than what is called pleasure, and longed for my work.

To Mr Blackwood.   WINDSOR, *27th January.*

. . . I think the Principal's little book admirable. The Goethe is very good, but I have taken the liberty to ask Mr Hayward (with trembling) to remember that we address a public which is not expected to understand allusions, but must have everything explained to it. He sent me, the other day, that potent, grave, and reverend signior, a little volume of society verses, the lightest of airy trifles, compliments, and gallantries. It took away my breath.

I should like very much to have ‘ Marmorne,’ please. Mr Pigott, the licenser of plays, was speaking to me about it the other day with the greatest enthusiasm. He says he has not seen anything so pretty for a long time, and asked me anxiously who was the author. I promised to ask you, though I told him I did not hope to get any information from you!

To Mr W. Blackwood.   WINDSOR, *14th April.*

. . . I hope to be able to get the ‘ Molière ’ done, but I am at present kept back from everything and kept in great anxiety by the illness of Cecco, who has got gastric fever, and who fully occupies all my time and thoughts. It is not as yet a very severe case, the doctor assures me; but it is always a very anxious business, and as I am painfully anxious by nature, you may imagine that my mind is not very free for work. He was taken ill on the 4th, on the day before the beginning of an examination for which, poor boy, he had been working so hard, but he has been too ill to feel this disappointment. Would you tell your aunt Isabella this when you see her?   I ought to have written to her, but cannot.

Cecco had been for some months working hard for the Newcastle Scholarship, to be even in the "select" for which is one of the greatest honours attainable by an Etonian. The night before the examination day he came home late from his tutor's, where he had been doing some final work in preparation. He was ill, but declared he would be all right next day. In the morning, however, the fever had declared itself, and for the following thirteen days he was very ill. Through this time and the early days of convalescence his mother nursed him unremittingly, leaving him only for the two hours after midnight, when she lay down, allowing "cousin Annie" to take her place. And she worked as well as nursed!

To Mr Blackwood.   WINDSOR, *17th April.*
I am very happy to tell you that Cecco is now on the way to recovery, the fever having subsided on Thursday—in thirteen days instead of the three, four, or even six weeks with which we were threatened. The relief, I need not say, is unspeakable. I shall hope to be able to get him away to the seaside in a week or ten days. After that, if he recovers his strength, we may or may not cross the Channel; in any case I will send you a paper for the June number.

Chez M. Develle, près du Casino Rosendael,
DUNKERQUE, *14th August.*
. . . We have got settled down in the sand here, and live roughly in a way which we should think very disagreeable indeed at home. I confess I don't much admire it here, but nothing better can be had. It is a very fine sea, and at the present moment much

ruffled and out of temper, and looking its best in consequence.

I have just had a little run in Bruges and Ghent. How delightful they are! One forgets the stateliness and old-world grace of them, so homely and kindly too. Please tell Mrs Blackwood that I was tempted and fell in the way of lace—old lace—and if she ever goes to the Béguinage, when they show her the commonplace productions of to-day, let her ask for a certain box of old lace which is kept in reserve. I wish I had *not* seen it, but she ought to see it. There is nothing so costly as bargains, and there are *such* bargains to be had ! Pardon an outburst of enthusiasm.

WINDSOR, 3*rd October.*

. . . I am planning to go to Oxford for six months or so in January if I can let my house here, which I hope to do. Cyril and Cecco will both be at Balliol, and I see no good in staying here when both the bits of my heart will be in another place.

I have been thinking of preparing the " Beleaguered City " in two parts, as it wants carrying out, leaving the supernatural portion for the January number. I almost fear, however, that you will not care for another story, now that you have commenced the " New Ordeal " (how capital it is !). Will you kindly tell me about this, whether you would have room for it or not ? as it seems to be specially suitable to the time of the year.

WINDSOR, 9*th October.*

. . . I think very highly of Daudet as a novelist, but I know nothing of him personally. Unfortunately for me, neither did I of Balzac, which has made Mr Reeve gum on a reminiscence of his to a paper of mine (which you would not have), and which I suppose will be in the ' Edinburgh ' next number — to my great discomfiture.

WINDSOR, *4th December*.

I am sending you, after all, the " Beleaguered City."
It is not quite enough for a volume, and perhaps it is
too much for two numbers of the Magazine. As I
think, however, that it is worth something, I send it
to you. If you like it for the Magazine, it might come
in very well for the "Tales" afterwards. It is very
much enlarged and altered, you will perceive. I have
wasted a good deal of time upon it, which is foolish,
but the subject struck my fancy.

The Principal [Tulloch] preached a noble sermon
in Westminster on Saturday. I never heard anything finer. The place was crowded, a great many
people standing ; and the nave of the Abbey lighted
up and filled with people, with all the misty distances
of the aisles, and mystery of the lofty roof overhead,
is a sight to see. The Principal had the sense, however, to leave the mist and mystery in the beautiful
arches above him, and himself struck the most clear
note of Christian sentiment and faith which I have
almost ever heard from him. I was considerably
nervous about the business altogether, not to say
highly antagonistic, but nothing could have been
finer.

1879.

To Mr Frank Wilson.   CRICK ROAD, OXFORD, *20th Feb.*

. . . I came here more than a fortnight ago. I
say I, for the boys had gone before me. It was
excessively cold at the time, the end of the frost,
and since it has been very wet and muddy. Unfortunately the house is a good way out of the centre
of Oxford, as far off as Windsor is from Eton, which
is much against us. On the other hand, it is pleasantly situated and among a great many pleasant
people. Many of the great persons of Oxford have
already called on me, and I have been asked to

several solemn dinners, to one of which I am going to-night and to another to-morrow. The people are all very civil, but I am sometimes doubtful whether I have been wise in coming. Cecco seems to have begun very well indeed. It is difficult to realise him as a Balliol man, but such he is, and has taken to smoking, which I never thought he would do, and talks about "other men" as if he had not been the baby a very little while ago. He has a good many friends, and seems to be quite cheery and happy, which is a great satisfaction to me, for I was always a little nervous about his start. . . .

Since I wrote the above I have been out to a dinner-party where all the people were profoundly learned and clever; the chief guest (after myself, in whose honour the party was given) being the rector of Lincoln, a man who is supposed to be the Casaubon of 'Middlemarch'—at least I believe his wife considers herself the model of Dorothea. He is a curious wizened little man, but a great light, I believe. He wrote a life of the great scholar Isaac Casaubon, which I reviewed some years ago, but this of course the good man does not know. I am going out again to dinner to-night. We leave here in about a month, and will return somewhere about the 18th of April.

To Mr Blackwood.   4 CRICK ROAD, OXFORD, *Feb.* 28.

I ought to have written last month to thank you and your able contributor for the flattering mention made of me in the article on Magazines, but the coming here complicated my other businesses, and I did not even read the article till somewhat late in the month. I am now again overwhelmed by Mr Shand's (is it Mr Shand?) civilities in the present number. It is very kind of him, and of you, to whose good word I am sure I am indebted for so honourable a place. My best thanks to both. It is very pleasant, especially when one's life has not been exempt from snubs, to have so kind and generous a recognition of one's efforts — not to say that it is always a feather in one's cap to appear as a member of that goodly fellowship, that noble army, which fights under the banners of 'Maga.'

Your contributor seems to know various secrets of the craft which I have not found out. I suppose Mr Trollope and Mr Reade are deeply learned in all those by-ways, colonial and otherwise, which a poor woman out of the way never hears of. I have had various colonial applications made to me, but they never came to anything.

I have been thinking lately of asking you whether you would mind introducing me to Lord Salisbury with the view of asking him for a Foreign Office nomination for one of my boys. As they are now both in the last stage of their education, and Tids will be done with his in June, the question grows more and more important. The Bar of course is the finest career of all *when* successful, and if Tids takes a *very* good degree it will encourage me to screw myself up for barrister's fees, and the legal education which has yet to come; but it is a horribly long process, and as there are two of them to provide for I should be very glad to have a public office nomination to fall back upon. Would this be asking too much of you? There seems no chance of getting at a Minister without introductions. Lord Salisbury's sons were in Mr Marindin's house along with my boys, and I suppose he will know my name. I do not care to ask a mere society acquaintance for such an introduction, but no doubt I could get it, if you don't care to do it.

To Mr Blackwood.   OXFORD, *16th March.*

. . . I am glad you like the " Hamlet " paper, proof of which shall be returned directly. I will say a word or two about Irving's unquestionable power over his audience. There is nothing so strange as popular success. I begin to think that it is only when one

gives oneself credit for doing a thing with great difficulty and labour that one gets due credit with the
public, and that what is apparently done with ease
is never so impressive, even where it may be really
better.

I have been seeing a great many notabilities here,
without, I am afraid, being very much impressed by
them. Almost everybody who is anybody has called,
I think; but intellectualism, like every other *ism*, is
monotonous, and the timidity and mutual alarm of
the younger potentates strikes me a good deal. They
are so much afraid of committing themselves or risk-
ing anything that may be found wanting in any
minutiæ of correctness. Scholarship is a sort of
poison tree, and kills everything.

To Mr Frank Wilson. OXFORD, 20*th March.*

. . . The term at Oxford is just finishing, and we
go home next week I can't say that I have much
enjoyed being here. There has been a good deal
of bad weather, and in bad weather Oxford is depressing to the last degree. Now spring is beginning very
unwillingly with many relapses into winter, but I hope
next term will be pleasant. . . . Everybody at Oxford
of any importance, or almost everybody, has called on
me, and I have been asked to a good many dinner-
parties, to which I have gone resignedly. My last
was at the Max Müllers to meet our old friend Mr
Ralston, whom you will remember. He came here
to tell stories, which has become his speciality. He
does it very well, and is very amusing. He had a
large audience in a sort of theatre connected with
the Museum here---heaps of children, whose attention and awe and amusement were very funny and a
very pretty sight. He is as long and as thin as
ever; but though he is always having bad illnesses,
he looks much better than he used to do. . . .

Cecco gave us a luncheon to-day at Balliol. Cecco
as a man continues to be a constant wonder and

amusement to me. His set is entirely distinct from Tiddy's.

To Miss Blackwood.   WINDSOR, 11*th April.*

. . . We came home about a fortnight ago, and in a week more will be back in Oxford if all is well, the vacation being so short. A great many people called on me; in short, everybody was very kind, and I got a great deal of attention. I rather think I was set up as the proper novelist in opposition to Miss Broughton, who has gone to live at Oxford and has much fluttered the dove‑cotes, though I don't exactly know how. Cecco was all the more comfortable in his beginning from having his home at hand, and has got thoroughly into the Oxford life, which is a great comfort to me, and I think Tids' work too was all the better for his mother's presence. The latter personage has his final examinations next term, which is a very anxious business. They all seem to expect him to do well. He is just now at Malvern on a visit to the Master of Balliol, who seems to have a very peculiar opinion of the meaning of the word holiday. He and his guests work all day with brief intervals for meals and walks. Tids regarded the prospect of this visit before he went with rueful gratification, but he does not seem to dislike it, being there, and I hope it will have done him good. Mr Jowett has been on the whole very kind. . . .

In the autumn of this year Mrs Oliphant lost her faithful and warmly valued friend Mr John Blackwood. He had been for a considerable time in failing health, and died at his house, Strathtyrum, near St Andrews, at the end of October 1879.

To Miss Blackwood.　　　　　　　　　OXFORD, *3rd Nov.*

MY DEAR ISABELLA,—So it is all over—all your anxiety and trouble, and dear John's suffering and patience. I felt that you were prepared for it, and that, notwithstanding the hope to which you clung, this was all that was to be looked for. What can we say but thank God that for him at least it is all over? We none of us can look forward to that passage with less than some pang of fear as to how we shall get through, and he has passed it safely and got over upon the other side. Amen. And thank God for him. . . .

In the meantime, dear Isabella, God be with you! Try to take what comfort you can in the thought that he at least, dear John—I can't call him anything else this sad day—is no longer in any pain or trouble. —With love from the boys, and the tenderest sympathy, affectionately yours.

November 4.

I have just got your letter. Very hurriedly I wrote to you yesterday, and was interrupted at the conclusion and obliged to end when I had much to say. I wish so much you had added the one word "Come" to your telegram. I would so gladly have gone to you; but knowing how deep your feeling would be, I could not convince myself that you would like any one with you but your very own, otherwise it would have been a comfort to me to be there. The flowers, a very beautiful wreath, were sent off on Saturday, directed 11 Charlotte Square. I hope they did reach in time; if not, and they still come, may they be laid upon the grave? I shall be sadly disappointed if nothing of me, not even my wreath, was there. I told you we had a little service in St Stephen's at two o'clock, and followed him in spirit with prayers for you all to that last resting-place. How grieved I am that I was not bold enough to go to you at once. I do not like to ask now what you are going to do.   Remember that you will always be welcome here. . . .

I am glad to think that dear John Blackwood was laid to his rest by his own chosen friends.   Every one of us, present and absent, feel what we have lost in him.   Thinking about my book on Cervantes the other day, I felt suddenly as if I had come to a dead stop.   Who is there now for whose opinion one will care as one did for his?

To Mr Craik.   WINDSOR, *December* 8.

I am most grieved to be so negligent.   For the last fortnight I have been, first in the most terrible anxiety and then in the deepest grief for my dear boy Frank Wilson, my nephew whom I brought up, and who died in India now five weeks ago of typhoid fever.   I had trained him with pain and trouble, and sent him out to India with every hope and blessing four years ago, and here is the end, so far as this sad world is concerned.   We were for a week waiting an answer to a telegram which never came — in an anxiety I cannot describe, and which ended on the 29th in an official announcement of his death.

This is my only excuse for the neglect.   The proofs came, I suppose, in the midst of this terrible suspense. I will get them off as soon as I possibly can.

To Mrs Craik.   WINDSOR, *Christmas Eve.*

It is very kind of you to write to me.   I have had a long spell of peace and quiet, all well with my children, which is the one thing that matters after all.   And of all the family my boy Frank was the one I was most secure about and had least anxiety for. All seemed so well with him, he was so robust and vigorous, nothing wrong about him either real or fanciful.   And now in a moment all is over—for this world.   It is the most inscrutable blow.   Thank you most warmly for your sympathy.   It is good to have an old friend to think of one in one's trouble.   We have seen little of each other for many years, but we will not forget how long it is since .we first joined hands, young and fresh to life. God keep your doors, dear friend, from the shadow that has so often darkened mine, and give you many happy years with those you love. I have my three orphan nieces, now deprived of the last prop that absolutely belonged to them, under my roof this Christmas. The children, thank God, always make shift to be happy, by times at least, even in the midst of trouble, but you will give a pitying thought I am sure to these three poor girls.

My best and warmest wishes for yourself, Mr Craik, and your child, and with love and thanks, believe me.

To Mr W. Blackwood.   WINDSOR, *Christmas Eve.*

I had not the heart to enter upon business matters when I saw you, the shadow of death was so much about us, and my own heart so full of anxiety. . . .

After all this long array of business it seems out of place to return to private friendship and good wishes. But at the same time these are never out of place, and I hope that under your reign, as under that of dear and kind John Blackwood, private and old friendship will always continue to sweeten our business transactions. Will you give your mother and sisters my kindest good wishes and greetings? —" Merry Christmas " is out of my way this dark and heavy year, but I wish you every blessing and prosperity.

1880.

Mrs Oliphant's Autobiography was broken off— as a connected narrative—at about the time when Cyril left Oxford. That he should have taken only a second-class was a disappointment to her, but yet, as she herself says, in no way a disgrace, and she was very hopeful of his future. He was to live at home and read for the Bar. Cecco had apparently taken to Oxford life with a certain amount of enjoyment. He was naturally a student, though perhaps not after the academic model, and there was no occasion for anxiety about him. A great grief fell on the household in the autumn of 1879, when Frank Wilson, the nephew whom Mrs Oliphant had educated with her own sons, died in India. He had been always a most satisfactory and delightful young fellow, full of talent and energy, and succeeding in whatever he undertook, so that the dreadful news of his death after only a few days of fever seemed almost incredible. Except for this sorrow and the void left by the loss of her old and faithful friend Mr John Blackwood, the time was one of peace, and the cheerful house at Windsor was brightened as usual by the comings and goings of visitors. Cyril went to town to work in the chambers of a barrister, and when he was at home his mother tried to keep him to his books, much as she had done when he was a very little boy, but with less success. Still she was happy in having him at home, and bore the tremendous burden of her own work with a light heart.

To Mr Craik.   Lowick Rectory, Thrapston, *25th Aug.*
. . Did you happen to see a story of mine called "A Beleaguered City" which was published last Christmas in the 'New Quarterly Magazine'? It is a story which I like—a thing that does not always happen with my own productions—and I should like to republish it. It would make, I think, only a *very* small volume, but I might add a short

new story of a similar description to make up. Would you care to undertake the republication? I have a fancy of making a kind of Christmas present of it to my unknown friends. I should like it to come out exactly at Christmas, and to be published quite cheaply, as an experiment. Please let me know what you think. I *fancy* it would interest *you*.

We hope to be in Golf Place, St Andrews, this day week, and perhaps you will reply to this there.

At the end of this summer Mrs Oliphant did what she could very rarely be persuaded to do—she paid one or two visits. The first was to Mr and Mrs Lucas Collins at Lowick Rectory; and while there she heard a legendary story of the neighbouring old house of the Sackvilles which by‑and‑by shaped itself in her mind into "The Lady's Walk." It is curious how constantly some real scene or incident gave birth to one of her stories, and yet how *very* rarely any real person appears on her pages. People often thought they found their own portraits in her books, an imagination which only goes to show how very little we know ourselves or how others see us. From Lowick Mrs Oliphant went on with her sons to visit Mr Woodall, M.P., at Burslem. She was much interested in the work of the Potteries—the "throwers" with their immemorial "potter's wheel" especially; but what makes this visit really remarkable in her life is the fact that for a whole week she laid aside her work! Never before, and never afterwards until the illnesses of her last year forced it upon her, did she take such a spell of idleness, and she gave herself up to the enjoyment of it with the zest that belongs to novelty.

From Staffordshire she went to Wales, and spent two or three weeks at Barmouth. The following letter refers to the great anxiety felt with regard to the fate of George Blackwood, brother of the Editor, and son of her first friend in the family, Major Blackwood.

To Mr W. Blackwood.   BARMOUTH, *Septr.* 9.

I send you now the final proofs of 'Cervantes.' I am very glad it is not too long.

I have been looking to see if any further news had come—with much anxiety. I can most truly enter into the long and painful endurance of your suspense, and I feel most deeply for *you* personally with so much work and so many anxieties on your head. I know well how every care is doubled by anxiety and grief.

14 VICTORIA SQUARE, GROSVENOR GARDENS, S.W.,
22nd September.

. . . I read with sad interest the references to your brother's[1] battery in the 'Times' this morning. If indeed he fell among his men so, it was a soldier's death, and one to call forth more envy than pity. "Here where men sit and hear each other moan" it is fine to think of a career so bravely accomplished.

The following letters explain themselves. The business caused Mrs Oliphant the most intense annoyance, and destroyed the pleasure of her short residence in town.

14 VICTORIA SQUARE, S.W., *Octr.* 4.

. . . I am greatly annoyed just now about a most arbitrary and unjustifiable proceeding on the part of the proprietors of the 'Graphic,' for whom I wrote a Life of the Queen some time ago. It was written

---

[1] Killed at Maiwand.

exclusively for the paper, and no idea of any further use was in my mind. I was horrified the other day to see it advertised in book form by Messrs Low. I immediately remonstrated, but was met by a copy of my receipt, in which I had, it appears, given the "entire copyright" to the 'Graphic.' I suppose I had never read the receipt at all when I signed it, and certainly no idea of republication had ever been suggested. I don't know what may come of it. I have asked Sir James Stephen to give me his opinion, which perhaps, as he is a judge, he may not like to do, but I shall certainly take legal advice upon the subject. I hope you will take my part in the matter. The thing was written with the idea of being a mere accompaniment to very good illustrations—in which point the 'Graphic' people broke their contract with me, to begin with—and is quite unfit to be published as a book. I am unspeakably annoyed about it, all the more that it was not even a profitable bit of work.

14 VICTORIA SQUARE, S.W., *22nd October.*

. . . I am in a great fright about the law business. I hoped the solicitor, who is a very moderate and sober person, and was greatly against proceeding to extremities, would have managed a compromise. This is still possible, but only by a sacrifice on my part—buying back the copyright, which I never had the slightest intention of selling. I have been entrapped by a supplementary receipt, which I suppose I signed without reading it. I am in great trouble about it. Harper's new proceeding is indefensible, I think, considering the line they have taken in the copyright question. I should like to write an article upon their circular which was sent to authors — I don't know if you ever saw it — saying that they were most anxious to favour *us*, but were determined to prevent English publishers from flooding the American market, which was their reason for standing out against our improved copyright.

14 Victoria Square, S.W., *Nov.* 3.

. . . I have been obliged to pay the 'Graphic' people thirty pounds to redeem the Queen's Life. I hear that some friends of mine are trying to represent that it is a shabby proceeding to take money from me, with some hopes of getting it back.

In the midst of her own troubles and anxieties she was never deaf to an appeal for help. The following refers to a piece of work which was her present to a less successful literary woman—a piece of work done too while her son Cecco was ill with a second attack of typhoid fever, and being nursed devotedly by her. His illness was, it is true, of a mild type, but she could never be less than acutely anxious.

To Mrs Richmond Ritchie.   14 Victoria Square.

Dearest Annie,—Mrs Craik writes to say that her name may go along with ours, and that she will send something if I can tell her the last possible day, as she is going to France to-day, and has nothing by her. Will you find out, dear, from Mrs Riddell, what time she must have the things? (It sounds like things for the wash!) I have done part of mine.

To Mrs Craik.   14 Victoria Square, *24th Nov.*

I have just been explaining sundry delays to Mr Craik by telling him about my Cecco's illness. He had been very queer and unwell some time, and on calling in the doctor at last a day or two after I saw Mr Craik, the boy was pronounced to have been struggling with an attack of typhoid for some time. It has turned out quite a mild case, and he is now getting better; but for a little while I was very anxious, and have been kept in constant attendance upon him all this time. The very name of course

brings one's heart to one's mouth. The grievous
thing is that he was just going in for " Mods," which
was of the utmost importance to him, and for which
he had been working hard. Alas! the examination
began yesterday, and here he is in bed tearing his
hair.

The very same thing happened to him once at
Eton.

I am very sorry to think I shall not see you, but
hope you will have less shutting up this winter than
you anticipate. Are you not tempted in such a case
to run away to the south ? After a month or two in
London I prize the sunshine more than ever.

To Mr Craik.   WINDSOR, *24th December.*

I don't know whether the ' Beleaguered City ' is
to be out immediately or not, but when it comes, I
should like to have a liberal supply of copies, for
which I must be charged if I ask too many.   I
have wanted to make a kind of present of it to my
unknown friends, as you will see by the dedication,
and there are a great many known friends to whom,
as about the best I can do, I want to give the book
itself. . . .

This is where men have such a huge advantage
over us, that they have generally something besides
their writing to fall back upon for mere bread and
butter. I think if I had enough of steady income
to justify me in getting a small house in town, I
should be thankful—but at least for the steady income I should be thankful anyhow. . . .

Oh, what a sad Christmas!—everybody mourning,
everybody fearing. I know two families who have
lost sons at this miserable Cabul. I take a little
comfort in thinking that my boy died in bringing
good and comfort to the district where he was in
India and not blood.

I am going to write a word for Christmas to your
dear kind wife. This will wait you at Bedford

Street till you go back to business again.   In the meantime may every good thing attend you at this season and all seasons.

To Mr W. Blackwood.   Windsor, *26th December.*
. . . Christmas is just over with all its many memories, and I am glad of it.   It will not have been very merry for you, and it is the worst of such anniversaries that they bring so strongly before us the consciousness of every empty place.   Accept my best wishes for the new year on which we are so soon to enter, and give my kindest messages to your mother and sisters.   I trust Mrs Blackwood, surrounded as she is with the devotion of the good children who remain to her, is strengthened to bear the griefs of which I know she has had no small share.   And let me congratulate you, on the other hand, on having got so bravely and prosperously through the first year of your great responsibility. It does not seem to me that the Magazine has suffered in the least, and that is a very great deal to say, and must give all concerned great confidence for the future. . . .

It seems to me while I write that probably you will be in London for George Eliot's funeral.   How sad it is! . . .   There is something very solemn in the thought of a great spirit like hers entering the spiritual world which she did not believe in.   If we are right in our faith, what a blessed surprise to her!

1881.

The following letter to Mr Craik is interesting, as expressing certain very strongly held opinions about what are called society papers.   Messrs Macmillan had some thoughts of publishing a weekly paper, with Mrs Oliphant as editor.

To Mr Craik.   WINDSOR, *January* 29.

I wonder how it would answer if a (I do not say *the*) projected new paper were got to be somehow under the patronage of the Queen? The idea has just shot across my mind, and I don't know if anything could be made of it, or if even that patronage could be secured. But I am sure her Majesty must feel (as she is one of the chief sufferers) the iniquity of these society papers which we would essay to combat on their own ground.

I should like very much to attempt some social sketches of an impersonal kind in the style (*con respetto parlando*) of the 'Spectator,' by which one might do all (I think) that the gossip papers pretend to do, without the gossip. How I might succeed is another question, but I should like to try.

And, I think, that a sort of creaming of the foreign press might be done, so as to give the public the chance of seeing what different parties say abroad of themselves, which is what it is most difficult for dwellers at home to know.

There are a great many other matters which would enter into the constitution of such a paper, or weekly magazine as you suggest, if you are really going to entertain the idea, which it would be a pleasure to work out in detail. I must say, however, that I don't think my name would be half so much good to it as that of your own firm. With the name of Macmillan to it as publisher the public would be sufficiently assured that it was neither to be scandalous nor impertinent. I see great capabilities in the social way, while entirely rejecting the vulgar aid of personality: the uses of fiction have not yet been half exhausted, and its legitimate licence is large.

This scheme seems to have been entirely abandoned, and Mrs Oliphant's next work for Messrs Macmillan was the 'Makers of Venice,'—a book which, however laborious it was in actual execution, gave her infinite pleasure in the collecting of materials.

To Mr W. Blackwood.

27 WELLINGTON SQUARE, OXFORD, 1*st March.*

. . . I am having a great pleasure to look forward to. I am going to Venice to prepare for a companion volume to the Florence one. I have just arranged about it, and will start in about a month, for a month's stay in that city of enchantment.

I congratulate you heartily on the prosperity of 'Maga.' You know I have borne a most delighted testimony all along to the way in which you were keeping up the old standard. It is a great pleasure to see it and no small triumph.

Mrs Ritchie's book will be delightful, and is sure to have a great sale. It is not only Madame de Sévigné, but it is thoroughly Sévigné-ish.

About the 1st of April Mrs Oliphant started for Venice, taking with her her younger son and the cousin who has been frequently mentioned. A little group of acquaintances gathered about her on her arrival, among whom were Mr Henry James, the novelist, and Mr Holmes, the Queen's librarian, who had undertaken to make drawings for the illustration of the book. There was also a sister of Mrs Oliphant's neighbour, Mrs Macdonald, with a son and daughter. The whole group often met in the evenings at Florian's, and some of them were frequently together in the afternoons. The weather was not very kind, but there were a good many fine days, and most delightful expeditions were made in search of notable or interesting spots. After staying for a time at the hotel the little party moved into lodgings on the

Riva dei Schiavoni, and had an entirely new and amusing experience. After a fortnight, it must be confessed, they were glad to return to more sophisticated ways of life but the whole time was full of charm and interest. They moved on from Venice to Verona, Florence, and Paris, staying a day or two at each, and reached England early in May.

To Mr W. Blackwood.　　　　WINDSOR, 17*th May.*

Laurence Oliphant and his wife are with me to-day. He tells me he is about to begin something in the Magazine, which I am very glad to hear. She is a very charming young woman. She has taken a little house in this neighbourhood, where she is going to stay till he comes back from America.

It was always a subject of regret to Mrs Oliphant's friends that there was no good likeness of her. She photographed very badly, and indeed only colour could have shown the beauty of her eyes and complexion. But she would never have herself painted, and the drawing alluded to in the following letters was the first ever made of her.

To Mr W. Blackwood.　　　　WINDSOR, 15*th July.*

. . . I am dreadfully sorry not to send to you the next number of the Autobiographies with this. I thought I would send you a short paper on Gibbon. It is half done, but I am entirely taken off work by the dreadful business of sitting for my portrait, which Mr Craik (of Messrs Macmillan) has asked me to do for him. The artist, Mr Sandys, who has just finished a very fine head of Matthew Arnold, is here, living in my house, and taking a great deal out of me. This joined to the heat of the weather has made me very late. If it is not too late I will try to send it to you by Tuesday. Will that do?

I hope you are having in Scotland the same steady brilliancy of weather that we have here, but here it is altogether enervating. Yesterday, with everything we could do to secure coolness — venetian blinds closed and every precaution — I "sat" in a temperature of 80°, and to-day it promises to be hotter still.

To Mr Craik.   WINDSOR, *17th July.*

Mr Sandys' work is going on admirably. He is making a most beautiful drawing, the most wonderful piece of workmanship I ever saw. He applauds me as a sitter, and intends, I hear, that this should be the best drawing he has ever made. The likeness everybody seems to consider very satisfactory. To me it becomes very touching from the fact that every day it is more and more like my mother, of whom I have no good likeness.

WINDSOR, *21st July.*

. . . I should give up my house here if I could, but the lease is a hindrance, and it is very difficult to let houses here. I have been in town to-day with my little Denny to see Dr Wharton Hood about her arm. Mr Sandys gave me a holiday, as the picture is just done—only an hour or two's work required about the dress. . . .

The drawing is quite beautiful. It seems to me much more dignified and imposing than I ever was, or could be; but barring this size and grandeur, which Mr Sandys seems to me to give to all the heads he draws, it is considered an admirable likeness, as well as the most beautiful piece of work I ever saw. I believe he intends to take it up to town to-morrow, and I hope you will allow me to have it photographed for the benefit of my immediate friends.

Unfortunately this drawing, though a very fine piece of workmanship, did not, as a likeness, quite satisfy Mrs Oliphant's most familiar friends. The very irregularity of her face—the mouth with its expressive if artistically faulty lines especially—had a charm which is lost in the "dignified and imposing" presentment.

The next letter is addressed to the mother of the present Editor of 'Maga.'

BINNY, *Sept. 6.*

MY DEAR MRS BLACKWOOD,—It is difficult to find words to tell you how much we enjoyed our stay at Colinton and felt your kindness in every way. I knew of old what a kind and genial house yours was, but it is a great pleasure to renew the knowledge. Both Cyril and I will always think of our visit with the greatest pleasure, and I can only thank you and your dear girls and excellent son for all your kindness to us. It does one good to be allowed to form part of such a household even for a little time, and I feel thankful that my careless boy, who has the gift of always appreciating excellence when he sees it, should have had the benefit of knowing Mr Blackwood at home. There is nothing that does a youth so much good.—With love and many thanks, believe me, dear Mrs Blackwood. . . .

To Principal Tulloch.

[*Probably Sept.* 1881],
WINDSOR, *Saturday night (or rather Sunday morning,* 2 A.M.)

MY DEAR PRINCIPAL,—I was delighted to get your letter, and now feel much comforted, and hope you will make progress daily. It wants patience, and I am sure you have had a very hard trial to go through in your banishment and loneliness; but God be thanked that it has had its effect, and I hope you will carry out your cure bravely, and not think of coming away till the doctors give you leave: as they have been justified in ordering you this very bitter medicine, it is only fair to let them get the full credit of their wisdom.

I wrote off to Sir Henry Ponsonby as soon as I got your letter. Unless it is promised to somebody, I think the mere suggestion that you would take this post of Historiographer should be enough. Is there anything to do? and is it worth your while?

What do you think of the appointment of the Master of University to the Deanery of Westminster? It seems a very curious choice. Mr Hale and I were regretting much the other day that you could not have got that. Mr Hale said boldly, "They ought to make the Principal Dean of Westminster."

Yes, it is evident that I am much stronger than you are. I fancy that women are stronger than men, after they get over their special danger, though indeed the dear padrona is not a case in point. But think, please, if it had been me who had been ill, what would have become of me?—no income going on whether one could work or not—no wife to take care of me. You are far better off than I am in these respects, and, to tell the truth, I am often tired to death of work and care — always work, work, whether one likes or not. But I am wicked to complain.

It will be very kind of you to write and let me know now and then how you are going on. Tids and I are all alone at present, living a sort of Darby-and-Joan life, which I enjoy much.

With very anxious wishes for your complete recovery, dear Principal, ever affectionately.

Letters such as the two following give an idea of the wide range of reading and of interests which Mrs Oliphant always maintained even in the heaviest press of solid work. She almost seemed to know books by instinct.

To Mr W. Blackwood. WINDSOR, *27th October.*

. . . For a New Books article I am somewhat divided in my mind between an article on Travels —including Miss Bird's books, Mrs Scott Stevenson's 'Ride through Asia Minor,' and Du Chaillu's new book on Scandinavia, which ought to make an excellent article—or Philosophical Romance, taking up Mallock's last production, the 'Romance of the Nineteenth Century,' and 'Clifford Gray'—or an article on French and English novels, taking up two or three of the latter, and Daudet's last two books, 'Le petit Chose' and a very recent one called 'Numa Roumestan.' Will you choose between them and send me which you like? About the ghost story, I am turning it over in my mind, and if I find it likely to work out well, you shall have it in good time.

To the Misses Blackwood. WINDSOR, *10th November.*

DEAR BESSIE AND EMMA,—I feel so startled and overwhelmed by the sad announcement I have just seen in the papers, that I have no words to say to you how I feel for you and how deeply I grieve in your grief. I feel more thankful than I can say that I saw so much of your dear mother this autumn, and so entirely renewed the affectionate regard which I had always felt for her. How kind she was! how thoughtful and good to everybody! I wish I were near enough to go to you and cry with you, dear girls. God bless you. I cannot say any more.— Yours in deep sympathy and affection.

The idea of the story of the Unseen called "The Open Door' was suggested to Mrs Oliphant by part of the grounds belonging to Colinton House, near Edinburgh, where Mr William Blackwood was then residing.

To Mr W. Blackwood.   WINDSOR, *20th December.*

. . . I am very glad that Mr Langford likes "The Open Door," and delighted that you are satisfied with your New Year number. The Magazine has been so successful during the last year that I have no fear of your keeping it up to the highest level.

The English books that I thought of taking up as a balance to the French ones are 'John Inglesant' (a very remarkable book), the 'Portrait of a Lady,' and 'Clifford Gray,'—these are all that occur to me at the moment, and I have got them all. I will tell you of any others I think of.

I am not going to mix up my Christmas good wishes with business, so I shall write again.—With once more many thanks.

To Mr Craik.   WINDSOR, *20th December.*

Your letter is exact to the terms we agreed upon, and I shall preserve it as my guide,—many thanks.

Let me wish you all kinds of good things for the season. I feel myself so struggling upon a stormy sea, so wildly afloat, and sometimes so little hopeful, that I am but a poor sort of raven to croak out good wishes. There are times when life is specially hard; but though you are safe and happy, you are not one of those who hug themselves upon their comfort and enjoy their peace all the more for the roar of the storms outside in which others are battling. Many thanks for the helping hand you have always been ready to hold out to me, and I pray that you may have for your share full measure, heaped up and running over, of all that is good and best, both now and always.

Entreat Mrs Craik in my name to come and bear me company in Mr Sandys' gallery. I don't think it is quite proper that I should be there alone. He is a dreadful tyrant, it is true, but it is only once in a way. I do hope she will be persuaded to sit. I feel sure he would make a beautiful piece of work of her. Will you greet her affectionately in my name, and give her my kindest and best wishes for the New Year and all years?

1882.

The work here referred to is the 'Literary History of England in the End of the Eighteenth Century and beginning of the Nineteenth.'

To Mr Craik.   WINDSOR, 1*st February.*

I can scarcely tell you how pleased I am by your letter to-day. I have scarcely had time myself to read the proofs, but I was quaking a little about them, and was on the point of writing to ask what you thought of them. If your opinion is so satisfactory about the first volume, I feel encouraged about the rest, which go upon fresh ground. I was half afraid of the many recent publications about Cowper, Burns, and the elder race. I have the second volume ready to send you, but the labour in preparing it has been immense, not only from the number of people to be taken up but from the difficulty of getting the books. I torment the London Library people, and have to wait, and to suffer, and to get all my notes confused by the sudden impossibility of getting exactly what I want at the time I want it, which is very bewildering. It is almost impossible to get everybody into his or her proper niche, and I am afraid the process of adding and dovetailing, as one after another turns up, will be a tedious business. The Wordsworths, &c., are very delightful work—one knows them by heart and knows what one thinks about them; but imagine me floundering among Godwin's set, all the grimy citizens of the end of the century and all the novel-writers! This is the real labour of the book. Pray, pray, say exactly what you think about the work—you cannot be too candid, nor can you do me a greater service than by mentioning every objection that occurs to you. About Wordsworth, I am very glad that the tide is turning again, but I think it had fallen a little. I meant to represent the needle of the popular compass as just trembling on the turn. It is curious how this return of appreciation begins really to tell upon Scott. I have not the least objection to cut out what I have said about Ruskin—probably I should have done it of myself, though to say it was a relief to my mind for the moment. You know that an utterance of the kind clears one's bosom, even if one throws it into the fire the next moment.

I wonder if you could lend me, or give me, a copy of the old edition of Gilchrist's 'Blake'? Not the gorgeous new one you showed me, which is too good; and have you *any* of those men [1] of the beginning of the century? This is vague, but I speak in a kind of despair, for their name is legion. *I do not believe you will get clear of me under four volumes.* Is this very alarming? I must have a chapter on Robert Hall and the Dissenters and the Slave-trade people before I get on to Byron and the upper classes, which I am eager to be at.

But, oh my dear Mr Craik! how much easier to spin a novel than to read and read—so much that there is very little interest in reading! I have had twice a little brief attack of what I believe people call overwork—a whirring and whizzing in my head which has compelled me to lay it back upon a cushion and do nothing for a whole day. You will have to send me to Venice at Easter to do that book and relieve my mind!

I will bring you the second volume. as soon as I can spare a few hours to come to town. In the meantime I have had to leave a little gap at Mary

---

[1] Dr Moore's 'Zelucco,' Hope's 'Anastasius,' Combe's 'Dr Syntax,' &c. &c.

Wollstonecraft, in the impossibility of getting a glance—I want no more—at her books.

This year Mrs Oliphant took her holiday in Scotland. Her friend Miss FitzMaurice was of the party, with Cyril and the two nieces, who were now beginning to fill the place of daughters in the family. Cecco was in Devonshire reading with a clergyman, and writing to his mother daily those letters which show, perhaps better than anything else could do, the dear and intimate friendship that existed between them. Only one or two short extracts from these are reprinted here. He never ceased as long as he lived to tell her everything that interested him.

Mrs Oliphant to F. R. Oliphant.

INVERCLOY HOTEL, ARRAN, *29th August.*
. . . We came here last night. . . . We had a terrible voyage here. The morning was grey but fair, and we started at eight o'clock for Helensburgh, hoping for good weather; but after we left Greenock it began to rain, and literally poured till we got here in bucketsfull. There was a large cabin, but it was crammed full and no windows open, so that it was very stuffy and various people sick. We went on deck accordingly, in mackintoshes and umbrellas, but got drenched notwithstanding, and passed through the Kyles of Bute without seeing anything but a few misty ghosts of hills. When we got here, after three-quarters of an hour of rather strong sea, it was found that my special boxes had gone astray, and on the return of the steamer from the further stations on the island, Tiddy and I rushed down to see after them. We lost each other, however, on the pier, and while he secured them, going on board by one gangway, I rushed over to the steamboat by another, and was carried off again, with only a light cloak on, and not

a penny in my pocket. Fortunately they touch at
Corrie, another place on the island, where we were
landed in an open boat, and I made my way to the
inn, and was received with open arms by a delightful
landlady, who wrapped me up in her own fur cloak,
gave me a cup of tea, and sent me over here in a
waggonette, lending me money to pay the boat, &c.
When I asked about the hire of the waggonette, she
said, "Never mind. Hoot, ye'll be coming this way
again," all this without even knowing my name. I
got back all right and got dried, but was very cross,
till consoled by this charming landlady, whose name
is Mrs Morrison of Corrie—make a note of it should
you ever be in these parts.

F. R. Oliphant to Mrs Oliphant.

IVYBRIDGE, Sept. 18.

. . . My work is progressing slowly. In fact, the
slowness is a more distinguishing characteristic than
the progress. However, if he will go on with Aris-
totle and Plato, which I am going over at present, I
shall not mind my work so much, but Heaven deliver
me from the English philosophers and Kant! I have
just been reading Heine's 'De l'Allemagne,' a very
amusing book, where, speaking of the influence of
Kant's system in literature, &c., in Germany, he says,
"Par bonheur, elle ne se mêla pas de la cuisine."
This is my only consolation. The philosophy which
colours everything, even in my walks, and reappears
in a chaotic state in my dreams, exerts no baneful influence over Mrs Creed's cookery.

Sept. 22.

. . . I think this extract from a western newspaper
pretty nearly beats the record (slang again) for confusion of metaphors: "He [Sir Stafford Northcote]
is a statesman, the blaze of whose parliamentary
escutcheon has never yet been dimmed by the bar-
sinister of inconsistency." What do you think of
that?

Nov. 1.

. . . Tell Tiddy that ever since I left Westward Ho, as throughout the time I was there, I have been unable to get out of my head the tune of "We'll all go a-hunting to-day."   But to-day all S. Devon is singing it, for is it not the great day on which the Dartmoor hounds meet for the first time? The scene described in the song I allude to, of the parson hurrying off after a wedding service to hunt, would exactly suit the vicar to-day.   To-day being All Saints' Day —the only saint's day which he observes—there was an early service before breakfast, a sort of hunting mass, after which, to save time, he breakfasted in his cassock, then disappeared for a few minutes and returned entirely transmogrified from the priest of the sanctuary to the sportsman eager for the chase. When he goes out cub-hunting he appears in a costume which is parsonic but shabby, but to-day he was in his braws, and presented such a fine sportsmanlike appearance that he might have been taken for Mr Mildmay's underkeeper.   To add a grotesque shade to the proceedings, he has to hurry back early for a funeral at half-past four, which seems to me a kind of grim satire on the whole business.

Mrs Oliphant to Mr W. Blackwood.

WINDSOR, *31st October.*

I want you to tell me what sort of paper you want from me for December.   There is a foolish story going about that the Glamis mystery has been cleared up by the death of an old man, either a criminal or a monster, who has been living all this time in the secret chamber.   I think it is simply nonsense, but it would not be at all a bad subject for a short story to be called " The True Story of a Haunted House." Would you like this, or do you think it would approach too nearly to the supposed story, or would give the Strathmore family reason to complain ?   I don't see that it should do so, and I shall of course take care to vary the circumstances. Or would you prefer a New Books article, or what? Give me my orders, and I will carry them out.

I heard from Mrs Laurence Oliphant the other day, from an island in the Sea of Marmora which sounds captivating. They seem to be getting along very happily; but I daresay you hear from Laurence often. I am very fond of *her*.

WINDSOR, *2nd November*.

. . . I wish very much to review Mr Howell's the American novelist's books with a reference to American books and magazines generally. This perhaps would require rather more research and consideration than there is time for for December, but I should be glad to do it for January, and to do my best to put these Jacobs of literature on their true level. I think fashion is going too far in this respect.

I do not see my way to getting my Leopardi ready before the beginning of the year. Cyril, like all in-experienced writers, has got a mass of material accu-mulated through which at present he is floundering, not seeing how to get it into bounds; but he is hoping to send the first portion, which of course he left to the last, ready soon. . . . We concluded, I think, that one volume more would be enough, which I thought I might perhaps do myself; but if you think that would be too much of me at the end, we might look out for another. I thought of the Great Preachers of France, taking Bossuet and Fénelon. This, I think, would complete the twenty volumes. Of course if Sir Theodore could be got to do that Heine instead, it would be much better.

1883.

In the beginning of this year Mrs Oliphant was in great anxiety, caused by Cyril's health. Two or three very alarming attacks of illness had followed each other, and Sir Andrew Clark had given a most serious report of his condition. In April his health was sufficiently re-established for him to accept an appointment as private secretary to Sir Arthur Gordon, who was going out to Ceylon as Governor. There was to be a delay of some months, however, and in the meantime Cecco went to Göttingen to study German, with a view to the examination for the British Museum, which he hoped to pass.

The family met again at Heidelberg in autumn, and only came back to England shortly before Christmas.

To Miss Annie Walker.   WINDSOR, 14*th April.*

. . . I don't remember even if I wrote to you that Dr Clark made, what it seems is his usual concession, . . . that Tids had made a remarkable improvement, and that he now thought he might say that with care he might shake off the complaint entirely. I hope I told you this, but I can't remember. If not, forgive me. We are such wretches, so much more ready to distress our friends with our troubles than to communicate our relief.

It is settled about Tids and Sir Arthur Gordon. He is to go out with that potentate as one of his private secretaries, with something between two and three hundred a-year. I suppose a private secretary lives with his chief, or it would not lighten my purse much to make such an arrangement. However, I think the value of the practical work for him is everything, and the entire change of scene an advantage too.

Mr A. W. Kinglake to Mrs Oliphant.

                    28 HYDE PARK PLACE, *April* 22.

MY DEAR MRS OLIPHANT,—I cannot help venturing to express the admiration with which I have been reading the 'Lover and his Lass.' It is by your powerful, truth-seeing imagination, and not by what pedants are prone to describe as "analysis" of character, that you enchant us. I know of nothing equal to the budding of affection in the heart of little Lilias which you enable one to see. The language seems to me beautiful, and I say this after having redoubled my enjoyment of some of the passages by reading them slowly. I delight in the Scotticisms. They all conduce charmingly to one's knowledge of the people presented to us.

I "pitied myself," as they say in Cumberland, when I got to the end of the book; but I hear of the 'Ladies Lindores' in a way that promises me pleasure to come. I say "to come," for I never read a novel that I know will delight me until it reaches the completed form.

Forgive my intrusion, and believe me, my dear Mrs Oliphant, most truly yours,   A. W. KINGLAKE.

To F. R. Oliphant (at Göttingen).

WINDSOR, *August* 18.

MY DEAREST CECCO,—I can't tell you how glad I am to get your letter, which has just come, and to see that you have got on so well. . . .

I certainly don't know any male creature who writes such satisfactory letters as you do, really telling one what one wants to know. . . .

Now about my own proceedings. I had a terribly hot and tiresome journey down the Rhine. At Cologne, where I rested a few hours, I was cheered by getting your telegram, and my journey home was tolerably comfortable. A sleeping-carriage, which I had at first thought of, proved impossible; for why? —it was taken up by men, so that even if there had been room, it would have been impossible for a woman to have any share, which I think is rather hard. I had, however, a carriage to myself, which was as good, though involving so many francs to a succession of guards that the sleeping-carriage would have been on the whole cheaper. At Brussels, at the first station we came to, I got out on the score of the *vingt minutes d'ârret*, and was left behind by my train! But fortunately it had only gone on to the Midi station, and after sitting for an hour and a half—5.30 to 7—watching the Flemish folk crowding to the early trains, I got on and recovered my carriage and all my belongings again, for I had left everything, even my boots, in the carriage. . . . .

I always feel very lost when your room is vacant, the blank is so very evident and always affects my imagination, besides the want of you in other ways.

God bless you, my dearest boy. — Your loving mother.

1884.

Mrs Oliphant began this year in a house which had been lent to her in Hans Place, and which was convenient, both because of Cyril's preparations for going to Ceylon, and of the marriage of her cousin, which took place in London. Cyril started on January 29th. Mrs Oliphant and Cecco went to Bordighera, and thence to Italy *viâ* Lucerne and Milan, moving later to Venice. They made at Bordighera the acquaintance of Lady Cloncurry and her daughter, Miss Lawless, and this proved the beginning of one of the warmest friendships of Mrs Oliphant's later years. She saw also at this time a good deal of Mr and Mrs George MacDonald. George MacDonald's first book, or at any rate his first successful book, 'David Elginbrod,' had been published many years before by Messrs Hurst & Blackett, at Mrs Oliphant's warm recommendation. She always spoke of it as a work of genius, and quoted it as one of the instances of publishers' blunders, for when the MS. came to her it came enveloped in wrappings that showed how many refusals it had already suffered. 'John Inglesant' was another typical case of the same blundering —less important, however, to the author than the former one.

To Mr Craik.   44 HANS PLACE, S.W., *January.*

I don't know why people should be so anxious to add to my age. I am quite old enough without any addition. I protested in the case of Mr Henry Morley's Tauchnitz book, and also as to an American one, but I did not know I had the honour of being included in the 'Men of the Time.'

According to my father's family Bible I was born on the 4th of April 1828—I understand that is legal evidence. I think I have heard that I was baptised in Tranent parish. I must write for a certificate, so as to crush the gainsayers.

Thank you for taking so much interest in the matter. . . .

I hope the rest of Professor Nichol's Literary Facts are more reliable. If I had done this, how all the critics would have fallen upon me!

When Mr and Mrs Craik were going to Rome, Mrs Craik asked if she could undertake any commission. This letter is Mrs Oliphant's answer.

To Mrs Craik.   *February* 19.

DEAR MRS CRAIK,—Only to make a little pilgrimage out to the sacred place where my darling lies by her father's side—that is all. You knew him too. Yes, I remember as if it were yesterday you sitting by my bedside holding that miracle of Heaven, my firstborn. What dark waters since then one has waded through!

Don't be nervous, dear friend, only take this one

precaution.   Carry a shawl with you for yourself and the child, and when you go into one of those ice-cold churches out of the warm Italian sunshine put it on. The cold is indoors, the warmth out.

I enclose a note for an old artist acquaintance who once lived in Capo le Case, close to the Via Sistina, and will be heard of no doubt at Spithoever's, an old Roman who knows all about the place.   Her husband is an American, a painter, she a sculptor—neither at all distinguished, but in her own particular way she might be of some use.   All my friends in Rome have died out.   I know absolutely nobody now, except one kind dear fellow, whom indeed I scarcely know, who watches over my little sanctuary in the English Cemetery with a delicate sympathy which that dear people has the secret of.   He is the Marchese Landolfo Carcano, and lives, when he is in Rome, at the Palazzo Carcano, Via dei due Macelli.   If you should meet him or hear anything of him, make friends with him, please; but I think most likely he may not be in Rome just now.

Do you know the W. W. Storys?   They are good people to be acquainted with.   I could easily get you an introduction to them if you like.

I hope—nay, I am sure—you will enjoy it when you are there.   I wish I were going with you.   "Buon viaggio, felice ritorno," as our old Capri friends used to say.

The *custode* at the Cimeterio Inglese will show you the place.

7th March.

My dear Mrs Craik,—Enclosed I send you a letter to Mr Story from William Blackwood.   I don't know the Storys myself, but they are intimate with the Blackwoods.

I hope you have got over your journey comfortably, and that you may get a great deal of pleasure out of Rome.   You will take your child to gather violets in the Borghese gardens, and watch the sunset from the

Pincio—how well I know what you will be doing.
I never did much sight-seeing in Rome, but go if you
can to Albano, and to Tivoli, and to the little town
on Lake Nemi—Genzano I think it is called. Nemi
is so lovely.

Think of me sometimes walking about those ways,
where I have shed so many tears. My kindest regards
to Mr Craik.

To Mr Blackwood.　　　　　　　　VENICE, *2nd April.*

I send you my certificate of existence, attested by
no less a personage than the Prefect of Venice, the
vice-king here. I don't know whether his certificate,
which he thought it better to put into divine Italian,
as he does not understand English, will be received by
the authorities at home, but if not I can send to
Windsor to get it done. My friend, Miss FitzMaurice,
who knows everybody, especially in Italy, has this great
functionary under her orders, so we are very well cared
for; and I have already made acquaintance with
several of the English and American residents, to
whom I had letters, chiefly by means of Professor
Villari, to whom I hope my friends in Edinburgh
will kindly repay his civilities to me.

My object in writing now, however, is to tell you
that we have at length acquired an address, which after
so many wanderings is quite a luxury. I shall be so
thankful to have the Magazine.

We have the most glorious weather, and Venice is
looking beautiful, notwithstanding the intrusion of the
steamboat, which is fortunately as little oppressive as
may be. We are on the Grand Canal, in a tolerable
apartment, after resisting the seductions of a quite
lovely little palace, which tempted me mightily, though
too dear.

I have heard from Cyril, who is already up in the
wilds of Ceylon, at a place called Cornegalle, with his
Governor, driving elephants! which sounds a very
extraordinary first step into Eastern life.

I trust you are all well, and getting no harm from the east winds. . . . What a sad, miserable thing poor Prince Leopold's death is!   He was the only one I knew of the Royal Family, and was always nice and pleasant.   Everybody will feel it, I am sure.

To Mrs Harry Coghill.   112 EBURY STREET, *July* 30.

MY DEAR COUSIN ANNIE,—I got your kind letter when I was in a state of great anxiety about Cyril, who has come back from Ceylon under doctor's orders, the climate having proved quite unfit for him.   By way of making me less anxious he did not let me know till the last moment, and I had to hurry back to meet him.   He had an illness some time ago, of which he made as little as possible, and I felt at the time that it must have been more serious than he would allow.   It turns out now that he was very ill indeed, and that after he got so far better he had repeated attacks of fever, and the doctor declared that Colombo would be fatal to him.   I had a very kind letter from the Governor—much more explicit, as you will understand, than Cyril would ever be—to tell me all this.   I got home last Sunday in consequence, not knowing when the ship would arrive, which it did on Tuesday morning.   I went down to Gravesend on Monday night, and so was in time to board the Cathay at seven on Tuesday morning. I found him looking better than I had hoped, the sea voyage having set him up again; but after we got home here, I was not by any means so well satisfied with his appearance as at first. . . . I miss you dreadfully here—it would have been such a comfort to go to S. Place and talk it all over : however, it would be selfish indeed to regret that, when all is so happy and well with you.

The girls—and boys too—send their love.   (By the bye, Cecco has entered the band of critics, and had a paper in the 'Spectator' the other week, and I hope will get on in that way.)

PILMOUR LINKS, ST ANDREWS, *Sept.* 7.

. . . I have been a month here alone with the
boys, and though they are of course out from morning
to night, I have really enjoyed it, strolling out upon
the sands by myself with great peacefulness and re-
freshment of soul.   It is half amusing and always interesting to see new developments of this kind in
one's self, and I am quite glad to find that age gives
this pleasure in silence and solitude, which I had not
anticipated.   The boys, especially Cecco, have been
very good, and now and then take me out for walks ;
and I have been much tranquillised and renovated
altogether by my quiet time here, and almost grudge
the modification of it now that the girls have joined
me again.   . . .

The sea is tumbling in with great white waves
before the window where I am writing, and the Links
have their usual Sunday look—very green with the
rain.   We had a catastrophe here the other day, a
poor boy drowned bathing at the Step rock, which,
though we did not know him, upset us all very much.
Cyril, out all day and golfing, is much better, and has
got his old mahogany colour; but he is still not very
strong—much less strong than he looks. Cecco is
very well, and fatter than is expedient at his age.   I
have got through the most portentous amount of work
in my long spell of quiet, but have still an intolerable
quantity before me, after the delays and idleness of
our long rambling.

To Mr Blackwood.   19 PILMOUR LINKS, ST ANDREWS.

. . . Do you think you could hear of a collie for
me ?   I should not like to give much for it, but I have
a great hankering after one—an honest fellow who
has worked for his living like my dear old Yarrow,
not one of the slim fancy articles.

I suppose you are immersed in odious politics—I
get more sick of them every day.   The Gladstone

fever is by far the strongest proof I have heard of the old slander that Scotland is without any sense of humour. I wish Lord Neaves was to the fore to immortalise the thirty - two bites which my grave young acquaintance Edward Lyttelton has had the solemnity to make known to the world.

WINDSOR, *October* 18.

I sent you my big photograph, enclosing one for Miss Blackwood. It makes me a much more imposing person than I ever was in reality, but on the whole it has been liked by most people, though I think the strength of jaw in it equals Father William's, or Mr Gladstone's, which is far from being the case in the original.

WINDSOR, 13*th November*.

I shall return the proof in a day or two, but in the meantime I want you to tell me whether you would mind me putting your dear mother's initials, E. B., with the date, Colinton, 188–, in the little dedication to the "Open Door"? I forget what the date was, but you could tell me—the year only, I think, but I should like to put the name of the place.

The following refers to the short story, "Old Lady Mary," which was dedicated to the memory of Mrs Duncan Stewart :—

WINDSOR, 3*rd December*.

You said I was probably preparing something for Christmas, to come upon you as a surprise. I had no thought of it at the time, but the enclosed has presented itself, and here it is if you like it. It wants the strong effects of "The Open Door" and the others, but still it may not come amiss. Look at it, and let me know—but soon, please. . . .

1885.

To Mr Blackwood.   WINDSOR, *29th January.*

Thank you very much for the 'Life of George Eliot,' and for the kind and flattering inscription. I am very glad to have the book, which is as curious a book as any I ever saw. The personality of the great writer is as yet very confusing to me in the extreme flatness of the picture. I don't mean by flatness dulness, though there is something of that, but only that it is like mural painting or sculpture in very low relief. I have just run over your reviewer's article and think it very good. He has most cleverly eluded the difficulties by making a picture of his own. I don't think that, from the point of view naturally necessary for 'Maga,' it could have been better done.

At the same time, I don't think any one will like George Eliot better from this book, or even come nearer to her. However, she is a big figure to be taken in all at once, and may grow upon one. I am glad that I have time to consider, should I make up my mind to say anything on the subject. Would you kindly say nothing about that, as very likely it will come to nothing? and even if it does, the excellences of anonymity are always evident. . . .

WINDSOR.

. . . Let me congratulate you on the great success of 'George Eliot's Life.' It was bound to be a great success in a pecuniary point of view, but not in a literary, I think. It is quite curious how much more interesting her correspondence with your uncle is than any of her other correspondences. He seems to have roused her out of that ponderousness which must have been natural to her. It is quite astounding to see how little humour or vivacity she had in real life. Surely Mr Cross must have cut out all the human parts.

I have the mother of your correspondent Miss Lawless—Lady Cloncurry—with me just now. She is the most charming old beauty of seventy—as bright as seventeen, and full of fun and cleverness. It was quite worth a journey to Italy to make friends with her.

Laurence Oliphant's sketches of the Druse villages are delightful, but his philosophy is something too tremendous. I am making the most prodigious effort to understand his book, but I have to catch hold of the furniture after a few pages to keep myself from turning round and round, and yet the absorption of such a man of the world as he is in a religious idea has something very fine in it.

The next letter refers to Cecco's candidature for the post of Secretary to the Society of Antiquaries. Failing the Heralds' College, on which his heart was set, this was the kind of employment most congenial to him, and naturally his mother greatly desired that he might obtain it. He did not, however, being probably too young and too little known; but he was now beginning to write stories and articles, some of them exceedingly clever and of great interest to Mrs Oliphant, who was no lenient critic of her son's work.

WINDSOR, 21*st July*.

. . . I enclose a list of the Council of the Society of Antiquaries. There are not many distinguished names. I know Mr Evans the President, Lord Carnarvon the late President (who has now too much to do, I fear, to take any trouble about this), and very slightly Dr William Smith, but none of the others. Please help me if you can. It appears that the appointment is more important than we supposed, and that many good men, of much longer standing than Cecco, are in for it, so that success is extremely unlikely. Still it can do no harm to try. Cecco was rather idle in his Oxford career, and did not do so well as he ought to have done; but I am happy to say he sees the folly of that sort of thing now, and is as determined to get work and to get on as I could desire, as well as being my almost constant companion and the greatest help and comfort to me. . . .

Here is a story on the best authority, told to the man who told it to me by one of the guests. At a great dinner-party lately the Prince of Wales took it into his head to inquire into people's incomes. He asked Sir Henry Thompson what a great doctor might make a year, who answered £15,000; then he asked (I think) Sir Henry James what a great barrister could do, who replied £20,000. Then the Prince turned to Millais and asked what a great painter could make: Millais said £25,000. The Prince took it as a joke, whereupon Millais explained. "For the last ten years," he said, "I should have made £40,000 had not I given myself a holiday of four months in the year: what I did actually make was £30,000, so that I gave an estimate considerably under the fact"! What do you think of this? It will be a long time before an author makes half so much, at least nowadays. George Eliot, I suppose, must have been almost the highest in our day.

The next letters are addressed to Principal Tulloch, and refer to his dedication of 'Movements of Religious Thought' to Mrs Oliphant. She was greatly pleased and touched by this proof of affection from so old and well-loved a friend. She would have valued it perhaps even more could she have known that it was the last of his long series of literary work,

To Principal Tulloch. WINDSOR, *4th August.*

MY DEAR PRINCIPAL,—I am very much touched and warmed by your letter. What you propose is a very great honour to me, one of the greatest possible. It is not in the least deserved, but as a token of a long and faithful friendship, the sort of brother- and sister-hood of so many years, I need not say it will be most sweet to me. . . .

No, do not send me the letter before it is published, only don't make me ashamed by saying anything of me that would imply knowledge I don't possess. Those old long talks were always delightful, but I am sure there never was anything on my side save a sympathetic understanding of what you said.

Thanks from my heart for so kind a thought. Ever affectionately yours, M. O. W. OLIPHANT.

My love to my dear padrona. I should have written yesterday, but I was kept anxious about Cyril, who was extremely unwell. I feared rheumatic fever, but he is better to-day.

To Principal Tulloch. ST ANDREWS, *October 2.*

DEAR PRINCIPAL,—I don't know what to say to you in reply to the words, more than kind and far more than deserved, by which you have placed our long friendship on record. As an outward sign and token of that which has been so large an element in my life for many years, it is very delightful and flattering to me, and to feel that you think anything like so well of me goes to my heart. I should break down if I spoke, so I write to say the poor little return I can for what is at once a great honour and an affectionate kindness which touches me to the very depths. Your friendship and that of my dearest padrona have been among the best things in my life, and I hope it will never, either here or on the other side, come to an end.   With thanks that are beyond words, and the warmest return of constant and faithful regard, believe me, dear Principal, affectionately yours,   M. O. W. OLIPHANT.

To Miss Bessie Blackwood.   WINDSOR, *October* 7.

We got home quite comfortably yesterday morning, a little cold, and thinking regretfully of the rugs you were so kind as to offer us, but still in very good preservation on the whole.   We find the trees still wonderfully green, and the Virginian creeper in great glory; but the skies are very much decreased in extent, which is a phenomenon I always remark in returning from Scotland!

I don't know how to thank you for the kindness which we always experience in your delightful house. It is a constant pleasure to see you all together in such a perfect home.   I hope the flowers may bloom and the animals thrive even better and better year by year.

To Mr Blackwood.   WINDSOR, *2nd December.*

I sympathise with you very much in respect to the obstinacy of Scotland about Mr Gladstone.   It is very strange, and if it brings about disestablishment it will be very unfortunate.   Still you know the upper classes in Scotland have separated themselves so long from the people in that respect that they cannot say much.   It has always seemed to me a great misfortune for the country that the Church of the nation was not the Church of the gentry: that, of course, is a standing weakness, and I have no doubt lies at the bottom of the separation in other matters.   I trust the Conservative majority in Scotland will suffice at least to keep Lord Salisbury in power, and to free him from Parnell, who is a fearful rock ahead.   I can well understand how disappointed you must be after all your exertions.   .   .   .

WINDSOR, *27th December.*

This is just a word to wish you everything that is good for the New Year. I hope you are better, and will begin 1886 in good health and spirits, and that you may find it a prosperous and pleasant year—the *anno venturo*, as the Italians say. I trust too that your last new contributor, Cecco, will give you and the public satisfaction, and that this may be the beginning of a long connection, though I do not think it will be in the way of fiction.

I wonder if you have heard the delightful story about Lady Randolph Churchill which is going about. I must tell you on the chance that you have not heard it. She was electioneering on behalf of Mr Ashmead-Bartlett, and some impertinent elector expressed his wish that ladies conducted their canvassing on the principles prevalent in former times, in the Duchess of Devonshire's way, in which case he should have been delighted to promise his vote at once. "Thank you very much," said Lady Randolph, demurely; "I'll tell Lady Burdett-Coutts!"

1886.

To Mrs Harry Coghill.   WINDSOR, *25th January.*

I ought to have written to you long ago, but I am indescribably busy, more than ever, with a batch of proofs always awaiting me, and other work going on. I have now the addition of the Venice book to bother me, which is under weigh, progressing slowly, and requires always bales of books about. .   .   .

I forget whether you know about Cecco's "Grateful Ghosts." We were discussing the question yesterday, and Cecco proposed to send you the number of 'Blackwood' containing it by Madge, but I recollect that you yourself get the 'Blackwood.' He has also a review of "Two Novels" in the 'Spectator' this last week, so he is getting his push off into literature. But his soul sighs for the Heralds' College ; he is set upon being Rouge Croix or Blue-Mantle, but in the meantime not even Madame de Montalembert, who is interesting herself strenuously in the matter, has been able to persuade the Duke of Norfolk to cut off the head of a pursuivant in order to make room for Cecco.   This is unkind of the Earl Marshal, but these high functionaries have no bowels. . . .

You will have seen, and you will have felt as I do, the death of Mrs Laurence Oliphant in Syria.   They were coming home this year for the season, alas !   I cannot think of her as dead, and I am sure that dying never represented itself to her as death.   If she was right she is more busy than ever somewhere, and nearer to everybody she cared for.   But to me it was a great and painful shock to hear of it.   Poor Laurence, though he too will be defended by his belief.

To Mr Blackwood.   WINDSOR, *February* 8.

I am very much interested by poor Laurence Oliphant's letter, which I will send you back the next time I write.   I should like to read a part of it to one or two friends of his here.   I quite felt that he would be sustained, as he says indeed, though I don't share, and even don't understand, their peculiar views.   The impression of reality in all she did and said and hoped for was so strong that I myself felt something of the same, as if death could not be anything but a trifling circumstance in the course of such an immortal creature.   I will write to him by-and-by. Strangely enough, I had just been putting into a little frame a sweet little photograph of her, very small but very like, which he sent me before they were married. . . .

On the 13th of February Principal Tulloch died at Torquay.   There never was a firmer or more affectionàte friendship than that which for twenty-five years had bound the Principal and Mrs Tulloch to Mrs Oliphant,—they were in all soberness a brother and sister to her; and this loss, almost unexpected, was not one of the smallest griefs of her much-tried life.

WINDSOR, 16th February.

I send you a very small notice, which might go upon the last page if you can manage it. I will set to work on an article for April. I don't think I could have done anything adequate in so much haste, and in all the sad excitement of the moment. Dear Mrs Tulloch has come to Eton with Mrs Tarver, and I have seen her to-day. I don't know how she is to live. She has known no existence apart from him for forty years. However, this I cannot enter into. The Queen has written them such a letter as *makes one love her.* I can use no other words. I will try and get leave to publish it in the article. It is full of feeling and tenderness.

To Mrs Harry Coghill. WINDSOR, 23rd *February*.

I have had no time to write to you about the great calamity that has fallen upon the Tullochs, and which I am sure you will take your full part in, with the rest of us. . . . The padrona, travelling night and day in her state of health, got to him when to all the rest of the world he was past consciousness. Fortunately he knew her, and had a rally after her arrival from which there were some hopes. They say he lay calling "Jeanie, Jeanie," until she came, and afterwards, if she was out of the room for a moment, began this piteous cry again, but never while she was there, so he must have felt her presence at least. Mrs Tulloch, as I have told you, came here with Sara and remained for five or six days. She was very quiet, entirely like herself. She never posed in her life, and she does not do so now. The Queen went to see her in the kindest way, remaining about half an hour with her, and talking, as the padrona said, rather like "a humble friend" than anything else, and expressing the greatest affection for him and gratitude. Mrs Tulloch went away on Saturday morning, going to York to Nettie's to break the journey. She got there, we hear, tolerably well, notwithstanding the great cold. She is going home, I believe, to-day. Think of her arriving there, at the desolate house, which is her home no longer. Dear old St Mary's, a place which it seemed so easy, so natural to go to at any time, but which we can now go to never again. The boys went to St Andrews to the funeral, which seems to have been a wonderful sight.

The Queen sent for me on Saturday, when we had a long talk—very different from my first audience: this was in a beautiful little room, where she was alone. She spoke to me a great deal about the Tullochs and also about myself, and was very sweet and friendly, hoping to see more of me, and other amiabilities. It alters one's idea of her when she is very pleasant to oneself, and I saw a great deal in her of the pleasantness which the Principal used to talk so much about. She seems to have been really attached to him. I hope there is no doubt that the dear padrona will get a pension. . . .

To Mr Blackwood.   *March* 8.

The Queen was extremely kind and gracious to me, so kind that all one's little embarrassments about such an interview went completely away. She talked, of course, a great deal about the Principal and his family, and told me about her interview with Mrs Tulloch, which seemed to have touched her much. She also inquired into my own movements, and expressed a kindly wish to see more of me, now that I had definitely decided to remain in Windsor.

I wish I could tell you one or two political questions she put to me, but I must not, I suppose.

A few days after this interview we were startled late one evening by a ring at the bell, and the maid came upstairs quite excited, carrying a large parcel, which she said had been brought by "two soldiers from the Castle"! and which proved to contain copies of Her Majesty's Journals in the Highlands, the special copy largely illustrated, which she has to give away, accompanied by a very pretty note from Sir Henry Ponsonby, evidently dictated by the Queen, saying that "she is well aware how humble her efforts are at authorship, but as a true Scotch-woman the Queen ventures to send them to you."

I thought it right, as I believe she likes to have one's thanks sent to herself, to write to her, thanking her for the books, and now I have a most gracious autograph letter. In short, my maids are getting quite used to the sight of the orderly.

Mrs Oliphant was suffering much at this time from rheumatism, which made walking extremely difficult and painful. As her old friend Miss FitzMaurice was disposed to try the baths at Wiesbaden, they decided to go together, accompanied by Mrs Oliphant's two adopted daughters.

To Mrs Harry Coghill.　　　　　WINDSOR, *August* 2.

We are, I suppose, just on the eve of leaving, which you will think rather a queer statement to make. But it is true enough, for I am going on preparing more or less in faith, but not very sure whether we shall not be stopped at the last moment. My purpose in determining to go to Wiesbaden was very much for Miss FitzMaurice's sake. . . . If she is well enough to start, and her doctor authorises it, we go on Wednesday. But it still remains doubtful. If you don't hear to the contrary, you may conclude we have gone, and are to be found at the Hôtel des Quatre Saisons (I really cannot write the German

name), Wiesbaden.   Do you still intend to go up
the Rhine on your way to Switzerland?   If so,
you should stay a night and see us.   Do you remember being there for a night or two once many
years ago, and how my maid Theodora lost her
own bonnet, and all my collars and cuffs, on the
pier at Biebrich?   .   .   .

The election must have been very exciting, and in
the end a great pleasure and triumph.   You must be
pleased to have a representative in Parliament.   We
are much interested in a humbler event, a possible
vacancy in the British Museum, for which Cecco is
held in suspense.   He is going probably to Göttingen
to brush up his German, in case he should be nomin-
ated.   There is an examination, a limited competition, and he has never been very happy in examinations.   This coming on makes my arrangement for
going to Wiesbaden still less desirable, and Cyril's
movements are uncertain too; so that I do not look
with much delight to the prospects of this week.

This is a queer budget of news, but I think
you will like to hear before I go away, if I do
get away!

The party arrived safely at the Hôtel des Quatre
Saisons at Wiesbaden, and after a short stay removed
thence into a very cheerful and comfortable-apart-
ment.   The baths seemed a success, and, in spite of
the tremendous heat of the weather, the experience
might have been a pleasant one, in retrospect at
least, but for one unlucky incident.   A jewel-box,
containing nearly every trinket she possessed, was
stolen from Mrs Oliphant's bedroom.   It is true,
as she said herself, that she was not rich in ornaments; but several of the things then lost were of
the utmost value to her—gifts of her husband and
of dead friends, or memorials of her little daughter.

There were two or three valuable rings also.   Not one of the things lost was ever recovered.

While his mother was at Wiesbaden, Cecco was making a second stay at Göttingen, and the next letter is addressed to him there.

Mrs Oliphant to F. R. Oliphant.

HÔTEL ROYAL, BONN, *August* 8.

MY DEAREST CECCO,—I have been thinking of you, and following you all the night, hoping you have had a good passage. . . .

We had a most amusing companion in the carriage with us as far as Dover, an old gentleman who informed us first that he was going to a presentation of colours at Dover, then that he had governed nearly all our colonies in succession, then finally that he was Sir George Bowen, and favoured us with various scraps of his speeches and verses of poetry, his own and other people's.   No such incident attended our farther journey, though we had an interesting old lady, the widow of Moscheles the composer, as far as Brussels. . . .

God bless you, my dearest boy.   I thank Him every day of my life that I can have full trust in my Cecco.   Write soon.—Your loving mother,

M. O. W. O.

To Mr Blackwood.

7 GIBSON PLACE, ST ANDREWS, 11*th Sept.*

I feel myself quite without excuse in not writing for so long a time, but I find my work so thoroughly enough, if not too much for all my time and faculties nowadays, that I literally never write a letter when there is any means of staving off the necessity for doing so.   Time begins to tell upon me in this as well as in other ways.   I was not aware, however, that I had not written in reply to your letter about the biography.   I decided, from a mixture of many motives, that it was incumbent upon me to do it, though of course it is not a remunerative piece of work. . . . The most important letters, however, will. be from Mrs Tulloch, who is working in the most touching way at her stores, and living over again her youthful life. I hope it is more sweet than bitter to her to have the necessity of doing so. She has given me the first set of letters, dating from '43, the beginning of their acquaintance, till their marriage in '45, from which I feel that a most simple and delightful picture of the young man may be made out.

To Mrs Harry Coghill.　　　　　　　　WINDSOR.

I ought to have answered your letter before, but I have got to that chronic and helpless stage of busyness (do you know it?) when one does nothing. My mother used to tell a story of some poor woman whom she found sitting down disconsolately in the middle of a disorderly cottage, having so much to do that she got hopeless and did not know where to begin. That's me!

To Mr Blackwood.　　　　　WINDSOR, *27th November.*

I see by the 'Athenæum' that the Magazine is to be enlarged (I think you might have told me, but that is neither here nor there). I wonder whether you would think well of a plan which has been long in my mind, and which, if I had ever had a magazine in my own hands, as I once thought I should, I should certainly have adopted. This is a standing article upon literature, a review of all the books of the month worth reviewing, with admixture of speculation and general comment, as would be natural, —not merely, however, an occasional paper like my own of this month, but a regular one, for which people would look. There is nothing of the kind anywhere. The reviews are essays on the subject of the book they nominally review, and I think the series I propose would be a popular one.

To Mr Blackwood. Windsor, 10*th December.*

I must throw myself on your indulgence in respect to the enclosed. I have been interrupted in finishing it by my cold, which is still very bad. . . . The Review article is going on: you will get the greater part of it by the 15th if possible. I see my way, I think, to making a good thing of it, but I very much want a good name. I should like to call it "The Saloon at 45," or something of the kind, and begin with a little sketch of that traditionary chamber. But perhaps you would not like this. Think it over, and if you can hit upon a good name tell me —"The Table of 'Maga'"? I am at a great loss for this. I write from bed; but whatever I do I cannot chase the oppression from my head, which is where it always centres.

I have got most of the books, but not Dowden's Shelley as yet. Lord Shaftesbury's Life is interesting—all the more as showing up the vile fallacy that all help to working men has come from so-called Liberal hands, which many misguided people believe.

The name finally chosen for this series of papers was "The Old Saloon."

Windsor, 20*th December.*

. . . Thanks for the old numbers; they are very interesting, and what vigour in them !—but one could not speak so strongly now.

Windsor, 28*th December.*

I have been stopped by a little absence from home from answering your letter. . . . It seems an excellent number, with the exception of the short story, which is not up to 'Maga's' mark. The article on Hayward is very good. Sir Edward Hamley, I think? I remember him telling me how dear old Mr Kinglake climbed up all those stairs to sit with the old man every night, which was very touching, and impressed me much.

Laurence Oliphant's narrative is most exciting— all those articles of his have been excellent. You should get him to begin a new series. I don't agree about John Knox with Mr Skelton. I think he exaggerates the share of the Reformers in the destruction of the churches, though what he says of their destroying the feeling of sanctity in the Church, and therefore indirectly bringing about their ruin, is fine, I think, and probably true. My own belief is that all the Reformers destroyed were the images, and decorations of the altars, which probably were very tawdry affairs, as well as abhorrent to their new-born zeal. I have strong leanings towards the Catholic Church in Catholic countries, but I can't say I should mind purifying a great many altars I know in John Knox's way.

1887.

To Mrs Harry Coghill.   WINDSOR, *12th February.*

I meant to have written to you at once on getting your letter, or indeed sooner, on getting your flowers, to thank you for them; but everything has been put out of my head by Cecco's illness, which makes me incapable of any other thought. He has had a cough for some time which was said to come from the throat; and though it gave me some uneasiness from time to time, yet, as I was assured the lungs were quite well, and that it was only irritation of the throat, I suffered myself to be quieted. Since Christmas, however, he has been getting very thin, and about a fortnight ago he was persuaded, or almost forced, to put himself under active treatment by a Dr M., whom he happened to have taken a fancy to —a young man supposed to be very clever—who came and told me on Tuesday last quite calmly that it was laryngitis with a tendency to tubercle, and all that follows.   I know you will feel for me.   You will imagine that every moment since has been spent in watching him, in thinking of him, in alternation from hope to despair.   He is going to town to see Dr Maclagan on Monday, and if he is ordered to go away to the Riviera or anywhere else, I of course will go with him and at once.   How I am to give up my work and do this I don't know, but I must and will, unless Providence absolutely forbids.   My mind jumps at everything that is worst and most dreadful, as you will readily understand.

I don't know how things will shape themselves in face of this sudden and unthought-of misery.   If we have to go, I will try to let my house in April when the Guards come.   But nothing is clear,—the means even of so far slackening work as to make my entire attention to him practicable are as dark as the rest; but it will be made possible somehow by God's grace, I hope.   This is too miserable a letter to send to an invalid.   I am very sorry you are ill, and hope that it may not be long before you mend.   You will not mind my selfishness in writing all this to you.   The comfort is that you will understand.

Windsor, 19th February.

I have arranged all my little affairs, and we start on Tuesday.   We think of going to Pau, where there is a golf club, which I think will be a good thing for Cecco.   He is a little better, I think, eating better, and his cough variable, sometimes not troublesome at all.   God grant that the move may do him good. You know how anxiety of this kind acts upon me. I am in a suppressed fever, and can think of nothing else day and night.   I watch every morsel he eats, every varying look and change of colour.   How strange it is!   All my troubles, and God knows they have been neither few nor small, have been repetitions

—always one phase or another coming back, and that makes it all the worse, for I know how far my anguish can go.

The following are addressed to Mrs Oliphant's adopted daughters:—

HÔTEL DE FRANCE, PAU, *March* 1.

MY DEAREST CHILDREN,—It is your turn to have the bulletin, and I am writing in the morning before breakfast, Cecco having not yet appeared. . . . I thought yesterday that through the whole course of the day he looked a little better; probably I shall be down into the depths again to-day. I don't think there is any torture in the world like anxiety: it rends my heart to pieces—I feel it *sore* in my breast. . . .

PAU, 23*rd March.*

. . We went upstairs to Mdlle. de Castelbajar's last night. There were about half-a-dozen ladies— Madame la Marquise That and Madame la Comtesse This—and *one* gentleman. The room very much crowded with furniture, nicknacks, and pictures, and two card-tables where everybody except me played whist; one of the games was honest bumble-puppy like our own, and great fun; the other serious play, Mdlle.'s own *partie*, to which Cecco had the honour to be promoted. I know that he is considered *très-bien élevé*, and that I too am approved of, but less warmly—this through the maids. Cecco lost 6 francs, but was amused and will go again, for which I am too thankful. If Heaven would only send a young man! not too good at golf.

After Mrs Tulloch's death:—

PAU, 30*th March.*

I have just been writing to Cyril about this terrible blow, but in the idea that he may possibly have gone to St Andrews before he receives it, I write to you too, and send you Mr Baynes's letter, which is very hard to read, but which contains a great deal you will like to see.   It was very kind of him to write so fully. . . .

I have been trying to say to Cyril that I am glad, —and so, in a sense, I am.   It seems the right thing and the best thing, but I don't think I shall ever want to go to St Andrews again.   To think one will never see her sweet worn face again is what I cannot realise.   It makes it more like a dream that I should be so far away.   I got a letter from her dated the 11th March, after which she had written to some people to ask them to call on me here, for Cecco's sake.   She wrote so tenderly and anxiously about Cecco. . . .

I think I told you, however, that when she bade me good-bye last in St Andrews I was very much struck with the emotion she showed.   She had never before showed so much feeling in parting with me, and that was why I said I would go and pay her a visit in February, which was stopped by Cecco's illness.   She had no heart to live any longer—and why should she?—her work was done.   God bless her wherever she is now — if we could only know a little where it is.   The two will be together, wherever it may be.   Of course you will see about a wreath.   I did the best I could here.   I made a little cross as big as the biggest flower-box I could get, and covered it with the pale Parma violets, which are so sweet, and I sent a box of anemones besides. . . .

To Mrs Harry Coghill.   WINDSOR, *26th May.*

Here we are back again with, thank God, the completest reason to be satisfied with the hurried and anxious step I took with trembling three months ago. Cecco is to all appearance quite well; his cough has almost disappeared, and his general health is quite satisfactory.   He has gained in weight, is in per-

T

fectly good spirits, and altogether is quite a different creature, thank God. The doctor at Pau said that he ought to spend next winter again abroad, but it is a long time before that question need be discussed, and in the meantime I am full of thankfulness. We got home on Monday night. Our Spanish trip was too hurried, yet we saw Burgos, Toledo, and Saragossa, all most interesting places, fairly well, besides Madrid and Barcelona, which are great flourishing modern towns, more or less like other places; and the sight of the country itself, even in the mere course of the journeys, was very curious and interesting. However, I need not say the best thing we saw was home, looking very bright and full of flowers, for a great part of which I have to thank you: they gave us the most fragrant welcome. Now, I want you to come to me for the great week here, the Jubilee. It begins, I believe, on Tuesday the 21st, and lasts the rest of the week. There are to be all kinds of *fêtes*.

In the cheerful and hopeful mood induced by the success of the Spanish journey, Mrs Oliphant was able to enjoy the festivities of the Queen's Jubilee and the company of the friends who filled her house. Of course she worked hard all the time, but work never seemed to exhaust her. "As long as the children were well," as she so often said herself, all was well. But Cecco, though he had greatly mended for the moment, was weak, and her fears were only lulled, not ended. He flagged before the summer was over, and the whole family removed in August to the Lake country, of which he was fond.

Mrs Oliphant to Mrs Harry Coghill.

ROYAL OAK HOTEL, ROSTHWAITE, KESWICK.

. . . We have been here about ten days in the very heart of the hills—in a very homely inn, where everything is a little frowsy, as old carpets, old furniture, &c., of the lodging-house kind are apt to get, but the food more or less good. Cecco had rather a roseate recollection of it, I suppose, and I was dreadfully taken aback when we arrived; but most things ameliorate by the great art of putting up with them, and we are not uncomfortable. The boys walk almost all day, though the weather has rather conspired against them, and they have had to postpone their big mountain climbing from day to day. This is our first absolutely and hopelessly wet day, and even now there are glimmers as if it might clear. Cecco, on the whole, is very well. I can't remember whether I gave you the doctor's last report of him or not. I suppose I must have done so, that he thinks him to have made great progress during the summer, but that, privately between ourselves, he *will not* let him live in London "for several years," though Cecco has not been informed of this definitely, the B. M. business not coming on till October. Nothing could be more entirely mountain air than we have here, and I don't think I was ever conscious of air so sweet: a sort of mingled balm of cow's breath and hay is in the whole atmosphere, the former predominant; and it is the most entire and perfect rural scene that could be imagined, hills, and very fine ones, rising up on all sides. The colour is cold, there is very little heather and too much green, but that is the only drawback.

This was the time of the British Museum examination about which Cecco had been very anxious. During a short visit which his mother paid to her cousin, Mrs Coghill, in Staffordshire, he passed this test brilliantly, earning a large number of marks in excess of what was required. He was naturally delighted with this success, and his mother shared in his pleasure, though she knew better than he did how much difficulty his delicate health might cause in the matter of an appointment.

And, as a matter of fact, he was destined to disappointment, the medical authorities deciding that his state of health was unsatisfactory. Against this decision he appealed, and gained permission to be re-examined. But the appeal turned out to be from Sir A. Clark to Sir A. Clark, and the decision was reaffirmed, to his great grief.

Mrs Oliphant to Mrs Harry Coghill.

WINDSOR, *December* 6.

I was just about to write to you when I got your note. I should have done so before if I had been sure that you were at home to tell you my tale of troubles. As you are so near, I shall run up to-morrow by the 1 o'clock train. It will be a relief to talk it all over with you, for all my hopes have come to nothing. Cecco has been rejected by the C. S. Commissioners on the score of health. Sir Andrew Clark has decided against him, and his work is made all of no avail. It has been a most bitter disappointment, though he has taken it very bravely. Sir A. C. allowed that he was quite able for the work now, but could not certify that he would be so uninterruptedly, as if that could be said for the most robust. I will tell you all about it to-morrow.

WINDSOR, 30*th December.*

I send you with this the 'Makers of Venice,' which I hope you will like. It has been out only a few days. The first opinion I have heard of it is Mr Gladstone's, to whom Mr Macmillan sent it, and who sent back to him at once a letter of four pages saying, first, that he was not going to Venice, as had been reported; and next, that he must contradict himself, and say that he had been in Venice, the book having quite given him that feeling; after which he enters into a question of Venetian political history about Bajamonte, whose very name, I should think, was unknown to most readers, but with whom this amazing old man seems intimately acquainted.

1888.

To Mr Blackwood.   WINDSOR, *30th January.*

I send you with this the conclusion of 'Joyce,' which I hope you will like. I have been so busy with it that I have put off for a day or two thanking you for your kind notice of the Venice book. It is most good and kind of you to have had it put in hand so quickly and given the book the advantage of such a valuable opinion in its favour. I hope I am not going wrong in writing to thank Mr Skelton for it. His hand is unmistakable, even had you not given me a hint. I hope you yourself like the book. You would see the insulting attack upon me in the 'Saturday Review,' which is not criticism at all but a personal assault. What I can have done to get myself such a bitter and spiteful enemy I can't imagine.

This spring, though Cecco's health had so much improved, it was thought advisable that he should again go to the south of Europe. He went alone, but, depending on his daily letters, his mother was satisfied that he should do so — more than satisfied, indeed, because his willingness to undertake the journey showed a hopeful increase of strength and energy. One of her letters to him is given here. Two of his, containing an impression of a bull-fight, were arranged by Mrs Oliphant, and printed in the 'Spectator,' to the great amusement of their author.

To F. R. Oliphant (then at Bordighera).

WINDSOR, 1st *March.*

. . . There is nothing new to tell you, nothing to say, except that I continue appallingly busy, and that now I have got well into the middle of the Principal's Life it is constantly becoming more difficult. There are endless allusions to public matters which I don't understand, and even in his own actual doings many things in which I miss the dear padrona's help. I have just been describing the beginning of our friendship, hers and mine, which was one day when we went up, she and I alone with you little children, to Whistlefield, and sat and talked there while you played. You were only a baby, so you can't recollect, though I think you were there in Jane's capacious arms. It all came back so clearly to my mind and caught my breath. Your sister with her bonny curls would be one of the chief. Somehow I never, as you may have noticed, can call her by her name. . . .

To Mr Blackwood.

WINDSOR, 30th *August.*

. . . Very many thanks for your kind invitation to Cecco and myself. . . . Could you introduce us to any Edinburgh antiquarian who would help us to see some holes and corners out of the beaten track? If Mr Cosmo Innes had been still alive I should have applied to him. . . .

But, oh, what is this dreadful business about Laurence Oliphant? Married after publishing his book to convince the world if possible that marriage should not be, and with such a wife so lately buried! Has he ventured to explain it to you? I suppose he has gone through the form merely to make it possible that he should have a companion and caretaker, for I can't suppose he is contradicting all the tenor of so many years at his age,—but he ought not to have done it anyhow.   I shall be very curious to hear what you know.

The following letter refers to the death of Laurence Oliphant, which took place on December 23, 1888 :—

WINDSOR, *Dec.* 29.

I have been quite anticipating your letter, and will give all the skill I possess to making such a sketch as I can of Laurence Oliphant.   His religious side, however, is to me of the very greatest interest, and I hope you will not object to a tolerably full description of it—not in its last development, with which I have little sympathy, but in the fundamental impulse which went before.   To have seen so little of him as I did, I happen to have seen him at moments and under circumstances which will give me considerable power, I think, in elucidating his life.   I am very sorry that I did not go to Twickenham to see him, as I had almost done, after I saw you last.   I think I could do this piece of work best by writing in the first person and with my own name, unless you have any objection.   I object to it on principle myself, but, as a point of fact, it would be less easy to make an interesting portrait of him in any other way.

The years do indeed grow sadder and sadder as they go on, and more still at my age than at yours.   I begin to watch them go, wondering if I shall see another end, and not very much wishing to do so, if truth must be told; for my path is clouded with anxieties and many disappointments, which I should once have thought insupportable, but which now, in the dreary philosophy of use, have come to be accepted more or less quietly.   I wish you and yours all that is good, as well as everything prosperous and pleasant for the new year.   Will you give my love to your sisters, and beg them to accept my affectionate good wishes, though at second hand?   I have caught another desperate cold, and even an additional letter becomes a burden in such circumstances. I am starting for Paris with Denny on the 3rd if all is well, intending to leave her there to study for six months in an artist's studio. I go on to Beaulieu on the 9th with the rest of my party.

1889.

The journey to Beaulieu was interrupted in a rather tragical manner, as the following letter explains.

To Mr Blackwood.   PARIS, 10*th January.*

I have a chronicle of misfortune to give you: in the first place, to explain why my article is late. I had hoped by this time to have been sending it to you from Beaulieu. We were all at the station on Wednesday night ready to start, our luggage all in the train, and ourselves eating something in the restaurant before setting out, when Cyril became suddenly and violently ill. This was about half an hour before the train started. I had no thoughts for anything but the sufferer, but Cecco saw the rest of our party off and then came and joined me. . . . I have now sent for an English doctor, who will, I hope, remove him to his own house; and if this gentleman gives a good account of him, as I hope, I will leave him in his hands and go on to Beaulieu to-morrow night. You may imagine what a dreadful business this has been — the horrible shock and alarm. . . .
The article on Laurence Oliphant is nearly finished, and leaving here to-morrow night, as I must do, if nothing very bad occurs, I hope to be able to send it off to you on Tuesday at latest. Cecco's proofs are in the same state, but the proof of course is not so urgent as the MS. I am sure you will be sorry for us. Cyril is very weak and exhausted, but quite himself,

and I trust will now go on well. We are in a dreadful French house, where there is not even a chambermaid; and our luggage is all gone, so that a clean collar seems to me the greatest luxury.

I will write with the article, I hope, on Tuesday.

VILLA DE FORESTA, BEAULIEU, 15*th* *January*.

I sent you my article in a great hurry to-day with no time to say anything. I hope you will like it. It is more a reminiscence than anything else, and it is rather remarkable, having really seen so little of Laurence Oliphant as I did, how completely my personal recollections follow the course of, and more or less elucidate the most interesting portion of, his life.

To Dr A. K. H. Boyd.   [*Jan.* or *Feb.*]

I have just been reading your paper about " Taking in Sail."   I think I have told you before how much I feel with and sympathise in your afternoon musings —the subdued thoughts that come to us with the decline of the day.   It is only this sympathy which makes me write now.   I wish I could take in sail, but it is not easy.   I almost think sometimes that to know the limit of years to which one had to reach, and so be able to regulate one's work to get as much done as possible without the vague horror as to years that may come after all ought to be over, would be a comfort; for at the end of all things the work is almost the only thing—is it not?—in which there is satisfaction.   Our children grow as old as ourselves, and friendship has its limitations, and the soul, even when most surrounded with apparent company, must live so much alone.   Your suggestion that something very good should happen to us as we get old once in every three years, is delightful, but almost ironical; this does not seem to me at least the end of life at which to expect anything good, but I hope that perhaps my experience is not that of others.   The one good thing that I am conscious of is the increased tolerance—nay, enjoyment—of the loneliness which is inevitable, and the great, calm, all-sustaining sense of a divine Unseen, a silent companion, God walking in the cool of the garden, which, after all, is the best.

Forgive me this return for your musings. I don't myself at all dislike the sensation and sentiment of getting old, and in many things I enter very fully into what you say on these subjects.

I have been here with all my belongings for the greater part of the winter, with January like June, and beds of violets and roses all through the dark weather, but the spring a little uncertain and trying even here.

To Mr Blackwood.   BEAULIEU, *4th March.*

. . . It has occurred to me that it might be worth while to publish the article on L. Oliphant a little enlarged as a small volume. What do you think of this? . . . I should add a greater detail of facts, and some criticism of his literary work, if you approved of the idea. . . . I heard a new piece of information about him on Saturday from Baron de Billing, a man high up in the French diplomatic service, and of whom people speak as future ambassador to St James's. He told me that it was M. Thiers who was really the cause of L. O.'s removal from Paris as 'Times' correspondent. Do you know if there is any truth in this? M. de Billing asserted it most positively, and said I might quote him to that effect. Mr Hamilton Aidé, who happened to sit on my other side, contradicted the statement, but only on his own authority. Perhaps you know which is to be believed. This took place at a magnificent luncheon at Monte Carlo given us by Mr Somerset Beaumont, at which Christine Nilsson was one of the guests. Thus we get glimpses of the world from time to time.

Mrs Oliphant to Mr Blackwood.   WINDSOR, *4th June.*

. . . After a conversation with Mrs Wynne Finch I put aside the idea of enlarging the article as quite inadequate, but hesitated a good deal about undertaking a larger work, feeling that it would cost me an amount of time and trouble which I could not afford to give except for a quite different remuneration.

I shall have to see all sorts of people on account of the book, and take a great deal of trouble, and my impression is that a real account of such a remarkable life would be very interesting to the public. . . . My own ideas are rather vague as to what size the book would come to, also now disturbed by some doubt as to what Mrs Wynne Finch's intervention will come to. . . . There is, however, no hurry about a decision. I should like to know definitely what is to be had of the letters at Haifa, and to see what comes from different quarters, and then perhaps we may be able to come to some mutual agreement on the subject.

WINDSOR, *28th June.*

I don't at all know the books you refer to—I have not seen any of them. Mr Barrie's 'Auld Licht Idylls,' &c., I think exceedingly clever. Indeed there seems to me genius in them, though the Scotch is, as you say, much too provincial. If you will send me the other books, I will carry out your wishes, if my opinion agrees with yours; but Barrie I must applaud, for I think his faculty is great. . . . He came here to see me one day. I have been rather nervous ever since, lest I should see myself in a newspaper, but he has been merciful.

1890.

To F. R. Oliphant.   WINDSOR, *Feb.* 17.

. . . I am correcting the type-written part of my 'Edinburgh,' half writing it over again, as I do not

like the John Knox bit at all. To tell the truth, I
liked John Knox so much less in going in to him
than I had done at a respectful distance, that it was
rather hard work to keep up a little show of approbation. He was a most intolerant bigot, and as dour
and obstinate as the nether millstone. The metaphor
is broken, but you will understand. I don't mean to
say he is not interesting, and his position often exceedingly humorous, though all the surroundings are
so grim. . . .

WINDSOR, *Feb.* 27.

. . . I wish, my dear, that you were less dis-
trustful of yourself. Every one must have felt the
same painful wandering of the mind, especially at the
most solemn moments. It has been my plague all my
life. What has been my consolation for a very long
time is the conviction that God understands what we
mean, or *what we want to mean*, so much better than
any one mortal can do. I have the most perfect reli-
ance upon His sympathy, so that I almost think He
must be more indulgent to us than we are to ourselves, and smile at things that horrify us, knowing in
His great understanding and tenderness all about it,
and that we prefer the good even when we don't succeed in doing it. Don't think lighter things, or the
lightest of all, without use, and have confidence in
our heavenly Father as, and far more than, you have
confidence in me, for He will never misunderstand
you.

Early in this year Mrs Oliphant found it necessary
to visit the Holy Land in order to collect materials
for her book on Jerusalem. Long ago, when her children were young, she had thought of this journey; but
circumstances had changed, and pleasure had little
to do with her present plans. She took with her her
elder son and niece, and Cecco, who was already in
Italy, joined her there.

To Mrs Harry Coghill.   WINDSOR, 11*th March.*

Many thanks for your kind wish to see us, and I wish very much I could have gone to you before leaving; but it is unfortunately impossible. I am up to my eyes in things to do, work to finish, and arrangements to make. How we are to manage to get under weigh by Monday morning is more than I can tell; but I suppose that we shall, as we generally do, though it always seems impossible the day before. . . . I am starting with a good deal of alarm both for the sea and the land, and a few thoughts of the possibility of never coming back again, such as are natural to a woman of my years. But the inducement to make the journey is strong, and I hope that by the blessing of God I may live and get home again, and see you and all my friends. All the same, I should have liked very much to see you before going away.

I have the very best news of Cecco. The renewed irritation in the lung, about which Dr Maclagan was so serious, has, he is told by a specialist in lung diseases whom he has consulted at Hyères, quite passed away, and he is doing as well as possible. We meet him at Turin on Thursday week, and we embark at Brindisi on Saturday 22nd. Burn a candle for us, that we may have a good voyage. I will write, if all is well, from Jerusalem. . . .

Mr A. W. Kinglake to Mrs Oliphant.

17 BAYSWATER TERRACE, W., *March* 19.

DEAR MRS OLIPHANT,—It is with ceaseless admiration that I have read ' The Duke's Daughter.'

My remembrance of what you had told me respecting the origin of your inclination to undertake the narrative put me into the mood for studying it, if so one may speak, instead of too placidly " reading " your delightful pages, and the effect of this special care was such as to make me think more—more even than ever before — of what — distinguished from " fancy " — I should call that sound, healthy, that strong Imagination of yours which tells you, and lets you tell others, the very, very truth.

To compare the few words I uttered to you in the course of perhaps some three minutes with your beautiful narrative is to make one remember that Shakespeare would look at some obsolete tale without perhaps any interest for any other live mortal, and then build on it or round it, a mighty work of genius.

To Mrs Harry Coghill.　　　　　　JERUSALEM, *9th April.*

MY DEAR COUSIN ANNIE,—Madge, I think, wrote from Cairo to tell you of our safe and pleasant voyage to Alexandria—that is to say, it was quite pleasant so far as calm weather was concerned, and I did not suffer in the least, nor did either of the boys. Madge was a little bad, but not much to speak of. I don't think, however, that I could be reconciled to a long sea voyage : the great monotony, the ceaseless round of the machinery, the longing one has to be quiet for a moment, to stop still and not feel the throbbing and swaying, get quite too much for me. I feel as if I could not put up with it for a moment longer, which is the most childish of sentiments, yet a very true one.

And so here we are in Jerusalem ! It is a wonderful place—wonderfully little changed in sentiment, I should think, since our Lord trod those solemn narrow streets, which probably would be filled with quite a similar crowd, strangers of all kinds, gazing and gaping when He was led through to His crucifixion. I insisted upon going along the Via Dolorosa on Good Friday, following what are supposed to have been His steps. I don't know that I could have done it had it not been for the boys, who took me by the elbows, one on each side, and almost carried me along. It was very deeply touching to toil along the laborious stony way, and to think, if not of what He felt, which is above our thoughts, yet of what Mary must have been feeling, and the others who were following through all the crowd of wandering strangers, and all the eager townsfolk taking sides for and against Jesus of Nazareth. The throng of Arabs, Jews, blacks—every conceivable kind of people, no doubt—must have been much the same. We only, unborn as then, so to speak, were new to the place. I envied the pilgrims who went along kneeling at the stations, kissing the stones. One would have been glad to have done it, to have been able to do it. My great pleasure is to see the poor Russians, shoals of them, peasants of the poorest class, who throng everywhere with a sort of passionate devotion in their faces, kissing the sacred stones as they might do a dear child, again and again.

The Church of the Holy Sepulchre is too confusing to be impressive. It is supposed to cover the site both of the Crucifixion and of the tomb; but there are many conflicting ideas, and these places do not feel like the real ones, covered as they are with tawdry shrines, and every kind of poor tinsel lamp and decoration. The recent explorers have a theory that the real place of Golgotha was a mound or little hill, most curiously like a skull in its formation, and which stands bare under the sky, not built upon at all. It was the Jewish place of execution—that is universally acknowledged. And underneath this hill, at a little distance, is a wild forlorn garden, and in it a tomb—not indeed a tomb new in which no man had yet been laid, but old, old, dark with the dust of centuries, and sunk under the heaps of rubbish that have invaded everything, yet so much more affecting, so wonderfully different from the feelings called forth by the Holy Sepulchre—so called—one cannot help wishing that this may be the true place.

We have been also at Gethsemane, a bright little garden full of flowers, but so possibly it might have been in the old sacred time. There are some very old olive-trees, and it lies low on the side of Olivet,

looking up to the city walls.   Another most affecting
spot was the turn of the road where our Lord, coming from Bethany, paused when the view of Jerusalem
burst upon Him, as it does where the pathway sweeps
round the hill, and wept over the city which would
not consent to be saved.   But indeed there is
scarcely a corner at which there is not some sacred
association.

Bethlehem, where we were yesterday, was very delightful, a little city on a hill—Christian—the women
pretty creatures with smiling uncovered faces and a
sort of innocent happy air about.   The place of the
Nativity is indeed built over and made into shrines
and chapels ; but the little inn, chiefly hewn out in
the rock, as is still common, can be easily traced, and
the little alcove where one can so easily believe Mary
to have been laid, and the manger where the Child
was placed, seem so credible and natural that one is
happy in believing.   The place is supposed by united
and invariable tradition to be quite authentic.

I am bearing the journey perfectly well, not feeling
the fatigue very much.   I have decided not to attempt
riding at all, but to have a palanquin for Galilee.
The others are quite well.   It is a little dreary being
here by myself. We leave Jaffa on Monday next for
Haifa, Nazareth, and the Lake of Galilee, if all is
well.   Should Cecco not feel equal to any more riding
he will return to Italy, but I hope this may not be the
case.   We expect to be in Constantinople about the
5th or 6th May, and I should be very glad of a letter
there to Cook's Tourist office.

I hope you are all well and enjoying the spring.
Of course it is full summer here so far as the heat is
concerned, but the country is very desolate, stony,
and grey, though the lower slopes of the hills where
there is grass are scarlet with anemones of the finest
growth, and clusters of cyclamen grow in many of the
crevices of the rocks.   The birds all about Jerusalem
are wonderful, chiefly swallows, and they are in all

the churches, flying about and adding a great charm. "The swallow findeth a place for herself, even Thine altars:" it is perfectly true.

To Mrs Tarver.   JERUSALEM, *12th April.*

I have been a long time in writing, which is partly because there has been so little time, and partly because the post is only once a-week, so that if one misses one there is no way of rectifying till another seven days are past.   We are now just on the eve of leaving Jerusalem, and this great end of the journey is accomplished.   It seems wonderful ever to get here at all, and now it seems equally wonderful that it should be all over, and that to-morrow our expedition here will be a thing of the past.   We have been in Jerusalem eleven days, and seen a great deal, and I am not disappointed.   In some of the holy places, indeed, it is difficult to feel all the solemnity of the associations, but with many others this is not the case; and the wonderful little inn at Bethlehem, though enshrined in a church, and the country road that leads to Bethany, and the Mount of Olives, and the splendid platforms of the old Temple, where the Mosque of Omar now stands, and all the other places which one is sure must have been trodden by those blessed feet, are impressive and touching in the highest degree.   To come round a sudden corner and realise that there our Lord paused and gazed, and wept over Jerusalem, is such a feeling as needs no words to tell.   The grey walls, the flat house-tops, the towers of Sion, the Golden Gate (now built up, because Messiah is to enter there when He comes again), breaking the long line of the Temple walls, all must be much as they were when He looked upon them.   And Gethsemane lies underneath.   It is a wonderful sensation.

All our journey has been prosperous: the sea was quiet, the landing at Jaffa easy, we have got one of the best of dragomen, and altogether would be very well off, if it were not that I am sadly disappointed about Cecco, who, though they say his chest is much better, has grown so dreadfully thin that it makes my heart sick every time I look at him. . . . This has been the terrible drawback of this time, which otherwise would have been all we could desire. We leave to-morrow for Jaffa, and go on by steamer to Haifa on Monday, where we begin the most novel mode of travelling, camping out and travelling—the others on horseback, I in a palanquin. This will last for ten days, ending at Damascus, and from there we drive to Beyrout and take steamer for Constantinople. We hope to get there about the 5th or 6th of May, and then home with very little delay.

This day has been a very fatiguing one. We were all over the Mosque of Omar in the morning, as it has been closed till to-day, and then went to the Holy Sepulchre to see the so-called miracle of the Holy Fire. The sight was a most extraordinary one. If you see Mr Holmes, tell him that his Greek Patriarch has been exceedingly civil, and done a great deal for us, though he has not been well enough to receive us. . . .

You will have got back again probably before this reaches you, as it may not leave Jerusalem till the 16th. One post a-week only! and not a book-shop in the place, which, as we have read all our books, is rather dreadful. Nor, I fear, is there any prospect of getting any, or of seeing a newspaper for a fortnight at least. Cyril, Cecco, and Madge went to Jericho and the Dead Sea in the beginning of the week, which took three days, during which time I was alone; and save for occasional flirtations with the American Consul and a Greek archimandrite, I don't know what I should have done. All the same, the hotel is half full of Scotch ministers and people from Dundee !

To Miss Oliphant.

HAIFA ENCAMPMENT, *Wednesday, 16th April.*

MY DEAREST DENNY,—I am writing to you from our first encampment close to Haifa. We have our tents pitched in a field with a beautiful view, just under our eyes, of the bay of Haifa, the white town and castle of Acre—besieged, Heaven knows how often, in all the centuries from prehistoric times till now—lying on the other side, and the mountains of Galilee behind. We came from Jaffa to Haifa yesterday on a perfectly smooth sea, and landed here at ten at night in boats. The pushing off from the big steamer in the dark (it was quite dark, the sky clouded, and the stars invisible), with a tremendous jabber of the boatmen, was rather terrifying; at least I confess that I was frightened and gripped Cecco, who was sitting next to me, hard. The lights of the little town guided us, and the water was like glass, but otherwise the sea all around was as black as could be, and looked like a mysterious infinite all behind and around us: however, we got in all right, chiefly by Jamal's good management, who is a treasure of a dragoman. I say he is my idea of a little Providence, for whatever we want we have only to refer to him, and all is supplied in a moment, or as near a moment as Eastern habits permit. He is a fine, grave, serious man of forty-five or so, and seems completely up to everything. It was a little strange last night sleeping in a tent for the first time, but we were quite comfortable, and took to it as if it were the most natural thing in the world, which is what one so easily gets to do with any exceptional circumstances. It rained, unfortunately, and blew a little, and it is still very windy and cloudy to-day. One kept wondering what would happen if the tent blew down; but this was evidently a thing which it had not the least intention of doing. We got to the tents from the landing in a rough sort of country carriage preceded by men with

lanterns. It was past ten at night, and we were by
way of having dined at five o'clock on the boat. I
expected nothing except perhaps a biscuit when we
got to the camp, but lo! there was a good dinner or
supper waiting for us, to which we did much justice
before going to bed. I think Cecco is a trifle better.
His spirits are so, and that is always a good test, and
he eats fairly well, and coughs scarcely at all. If only
he were not so awfully thin! but I hope that this out-
door life may do him good.

We have been to-day to the Friedhof, where Alice
Oliphant lies. Madge made a white wreath and I
a red cross, entirely red, to lay on the grave; and
afterwards we saw their house, a house full of nice
airy rooms, which I am sure they must have made
the most cheerful place. I thought I could see her
flitting in and out, on household cares intent. You
remember what a taste for cooking and managing
she had. Round about their house are the prim, red-
tiled houses of the German colony, looking like a
village emigrated bodily from the Fatherland, and
everybody about is German.

Since we came here last night another encampment
has been set up beside us, which is said to belong to
a father with seven daughters. It is bigger, but not
nearly so well placed as ours. I must try and get
Tiddy to take a photograph of our encampment. . . .
We are on a sort of natural platform, the field sloping
downwards just beyond. There is a tent for Tids and
Cecco, one for Madge and me, the dining- and sitting-
room tent, the kitchen tent, and another big one beyond, which I suppose is for Jamal and the servants.
There are lanterns hung round at night, and I think
two of the men watch. The horses, mules, &c., are
in the field before us, increased now by a multitude
of mules and donkeys, the beasts of burden of our
neighbours, who, by the way, are just arriving. I am
sitting out at the door of the tent watching them come
in.

This summer, after Mrs Oliphant's return from the Holy Land, was one of renewed anxiety. It is probable that though she had enjoyed it much, she had also suffered a good deal from the heat and fatigue; and a very disagreeable accident (to call it by its mildest name) which she met with must have shaken her nerves. She was being carried down a slope on Mount Carmel, the younger members of the party being on horseback a little in front, when the pole of her chair broke, and she was thrown to the ground. Though she fell so as to get scratches about her head and face, she had no actual damage, except indeed the jar to her nerves. She was much more occupied with her son's ailments, however, than her own, and it is in reference to them that she writes to Mrs Coghill: "Won't you come down here if you are in town? I should like so much to have a talk with you over everything: there is scarcely any one else with whom I can give myself this indulgence."

On the 7th of August, when Cecco had been sent away to the Engadine, she writes to the same correspondent:—

To Mrs Harry Coghill.   WINDSOR, *7th August.*

. . . Cecco I don't know what to say about. He startled me by saying he was going on a mountain expedition, after complaining of the almost impossibility of going uphill at all on account of his breath, and I fear it was more than he ought to have done— and he is very impatient of being questioned. I am more anxious than words can say, but say very little about it, and try to be patient. God knows whether I have yet accomplished the tale of my sorrows.

Cecco in the meantime was undergoing a sort of

Arctic experience, which could not have been pleasant, and was certainly not beneficial.

One of the notes in which Mr Kinglake expressed his warm admiration of Mrs Oliphant's work belongs to this date, and must have given her pleasure.

Mr A. W. Kinglake to Mrs Oliphant.

17 BAYSWATER TERRACE, W., *August* 25.

DEAR MRS OLIPHANT,—It is so long since I heard from you that I venture to ask how you are.

Some little time since, I had the good fortune to find that there was at least *one* of your delightful books which I had missed—I mean 'In Trust'—and I am only now towards the end of the second volume. I am greatly interested, and more than ever admiring the way in which your powerful yet truth-loving imagination proves able to deal with the mazes of Human Nature.—Believe me, dear Mrs Oliphant, most truly yours,   A. W. KINGLAKE.

To Mrs Harry Coghill.   WINDSOR, 28*th August.*

I ought to have written sooner to announce my safe arrival at home, but I had to make such a leap among the lions of retarded work that I have scarcely had a moment to myself. I found Cyril not very well. He has run down somehow and got below par, as the doctors say, but he is now better again. And Cecco's letters are far from satisfactory. I feel as if he were coming back less well instead of better. God grant I may be wrong, but my life seems sometimes almost too full of anxieties to be borne. The little rest with you, though it does one so much good, perhaps makes the return for the moment more acute. I hope that in a week or so Cecco will be back, but I almost fear the sight of his dear thin hands. I am cheerful enough, you know, outwardly, and don't talk of my troubles, but they are very heavy and sore. The mountains of work I have to toil through are the best help I could have.

It had always been the custom of the house at Windsor to keep the birthdays of the two brothers together. The dates were but three weeks apart. Cyril's fell on the 16th of November, and sometimes that was the day chosen. That day, at any rate, had been always more or less a *fête* in the family circle, and it was no small shock to the one nearest to that circle, though no longer of it, and herself at the moment in deep grief, to receive on the 10th the following note — a mere cry of distress from the agonised mother :—

To Mrs Harry Coghill.   WINDSOR, 3 A.M., *9th November.*

DEAR COUSIN ANNIE,—You are in trouble, but in no such trouble as I am. My boy, my Tiddy is gone !—a few hours ago—dead ! You will not believe it, nor can I. You will wonder at my writing to you myself, but I can't sleep or rest, and I can only talk of him—my bonny boy—my darling ! I am like stone —I can't feel it—but it is true.—Your affec.

Many of the letters conveying this sad news were naturally written by Cecco, in every emergency his mother's loving and dearly loved helper.

F. R. Oliphant to Mr Blackwood.   WINDSOR, *Nov.* 9.

DEAR MR BLACKWOOD,—I have to give you the terrible and unexpected intelligence of my brother's death, which occurred at one o'clock this morning, after a short and apparently unimportant illness. On Tuesday he was suffering from a very heavy cold, and complained of pains in his head ; he then took to his bed and remained in a rather prostrate condition, but gave us no great alarm till Thursday, when there were several degrees of fever, and the doctor declared that he had congestion of the lungs. The fever subsided yesterday, but left him in a terribly low condition, and the ultimate cause of death was apparently suffocation through the obstruction of the passages by some matter which he was not strong enough to force up. The end was quite peaceful and (presumably) painless. Only yesterday morning he was well enough to read out to me a little notice of his ' De Musset ' which appeared in a Glasgow paper ; no one of us had any suspicion of what was at hand. My mother is in a terrible condition of grief, but bears it with her usual extraordinary strength and courage. It seems almost impossible to realise what has happened. —I remain, yours sincerely,   F. R. OLIPHANT.

I am very glad that his ' De Musset ' had come out.

Mrs Oliphant to Mrs Harry Coghill.

BOURNEMOUTH, *November.*

. . . All is over. I am very quiet—I think unnaturally—I hope supernaturally so. All the time of the burying I thought I saw my Tiddy and Frank looking on, and was sustained as if they were holding me up. I would like to tell you all about it, but I cannot write. All his temptations and dangers are over, his feet are in a sure place, a better life has begun—that is what I think most. God bless my boy—life was hard upon him ; so many people have written to me so sweetly and tenderly of him.

All was over. A career so brilliant in the hope and promise of its beginning had ended in barren disappointment. One little volume and a few verses were all that was left. Yet there are still some living who can testify that Mrs Oliphant's pride in her son, and ambition for him, were not unreasonable—who can recall the handsome brilliant boy, his lovely voice, his quick sympathies, his generosity in the small things of daily life. And it is they, alas! also who can recall the falling away from that bright youth—broken health, broken hopes, a dismal resignation to inactivity—which was more tragically painful than words can say to the mother whose toil had been so gladly given for him.

Mrs Oliphant to Mr Blackwood.

DAVOS-PLATZ, *November* 30.

. . . I am glad to say that I have a most favourable opinion of Cecco here. . . . This is all the consolation I can now have in this life, and I thank God for it.

If it had been possible to have published the 'De Musset' book a little sooner, that my dearest boy might have had the pleasure of seeing what was said of it, I should have been thankful; but that is but a small matter amid all the anguish of this dreadful month. Please give your aunt my love, but tell her I cannot write. I can work enormously, which is the only opiate I can take, but no more.

To Mrs Harry Coghill.   DAVOS-PLATZ, *November* 30.

The reason of our leaving so soon was that Cecco had been ordered to go off in the beginning of the month, and was only hindered by some apparently accidental circumstances from leaving on the morning of the day his dearest brother was taken ill. I had no thought, after all that we could do was done for him, but to hasten Cecco's going and to go with him. We left the house with my good Esther in it, and there was no occasion for any delay. I fear there is little likelihood of letting it before April. I would with my own will go back to it no more. It is too full of associations, so many of them of pain and sorrow; and I think that to sit alone at night at my work, and feel those two empty rooms blank and dark, would be more than I could bear. I find everything grow harder and more crushing as the heavy days go on. At first I had a kind of exaltation—of support, and consent to what God had done, believing, as I still believe, that for him, my dear boy, the only person to be considered in the matter, it was best. But nature will not be balked, and my heart is broken.

I have, however, the only consolation this life can now give me in what is said about Cecco here. "The disease has passed off nicely," the doctor, the best here, a Swiss, says. He will not be so strong as other men for a while, but eventually he will be so. Koch's cure is the only matter that is thought of here, and it is now beginning to be applied; but the doctors say there is no occasion to try it for Cecco—that it is better to let well alone. This is, you may suppose, balm to my heart, as much as I am capable of, and I hope I shall live a year or two more to make things as smooth as I can for my Cecco. . . .

I am simply working like,—I don't know any simile to use—working always; it is the only prop for my mind, and my body feels no harm. I am always quickened into intolerable life by calamity. It is impossible to conceive anything more miserable than this abode of snow, with all the poor people coughing their lives away. I sometimes think if I could hear the howl of the sea, and see a green world again, that it would do me a little good, but I don't imagine that or anything would make much difference.

HÔTEL VICTORIA, DAVOS-PLATZ, *Dec.* 2.

MY DEAR BLANCHE CORNISH,—I cannot call you by any formal name. All your family have been so sweet and so dear to me in my anguish and trouble that I feel as if you belonged to me a little, and you know I told you that you were the only person of whom my dearest boy thought when he was bringing souvenirs from the East. I want you to ask Emily sometime when she sees Lord Tennyson to tell him that for the last two months of his life, I know not whether by any presentiment or not, my Cyril almost every evening sang Elaine's song, " Oh love, if Death be sweeter, let me die," till it got so into our ears that we all kept singing it involuntarily, with no thought—God knows—in my mind of what it meant for him, though I often thought of it for myself. Perhaps it may interest the poet, who knows what this anguish is. My thoughts, which are always circling round and round the one subject, are twisted through and through with lines of " In Memoriam"; and Elaine's song will always now be Cyril's song to me. It was not that he was melancholy or downcast, for that was not so. I wonder sometimes if it was one of those unconscious prayers which God seems to thrust into our hearts, and answers, though we don't know for what we are asking. This has been my case in the most wonderful and heartrending way.

Give my love to all your dear people, and thanks a thousand times for all your sweet words about my dearest Cyril. His name opens up the fountains of tears, which at my age are deep down and hard to come. It is my indulgence in the night, when my Cecco and Denny have gone to bed, to write a letter now and then and let them get vent, for the after-days are worse than the first.

God bless you, my dear.—Your affectionate,

M. O. W. O.

To Mrs Valentine.　　　　　Davos-Platz, *15th December.*

 . . . Our days are very monotonous: this is how we go through them. I have my breakfast before I get up, but the others go downstairs for theirs. C. goes out for an hour's walk by the doctor's orders immediately after breakfast; then he comes in and generally sits a little on the balcony, and goes out for another dander with D. Then comes lunch at one o'clock, to which we all go down. The company at table are all very friendly, even intimate. . . . Then

we return upstairs, and in about half an hour C. and
D. take me out for a walk. We turn the sunny way
down the valley, along the road, which is hard snow,
and crossing one or two toboggan runs, as far as I am
able to walk, which is a good way now. Then we
come in and have tea, and I get to work again, and
generally finish my chapter before dinner, which is at
half-past six. Our letters sometimes come—they did
to-day—at half-past two, sometimes not till past six,
and we look for them eagerly; then C. stays down in
the smoking-room a little time after dinner and plays
a game with the other men. All this sounds cheerful
enough—doesn't it ?—and though we often flag in the
way of talk, we do support each other, and keep very
steady. But when they leave me and go to bed, then
I confess I do put off my mask, and give myself up to
the thoughts that have been besieging me through
everything. It is the only time that I let myself go.

To Mr Craik.   Davos-Platz, *28th December.*
    . . . I am very glad to hear that ' Edinburgh '
is doing well. . . . Have you thought yet of any
one to do the pictures of the ' Jerusalem ' ? I should
like, whoever it may be that is chosen, to have an
opportunity of seeing him and talking the matter over
with him, which I think could not but be to the
advantage of the work.
    I see that the ' Athenæum,' by the way, has noted
one real error of carelessness on my part, among
many which are not so—about Duncan Forbes, who
of course I know very well to be a contemporary of
Allan Ramsay, and Fletcher of Saltoun older. I don't
know how I can have been so careless as to represent
them as reading his ballads in their childhood. By
the way, if you should know any one who is reviewing
the book, could you have it said that my George
Buchanan chapter was written, corrected, and out of
my hands before the recent book about him was
printed ? I put this in a note, but it might be well

to mention it over again, and I would also like to correct the paragraph I refer to about Forbes and Ramsay before another edition comes out.

Every good wish.

1891.

To Mrs Harry Coghill.   DAVOS, *January.*

My news about Cecco is all that could be desired. Dr Ruedi has seen him again, and finds the improvement progressing so well that he says, if all continues in the same way, he will be *well* in spring. I am very, very thankful, though my heart seems so dead to all thoughts but one that I scarcely seem to feel it. This is one great and strange consequence of the great parting, that the one who is gone, and who while he was present with us was the subject of many thoughts indeed, yet thoughts crossed and broken with a hundred other interests, becomes far more present, close, and intensely felt in every movement of life than if he were by one's side. The first result of the separation is thus to make all separation impossible, to bring him nearer and make him dearer than ever before. It shows how little death is, and yet how unspeakably great, cutting off all response.

I am very well, all the same, nothing touches me, and working very hard. I sometimes think that to be made ill by suffering, as other people are, would soften a little the pain; but I get the full sharpness of it in every way, though it is different at my age from the tempest of younger days. I think I am learning patience, and am soothed by the thought that it cannot be a very long time. I used to be appalled at thought of the long years to come when my Maggie died; now, they can't be very long.

Pardon me for dropping into the usual weary strain. I shall have to give up writing letters, for I feel that I must weary out my friends.

The health Mrs Oliphant thought so cruelly strong did give way at this time, and she had a sharp attack of illness, to the great distress of Cecco and her adopted daughter. The bad effect of the climate on a system so hardly tried was very nearly fatal in this case, and the little party moved as soon as they possibly could to a milder air.

To Mr Blackwood.   DAVOS-PLATZ, *24th February.*

. . . I am still very far from well, and the doctor tells me that I must not expect to be so till I leave here. It appears that the High Alps are not good for elder people, and almost always produce a collapse of some kind. I tried very hard to finish your article, and was in hopes to have done it till the last moment, when another attack settled the question. I am better now, but in an irritated and feeble state, afraid to eat anything. Half in bed, however, I have managed to get through the proofs, and on next Monday, the 2nd March, we are to get off to San Remo, where the doctor says Cecco will do as well as here for the rest of the spring, Davos having strengthened and set him up so much. This of course removes all my objections to leaving. For many reasons I shall be very glad. These months have been very dreary ; and to see the fair face of nature again after looking on nothing but dazzling snow, may convey a little solace to the sick soul as well as body.

VILLA DEGLI OLIVI, SAN REMO, *March* 23.

. . . This reminds me of my great negligence in not having thanked you before for the review of 'Royal Edinburgh.' I should have credited Mr Skelton with it, but that his own work was included with mine. In any case, whoever executed the work, many thanks for having it done. I presume the article on dear Mr Kinglake was Sir Edward Hamley's, and I am grateful to him too for what he says

of our dear old friend's kind interest in my books.
I was so ill when the Magazine arrived, and so altogether out of sorts, that I had not the heart to write
to you about them, as I ought to have done. Pray
forgive me.

To the Hon. Emily Lawless.

WINDSOR, *Saturday Night, late, 30th May.*

DEAR EMILY,—The sight even of your handwriting
is a pleasure, and your praise is very delightful, and
gave me a surprised sensation of real pleasure still
more warm. I had not, somehow, expected it. Pray
believe, what is most completely the truth, that there
is no one whose opinion I believe more, or whom
I am more glad to please, and what you say of the
book[1] is exactly what I should have most wished
to accomplish. I am very glad that you think I
have succeeded. I quite recognise the truth of your
affectionate blame, that I don't care much about my
own standing as an author. It would have been
more sensible to have done so — to have shown a
more proper regard for it when I was younger; but
then life has always been at hard if not high pressure for me, and there have always been so many
other things that were more important. Do you
know, I am sometimes inclined to think that a little
pomposity is coming on! I begin to have a faint
consciousness of stilts, and of an inclination to
think that a person of my standing should be treated
with respect, which amuses me, as a new feature
in what Colonel Lockhart used to call "the other
fellow" who is one's self.

Mrs Oliphant to Mr Blackwood.   WINDSOR, *17th October.*

I send you my Old Saloon paper, which I hope
you will like. I have used, as you will perceive, few
books, and I trust you will not think I have done

---

[1] Life of Laurence Oliphant.

wrong by bringing in Rudyard Kipling, who I think wants something more than the praise which is so liberally dealt to him in the newspapers. You will think, however, that I am still more liberal in my praise. . . .

We are leaving here (this house) in about a fortnight, and Windsor in the middle of next month, and it is on the cards that we may not return again here, where so much of our life has been spent. My own house I will never go back to, and the whole place has become unutterably sad.

This decision could not be adhered to, and the diminished family returned to the old home at Windsor late in the summer of 1892. The Jerusalem book was published by Macmillan at this time.

The Right Hon. W. E. Gladstone to Mrs Oliphant.

BIARRITZ, *December* 28.

DEAR MRS OLIPHANT,—The beautiful volume which you have so kindly sent me came, I need hardly say, introduced not only by your much too flattering note, but by abundant recollections of knowledge and of pleasure derived from you on many previous literary occasions.

I have begun the perusal, and I much hope, and cannot doubt, that your living portraitures of Scripture characters will impress upon many minds an important portion of those evidences of the sacred volume which are so much higher than the "higher criticism," and which have a range of flight beyond its reach.—Allow me to remain with many thanks faithfully yours,

W. E. GLADSTONE.

1892.

To Mr Blackwood. WINDSOR, 25*th August.*

I have been a long time of replying to your letter. Books do not seem very plentiful just now, and I don't know whether you would like me to take up a handful of novels, and perhaps a few poetry books. I should like to say my mind about Louis Stevenson's 'Wrecker' and the 'Naulakha,' both of which are striking instances of the evils of collaboration, and I think would furnish good materials for a little slashing. As I am very fond of the principal authors in both cases, I should not go too far. I will send a list of some others if you feel inclined for this. . . .

WINDSOR, 15*th September.*

. . . By the bye, I have thought several times of collecting—only for private circulation—my own verses scattered through many years of 'Maga.' Could you bid some of your attendant spirits look them out for me, tearing out the page or making a rough reprint?

Thanks for the volumes received yesterday of 'Valentine' and 'Katie Stewart.' They are delightfully printed, and nice volumes, though I don't care for the binding. And I wish, I wish you had printed 'Katie Stewart' by herself.

The death of Tennyson and his funeral are the occasion of the next two letters.

To Mr Craik. WINDSOR.

I telegraphed to you yesterday in the evening, fearing that there might be a great rush, as no doubt there will be, for places in the Abbey on Wednesday. I hope my application would be in time. Mr

X

Blackwood wants me to write something upon Lord Tennyson (not the funeral), and I should be grateful if you would send me the new volume when it is ready as well as a copy of the 'Foresters.' What a pity that he was not gratified by seeing the latter performed in England in a becoming way! If we knew when our great men were to be taken from us, how much more we might do to give them a pleasure before they go.

All seems most nobly appropriate in his end, and nothing but congratulations seem to me to be applicable to him. He has met his pilot face to face. How entirely that last wonderful poem of his seems to have taken possession of everybody's imagination, and how fitly! Is it true that Hallam Tennyson has wished it to be set to music and sung at the funeral? I can't think it very suitable for that. I suggested to Dr Bridge those verses from " In Memoriam " :—

> " Peace, come away, the song of woe
> Is after all an earthly song."

To Mr Blackwood.   WINDSOR, *7th October.*

Your letter this morning has thrown a different light upon the Tennyson article. I thought of it in the shock of the moment as a mere obituary notice, such as you sometimes put in at the end of the Magazine. This was a foolish mistake on my part, for of course our great poet was not one of ' Maga's ' men. But I am rather afraid of the inveterate want of accord between you and me on the subject of poetry. I had forgotten Christopher North's strictures, in which I think that great critic must have been wanting in his usual insight; but in any case I fear I can't agree that " Maud " is anything but an exquisite piece of art and melody, and " Locksley Hall " a very fine poem.

. . . He was once most amusingly rude to me, for which I bore him no malice, for it was exceedingly

funny; and last time I saw him in the Isle of Wight he
was delightfully kind, and took the greatest trouble
in making our little visit pleasant. He read two of
his poems to me, one a long and difficult one, the
" Ode on the Duke's Funeral," which must have been
very trying and exhausting to read : so my last view
of him has left the most delightful impression on my
mind. Now it is in your hands, let me know what
you wish me to do. . . .

1893.

To Lady Cloncurry.　　　　　　ST RAPHAEL, *February* 4.

I have been delaying to write to you until I had
an address! A family wandering about the world
without an address is a comic, but at the same time
almost a tragic thing, and I think I must make something of the predicament. However, for the moment
this is ended, and I have not only an address, but so
impressive a one that I hope you will be quite struck
by it. *Château La Tour !*—that is the name of the
house—Château La Tour, Mont Boron, Nice. It is
close to our former villa, much more showy, but not
so big, though also, alas! considerably dearer. We
found no villas at all to be had on that spot except
this one, and we have been going through a course
of bargaining, which, you know, by degrees heats
one's blood! You go on and the owner goes on, he
falling and you rising, till you find that you have
gone a great deal farther than you had any intention
of going. You would laugh at our Tower, which is
very French and fantastic outside, but very nice
within; and the view is superb, the same we had
last year, but a little more so, please tell Emily.

I thought Cecco looking very well when we met,
but I fear, from being out two or three times at
sunset, he has caught another cold, and his cough
is bad. When it is better, I am better; but when

it torments him, as it sometimes does, I become a very poor creature indeed, and good for nothing. Still I can't say that he is not well on the whole.

I found here established Mrs Harrison and Miss Kingsley, the latter so like her father that there could be no doubt who she was.

To Mr Craik.

VILLA LA TOUR, MONT BORON, NICE, 17*th February.*

We have settled down here for the spring in a beautiful corner, with the most delightful view of the sea and the mountains and the lights of Nice at our feet, very near the place where we were last year. Cecco is very well on the whole, and he has sent or is sending in an application for the vacant librarianship at the London Library. It is expressly said that no private applications are to be made on behalf of any candidate, so I do not ask you to use any interest of yours in his behalf, and I have not written to anybody on the subject, though no doubt you will know all, and I several, of the judges. I scarcely know what kind of post it is, and probably they will want an older man; but in any case I think it was right for him to try for it. He has excellent testimonials.

My chief disadvantage here is the difficulty of getting books. Will you please whistle for one of your slaves, and bid him inquire whether there are any translations of the life, letters, and works of St Gregory the Great, or of St Jerome, in English? I have the Latin, but a crib is legitimate for me, as I can't have Cecco tied to my apron. He begs me to ask whether you would be so very kind as to send him the 'Agricola' of Tacitus, of which he says you have published an edition, and which he has at home, but I could not find to bring him. He would be very much obliged.

Madge is getting on wonderfully with her engraving, but is more than likely to exemplify over again the foolishness of giving expensive training to young women, by turning her thoughts in quite a different direction.

To the Hon. Emily Lawless.   VILLA LA TOUR, 12*th May.*

It seems years since I have heard from you, and as this is the most inappropriate moment possible for writing letters, seated among the ruins of this three months' home, I naturally take advantage of it to send you my *Ave* in your new house.   Going away is always a horror, especially that *mauvais quart d'heure* of the reckoning!   I have been paying and paying till I am quite sick.   .   .   .

We have had a checkered season altogether.   Cecco has not been at all well.   He has given me moments of great anxiety: even the doctor thought the old mischief was beginning again, and I had a week of such misery as I cannot describe.   It is all right, I believe, but he is very thin and weak.   This place, I think,—I almost hope,—has not suited him, and that he will be better elsewhere.   I have been anything but well myself in consequence.   And yet it is so beautiful, that to leave this glorious bay and the mountains and the lighthouses and all the villages on the hillsides, and the flowers rioting everywhere, roses flinging themselves about in every direction, is a pity too.   What a thing it would be to live a week, a day, without some anxiety tearing at one's heart!   It would almost be heaven enough for a poor mortal of a mother, at least.

This summer was one of a little revived cheerfulness.   The elder of Mrs. Oliphant's nieces (who were also her adopted daughters) was married on the 26th of July.   There is always, or almost always, a certain amount of pleasant excitement in preparing for a marriage—the gathering together of the bride's pretty things, the summoning of friends, and the arrangement for the ceremony. Into all this Mrs Oliphant threw herself, determined that the girl she had brought up should go to her husband surrounded by all that love and care could do for her. A very large party assembled, and for the last time the house, which had known so much happiness and so much sorrow, was filled and overflowing with guests.

In all that was to be done Cecco took the part of master. He was far from well, and on the day of the wedding his looks alarmed some of those who loved him. Almost immediately afterwards there was an evident failure of his health, and his mother's anxieties became again as acute as ever.

To the Hon. Emily Lawless.   WINDSOR, *3rd August.*

I hope you are now safe at Niton, since you are going there, though I also wish you had not gone there with a raging sea between us. I hope my dear Lady Cloncurry has got there safely, and I hope you will like it. Cecco is very, very poorly. It was found he had dilatation of the heart, which is the immediate cause of his low state; but I am more anxious about him than any words can say. It seems to me as if my sorrows were never to have an end as long as my life lasts.

"The Valentines" are here and look very happy, tell Lady Cloncurry, which it is a comfort to see. Much love to you both.

To Mr Blackwood.   WINDSOR, *27th August.*

. . . The two Hamleys make a great gap in the old band of contributors. I hope you pick up new ones to fill up the vacant places. One always regrets the days that are gone, but it must be "Le roi est mort, vive le roi!" in literature as well as in all other things. . . .

The last time, I think, that I saw Sir Edward was

at a Royal Academy soirée in the Jubilee year, when he was blazing with all his stars and orders, and a most distinguished figure, whom one was proud to stand by. I have just been recalling this in writing to his niece. I am glad to have that last recollection of him.

1894.

To F. R. Oliphant. WINDSOR, *9th January.*

. . . I have done nothing but wade through Dean Stanley's Life this last week in the intervals of doing perfunctorily a little work in the mornings. What a queer little being he was,—quite uninterested in any argument or harmony of religious opinion, but up like a little turkey cock at the first note of discord, and grappling all dissentients to his small bosom— Maurice, Colenso, Père Hyacinthe, Pusey, Newman, in their times of contradictiousness. Hampden and Goring (which are names you will know nothing of), every man who fibs—which is a wrong word to use— is in the moment of his fibbing a delight to Stanley. It is a curious characteristic.

To Mrs Harry Coghill.

HÔTEL D'ITALIE, MENTONE, *March 4.*

I have been rather a cripple ever since I came here, very much taken up about my knees, which gave way in the most ridiculous manner when I attempted to walk, and gave me great pain; and though this of course did not prevent me from writing, it hampered me in many ways. However, I have been in the hands of a *masseuse* for ten days, and am getting right again, which I really did not think I should have done. And now we are approaching the end of our stay here, Cecco being anxious to go on to fresh woods and pastures new. He is tolerably well, but still much troubled with his breathing;

and he has not gained much strength, I fear, but he is very full of Riviera work. I get him to drive as much as possible, and fortunately he begins to like driving. I must get him a little trap of some kind when we get home. He is so tremendously conscientious about seeing with his own eyes everything he intends to mention in his book, that he gives himself more labour than he need do. We have had warm and fine weather on the whole, but with many misty grey days such as I have never seen before on the Riviera—they must be peculiar to Mentone. We are on the east bay, which is much the finest so far as the view goes, though not the fashionable end. We have a tiny little sitting-room, but with a balcony attached, the view from which is wonderful, the old town rising up to the right in all its wonderful glow of colour, and the coast on the other side ending in Bordighera, which is the most persistently shining and smiling place I ever saw. . . .

To Mr Blackwood.   WINDSOR, *9th July.*

. . . I had been thinking of offering to you a series of perhaps four articles, to appear at intervals, called the " Spectator " or the " Looker-on," or some such title, a sort of review of the three or four months preceding,—the season, the autumn, the winter season, &c.,—with a reflection of the Society and lighter morals, politics, art, and literature of the time. I don't know if you would care for them, but I have rather a fancy for doing them, and there is plenty of material, Heaven knows. Let me know if you would like them, for in that case I should look again at some things before the season is over.

WINDSOR, *22nd August.*

I have an offer from America for a novel to begin in the end of next year or beginning of '96. As the New York people ask in what magazine the story would be published here, and at what time, I think it best to ask you if you would be inclined to make any bargain with me before answering them. Would you then kindly reply to this as soon as possible?

I have been thinking of sending you a paper for Christmas to be called "The Words of a Believer" —not of the class of the stories of the Seen and Unseen, but yet something in that way, containing, in fact, my own theories of the world and its management. Should you care to have it?—of course I give you the first offer; and will you give me your advice whether the Believer should be a man or woman? Naturally I should say the first, but the tendency of the day is so much (apparently) in the other direction that I hesitate. Of course it would be more actually true to make a woman the speaker, but a generation ago it would have given the adversary an occasion to blaspheme against old women and their maunderings. I doubt whether this would be the case now; but it is a curious question, and one on which I should like to have your advice.

At this moment, when, though she did not know it but was still fighting to keep her terrible anxieties at bay, the last and crowning sorrow of her life was approaching, Mrs Oliphant was cheered and interested by a suggestion made to her by Mr Blackwood. This was that she might undertake the history of the great publishing house with which for forty-two years she had been so closely connected. Many of the old friends of that house had passed away; she herself was to lay down her task unfinished. But there could be no question of her superlative fitness for the work, and though it proved extremely laborious, it was more congenial to her in the last sad days of her life than the lighter kinds of writing from which

she began to shrink.　The following is her answer
to Mr Blackwood's first letter on the subject:—

WINDSOR, 26th August.

I like your proposal, or rather suggestion, very
much indeed.　I have often wished that you would
think of doing something of the kind.　It ought to
make a valuable as well as very interesting book,
for the history of the Blackwoods would involve a
most important piece of the recent history of literature, as well as many extremely interesting figures.
Your grandfather and elder uncles must have been
men full of character, and few people living can have
a clearer recollection than I of your Uncle John,
—your father too, always so kind, the kindest of all.
I should undertake the work with the greatest of
pleasure, and I think I could do something worthy
of the subject.　It is possible that I may be going
to Dundee in the beginning of the month if Cecco
keeps well, and on my return I might perhaps stay
for a day in Edinburgh, but that would depend upon
Cecco.　He is tolerably well, but the terrible weather
we have been having is very trying and depressing,
and affects him a good deal.　To-day, after nearly
a week of rain and cold, it is quite hot again, and
as bright as possible, which does one's heart good.
I hope we are going to have a good September.　It
is dreadful to see the golden sheaves getting all
brown and shabby and soaked in the wet fields.　I
hope you have not felt the evil influence of the
weather. . . .

It is curious enough that the idea of a book on
the House of Blackwood as a thing that should be,
though not in any connection with myself, passed
through my mind with some vividness a little while
before I heard from you.　It must have been a
brain-wave!

A gleam of something like happiness, or at any

rate pleasure, came at this time with the birth of a little daughter of Mrs Valentine. It was only a gleam lost in the terrible grief that followed, but still the little Margaret was very sweet and interesting to her " Grannie."

To Mrs Harry Coghill.

ELMWOOD, LOCHEE, DUNDEE, *Sept.* 13.

I feel myself unpardonable not to have written to you at first hand to tell you about Madge, but I was at the moment distracted by bad news from home, and lost my head, I fear, altogether. . . .

I came on the morning of the 3rd September, leaving home with very great reluctance, for Cecco had been ·very poorly. Since I came he has had another bad turn, and I have been torn in pieces between the two. Thank God, my news since Sunday has been better, but he is in so weak a state that any additional trouble breaks him down altogether. I have been myself so worn out with the constant strain of anxiety and miserable helplessness, that the relief of the good news almost broke me down also. And I feel as if I could not get up my hopes again as I used to do: however elastic a cord may be, it breaks its fibre at the last, and I feel the prospect very dark before me. . . . The baby will be Margaret, I suppose, like all her female forebears. I am going home on Tuesday, 18th, at the latest.

On the 1st of October Cecco died. Even now the words cannot be written without a pang, though the desolate mother found courage to tell the sad story herself to the one who writes them.

WINDSOR, *2nd October.*

I am writing what letters I can myself simply to keep me from distraction,—I must do something, whatever it is. My Cecco died last night. He is gone from me, my last, my dearest, and I am left here a desolate woman with the strength of a giant in me, and may live for years and years. Pity me, —it seems as if even God did not, and yet no doubt He had a higher reason than pity for me. The dreadful thing is that I can't go too: I am forced to live, though everything in life is gone.

You know that my dearest boy has been very poorly all the summer—not from the complaint which we were all so much afraid of, which I believe was as much got under as it could be, and in complete abeyance. Monday night, the 17th, he was taken ill with inflamed throat and tongue, and I got home from Scotland on Wednesday morning to find him ill in bed, but nothing to be alarmed about. He got well of that, though very weak, and was downstairs for two or three days. Then he had a relapse, but got over that too. Yesterday morning, after a bad night, he was so ill and restless that I sent in a hurry for Dr Miller, who said it was exhaustion, and poured in stimulants, but with little or no effect. At about half-past eleven at night, after he had been. quite given up, he made a wonderful rally, and even I was for a moment deceived. The doctor left expressing hopes, but had not been gone ten minutes when he sank again all at once, and peacefully like a child breathed out his last breath. He lies now on his own bed, a perfect image of repose, his face rounded out as if he had never known illness, his look so peaceful and so sweet. And here am I, his desolate, heart-broken mother, childless, and yet as strong as iron, as if I should live for ever. . . . My Cecco, always my baby, never parted from me, always mine; and now I shall never hear his constant call upon me again, never until we meet where all will be so different. I write to try and deaden myself a little, and in the hope of getting tired and done like other people, but that is what I never seem to be.

It is indeed a sad task to recall the silent house: the mother sitting desolate, deserted by all the children who had been the heart and soul of her life; feeling herself physically strong still, though she seemed to others only the white shadow of what she had been; able to talk of her boy with tears, indeed, but with calmness, until some too poignant thought made her start up and steal away into solitude. And close beside her, in the boy's room which he would never consent to have altered, lay the last of all her treasures — those treasures that were her very own, and for which she had waged so brave a fight. Day and night she scarcely left him for an hour, until he was carried away to be laid with his brother at Eton; and even then she stood beside him, feeling, as she wrote afterwards, as if the "two other boys," her own Cyril and Frank, long ago dead in India, stood one on each side of her and supported her through the anguish of the parting.

For a week or two after this there was a stillness and exhaustion of grief over the house. In the quaint study in which Cecco had gathered his books, queer volumes of heraldry, special editions of his favourite classics or his best beloved poets—where all sorts of weapons, pipes, and curiosities decorated the walls—his chair still stood by the writing-table, and, left as when he had risen from his last day's work, the half-written page, and the pen laid down for ever, seemed only waiting for his accustomed presence. But it was all over. The goad, urging her to perpetual exertion, which his frail life had supplied to his mother, had failed her suddenly and completely. There was no longer pleasure or hope either,—nothing but such patient endurance as God's grace might vouchsafe to her.

But after that dreadful pause work did begin again: a paper called "Fancies of a Believer" came from her heart, and was perhaps the very best kind of occupation she could have found. And she finished and sent off to Mr Blackwood a paper called ".An Eton Master," a sketch of the Rev. Edward Hale, one of the earliest and most valued of the friends who had gathered about her during her boys' school-life. Mr Hale had died shortly before Cecco, and this little memorial of him was really a labour of love.

To Mr Blackwood.   WINDSOR, 10*th October.*

It grieves me not to be able to keep my engagement about the "Looker-on," but you will feel that it is impossible at present. God has stricken me so sorely that I am sure you will excuse and forgive. As soon as it is in flesh and blood to do it, I will. I have sent the little article on Mr Hale, and I shall, if I can, send "The Words of a Believer" before Christmas. I received your box safely. If I live— which I most heartily pray God I may not, but one knows how vain are one's desires in the face of His decrees—it will be a great relief from other work to undertake your family history: in any case, I will keep the materials safely and in their proper order. I have never been able to thank you for the kind thought that made you suggest this work to me as a kind of prop and support in the midst of my many expenses and cares. These are now diminished along with my life, and I earnestly hope that the blow which has taken my all from me may have so loosened the tenacity of existence that I may not abide long after him; but God only knows. In the meantime, bear with me in respect to the other things which I had pledged myself to do.　Thank you for your sympathy.

To the Hon. Emily Lawless.　　　WINDSOR, *15th October.*

DEAREST EMILY,—I send a little note to be given to your dear mother if you think it fit.　The girls, Denny and Fanny Tulloch, who has made herself so one with us in our calamity that we are never likely to part, have been looking for a house in London to which we could remove at least for a time, partly to make the journey a little more easy for Madge, who, we have been hoping, would come to us soon, partly in the first impulse of leaving this desolate house.　But both these motives have been shaken in the last few days.　Madge is not doing so well as we hoped, and has got at present an attack of rheumatism about which I am anxious, and we may go to her instead of waiting for her to come to us. And I begin to feel that the world outside is more desolate still than this poor bereaved house, which was my boys' home for almost all their dear lives, and where their trace is upon everything.

BIRNAM HOTEL, BIRNAM, *Oct.* 25.

. . . You ask do I read?　I would read night and day if I could, or work—these two things keep me going, since go I must, and no softening of incapacity or weakness is ever allowed me.　You can't imagine how I long to be ill or stupefied in some way; but, on the contrary, I am all strung up, and fit for everything.

I can't write, and yet I can, and feel as if it were a moment's ease to let my heart overflow to you. But I will not say any more, dear Emily, for your sake rather than mine.　I hope that 'Mælcho' will do very well, and that you will be pleased with it in print, which always makes a difference.　God bless you for all your kind thoughts.

To Mrs Cornish.   BIRNAM, *Sunday, 28th Oct.*

I have meant to reply to your kind letter for some time, but the courage has always failed me. When last God called upon me to give up what was the half of my being, I could speak a little and express the anguish that was in me; for then I had still my Cecco, his ever-ready arm to lean on, and a motive and object for every self-denial. But now I have lost all, everything on this earth that came from me and was wholly mine. I thank God for my dear little Denny, to whom I seem to do wrong by speaking as if she were not mine, which she is by every tenderest tie. But only God knows, who has not spared, what Cecco was to me—my child still, though a man, my dearest friend and closest companion. It seems strange that with all the assurance I have that God would not have stricken me with this dreadful blow had it not been best, and indeed necessary for him, I should bear it no better than if I had no hope at all; but nature is very weak and humanity very short-sighted, and the distance that is between him and me and the silence seem more than flesh and blood and an old worn-out soul can bear. There was never a day when he was away from me that he did not write to me; during these years of his weakness he has liked always to have me by his side, his call to me, "Mamma," as he always said, was continual, in everything he wanted me, till we made a joke of it, in the happy days in that other world which came to an end scarcely a month ago, though it looks like a hundred years. Yes, you are right; I was more blessed in him than most mothers are, the more and the greater is my desolation now. But yet I know that I ought to bear it better, only that my prayers are all silent—I seem to have so little now to ask for, nothing but that I may soon be united again to my dearest boys in that little house at Eton where they are waiting for me, and in that above, which is dim, of which we know so little. And the less prayers one has to say the farther off one seems to get from God, who is all that is left in the ruin of my earthly hope.

Since I wrote this I have been called down to see Bishop Wilkinson, who is a good man and has said many things to me which will perhaps do me good after a while; but, alas! one knows everything or almost everything that can be said, and has said it to oneself over and over with so little effect. I find a little comfort in fantastic thoughts that float into my mind I cannot tell how. You and your dear husband say many kind things to me of my Cecco, and Mr Cornish bound me to him by saying how he had wished in the time to come to make a friend of my dearest boy. And I know my Cecco in his heart loved good company and was fain to make friends, but was kept back by the reserve of his nature and a shyness to believe in the interest of others in himself. And the other morning it came into my head that he would now have the noblest of company, and would doubt no more of the affection of others, but know as he was known. And this for a little gave me great and sweet consolation, to think of him among some band of the young men like himself whom I have a fond fantastic thought that our Lord draws to Him, because He too in His flesh was a young man, and still loves His peers in human age, and gathers them about Him, for some great reason of His own. You will feel how fantastic all this is, and yet it gives me more gleams and moments of consolation than anything else.

I want to send Mr Cornish the last book which my Cecco ever bought, which had been taken to his bedroom for him to see, and was still there when he passed away from all the fancies and likings of this life. It is a Baskerville Ariosto, valuable, I believe, for the printing: your husband, I think, shares that taste too.   Give him my love and thanks for all his good thoughts of my dearest boy, and to you too, dear.

When the visit to Scotland was over, Mrs Oliphant took possession for a few weeks of a house in London, where her two adopted daughters and little Margaret, the baby whom she could not but care for and pet, were her companions.   Thence she writes :—

To Mr Blackwood.   85 CADOGAN PLACE, S.W., *Nov.* 3.
. . . I am working now at the "Words of a Believer" with, I fear, but indifferent success; for I am very restless, and find it difficult to settle at my work for any time, even though it is the only thing that does me any good.

I hope to begin your work, 'The House of Blackwood,' early in the year.   I would very fain make this my last work, if God will be so good to me as to let me go by the time I have finished it.   I should not in any case take more than two years to it, and would probably do it much sooner if there was any need for hurry.   I can think of nothing better, if I must go on with this weary life so long, than to conclude everything with this book.   We rarely get what we wish for in this way, but it would be very sweet to me, and I can at least hope for it.

For once, at least, her desires were accomplished. This book was the last.

"The Words of a Believer"[1] appeared in 'Blackwood' for February.   Certainly it appealed to many hearts.

---

[1] "Fancies of a Believer," 'Maga,' February 1895.

85 CADOGAN PLACE, S.W., *Nov.* 16.

I fear that you will perhaps find this too serious, and perhaps will agree with it too little to put it into the Magazine. I don't even know if it is very suitable for the Magazine. You must decide solely as you think best. It is not what is called orthodox, nor is it unorthodox, and it is perhaps fantastic—that I am sure it is anyhow. It is even perhaps too much the musing of a very sore heart to be fit for the public at all. But only there are so many sore hearts. I do not, however, wish to bias your judgment in any way.

In the midst of her sorrow she was never insensible to the sufferings of others, and the following letter, written to one in great trouble, will show how keen her sympathies were :—

To Mrs Harry Coghill.   85 CADOGAN PLACE.

Seeing you yesterday was such a mere flash, like a dream of trouble and pain, that I must say a word to you to-day, though indeed I have very little to say. It is so easy to bid you have courage. It was the first thing that came into my head this morning . . . How full the world is always of trouble and sorrow! I don't know how I shall get through Sunday, knowing what I know. I steal out now in the early morning to Mr Eyton's church, round the corner, to the early communion. I have lost confidence in any prayer of mine, but as one must pray whether one will or not, I will carry you there with me, my dear, and ask strength for you and ease and complete restoration, and you may be sure, if they know, the boys will add their word, knowing better than we do. I dreamt this morning I was reading one of Cecco's letters, and he said, " Everything here is covered with gowans, as you call them."

Now, I never do call daisies gowans; was it not strange? and doesn't it give you the idea of a great sunshiny flowery mead that he must have been in?

God bless you, dear, and give you strength. You came to me in my great trouble. I hope all good angels will be with you.

An article entitled "In Maga's Library," published in the Magazine for December, has a notice of Mrs Oliphant's work, and—what she valued much more—a short but very just appreciation of such writings of Cecco's as had appeared in those familiar pages.

To Mr Blackwood.   85 CADOGAN PLACE, *Dec.* 4.

You will be surprised that I have not written before to thank you and your contributor for what he has so kindly said both about me and my dearest boy. Will you say to him that I shall be ever grateful to him for his kind words? Whatever touches my Cecco is precious to me, and·about the only thing in which I can take any real interest in these dark days. It is only this moment that, turning to the article to see whether by any chance I might have mentioned in mine any book already mentioned in that, I found my own name and my Cecco's. I presume it is Mr Allardyce who is the author: I am very grateful to him, and do not delay a moment in saying so, though you must have thought me very indifferent. There have been several very kind notices in the papers. It is a pleasure, if anything can be a pleasure, to see it in "the Magazine," as my boys used to call it, as if no other magazine existed.

85 CADOGAN PLACE, *7th December.*

I said to you that I hoped 'Who was Lost,' &c., would be the last novel I should write. (There is, however, one to come out in 'Longman's Magazine' which was written before.) I have a Life of Joan of

Arc to do, one of the Heroes of the Nations series, and a child's book about Scotch history, and besides that my desire is to undertake nothing but to give myself up to your great book.   I had calculated I might take two years to it, and though the other calculation I know is presumptuous, I had hoped that these two years might perhaps see me to the end of my life. . . . It seems in my mind to shape itself to three volumes, and it would please me thus to bring my life's labours to a conclusion.   It is true that this is calculating without the will of God, which is, after all, the great thing, and He has refused so many of my prayers that I have perhaps no right to expect better for this; but still, as I am nearly sixty-seven, there seems reason for hope at least.

85 CADOGAN PLACE, December 19.

. . . I forgot to say to you when writing last that I have various chapters of my own experiences written, which if I live long enough to finish them might make a book not without interest.   It has sometimes given me a little amusement to write it, meaning it for my sons.   Its character may be changed now, but it will be more adapted perhaps for the public. . . . It is premature to speak of it in its present state, but I think it well to let you know that there is such a thing to be calculated upon.

The autobiographical work, never completed, forms the first part of this present book. What Mrs Oliphant says in these letters she repeated without word of change on her deathbed. Only it would seem as if in those last hours of failing strength she did not quite remember how prematurely her narrative broke off.

To Mrs Harry Coghill.   85 CADOGAN PLACE, S.W., Dec. 31.
I must go home after all. I do not know how I will fare when I get there. If I can bear it at all, it will probably be better and sweeter to be there than any-

where else. It was the home of my dearest boys, to which they were both attached and liked better than any other place. Cecco said to me a few days only before he left me, when I was talking about changing the position of his bed, that he had slept there for more than twenty years. All the associations of his life are there, and I should like to die there. I think it will be better for me, for the little time that remains to me, there than anywhere else. . . .

I am instinctively forming all my plans for two years: it would be so comfortable if all should be wound up then, and myself dismissed to the narrow little house at Eton and all well. God grant it may be so! It would be dreadful to begin all over again, and struggle for work once more. Then another reason: if I stay at home, I may be able to afford to go away here or there when it becomes intolerable, which with a more expensive house and a new settling I could not do. This looks a little like a bull, that I should stay at home in order to be able to go away, but you will know what I mean.

1895.

The proof referred to in the following letter was that of " Fancies of a Believer " :—

To Mr Blackwood.   WINDSOR, 11*th January.*
I send the proof corrected—but pray don't publish it unless you think you can risk it. I should much prefer not putting any name, but if you prefer that I should take the responsibility, as is quite right, put the initials only. It seems to me, however, that any name would spoil the effect. It is sure to be attributed to me. My " Little Pilgrim " has never had my name, but nobody ever doubted that it was mine; and this too would be better for being without a name, but I leave it to you — nothing more than initials in any case. . . .

There is a phrase in Mr Skelton's very interesting article about Mr Froude which shows that gentleman's usual methods—I mean Mr Froude's methods. He says, "'A good joy,' as Mrs Carlyle used to say." Now Mrs Carlyle did say it in her sarcastic way as an absurd expression used by Leigh Hunt's children, who lived near her, and who, when they were coming back from their walk, used to run in and tell her they had had such a good joy. She quoted it in illustration of the high-flown talk in which they were trained, and here it is put into her own mouth as if she had ever spoken in that way.

To Mrs Harry Coghill.   WINDSOR, *27th January.*

I should have answered your letter at once. It occurs to me to say that I waited for Sunday, which somehow seems the appropriate day for *lettres intimes;* but that really would not be true, since it is only a sort of languor of soul which makes me put off everything —a restless languor, idle and yet incapable of keeping still, which makes me break off as soon as I come to the middle of anything I am doing and turn to something else, as if one could cheat one's weary soul to a sense of novelty in that way. But I need not tell you over and over again the vagaries of that weary soul. Thank you a thousand times, dear Cousin Annie, for your letter and for your most kind invitation. I think I am best where I am, wherever that might happen to be. It is no use for me to stir. We should change the skies but not the mind, and in my present condition one place is much the same as another. I can't be much worse; I don't hope, nor indeed scarcely do I wish, to be any better. I just get through every day as I can, not easily, but somehow. The corner that I have crouched into is the best to stay in, especially in this awful and blighting cold. For years past, you know, by this time we have been away to the South, and that, perhaps, makes me feel the look of the cold and the sensations of it more bitterly. . . .

I for my part am always telling myself that the new
life must be so much better, more blessed in every
way for those who are gone, and then return to break
my heart over the petty things left behind,—the lives
like other men, the work half done or never begun,—
when if I could only feel what I believe I should be
quite happy. . . . Do not let yourself think, dear.
In some cases there is no such evil exercise, and it is
wonderful what control we have over our thoughts
when we exercise it steadily. I used almost to brag,
though sadly enough, in the time of those anxieties
which you know of, which were to my present state
what the height of a battle is to the dreary sighing of
the captives in prison—that I had got to be able to
stop the course of my thoughts, and think of something
else, even when the strain was fiercest. Don't be vexed
if I preach. Have not I a little right? though in respect to illness I know it is you who are the professor
and I who should be the pupil, and I should not bear
physical pain half so well as you do: to tell the truth,
I don't bear anything well nowadays, so that I am
little better than a humbug when I begin to advise.

March 3.

. . . Denny has made an extremely successful drawing of me in pencil—very simple and exceedingly good,
I think. It seems to me rather original altogether:
I have seen nothing like it. I am anxious to have it
shown to the Queen. I like it better than her painting. Perhaps this may turn out the thing she can do.
We must have it photographed. She thinks of sending it to the Academy, and Mr Holmes says certainly
she must do so. I am very much pleased with it as
a drawing, and people seem to think it is like. It
would give me as much pleasure as anything in the
world can nowadays, which I fear is not saying much,
to see her get into an assured way of doing good
work.

I am not much to brag of in any way. Did I tell

you of my great piece of work, the 'House of Black-wood'?   I am dreadfully busy, and get on with my work well enough, but do it with very little heart.

The first anniversary of Cecco's death, October 1st, was a day of terrible suffering.   Mrs Oliphant, with her adopted child, made a pilgrimage to Eton to visit the cemetery where her two sons had been laid.

To Mrs Harry Coghill.

42 ALBION STREET, IIYDE PARK, W., *October* 2.

I have not been up to writing, as I am sure you will understand.   I am thankful that the immediate moment is over, and that all the details of the an-guish of the past can be laid aside, at least as far as they ever can be.   I cannot bear to think of my Cecco as—I can't write the word.   He is always living to me, and that is what makes it so dreadful when the mind is forced upon all the last circumstances.   I say to myself I will think of them no more, but only of him in the new life; but, alas! how to keep to that? There was a wreath which we think must have come from you.   God bless you, and thank you, dear Cousin Annie—I know you think of him.

The short visit to London, during which this last letter was written, was made on the way to Paris. Mrs Oliphant thought it advisable for her adopted daughter, who had already had some training in a Paris studio, to work there again for a short time, and they went to France, accompanied by Miss Tulloch.

To Mr Blackwood.   PARIS, 26*th October.*

Thanks very much for your long letter, which is full of information and interest.   I am sorry that you find

it needful to go away, yet I am half disposed to congratulate you on it.   It is dreary to spend these long
cold months in the North after one has acquired the
habit of migrating to the South and the sun.   It
seems to me, however, that it would be agreeable to
you to see part of this book in print before you go
away, so that I will strain every nerve to get the first
three chapters ready to send by the 1st or 2nd
November. . . .

To Mrs Valentine.   PARIS, *12th December.*

. . . I had hoped much to get out to Notre Dame,
but it is impossible, and I must just give it up.   The
last of these days of remembrance—my dear Cyril's
birthday—it was a comfort and very sweet to me to
spend an hour in the old, old church laden with the
prayers of generations; and now my Cecco's day has
come, and I must just content myself to thank God
for him as I may at home.   It is a dark day, and yet
it must always be a bright and blessed one which
gave him to me.   I think all sorts of thoughts, as you
know, all centring round the one great thought, and
lately I have been saying to myself that God separated
Himself from His Blessed Son for our sakes for thirty-
three years, and I have been parted from my Cecco
only for one.   It could not be separation to God, who
is everywhere; but it must have been to our Lord,
who for our everlasting consolation was a man.   So
He must know, as I am often tempted to say of myself, all the ways of it—parting of every kind!   The
thing I dread most in the world is to live long, and
to be swept as it were away from them, and things
dulled to me perhaps by the passage of time, but I
hope in God this may not be.   I ought not to speak
to you like this, perhaps, but I am sure you would
rather share my trouble, my dear child, than be left
out.

1896.

Those most attached to Mrs Oliphant had been anxious ever since her last loss that she should find, temporarily at least, a home which would not at every turn and in every corner recall those gone from her. Her long nights of sleeplessness and tears were enough. We tried to persuade her to find new surroundings for her days, and at this time the scheme was carried out, and she moved to the little house on Wimbledon Common, where she spent the remainder of her life.

A sharp illness which attacked her in the summer of this year should have done something to break her confidence in her own health. She was really in a condition to cause great anxiety, and her sufferings at times were most severe. The next letter is written by her much-loved niece and adopted daughter, who with Miss Tulloch and herself made up the little family at Wimbledon.

Miss Oliphant to Mr Blackwood.

WIMBLEDON, *3rd July.*

I think my letter must have crossed yours, but I know you will want to hear how my aunt is getting on. She is very weak and pulled down—unlike herself in every way; and the doctor evidently thinks it will be some time before she is well again. I can't help feeling very anxious about her, and the doctor has absolutely forbidden work or even talking; but she must be kept quite quiet, and she is too weak to wish for anything else.

After a week or two Mrs Oliphant was able to resume work, though shaken and very feeble.

To Mr Blackwood.   WIMBLEDON, 25*th August.*

. . . I have several times intended to speak of the very great vigour and fresh start which the Magazine seems to me to have taken during the last year. It has been more full of interesting articles, and altogether stronger than for a long time before. I have also for some time back intended to tell you, but always forgot, how much struck and amused I was by the pride and eagerness with which the young men jumped at the idea of being admitted to ' Blackwood.' They evidently looked upon it as a chance almost too good to be true, which I don't think is at all the sentiment with which they regard the other magazines. What a very remarkable story that is in the last number of Sir James Brown ! I don't know when I have read anything so striking.

WIMBLEDON, 3*rd October.*

I have received the book,[1] and will take care of it, as you say, till it is published. Mr Lang sent me several chapters to read in the early summer, which I thought were rather dull—tell it not in Gath—with much virtuous indignation about 'Maga's' personalities. . . . He has been very good-natured to me, and I shall say all I can for him. The illustrations seem to me at a first glance hideous,—he said they were so clever.

I have worked a hole in my right forefinger—with the pen, I suppose !—and can't get it to heal,—also from excessive use of that little implement.

WIMBLEDON, *October* 16.

. . . I have been much touched by finding several very kind allusions to my youthful self in your father's letters. It is strange to look back upon the beginning of a career, when one is so near its end.

---

[1] Life of Lockhart

WIMBLEDON, 11*th December.*

I send you the enclosed[1] without having taken time to read it over, and it will, I fear, want a great deal of revision. It has been written not from the head but from the heart, and I am unable to form any impression whether it is good or bad in the hurry of my feelings, but no doubt I can much improve its form in correcting it.

The letter that follows is only inserted because it is a kind of return to the brightness of past times. The gifts alluded to were to be the last Christmas gifts of a very long series.

WIMBLEDON, 24*th December.*

MY DEAR ———,—I really don't know how to find words to thank you for the magnificent chair—nay, throne—which you have sent me, and which still over-awes us all with its splendour. I hope by means of familiarity to get accustomed to the idea that it is for use, and a real seat to sit upon, and not an idol to which sacrifices of respect and admiration should be paid.

And now, as if that were not already too much, here comes in a noble turkey fit for the biggest and the happiest Christmas table. Alas! we will do it no justice. I only wish the Queen or some other distinguished person would pay us a visit to sit in my chair and eat of my good cheer.

Much happiness and prosperity and every good thing. With love and thanks.

1897.

To Mr Blackwood.　　　　WIMBLEDON, 5*th January.*

I was just about to write to you on other matters when I received Emma's letter with the news of your

---

[1] “The Land of Suspense,” ‘Maga,’ January 1897.

aunt's death—I will not say the sad news. It is very solemnising to hear suddenly of one so long known and familiar passing into the world unseen; but you, I hope, feel as I do, that except for that shock, it is a blessing and comfort to feel that, having outlived herself so long, she has now recovered, as I hope, all that is best in life.

In Mrs Oliphant's younger and brighter days she had had four dear and intimate women friends—Mrs Macpherson, Mrs Tulloch, Miss Blackwood, and Miss Fitz-Maurice,—and with all four her friendship had been long and unbroken. Two, and those the best loved, had at this time been dead for some years; now both the others passed away in quick succession. Miss Blackwood had been lately too great a sufferer for her death to be regretted, yet it made another gap; Miss Fitz-Maurice, who had been much with Mrs Oliphant in recent years, died at Ealing at about this time.

To Mr Craik.   WIMBLEDON.

Would you kindly send a copy of the ' Land of Darkness' to ——, an unknown correspondent of mine, to whom in great trouble these books seem to have been of some use?

I do not know if you will care to have the ' Land of Suspense,' to complete the series. It hurt me to publish anything so personal, but if there is any comfort in the communion of sorrowful souls, it was perhaps worth doing, and one's personality will be so soon blotted out.

WIMBLEDON, 13*th January.*

Thank you for the kind feeling and sympathy. I don't know very well what I have written, except that it is the overflow of a very full heart—perhaps too individual for publication; but there are always many

who are desolate to whom one puts out one's
hand.

From this thought we may perhaps put it with
the 'Little Pilgrim,' in that series, if it is not too
short, sometime.

To Mr Blackwood.   Wimbledon, 14*th February*.

I feel that I have behaved very badly about this
article, and I almost hope you will reject it. These
"Looker-on" papers become very difficult to me: I
feel as if I had no longer the lightness of touch necessary for them, and there has been a want of topics
to comment upon. Of the enclosed pages one should
be inserted after the review of 'Margaret Ogilvie';
the other is the conclusion of the paper.

For two years Mrs Oliphant's health had been
slowly but very visibly giving way. She was subject
to attacks of severe pain, and was unable to walk
more than a few yards. Work, which had been her
comfort and stimulant, was beginning to be evidently
burdensome. Even the crippling of her finger, where
the pen seemed to have really worn through the skin
by long usage, was both a symptom and an aggrava-
tion of her depressed physical condition. Her talk,
however, if less bright, was as delightful as ever, and
she retained the charm, which is surely the best of
all social qualities. She paid a short visit to her
cousins at Coghurst, but was very weak and suffering. Her work was done almost entirely in bed or
on a sofa; but she would come downstairs when the
morning's task was finished, and be ready for bright
and pleasant talk, and to interest herself in all our
doings. In her company and in that of her host there
could be no dulness: how could any one guess that

in six months both the homes they brightened would be left desolate?

To Mr Blackwood.   COGHURST HALL, HASTINGS, *Feb.* 19.

. . . I write to you at present to ask a question, for which I want a speedy answer if possible. If I am to write something for May about the Queen and her Jubilee, how would it do to throw that into a "Looker-on"? This would prevent my name being put to it, which I don't wish—that is, I should prefer the paper to be anonymous. There will be so much flummery written everywhere on the subject that I had thought of a more serious article, noting all the important changes that had taken place in the Queen's reign, and called "'Tis Sixty Years Since."

I should like to know what you think of this. In the meantime I have had a letter from Dr Macleod of 'Good Words,' asking me to do a short article of 4000 words on the same subject. If you wish me to write a signed article on the Queen's Reign, of course I should refuse Dr Macleod at once: if, on the other hand, you like the "Looker-on" form (which I do myself), I might consider what he proposes. If you would be so kind as to telegraph to me to-morrow, on receiving this, "No" or "Don't," I will write to him at once declining. He is anxious for an answer.

The article called "'Tis Sixty Years Since" ap-. peared in 'Maga.'

It was with no little dismay that Mrs Oliphant's friends heard of the suggestion mentioned in the next letter—that she should take the journey to Siena. These hurried journeys for the purpose of gathering materials had been formerly easy enough to her, but she was now in a condition requiring rest, care, and warmth. Most unfortunately she did go, and it was the last journey she ever made.

Wimbledon, 19th March.

. . . I undertook some time since to write a little book for a series, upon the subject of Siena—a place which I do not know, having only once been there,—and I shall be obliged to go there to study the place a little. It is a very long and expensive journey, and I am not perhaps in strong enough health to risk it, but I fear it is quite indispensable. . . .

I shall go to Siena, if I find it possible, about the second week in April.

We have got Madge and her babies here, which makes the house lively. . . .

I am by no means well, and easily worried, which is so different from all my habits; and I seem to avoid everything I can possibly leave out.

In the second week of April Mrs Oliphant started for Siena. She had with her Miss Tulloch, who had chiefly lived with her for the last year or two, and her youngest niece. She was much fatigued by the journey, and had one of her frequent attacks of illness on her arrival; but she managed to do what she thought necessary for her projected book, and returned home, with her gathered materials, at the end of the month. She had been much interested and charmed by the details of St Catherine's life and by some other gleanings from the Sienese chronicles, and came back to Wimbledon feeling a little better, and able to set to work.

But the improvement was of the most temporary kind, and a sharp attack of illness seized her directly after. Each of these attacks left her whiter and weaker, and, in spite of considerable divergence of medical opinions, it was impossible not to feel that most serious and probably fatal mischief was going on.

z

To Mr Blackwood.

GRAND HOTEL, SIENA, *Good Friday, 16th April.*

I was pleased to get your letter yesterday. I send you with this a further despatch of proof, and should indeed have completed the volume, but that I have been a little upset with the long journey, which, however, I have got through better than I expected. This is a very interesting place, though there is an element of guide-book in what I am desired to do about it which does not please me much, and to which only my poverty, and not my will, consents. I will probably one day or other send you an article about Siena and its saint. I hope to get home again on or about the 24th, but may be a day or two later.

WIMBLEDON, *30th April.*

I got home on Monday night feeling tolerably well; but over-exertion seems to have acted upon my weak point, and I have been laid up by a small bout of my last summer's trouble since then. I am not out of bed, but I hope the worst is over. . . .

I think your writer on fiction might have made his article more interesting if he had gone a little further. He might quite well have taken in Anthony Trollope and Charles Reade, whom I am always on fire about: they have never had justice done them, being both most admirable novelists, full of insight and power, the latter especially. And what was Dickens if not early Victorian ? Besides, the writer is very unjust to Bulwer, classing him with Lady Blessington. Bulwer was of course full of sham and cheap melodrama, but he knew what he was about, and his last books (the Caxton series) are of a high order. I suppose there was no man who had a greater command of the public in his day. To be sure, one might say the same of Miss Marie Corelli, who, by the way, in the

only book of hers I can read, seems to be founded
upon Bulwer.

On the 19th of May, the Princess of Wales held a
Drawing - Room, and it had been arranged that a
number of Mrs Oliphant's friends were to meet at the
house of her cousin after it. She had long promised
that if possible she would be of the party, and she
kept her word, really enjoying the little festivity—
the last social occasion at which she was ever to
assist. She was looking fairly well, and apparently
moved about with less fatigue than she often did.
She greatly enjoyed having both her nieces with her,
and Mrs Valentine's two tiny children — the little
Margaret especially, who was brought up to town
to see the pretty dresses and play with another
maiden of her own age. It was a very bright
day, not presaging any evil, yet three of the
most valued and beloved lives that went to make
up its brightness were close to the end of their
pilgrimage.

.She was none the worse for this expedition, for
it was the very next day that the spirited verses for
the Queen's Jubilee were written. They are given
here, with the note that accompanied them to Mr
Blackwood :—

WIMBLEDON, 19th May.

The enclosed little rant came to me, and wasted
an hour or two of good time this morning. It
is not worth sending to you, but there is a sort
of a lilt about it. It might go in a fly-leaf, and if
some one who knows my hand well would read it
carefully there would be no need of proof. In great
haste. . . .

Send it back if you don't like it.

22nd June 1897.

The trumpeters in a row,
　　With a note as clear as a bell,
And all the flutes and the fifes below,
And the brazen throats, and the strings of fire,
　　To let the people know
That the Mother, the Queen, the heart's desire,
　　From her palace forth doth go.

Princes, form in array!
　　Great ye are, and greater may be;
But only guards and vassals to-day
To the Lady enshrined in duty and love,
　　Pacing forth on her way
In weakness of age, and in power above
　　All words we can sing or say.

The streets that sound like the sea
　　When the tumult of life is high,
Now, in a murmur of voices free,
Hum and ripple and rustle and stir,
　　Straining each eye to see—
To gaze and to watch and to wait for Her
　　Whose subjects and lovers they be.

Sons and lovers and subjects all,
　　The high and the low together—
From Princes that ride in the festival
To us in the crowd who but shout and gaze;
　　Rendering, every man and all,
Thanks to our God for her lengthened days
　　And the nation's festival.

Hark! what is this which hushes the crowd?
　　A sound of silence amid the noise;
The sweep of a pause through the plaudits loud—
A moment, a stillness, a start, a stir—
　　The great heart of the multitude
Holding its breath as it waits for Her,
　　One being in all the crowd.

> She is coming, is coming! The Queen! the Queen!
>   Here is our moment in all the day.
> One voice for all, and the air serene
> Quivers, as if a storm blew by:
>   A little more, and there had been
> Gates burst apart in the very sky,
> To hear a whole nation shouting on high—
>   "The Queen! the Queen! the Queen!"

A week or so after the party just mentioned Mrs Oliphant again drove up to town to her cousin's, in order to have a fresh and careful medical opinion. This opinion, which was of the most confidently hopeful kind, proved to be entirely wrong, and early in June the doctor who attended her at Wimbledon, in answer to her questions, told her he believed her state to be hopeless. Other opinions—one that of a distinguished surgeon—showed equally that what she called "the beginning of the end" had indeed come. Her niece says: "To her this was longed-for and welcome news; and when she had ascertained that no medical help could give her any permanent relief, she made up her mind, in the greatest serenity and happiness, to await the end. After the first week or so she was able to take very little nourishment. She was daily lifted to a sofa near the window, where she lay in great peace and content, sometimes reading or being read to, herself writing some letters of farewell to friends, or dictating others; glad to have the letters read to her that came, as she said she wished to have their messages. Many times she said that she was at perfect ease in body and mind. All care and worry seemed to leave her. She said she felt as if she were lying somewhere waiting to be lifted up; or again, as if she were lying in the deep grass of some flowery meadow, near the gate, waiting for our Lord to pass by. Her sleepless nights were filled with wonderful imaginings. She spoke of thinking herself in a ship in which was our Lord, who made with His robe a great white sail to carry her across a river. She said she could not think of God as the Almighty God of all the world, but just as her Father, and that at this moment even the thought of her children seemed to cease in the thought of Him."

In this serene atmosphere of perfect peace—satisfied that all was arranged as was best for her—she lay day after day waiting for the end. "I have no pain," she said one day; "I am only waiting, and I hope I shall not have to wait very long, lest I should get impatient." One of her last letters is a short one to Mr Craik, in which she suggests the republication of some of her magazine stories, and adds, "Perhaps some one would write a small preface of my life to enable you to add £100." "I am dying," she concludes, "but not suffering much. Good-bye."

When she could no longer write she dictated some notes, and on the 21st of June some verses, which, broken as their music is, are strangely touching. She desired that they should be sent to Mr Blackwood, thinking they might be printed as a sort of *Envoi* to the Jubilee verses already in his hand. This was not judged possible, but the lines, as her dying voice uttered them, may be given here:—

> On the edge of the world I lie, I lie,
> Happy and dying, and dazed and poor,
> Looking up from the vast great floor
> Of the infinite world that rises above
> To God, and to Faith, and to Love. Love Love!

> What words have I to that world to speak,
> Old and weary, and dazed and weak,
> From the very low to the very high?
>   Only this—and this is all:
> From the fresh green soil to the wide blue sky,
> From Greatness to Weariness, Life to Death,
> One God have we on whom to call;
> One great bond from which none can fall;
> Love below, which is life and breath,
> And Love above, which sustaineth all.

She liked to be read to, as it wearied her less than talking; and her little well-worn Bible, out of which all through their Eton lives her boys had daily read a verse or two to her before their terribly early start from home, lay on her bed, and was the best-loved of her books. One passage which she refers to in her Autobiography seemed to be often in her mind. It was the one in the 1st Epistle to the Corinthians beginning, "For other foundation can no man lay." And she dwelt on the words, "If any man's work shall be burned, he shall suffer loss: but he himself shall be saved; yet so as by fire." The death of St Catherine of Siena was one thing she reverted to; and another, Lockhart's account of Sir Walter Scott's last days. One afternoon, very near the end, she begged to have "Crossing the Bar" read; and while the reader, painfully keeping her voice steady, repeated the last lines, the listener fell suddenly into a calm sleep.

She wished at the last to live over the great day of the Queen's Jubilee; and speaking to one of her little circle whom she was urging that "to please me" she should not disappoint her husband by staying away from the scene of the procession, she added, "I promise you shall have no bad news on the 22nd."

She bore with great patience the noise of bands and fireworks on Wimbledon Common, though her windows looked full towards the scene of the merrymaking, only remarking how little we who used to enjoy the fun and noise of an Eton 4th of June had thought that there might be some poor soul lying dying close by. "Through all, her wonderful security and absolute certainty that she was so soon to recover what she had lost seemed almost to transfigure her, making her room, which she loved to have filled with flowers, the one cheerful spot in the house."

She lived till June 25th, and then softly passed away. The names of her boys were on her lips almost at the last, though she had said repeatedly, "I seem to see nothing but God and our Lord."

PRINTED BY WILLIAM BLACKWOOD AND SONS.

Catalogue

of

Messrs Blackwood & Sons' Publications